DARE YOU TWICE

Also by Murray Bailey

I Dare You
Map of the Dead
Black Creek White Lies
Singapore 52

DARE YOU TWICE

Murray Bailey

Heritage Books

First published in Great Britain in 2017 by Heritage Books

1

ISBN 978-1-9997954-1-2
e-book ISBN 978-1-9997954-2-9

Printed and bound by Clays Ltd, St Ives plc

Heritage Books, Truro, Cornwall

Mostly for my amazing sister, Kerry
but also David, Nia and Cara

ONE

Cristina placed the fresh corvina in her basket and thanked the fish seller. She would make a spicy garlic sauce, pan-fry the sea bass and have it with the tomatoes, onions and peppers she'd just bought. She smiled at the thought of impressing her new man, Xavier, with her cooking.

Three years after the climax and she was finally starting to relax and enjoy life. It had begun by two men stopping her in the street and asking her to get into their car. One was short and fat and white. The other was the complete opposite. It was as though someone had put them together as a joke—or a weird company policy to balance something out.

They never said they were CIA, but that's what they were. She knew. They said they worked for the government but they were clearly American. At first it was easy to do what they said. All they wanted was information on the man she worked for. He didn't seem to do much except enjoy life on the Panamanian coast. He was rich and reclusive, so who was she to complain? But he had a secret past and a room with computers and other devices she didn't understand.

The CIA men wanted her to report what he did, and each week she left a message for them when she went into town for groceries. In return for her boring updates about what he ate and where he went, they paid money into an account for her. Everything was perfect: she could pay for her mother's palliative care and save for her own retirement.

And then her boss had received a mysterious message. He changed overnight, like a man who had been on a long vacation and returned to work. He planned and he travelled. The CIA guys picked her up again and asked lots of questions. They said his name wasn't Señor Max, but they didn't give her his real name.

"It doesn't matter what names he uses," the thin black one said, "just what he does."

They told her what to look for and what to report on.

She gave them the names she overheard when he monitored people: US politicians, the CIA and two people he called Tango One and Two. Over time she worked out that Two was looking for Tango One. Two was called Kate Blakemore, and Señor Max secretly helped her—although Cristina guessed it was for his own reasons.

Then he said he needed to go away, didn't know how long for, but asked her to monitor the news and gave her a batch of names to check on the Internet four times a day. She was also shown how to redirect encrypted messages received on his equipment.

She still had no idea what was going on. Except the CIA men got even more excited. They turned up one afternoon, sweating due to the intense humidity or a race between them to Señor Max's front door. Or maybe both.

"Send this message," the tall black one said as his colleague caught his breath. "Send it now."

And so she sent **Hamilton's dead** to Señor Max's phone. Hamilton was one of the names she was looking for.

"*¿Como murió?*"

"In English, please," the white one said.

"This Hamilton—how did he die?"

The CIA men exchanged glances.

She said, "I can't just say this. *Necesito pruebas.* I need proof, to have seen it for myself. The news..."

They understood and said they'd provide something. Less than an hour after they left, Señor Max's computer pinged with a report of the news that Grant Hamilton, congressman and ex-CIA head of Middle East operations, had died of a heart attack.

Her boss returned home two days later, but he wasn't the same relaxed man she had first worked for. She sensed he'd intended to come out of retirement one last time but something had gone wrong. Something to do with the message she'd sent. And after that he seemed to work to distract himself from the failure. At least that was her judgement.

She'd wanted to leave then. The fear of being discovered began to eat away at her. She dreamed that he knew she'd betrayed him to the CIA, and each day became an uncomfortable act, like walking on broken glass. At any moment, he would look at her and realize she was the one who had broken it.

"Leave now and you'll look guilty," the black guy had said when she told him. "Bide your time, Cristina. Just keep smiling, tell us what he does and bank the cheque."

And then she found an excuse. Four months later her mother died, and she needed to go back home.

Señor Max accepted it. He even sent flowers to the funeral. So she moved back to the village. But she was still afraid that he would find out. Her biggest worry was the timing of her message and the release of the news item. But he never queried it.

She moved and moved again and then realized she'd be safest in the city; just one middle-aged spinster, a nobody, in a population of over forty thousand.

Cristina was interested to find out that Kate, the girl she'd known as Tango Two, had written a book—or at least someone had written it in her name—about finding her boyfriend. The story ended with her tracking him down by following his clues. There were hints of a conspiracy but it wasn't explained. And there was no mention of Señor Max.

The book was a bestseller and now they were making a film with A-list stars.

She reached her apartment and started up the stairs. What should she make as a dessert for Xavier? Maybe her mother's favourite cake. That would seem fitting since Xavier had mentioned he liked coconut.

Cristina opened the door to her one-bedroomed apartment and told herself for the hundredth time to get the door painted. Maybe, with a man around, things like that could be done straight away?

The curtains were drawn. The shafts of afternoon sunlight picked out the shape of someone sitting in her armchair. For a fraction of a second she smiled, assuming it was Xavier, before grasping the impossibility of the thought. Xavier didn't have a key. Xavier wouldn't just let himself in. Xavier wouldn't be there for at least three more hours.

With her hand shaking, she turned on the light.

"Señor!" She tried to mask the fear in her throat, hide the quaking of her body. Not looking at him, she hurried too quickly into the kitchen and poured herself a glass of water. She put it down immediately in case the trembling was too obvious.

4

Señor Max stood and pointed at the chair. "Sit down, Cristina."

She shook her head but found herself walking to the chair and sitting. She looked up at his cold, hard face.

"How did you find me?" Even as she said the words, she realized how foolish she sounded. Of course he could find her. "Señor, I am just a poor peasant girl."

"Not too poor to afford a nice apartment though," he said. "But I'm not going to hurt you. Tell me everything and I'll leave you in peace."

She swallowed hard and wished now that she had the glass of water.

"Who are they?" he prompted. "Who are the people you worked for?"

"I... I don't know."

He waited, and she looked into his eyes. She felt tears prickle and they began to blur her sight.

"The message," he said eventually. "Tell me about the *Hamilton's Dead* message."

For a moment she thought desperately for a reason. Why hadn't she planned for this confrontation? Why did she think he wouldn't track her down?

"Two men. Two Americans," she blurted.

"What about them?"

"I think they were CIA. They just wanted to know things. I didn't tell them anything. Not much. Just when you were away, where you went." She was speaking too fast and then her mouth dried up.

He broke eye contact and fetched the water she'd poured. She gulped it down, her hands still shaking.

"I'm sorry," she said. "I didn't have a choice. I'm sorry I let you down."

He squatted opposite her and nodded. "Start from the beginning. I just need to know everything you told them and everything they said."

She did her best to recall everything and she could see he believed her.

"How?" she said when she'd finished. "How did you know?"

"Because Hamilton's not dead."

She shook her head, not quite understanding. "I don't—"

"It doesn't matter." He stood and she expected to see a gun levelled at her. There wasn't. He simply walked away.

"I thought... I thought you'd shoot me."

He stopped and half turned. "No, Cristina. How would that look?"

Cristina cancelled dinner with her boyfriend and it took a couple of days for her to calm down and come to terms with what had happened. She knew she'd been lucky. Señor Max was a killer but he'd spared her. It was a miracle. She went to the old town and prayed at the basilica and thanked the Virgin Mary for her life. And it was as though she listened because Cristina felt a great sense of calm emanating from the statue as she kissed her feet.

Outside again, Cristina stood on the steps and sucked in the sea air, the feeling of warmth and the smell of ozone. She should get on with her life and put the past behind her. She would call Xavier and rearrange that dinner. Maybe it was time to settle down, and maybe Xavier was the one.

She stepped onto the pavement and never knew what hit her. A car lost control, bumped over the kerb and mowed her down. An old burgundy Ford, witnesses said. A freak accident on a busy street. But the driver didn't stop and the car was never found.

TWO

Vancouver Island, Canada

Kate looked out of the window and took a breath. The detective opposite her was either trying to wind her up or was just an arse.

"You understand? You're attending as our guest," he said again.

Detective Stanley had short, spikey blonde hair and a face that looked like it had been scoured and polished. She judged him to be in his late twenties and he had the arrogance of someone who had risen quickly through the ranks.

"No," she said and pulled a piece of paper from her bag.

"Ms Blakemore, you are here with the backing of the Integrated Major Crime Unit. And"—he flashed a thin smile—"let's be honest with one another. We only tolerate you and your ex-Special Forces boyfriend because of your celebrity. Where is the action man, by the way?"

"OK, enough of the attitude, Detective."

"Attitude? I'm justified in being a bit pissed off, don't you think? I'm wasting my time with an amateur rather than getting on and doing my damned job. And your cute English accent doesn't carry any weight with me."

Kate shook her head. "You're convinced it's murder."

"To my mind, it's definitely abduction and probably homicide."

"Let's take a step back," she said, and handed him the piece of paper. It was an email from Grace LaBelle, mother of the missing girl. "This is a request for us to get involved."

"Dare Services," Detective Stanley scoffed. "DARE stands for Don't 'Ave Real Experts, doesn't it?"

Kate ignored the jibe. "We offer an alternative, that's all. People seem to want someone to help when they feel let down by the authorities—that's you, by the way. The very fact that Grace emailed us tells us something."

"Enlighten me."

"Why ask for help finding your daughter if you've killed her?"

"I didn't say we thought the mother was the killer."

"Who then?"

"Anyway, one reason for the email could be as a distraction?"

"So who do you suspect, Detective Stanley?"

Stanley said nothing, his eyes fixed on hers.

Kate waited. She didn't know what he or the Vancouver Island RCMP were thinking. All she knew was that the girl had been missing for two weeks and Grace LaBelle feared the police suspected her. The very fact that they didn't appear to be searching for the girl was evidence enough.

Stanley said, "I see the email was sent three days ago. Took your time coming."

Kate glanced out of the window, watched the rain and bit back her frustration with this imbecile. It was like when they first started, almost three years ago, before other police departments started to accept their help. This was their first time dealing with Vancouver Island authorities and the barriers seemed to be up.

"I don't need to work with you," Kate said, snapping her attention back to him. "You want to know why a three-day delay? Purely because of workload. There's just the two of us and we get a whole bunch of emails every day. There's always someone not happy with how their case is being handled."

Stanley shrugged. "The husband, not the wife. We arrested him yesterday. Maybe the mother doesn't know he's guilty. Maybe she's complicit—an accomplice. Asking for you to investigate takes the pressure off. Getting the famous Kate Blakemore involved? Well, the media are going to focus on how we do our job rather than the crime."

And there we have it, Kate thought. Detective Stanley wasn't just pissed off because he'd decided it was a waste of time. He was worried about the media attention, worried about screwing up.

Kate said, "Look, just treat me like a silly girl who's a trained physiotherapist. Ignore the fact that I got my PI licence—"

"Whoopeedoo. You did the fifty-hour course and passed the test. That makes you a professional investigator."

She ignored him. "Maybe use me as a sounding board—someone who might shed a bit more light on your case. I'm not trying to trip you up or catch you out. I'm just here to help justice be served."

"And get paid for it."

"Firstly, correct me if I'm wrong, but you're being paid by the community... to do the right thing on behalf of the community. And secondly, actually, this isn't a paid job for us. We don't charge, but we do accept donations. Pro bono, as the legal guys call it."

"Because these people can't afford a proper PI."

Kate felt the anger rise in her chest. She was doing her damnedest to be reasonable. She slammed her hand on the table and glared at him. "Listen, arsehole, I don't like you and you don't like me. Now let's cut the crap and tell me about the case."

Stanley held her stare for a moment and then shrugged. "All right, since you're the intelligent one, you tell me what happened." His voice switched to monotone as he began to describe the case.

Fourteen days ago, Jemila Dacks had gone missing from the family home in Colwood on the island. A call was made by Mrs LaBelle at eleven minutes past eight on Wednesday morning reporting that her fifteen-year-old daughter was missing. Two officers from Saanich Police Department attended and identified that the girl appeared to have disappeared sometime overnight from a locked room.

Stanley concluded with: "The door had been locked from the outside and the windows were also locked."

"Was the door locked when the police got there?"

Stanley scoffed, "Of course not. That would have been suspicious in itself. No, Mrs LaBelle had opened the door to check why her daughter hadn't answered when she banged and said she'd be late for school. Dacks went to her room at about seven at night and her mom was the last person to see her."

"That's early for bed for a teenager."

"She had her computer and comics," Stanley said, and shrugged. "Seems she liked to lock herself away, be on her own. Nothing unusual there—for a teenager."

"But she didn't *lock herself away*, did she? You said the lock was on the outside."

"Mrs LaBelle locked it at about eleven."

Kate raised an eyebrow.

Stanley said, "The girl is a delinquent. She's known to the Saanich Police for disturbance of the peace, minor damage to property and theft. Nothing too serious, but enough for the parents to be warned, and their solution was to lock her door when they went to bed."

"So she somehow got out of a locked room."

Stanley gave her a proper smile for the first time. "A regular Harry Houdini vanishing trick. No way out of the room. Windows and door locked—and still locked in the morning. So what, Ms Blakemore, does that tell you?"

"That she wasn't in the room when her mother locked it at eleven?"

"Mom swears she checked."

"Then the girl used something to knock the key out. It fell on the floor and she somehow pulled it back under the door."

"That would work," he said seriously.

"Really?"

"No. There was no key. It was bolted. And the window needed a key and was also still locked. And before you suggest it, she couldn't have climbed out of the window and then relocked it. No, someone opened the door from the outside and let her out."

Kate leaned back and studied the detective. "And you have a theory—a motive, means and opportunity?"

"Yes."

Kate waited. "And...?"

Detective Stanley smiled. "The reason you're here— the reason I'm talking to you—is that we want to deal. We want you to understand what we think. We want to make sure we're working together on this." He paused a beat and watched for her acknowledgement. "The deal is that I show you what we have."

11

We want to deal. Stanley had switched from first person. He wasn't totally on board with this but someone higher up had insisted.

She said, "And in return?"

"You don't undermine it."

"OK," Kate said. It sounded reasonable but she knew what it really meant: they had a theory but it was weak and maybe she could help them. By appearing independent she might elicit a statement or evidence that would close the case. It also meant they were worried about their evidence—worried about the media's assessment.

Stanley pulled out a three-page document and handed it to her with a pen.

"We need to make this formal."

Kate took her time to read what had been written by a lawyer with the apparent intention to either hide the main purpose by obfuscation or cover so much that the objective was just lost in the morass of jargon. However, eventually she had the key clauses: she couldn't share any information—with any party, including the media— that wasn't already in the public domain. Furthermore, any interview she had with the parties involved— meaning the parents and anyone else she met in relation to the disappearance—had to be accompanied by an officer from the police department.

She said, "You do appreciate that I could just ignore this and go straight to the LaBelle's place?"

"I do, but then you wouldn't hear our theory."

"Which could be a crock."

Stanley smiled. "Just sign it."

Kate held her pen over the signature line and watched him. He was desperate. They needed her far more than she needed their opinions. She put the pen down.

She could see irritation in his eyes, and his shiny, scrubbed face looked even more polished, tinged with redness.

"Sign it."

"Give me something first. Convince me it's worth it. We both know the stats. Three-quarters of missing kids are runaways, and the vast majority of these are between the ages of fourteen and fifteen. It's by far the most likely scenario."

"But at the last count eighty-seven per cent were found within a week. It's been fourteen days. This is different."

"Because?"

His neck was flushed now and he was fighting back anger. "Because the kid was locked in the room. No way out. Because Mr LaBelle is guilty as hell. Because there's something else that points to him."

THREE

Kate called Scott. She'd told Detective Stanley she wouldn't sign and now she was standing in the corridor outside the meeting room.

Scott said, "How's it going, honey?"

"It's bullshit. They want to trade. They show me what they have on the father and in return I give them control over the interview with the family. And I'm pretty sure they have nothing concrete."

She talked him through what Stanley had said about the case.

When she finished he said, "What about this *something else* he mentioned?"

"Just a tease to get me interested. I'm not convinced I should be signing that contract."

"Remember it was like this in the early days? It's taken a while to build a good relationship with the IHIT. The first time with a department is always the toughest." The Integrated Homicide Investigation Team was their local and the largest homicide unit in Canada.

"Maybe the problem is with Stanley rather than the whole of the island's IMCU."

"You could make the deal based on having a different detective."

"And get someone less close to the case, maybe? If it's anyone, I think it has to be this guy unfortunately."

Scott agreed. "They think it's the husband. See if you can persuade him to tell you what they actually have. But I don't see any reason to sign that contract. You know how to play this better than anyone, Kate. Go with your instincts on this."

Kate said she loved him, and she was about to end the call when Scott said, "Ben Hurwitz is coming over later."

"Oh." She had an uncomfortable feeling. Ben was a nice guy, but he was Agency and he was the past. If he was visiting then it was unlikely to be purely social.

"He said he had something to show me," Scott said. "I've no idea what. Now go back in there and give that jerk some serious shit."

Detective Stanley was standing in a pose reminiscent of someone about to be searched. He had his hands on the window looking out at the dismal weather. He almost jumped as the door clicked open.

"Here's the deal," she said. "Tell me what you have and you can accompany me when I interview the family. You can hear what they say. I have every right to talk to them, so you can either be there or not. Your choice. But if you're coming with me then I want what you have on the husband."

He pointed to the chair but she didn't sit.

"Sign the agreement," he said again, although the conviction was gone.

"I almost walked just now. If you want to hear what anyone has to tell me, then you share and you share right now."

She watched his jaw tense as his teeth ground. Then he picked up a remote and a TV on the wall came on.

"The husband—Mike LaBelle—works at Stones Bakery. His shift starts at four each morning. He leaves

15

the house at around three thirty. That's what he told us, and Stones have confirmed it."

He pressed play and the screen lit up, grey and grainy, showing a gas station forecourt. A time stamp in the top right-hand corner showed 2:43. On the left it had a date stamp. The morning that Jemila Dacks had disappeared.

A car pulled in and a man got out and began filling up.

Stanley said, "That's Mr LaBelle."

"He left earlier that day."

"He lied. Told us it was three thirty, like always. Question is: why?"

She watched the image for a while as LaBelle finished and paid the night clerk. Then he drove away. "Doesn't look like anyone else in the car."

"I agree."

"Which gas station is it?"

"Ah, now you're on to it," Stanley said with a hint of sarcasm. "Peninsula Co-op on Highway 17."

"And?"

"And that's not en route to Stones Bakery. There are lots of other, more convenient gas stations. In fact, you saw he turned left when he exited. That's heading north, away from Victoria. About a mile from Beaver Lake. We checked the CCTV at the next gas station, two miles up the road, and LaBelle's vehicle never gets that far."

"So, you think he stopped off at the lake."

"Yes, I do."

She guessed what Stanley considered happened but waited for him to say it.

"My working hypothesis: it was to dump the body."

Kate looked back at the screen as it continued to show cars pulling in and filling up with gas. She could see a

16

portion of the road. "Presumably you tracked this forward and watched him come back?"

"He flashes past at three twenty-eight. Speeding, I figure, and late for work."

"Three-quarters of an hour. That seems a long time to dump a body—if he was that close to the dump site."

"Maybe. Maybe he went on foot across the park to find a secluded spot. Maybe he drove around a bit to make sure no one saw. Or maybe he had second thoughts and delayed." Stanley fast forwarded and then froze the screen at 3:28 with LaBelle's car clearly illuminated by the gas station's grey light.

"Obviously we've searched the car, but we found no evidence of bodily tissues. But that's not unfeasible. We also checked the car and his shoes for mud that might be from the park. Nothing."

Which was a good summary of what they had, Kate thought. They had nothing. No wonder they wanted to be involved when she met the parents.

She said, "What did Mr LaBelle say about the time discrepancy."

Stanley fake-laughed, "He said he forgot he'd gotten up early that day. He couldn't sleep so went for a drive. Said he wanted some air from the bay. Wanted to do some thinking."

"So, you arrested him for that?"

"And the other thing."

"Which is?"

Stanley gave her a crocodile smile. "Tough. You sign and I give you everything."

Kate shook her head. "More bullshit. What else do you have? Let's for a minute consider that Mike LaBelle didn't kill Jemila. Who else is a suspect?"

"The mom."

"As I said before, it's unlikely she would have asked us to get involved."

"But we arrested her husband. Could be to protect him."

"Again unlikely. The timing doesn't work since you just arrested him. What about the genetic father?" Kate asked. With a different surname, she was sure Mike LaBelle wasn't Jemila's father. "What do you know about him?"

Stanley looked like he considered stonewalling again but then relented. He said, "According to Mrs LaBelle, her first husband didn't stick around long after the birth. She has no idea where he is and he hasn't been in touch since the day he walked out. Her second husband—yes, she's on her third go around—was an alcoholic and couldn't hold down a job. They were married for less than a year before she kicked him out. He's now believed to be on the mainland."

"Have you interviewed him?"

"Not yet. We'll trace him if we need to."

Kate made a mental note that Scott could probably trace the ex faster. "Name?"

"Steve McNamara."

"Any other suspects—assuming it's abduction?"

"A neighbour."

"Anyone in particular, or a *neighbour* generally?"

"Specifically. Mr Caan. And yes—before you ask—of course we interviewed him. He and the girl had history."

"History?"

"Of conflict. According to him she was regularly abusive, and he'd made numerous complaints about her to the police. It looks like things got bad a couple of years ago when his dog jumped up at the girl. Since then things have escalated. He says she's spat at him, called him names and thrown stones at his house. The worst, he reported, was that she posted a packet of burning shit through his letter box. He had no evidence it was her and she denied it. In one report, she says Mr Caan threatened to kill her."

"But you've ruled him out."

"No one is ruled out unless LaBelle is convicted."

"I'd like to speak to Mr Caan," Kate said.

"Then it's a good job you aren't on your own. He's unlikely to relish speaking to you—and he only spoke to the police because he had to."

"OK," Kate said, standing. "Let's go and see Grace LaBelle. Let's see what she'll say to me. Then afterwards we'll speak to this neighbour."

Stanley picked up the contract and waved it towards her. "You going to sign this now?"

"In your dreams."

"What about the other thing? Don't you want to know what we have?"

Kate ignored him. She was already striding out of the room.

FOUR

Kate followed in her SUV. Having her wipers on at high speed made barely a difference to the sheeting rain on the screen. She fixated on the red lights of Detective Stanley's car and accepted he knew the way.

When they reached the estate where the LaBelles lived, the rain had eased off to large, slow drops that splatted on the glass.

The properties were single storey and had metal fences for boundaries. There was junk in most of the yards, which were either bare or overgrown. To Kate, it said they were not only poor but also rough. It was what she expected. It was why Grace LaBelle was sure she wasn't being treated fairly. If this had been a rich neighbourhood, her email had said, the police would have responded quicker and focused on all possibilities. Focused on the highest likelihood that Jemila had run away rather than been abducted.

Detective Stanley stopped and Kate pulled up close behind. A couple of kids sat on a wall on the corner of the street up ahead, oblivious to the rain, it seemed. Although Stanley was in plain clothes, they knew who he was, what he represented, and Kate heard shouts of abuse as she climbed out.

"They're harmless," Stanley said. "At that age, and this time of day, they wouldn't dare do anything."

"Good to know."

Stanley opened the metal gate next to his car and led the way up a path to the LaBelles' home. Kate noticed the yard didn't have much junk and, though patchy and weed-ridden, the grass had seen a cutter in recent weeks. There was a hard standing for a car but it was vacant.

Grace LaBelle opened the door with a sad smile for Kate. She shook her hand and welcomed her in, apologizing for the state of the house. There was a smell of polish over something that could have been a cross between stale cigarettes and old cooking fat.

Kate explained that the detective was only there as a witness. "Just to help me by filling in the gaps."

Grace looked at him suspiciously but after a moment accepted the situation.

"Thank you for coming," she said to Kate. "I didn't read your book but I watch TV. I saw you on there. I remembered after Jem disappeared. I remembered you saying how frustrated you were with the police—" She glared at Detective Stanley, who shrugged. "It's like they don't care. We're just another case. A number. Not real people who need to be helped. They don't care: the social service bureaucrats and the police, who just see the bad in people."

Stanley went to respond, but Kate raised a hand to stop him.

Mrs LaBelle said, "I looked you up on the Internet and watched some clips. Then I remembered. You found that kid in Pakistan. Her father had abducted her from her home in Toronto and no one knew where she was. You and your Special Forces partner found her and brought her home."

Kate nodded. It had been two years ago and their first successful case. Scott had done most of the work and tracked the girl down. Court proceedings take forever and even with an order for her to be returned, the likelihood of success was miniscule. So Scott had located the father and extracted and repatriated the girl.

"So that's why you emailed me."

"Yes, I need help." For the first time, Kate heard emotion in Mrs LaBelle's voice. "She's my girl, my only girl, and I don't know what to do. You were the only one I could think of turning to."

"Has anyone from the Bureau of Missing Persons been to see you?"

"Yes, a week ago. He was a nice young man, but he just asked a bunch of questions and wanted a recent photo of Jemila. Like I said, he was nice, but I don't think they do anything, just post her details on their website."

Stanley said, "And they communicate with the police departments and other authorities."

Kate glared at him and he leaned back. He wasn't supposed to say anything unless she prompted him.

"Other authorities," Mrs LaBelle said. "That's what they are—authorities. They're the same bunch who want to put my Jemila in juvie. Their so-called help is psychoanalysis. Behaviour modification was what they told me. Damned social services. They're just an arm of the law, that's what they are."

Kate said, "Shall we have some tea?"

Mrs LaBelle seemed to snap out of her bad place. She almost smiled. "Tea," she said with a laugh. "You are so English—not like the people from Victoria who think they are. I like you."

She left them for a few minutes and returned with a cup of hot water and a tea bag on a plate. She had nothing for the detective.

Kate said, "I apologize for asking, because you must have been over this a hundred times, but would you mind just talking through what happened on the night Jemila disappeared? In your own words and slowly. Please try to visualize everything as though you are there."

LaBelle started talking about bolting Jemila's door.

Kate interrupted. "Could you start a bit earlier? What time did you get home?"

"About six fifteen. I got home from work about six fifteen. That's the time I usually get back from the supermarket where I work on the checkout some evenings. It wasn't raining. I remember because I didn't have a coat and was worried I'd get wet, but the rain had stopped. I opened the front door—"

"Was it locked?"

"It's always locked. I unlocked the front door and went into the kitchen to prepare supper."

"Where was everyone else at this time?"

"Jem was in her room on the computer and Mike was in bed asleep."

"Do you know this because you checked?"

"No. I guess I figured that's where they were because that's where they always are."

Kate nodded. "Sorry, you were saying?"

"I came in here and put the TV on and watched it while I waited for the supper to cook."

"What were you cooking?" Kate wasn't really interested, but she knew that the more detail a witness remembers, the more likely it is they'll then recall something that turns out to be important.

"Pie—steak pie—and fries with vegetables."

23

"Oven fries?"

"Yes, and the peas and carrots were in a microwave bag."

"So dinner didn't take long to make?"

"No, it was done by maybe six forty-five. I only make it for me and Jem because Mike eats when he gets up around three in the morning." She hesitated, perhaps having got a bit lost with her train of events. Or maybe it was because she knew he'd left the house earlier that next morning.

"Go on. You were saying about serving dinner. Did Jemila join you then?"

"Yes, I called her from her room. Usually she'll just take it to her bedroom without so much as a thank you, but that evening she stayed. We had supper on our laps watching TV."

"What was on?"

"*The Young and the Restless*. I record them."

Kate had never watched the soap but Mrs LaBelle provided a bit of detail about the episode.

"Jemila doesn't like it, and to be honest I think she went after maybe quarter of an hour—she always was a quick eater."

"So, she went back to her room at seven?"

"That's right."

"How did she seem?"

"No different from usual. Typical grumpy teenager who doesn't say much. Like I said, I was lucky she sat with me while she ate."

"And you checked on her at eleven?"

"When I went to bed. I looked in, said goodnight and locked the door."

"And that was the last time you saw her?"

"Yes."

24

Kate asked to be shown the room. It was right opposite the lounge. It was a small house with a kitchen, lounge, two bedrooms and a bathroom. Kate had noticed the door with the bolt on it as they came in. She studied it now. She'd assumed it would be a little thing that could be easily broken—like a bathroom bolt perhaps. But it wasn't. This bolt looked substantial, like it had come off a garden gate.

Mrs LaBelle opened the door inwards and Kate saw a single bed, a built-in wardrobe and a desk with a computer on it.

Kate said, "Where was Jemila when you said goodnight?"

"At her computer. She was always either at the computer playing games or on her bed reading her comics or painting."

There were superheroes painted all over the walls.

"Did your daughter paint these? They're amazing."

"Yes, she wants to be a graphic artist. It's a competitive market though—hard to break into."

Kate shook her head, impressed by what she saw, then switched her attention back to the computer and its table and chair. "She was definitely there—at the computer?"

"Without a shadow of a doubt."

"And you definitely bolted the door."

"A hundred and ten per cent sure. And it was still bolted in the morning."

Kate looked around. "And you're sure she ran away. So somehow she got out."

"I know it sounds crazy." Mrs LaBelle took a long breath and Kate realized she'd been holding herself together. "But yes, I think she somehow got out."

Stanley scoffed. "Apart from the other thing."

Kate remembered him saying there was something else, back at the station. "What?" she said.

The detective ushered them all further into the room so he could close the door. On the inside was a brown mark on the off-white paint. It was an X.

Stanley said, "It's blood. And it's been tested and confirmed as the girl's—Jemila's blood." He looked hard at Mrs LaBelle and her eyes filled with tears. "And the X is relevant, isn't it?"

Grace Labelle said nothing.

"Mr LaBelle wears a gold chain with a pendant. Doesn't he, Mrs LaBelle?"

She nodded slightly.

"And that pendant," Stanley said with his crocodile smile, "is a circle with an X."

In that moment, Kate didn't just dislike the detective, she hated him. She despised him for his lack of empathy.

FIVE

Kate looked hard at the detective but kept her voice neutral. "I'd like to spend some time alone with Mrs LaBelle," she said pointedly.

For a moment, Stanley looked like he'd make a stand. Then he bobbed his head and ducked out of the room.

"I'll be in my car."

Kate waited until she heard the click of the front door. "Just a thought, would that sound wake you up?"

"What, the front door closing?"

"Or opening?"

"Yes. I hear Mike when he leaves for work. And in the past, I've heard Jemila slip out in the night."

"What about the night in question?"

"I just heard Mike go."

Kate nodded thoughtfully and then turned her attention back to the mark on the door. "What do you make of this?"

"Just a mark." Mrs LaBelle fought back tears. "I didn't mean…"

"It's all right," Kate consoled her. "I understand."

Mrs LaBelle said, "If it is blood then it could be old, couldn't it? And anyway, I can't believe Mike did this."

Kate went over to the window and checked it. It had one of those catches that was locked by a small Allen key. She tried to wriggle it free but the lock held tight. She looked out of the window at the backyard. There was a patio and then a patch of grass. Beyond the plot was a strip of common land and then trees.

"What's that sound?" Kate had become aware of a faint high-pitched whine.

"I'd forgotten about that. I don't hear it any more. Not heard it for years. There's an electrical substation just the other side of the trees. I think it's that. I think it's worse when it rains."

Kate turned back to the room. The floor was strewn with comics that she'd had to navigate around. She picked one up. It was called *The Inhumans*. "I don't know this one."

"Like the *X-Men*, I think. I'm not too sure but Jem was obsessed with a character called Rogue." Mrs LaBelle pointed to one of the paintings on the wall—a young woman on the front cover in green Lycra and a typical superhero pose. "That's her. Jem coloured her own hair grey at the front just like this." She waved her hand around. "Jem was normally much tidier than this. She treats these comics like gold dust or something. Most of them are normally stored in the cupboard. It's not like her to leave them like this. I want to tidy the room, put them in piles, you know, but the cops said I had to leave them."

Kate reached over to the PC and switched it on. She was surprised the police hadn't taken it for evidence. It seemed most kids these days lived their life on social media—something that could be hacked and traced.

The screen burst to life with comic book characters and required a password. Kate looked at Mrs LaBelle.

"I don't know it," the mother said.

Kate wasn't surprised. No teenage kid would want their parents snooping around their private life—which was ironic considering how they were barely private at all.

Kate asked, "What did Jemila do on the computer?"

"Gaming mostly. *Marvel Heroes*, I think it's called. She would also stream TV, YouTube and stuff. She was always talking about the latest movies, so she was getting them somewhere too."

"Not see them at the cinema with her friends?"

Mrs LaBelle looked askance. "Jem didn't... I mean doesn't..." For a moment she choked up and sat on Jemila's single bed.

Kate said, "It's all right, take your time."

"Jemila is a loner."

"What about Facebook friends?"

"Not so far as I'm aware. She never mentioned anyone."

"People she called?" And then Kate realized she hadn't asked a pertinent question. "Grace, what about Jemila's phone? Did she take that?"

"She didn't have a phone."

"Oh, shame."

"Yeah, the cops said they could trace her if she had one with her. I just wish I'd let her have one now. But then she never pestered for one like other kids. Again, who was she going to call?"

Kate opened the wardrobe. It was crammed with hanging clothes, clothes jammed on shelves and an empty top shelf. There was a backpack and array of footwear at the bottom.

Kate moved the desk chair to the wardrobe and stood on it. She hoped there would be something on the top shelf, hidden at the back. A shoe box, perhaps, with a clue in it. There was nothing except cardboard.

"Why the empty shelf?" she asked climbing down.

"I think she'd been having a clear-out. I think she was planning to put her most precious comics up there for safekeeping."

Kate looked under the bed and lifted the only floor covering: a five-by-seven-foot threadbare rug. She walked around the room, checking the walls and ceiling, and stopped at the door. After checking the frame and bolt, she sat on the bed next to Mrs LaBelle.

"The door was bolted from the outside," Kate said. "I've checked and it's some sort of alloy. Not magnetic— even if it was possible to move such a thing with a magnet, which I don't know. It's also firmly screwed in and would show damage if it had been pulled off.

"The window is locked, and if someone got out through it, it's not one that would self-lock. How do magicians get out of a locked room? There's a trap door. I've checked the floor and there's no sign of any opening. The ceiling also looks intact, so I can't see that she went through there." Kate turned to the mother and shook her head in defeat. "You're convinced she's run away?"

"Yes." A small voice.

"So what's your theory?"

"I don't have one. I have no idea. I just feel it. You know how a mother knows things. Like I know she's alive." She choked up again.

"Let's go back to the living room," Kate said. "I want you to tell me more about Jemila."

Kate's approach was to try and think like the missing person. That's what she'd done to find Scott. She'd solved his clues by understanding him rather than by using any clever mathematics. Whether someone wanted to be found or not, they left a trail. The authorities were experts at electronic footprints and locating CCTV images, but they often failed on the human side.

Grace LaBelle sat in the lounge and took a long drag on a cigarette.

"Sorry for smoking," she said. "I've been trying to give up for... well forever. I usually don't smoke in the house but... you know... the stress."

Kate smiled. "Sure."

"It's ironic, don't you think? The people who have the least money are the most likely to spend it on cigarettes and liquor."

And drugs and gambling, Kate thought, but kept it to herself. "Tell me about your daughter. Everything. Start from the beginning... When was she born? How much did she weigh? Did you have her at home?"

Kate looked at the face of the girl in a recent photograph she'd been given and tried to understand her as Mrs LaBelle spoke. The mother started talking freely, covering everything from her daughter's first word to the first signs that she was a loner and how independent she was. "By the age of four she was letting herself out of the house to go play in the woods. She's always been such a tomboy. There was never any question of dressing her in girly clothes. 'I can't climb in those,' she would say."

Most of Mrs LaBelle's stories were about Jemila's formative years. "What about more recently?" Kate asked. "What about her birthdays?"

"The last proper party was when she was ten. We took her to Pizza Hut with a bunch of kids from school. Afterwards Jem said they weren't her friends and didn't want any more parties like that. So, yeah, that was the last one we bothered with."

"You said 'we'. Was that with your husband?"

"Husband two. He was a boyfriend at the time."

"Tell me about Mike."

31

Mrs LaBelle suddenly welled up. "Sorry, sorry, it's just that it's our wedding anniversary today."

Kate didn't comment. She waited while Mrs LaBelle composed herself.

"It's been so hard. Not only missing Jem, but having had Mike arrested yesterday. It's all just so unfair."

Kate knew she'd made a mistake mentioning Mike LaBelle so soon so she switched back. "Tell me about the first two husbands."

"Jem's father, Bob, just walked out when she was five months old. Said he wasn't built to be a father. What a joke. Too damned late, I said. But he walked."

Kate asked for some details, including his name, date of birth and where he was from.

Mrs LaBelle didn't know where he'd gone and he'd never been in touch since that day. "Oh, except for a birthday card he sent Jem a few years back. I forget when. I noticed the postmark was Ruby Creek. Jem took one look at the card and binned it."

"So you don't think she's gone to find him?"

"Not a chance."

"And husband number two?"

"Gone to find him? No."

"OK, but I just meant generally about him." Kate knew it but she asked anyway. "What was his name?"

"Steve McNamara. It all happened too quickly, and I thought he was OK but he wasn't. I kicked him out once I realized what a bum he was. He did nothing, just sponged off me, watched TV, drank and smoked weed."

Kate was interested in whether Jemila had bonded with him. She asked the same questions about him and again got his name and date of birth.

"And how old was Jemila when you kicked husband two out?"

"Thirteen."

Kate processed that it had taken Mrs LaBelle three years or more to realize he was a bum but didn't comment.

"What was Jemila's relationship with him like?"

"She didn't like him much."

"And what about husband three. How was Jemila's relationship with Mike?"

Mrs LaBelle looked taken aback by the question, which was odd since it followed from the questions about the past relationships. Any sensitivity about the wedding anniversary was surely over by now.

She said, "He acts like a father. He helps provide. In fact, we're saving now. We should be able to move from this shithole and buy some place in a better neighbourhood."

"And how does Jemila feel about that?"

Mrs LaBelle shrugged. "Couldn't say. She never showed any interest. We never discussed it."

"You know Detective Stanley is convinced your husband abducted her..." She avoided mentioning his frequent reference to homicide. "The most incriminating thing is what he was doing on Highway 17 that morning."

Mrs LaBelle said nothing. She lit another cigarette but didn't apologize this time.

Kate waited.

Mrs LaBelle said, "I think you should leave now."

"I'm sorry, but why?"

"You aren't really here to help, are you? Jemila has run away. She's not been abducted and Mike has nothing to do with it."

Mrs LaBelle was getting herself worked up. Her neck flushed; her eyes widened.

Kate said, "I'm sorry you think—"

But she didn't get to finish her apology because Mrs LaBelle said, "Leave. I want you to leave now. And tell your friend the cop that I want our car back."

SIX

Detective Stanley was leaning against his car when Kate approached. There was now a gang of eight kids watching him, their poses threatening. They were a stone's throw away. Literally.

"Don't worry. It's just bluster—for now," he said. "How did you get on?"

Kate shrugged. She felt deflated and confused. "Didn't end well. She asked me to leave."

He smirked briefly before masking it. "You've been as useful as a Chinese teapot," he said.

"You mean chocolate teapot."

"Yeah, whatever. You've been no use to me."

She bit back on the anger that rose in her chest. "I'm not here to be of use to you. It's the family I want to help."

"Yeah, whatever," he said again.

She said, "I'd like to see the neighbour—Mr Caan, wasn't it? Which house is his?"

"I tried him, he's not answering. Just his Doberman." He pointed to the fourth house along. It was just like the LaBelles' but had higher metal fencing and seemed to have a large vegetable garden at the rear. There was no vehicle in the front yard.

Kate stepped over to her car. It felt like she'd just wasted a day. A girl was missing, she'd upset the mother and—if Stanley was anything to go by—the police were insensitive and obstinate.

He said, "What time's your ferry?" For a second he sounded almost friendly. Perhaps he regretted being so difficult.

Kate checked her watch. "I've about an hour."

"OK, follow me. It's on the way."

Stanley led her out of the estate and a few minutes later they were on Highway 17 heading north.

Kate realized where they were when they passed a Peninsula Co-op gas station and saw signs for Elk/Beaver Lake—one lake, two names. Stanley pulled off on a parallel road and then turned into Beaver Lake Road. He led her into a car park and picnic area.

Kate got out and joined him by a bench.

He said, "If I was dumping a body I'd have come down here. Easy to bury a body here. And it would have been deserted in the early hours of the morning."

"You've taken their car in for forensics?"

"His nice new Dodge, yes. Any trace of this soil— better still, her blood—and we have him. We get that and hopefully we'll get a confession."

"Mrs LaBelle was agitated when I asked what he'd been doing."

"He's guilty."

Kate had been thinking about it during the drive. She still wasn't convinced. The overriding factor was the mother's belief that Jemila was alive. That came across as so genuine. Maybe her annoyance was purely frustration at the direction of the investigation.

She said, "The door was locked. If Mike LaBelle took her, why was the door locked?"

"People make mistakes. All criminals make mistakes all the time. You'd be surprised how stupid they can be. So focused on one part of the plan that they forget something basic. Maybe it was habit. He's so used to locking her in that when he closed the door he locked it."

He pointed to the lake. "But you know what? I don't think he was so stupid as to bury her. We've got his tools too—checking the spades for this local soil. But if it was me, I wouldn't have buried her. I'd have taken her out into the lake. Dumped the body dead in the centre just to frustrate us."

He got up and walked to his car, put his hand on the door. "You've still over half an hour. Take a row boat out. See what you can find." He laughed, got into his car, spun it around and left her feeling even more frustrated and annoyed.

She walked down to the water's edge. The surface was dark and choppy. What had the detective said? *Dumped the body dead in the centre.* It reminded her of something.

She watched a couple of coots struggle against the choppy water and disappear into the sanctuary of a clump of reeds. Runaway or abduction? God, Kate desperately wanted the mother to be right. Not just for the girl's sake but so that the supercilious prig of a detective would be proved wrong.

Start with a hypothesis and test it. Look at the problem and challenge it. Eliminate the impossible and consider the alternatives. That's what she had learned over the last three years of detective work. But how could Jemila have escaped from the bedroom? It was locked, and she certainly couldn't walk through walls!

So, just accept that she did run away and she did get out. What else could she have done?

Dumped the body dead in the centre. Then she had it. The phrase reminded her of a conundrum she'd been told as a kid: There's a lily pond of a certain size. There's a frog dead in the middle of the pond on a lily pad. How many hops does it take the frog to reach the edge?

It was a play on words. The answer: none. There would be no hops because the frog was dead in the middle. He was *dead.*

Semantics yes, but it required lateral thinking. Look at the problem in a different way.

How do you get out of a room with no obvious means of escape?

Kate was trying to recall some lateral thinking puzzles when her phone rang.

"Found the body?" Detective Stanley said, laughing.

Any creative thoughts she was about to have evaporated. She bit her tongue. "We need to stay open-minded," she said.

He scoffed but she continued: "There are three possibilities. One: the mother is lying or is mistaken. Two: someone let her out and then locked the door afterwards."

"Like I said, criminals make mistakes." He sounded more mature now, reasonable. "You don't think the mother is lying so it must be door number two."

"And the third option is that Jemila got out of the room herself."

"Which is impossible. Are you driving?"

Kate had started the car and pulled onto the lake road.

"Yes, why?"

"I hope you're hands-free." There was irony in his tone.

"Yes, I am. Thanks for your concern."

"It's most likely the husband. He was in the house. He left earlier than usual. He didn't go straight to work. And he's lied to us. I'll grant you that the girl hasn't definitely been murdered, but the stepfather took her."

Kate waited for a gap in the traffic and turned north onto the highway. "But what if?" she said, a lateral thinking problem coming to mind.

"What if what?"

"Let me give you an example. Let's say you see a truck driver going the wrong way down a one-way street. Would you stop him?"

"Of course."

"You'd arrest him."

"If it was a serious traffic violation—"

"I'll take that as a yes. Even though he's done nothing wrong."

"I'm not following."

Kate said, "What if he wasn't driving? He was walking the opposite way. You've just arrested a man for no good reason."

"That's just stupid. You're wasting my time."

"No, the point is to think beyond what you expect."

He scoffed again. "I expected you to be a pain in the ass. Oh look, and I'm right!" He paused for a second and then said, "I'll tell you what. I'll give you a what-if."

Kate watched the road and said nothing.

"What if..." Stanley paused for dramatic effect. "What if you just leave the experts to do our job?"

Kate ended the call, cutting off his laughter.

SEVEN

Kate stopped in the queue for the Tsawwassen ferry.

She paced around the front of the car and finally called Scott.

"Hey, baby. On the ferry?"

Kate said, "The RCMP—at least Stanley—is totally focused on one scenario. The most likely suspect is the stepfather. He lied about the time he left home. He lied about where he went and there's a bloody mark—her blood—that points to him. Their conclusion: he killed her and disposed of the body."

"And you think?"

"I don't deny the possibility but I don't see that we can help much there. If she's alive, and especially if she ran away, then there's a role for us."

"You sound deflated."

She looked at her reflection in a window and thought her eyes looked more tired than usual.

She sighed. "I'm afraid Detective Stanley got to me big time."

"So, is there a possibility she ran away?"

"I think so. I just can't work out how. It's like a lateral thinking puzzle. Know any?"

"Well let's see... I remember one from when I was a kid. It went something like: Jack and Jill are found dead on the floor. The only evidence of foul play is a pool of water round them and broken glass, but they didn't drown, so what happened?"

"Not killed each other, or suicide pact?"

"Nothing like that."

"OK. OK, I need to think laterally." But Kate's mind couldn't see anything but two bodies on the floor surrounded by water.

Scott said, "Are there any leads?"

"About Jack and Jill's deaths?"

"No, about the missing girl. Let's focus on being positive. What other information do we have? I'll leave the other problem with you."

Kate relayed the detail about the two ex-husbands.

"OK, that's something to go on. I can start trying to locate those guys and we can take it from there. Did the police look at footage from the ferries?"

Kate glanced around and spotted a camera by the tollbooth. Damn, she hadn't thought about that.

"Detective Stanley didn't mention it, but then he didn't offer anything I didn't ask for."

There was dead air for a moment. Although talking to Scott helped raise her spirits, Kate still felt bad. And it wasn't just because of Stanley. She said, "Scott..."

"Yes, baby?"

"I screwed up. We're all about the human-touch. We're supposed to be on their side, but I screwed up. I upset Mrs LaBelle."

"You can't please all of the people all of the time, honey. Abraham Lincoln said that."

She knew he was winding her up in a nice way and it brought out a smile. "Lincoln said 'you can't fool the people'."

"Which is like lateral thinking puzzles, isn't it? They fool you into thinking something. Into making an obvious but incorrect assumption."

"You're right," she said. "But coming back to me for a minute. It wasn't about pleasing the mother. It was because I handled it badly. I had her talking freely and sharing minor details and then she just clammed up." Kate described the conversation that ended with Mrs LaBelle asking her to leave.

He said, "I see."

She said, "I think I need training."

"You've passed your exam."

"I don't mean as a PI. I mean in understanding people better—you know, psychology, behavioural stuff." She knew Scott wasn't interested in that side of things, but then he had his skill set. He was the tough guy. He did the legwork and the dangerous stuff. She just acted as the face of the team—the frontman. She asked the questions and gathered the information. She got into their heads and solved the clues. And the getting into people's heads required a better structure than her amateur approach. She didn't know if Mrs LaBelle had been lying. She didn't know if she was covering something up. She didn't know how to keep her talking.

Kate said, "Maybe if I knew that, I'd know the why. And if I knew the why I might know where she's gone."

"Sounds like a good idea to me. If you think you need to do a course in psychology then let's find you the right one."

"Great. When I get home." She got back in her car.

"Honey? What aren't you telling me?"

"I'm going to stay a night."

"That's a shame because Ben's on his way. You'll miss him. But do what you think is right."

"I need to do this."

"I know."

"I need to go back to Mrs LaBelle and find out what she's not telling me. I also want to speak to the neighbour."

"Neighbour?"

She told him about Mr Caan and his supposed feud with Jemila.

Scott said, "But if he's involved, it can't have been a runaway."

Kate knew there was a contradiction there, but until she knew everything, she shouldn't totally rule out abduction or worse.

"I'll call you from the hotel tonight," she said. "Have a good evening with your old buddy and tell me all about it. Now, what was the answer to the Jack and Jill murders?"

"Think about it."

The light was fading by the time the doorbell chimed. Special Agent Ben Hurwitz stood at the door beaming.

"Good to see you," he said.

Their handshake became a hug. Then Scott stepped back, appraising his friend. Ben was a few inches shorter than Scott's six-one. Ben's had tight curly brown hair, whereas Scott had let his hair grow. Ben's eyes were warm—the colour of walnut. But they looked tired. He had a satchel over one shoulder of a crumpled grey suit that looked like he'd slept in it.

"You're looking good," Ben said. "The beard suits you."

"I can't say the same for you."

Ben laughed. "A lot has happened since we last met. If you'll invite me in, we'll catch up."

Minutes later they were in the lounge looking out through a wall-to-wall window at the expanse of nature. They chinked beers and smiled and Scott had his first sense that Ben was concerned about something.

But when he spoke, Ben said, "I see you're still basically out in the country even though you're just a few miles from Vancouver."

Scott nodded. Whatever Ben had really come to talk about would have to wait. "Best of both worlds," he responded. "It feels remote but we're only minutes from civilisation. And we have neighbours. You'll have passed their lodge on the road here. The Delahunteys help out—cleaning, gardening—and when we're away they feed Tolkien." Tolkien was Kate's chocolate Siamese cat.

"How is my old buddy?"

"Tolkien? He loves it. Typical cat, spends most of the day out hunting or sleeping and comes in at night for food and a cuddle." Scott took a slug of beer. "So, what's this news you have? Why do you look like an old worn-out shoe?"

"Thanks a bundle! But you're right. I moved up to the New York office, met a girl, got married and I now have a bouncing baby boy—well actually he doesn't bounce yet. He's three weeks old and just lies there." Ben grinned. "Wouldn't have it any other way though. We live in Manhattan in a fabulous apartment. Jody's a budding interior designer..." He whipped out a photo of mother and baby. Both very cute.

"Pleased for you." They chinked bottles.

"Tired but exceptionally happy," Ben said. "What about you? Tell me all your news. I've watched the development of Dare Services with interest, though I notice it's always Kate's photo, never yours."

44

"I can't risk celebrity—surveillance would be a little tough if everyone recognized me." He pointed to his beard. "I try and vary my appearance too."

With Ben's prompts, Scott went on to talk through some of the cases. Only the achievements got the big publicity, and there were more failures than successes.

"That's the downside," Scott said. "Not every job is satisfying. Maybe one in five turns out as we'd hope. The trick is picking the right ones, and we're getting better at spotting them." He went on to tell Ben about Kate's current investigation and passed on her disappointment that she wasn't here to see him.

Ben shook his head. "Escaped from a locked room? Sounds to me like the mother is lying. Maybe she's a drinker and imagined she'd checked before she locked it. Or maybe she's lying about it being locked in the morning."

Scott laughed. "There you go. That's where we come in. You're thinking like the *authorities*. However, Kate did mention she could do with a better understanding of people. Her skill is natural but sometimes lacks a bit of structure, proven techniques, the principles, you know. She'd like some training to give her that without becoming institutional in her thinking."

"I might be able to pull a few strings. Get her on a behavioural analysis course."

"Would appreciate anything you can come up with," Scott said. Then he realized he hadn't offered Ben food. Kate would have thought about it immediately. She'd also have checked if Ben wanted to stay over. "You must have flown New York to Vancouver and hired a car? I assume it's on the company, but you should stay over—the spare room is made up already."

"I flew United, but at my own expense, and I could do with getting back as soon as possible." Ben suddenly looked serious. "There's something I urgently need to tell you."

Finally. Scott leaned forward. "What is it?"

"It's about your brother. He's alive, Scott. Your brother Joe is alive."

EIGHT

Joe couldn't be alive. Scott had last seen his twin brother in Iraq. Killed on a Black Ops mission.

Scott's head felt like he'd had one beer too many. "He can't be. I saw his body."

Ben pulled an iPad from his satchel and set it down in front of Scott. He opened a video and hit *play*.

The short clip showed an aid convoy in Syria. Scott had seen it on the news: the convoy of eight trucks had been attacked by IS fighters. There had been a firefight and six of the trucks had been destroyed. The report didn't mention who was firing back. Scott had wondered at the time which army was escorting the convoy. The aid charity wouldn't be so bipartisan as to be associated with any side. Not officially anyway.

The news had just shown the burning trucks and reported thirty dead, including nineteen of the enemy.

Ben's footage started before the attack. It was almost pitch-black, and the surveillance, which Scott guessed was a satellite, used infrared to observe.

Bright lights approached and stopped at the head of the convoy. The new vehicle looked like an army jeep. Scott judged there were two men in it, and it was met by three on foot. The passenger got out and there appeared to be a discussion between the passenger and the men on foot—presumably aid workers. Then one walked back to the trucks.

He returned, and for a moment they appeared in deep conversation. The man from the jeep raised his hand and Scott saw the flare of three shots. The aid workers dropped. The shooter jumped back into the jeep and it accelerated away, lost in the night as it turned off its headlights.

Seconds later, men rushed out of the darkness, firing guns towards the convoy. Shots were returned and momentarily the attackers halted. But then they started again with more men arriving. They advanced and took the first truck. It burst into flames. And then the next. Three more quickly followed.

The defenders had retreated to the rear of the convoy but then started to advance. There were more explosions and another truck caught fire. The firefight continued and the tide appeared to turn. The attackers became more ragged and thinly spread. And then they started to run away. They disappeared into the darkness.

The defenders didn't follow. They formed up in case of a further attack.

Ben ended the video. "What do you think?"

"That wasn't an aid convoy. Am I right?"

"Not officially. There was aid that would have been distributed if the convoy hadn't been attacked by IS fighters." He raised his eyebrows.

Scott sat back. "So, the media got it wrong?"

"They reported what they were told. Won't be the first time, won't be the last. But there was something else."

"The jeep that originally approached, was that ISIS?"

"Have you heard of al Amriki?"

"It means 'the American'. The locals used it all the time to refer to us—the army."

"But specifically about one man?"

"No."

"Again, the media. Only this time it's something they haven't been told. Of course, the latest count is that about two hundred and fifty Americans have tried to join ISIS, but this one is different. This one has gained a reputation—a bit like the Brit a few years back. Mohammed Emwazi—or Jihadi John as he was known by the press—was perfect for the ISIS propaganda machine and the British media couldn't help themselves but lap it up and fuel the fire. It's ironic that the very act of reporting atrocities in fact assists the terrorist with his goal of instilling fear and hatred."

"But he's dead now, right?"

"Killed in a drone attack at the end of 2015. He was an embarrassment and deliberately targeted—on the kill list."

Scott knew all about the kill list, having been on a tour of duty in Iraq. What was it—almost five years ago? A lifetime.

He said, "What's this got to do with the guy called al Amriki?"

"The shooter—the passenger from the jeep—is believed to be al Amriki. He's been associated with many atrocities over the past year and sources say he's ex-US Army."

"But I've not heard of him."

The agent nodded. "To restrict the propaganda, it's been kept out of the media. No doubt the reporters on the ground have heard of him, but they've agreed to say nothing. Even Al Jazeera."

Scott had an odd feeling about this, about why his friend was telling him all this, but he decided to wait. He wanted Ben to tell him the whole story in his own time. He stood. "Shall we have another beer?"

"Something stronger," Ben said. "Pour us both a Jack."

When Scott returned with the drinks, Ben said, "I can't tell you directly, but let's assume the convoy did have aid but was also a cover for our boys."

"Pretending to be from the aid charity?"

"No pretence. It was just an aid convoy for people near a town called al Mayadin. Only we happened to be supporting it."

"I don't know it. Wait, I've been a bit slow. This is Syria. What are we doing in Syria?"

"Just over the border about forty miles from Iraq. So, yes, as sensitive as hell and hence no mention of our connection with the attack. The US is officially just advising and is based in Northern Syria. It's the first time this al Amriki has come into direct contact with us. Unfortunately, not one of the three men who spoke to the passenger from the jeep survived, so we have no direct confirmation, but we do have this."

Ben opened another clip and played it. It was daylight but the picture was poor and it was difficult to discern much detail. There were two men, one with something red around his neck—a bandana perhaps. They climbed over the rubble of a wasted building and joined a group of others who were in the process of stripping dead bodies and burying them in the rubble. Some men wore the typical black clothes of IS fighters.

"We believe this is al Amriki," he said, pointing to the one with the red bandana. He brought up the first video and zoomed in on the jeep passenger. Scott could see something like the bandana around the man's neck.

Ben said, "It's the same man who led the attack on the aid convoy."

Scott waited.

Ben said, "The smart guys in Quantico have zoomed in and cleaned this up." He clicked on a jpeg and the face of the man with the bandana. Close up, Scott could see it was actually red, white and blue.

Ben said, "I'm sorry."

Scott stared at the picture until his eyes prickled. His brother. There was no doubt about it; this was Joe Ranieri, the man who had died five years ago.

NINE

Scott tasted bile. "It can't be. There has to be some mistake." But even as he said it, he knew this was his brother and the DOJ wouldn't identify him—even internally—unless they were sure. He took a gulp of whiskey and focused on the burn in his throat.

"You OK, buddy?"

Scott took long deep breaths. "It doesn't make sense," he said eventually.

"I know. But here it is, and we need to talk about the implications."

"Implications?"

"The kill list."

Scott shook his head, trying to clear the fog that suddenly filled his brain.

Ben said, "As an enemy combatant there is legal justification to kill him. The question is, has he materially and purposefully supported hostilities against the US? The secret DOJ committee who decides these things have said that al Amriki meets this criterion."

"But this isn't... he's a US citizen... I thought..."

Ben raised a hand. "Look, it's not been decided yet. Joe has not been put on the targeted kill list, but my understanding is"—he pinched his fingers together—"he's this close to it. But he's a US citizen and there are three conditions that have to be met for him to be targeted."

Scott nodded. They both knew that targeted meant a drone strike—vaporized like Jihadi John had been.

Ben continued, softening his voice perhaps hoping to ease the impact: "The three conditions are: the individual poses an imminent threat of violence against the US; that capture of the individual is not feasible; and, three, that the operation is conducted in a manner that is consistent with the laws applicable to war. In other words, the act itself must not be a war crime. Those three rules constitute what's called due process to protect the specific targeting of US citizens in the event of them joining the enemy."

Scott said, "So the key one is the imminent threat?"

"Yes."

"Is he... could he possibly pose an imminent threat?"

"It depends on the definition of imminent."

"About to happen, surely?"

"You've got to remember that we have a new administration. The hawks are in charge now and imminent has been loosely interpreted."

"How loosely?"

"To mean any threat that could happen in the future... at any time."

"Jeez."

"Yes, it's basically undermined the due process, but only the committee that determines such things is in a position to argue otherwise."

"Jeez," Scott said again. He refilled his glass, took another slug and relished the fire that rolled down his throat.

"There is good news... of a kind."

Scott turned to his friend and waited.

"As I said, your brother isn't on the kill list *yet*. They know about you, of course, and there's the question about capture."

"What are you saying?"

"You have two weeks to find him and bring him back."

"Or he'll be vaporized." Scott shook his head as though dispelling the image of his brother blown to smithereens.

Ben opened his satchel again and pulled out a folder. In it were plane tickets. "I assumed you'd want to get out there ASAP so I've got you tickets to Germany on Air Canada with one change. The flight's in the morning I'm afraid. From there, I've arranged a military plane to take you to Turkey. Then you can take a short hop to an unofficial US base in north-eastern Syria. You'll be going as an embedded reporter for CNN. As far as everyone over there is concerned, that's who you are, except for a unit who'll meet you. When you get there ask for Lieutenant Morrison. He's the man for dealing with anything you need."

Scott's fingers tingled as he took hold of the folder. It was as though they would start to shake at any moment. He felt sick and dizzy. His brother was alive but was soon to be a target.

Ben was speaking again.

"Sorry, what?" Scott said, shaking the fog from his head.

"You are going, aren't you?"

"Yes, I'm going. If Joe really is alive, I can't leave him out there."

"But what if he has joined the terrorists? What will you do then?"

Scott took a long calming breath and felt his head clear, the knot in his stomach ease. "No way has Joe joined ISIS. No matter what it looks like, he wouldn't do that. Hell yes, I'm going! And I'm going to prove he's innocent."

TEN

Kate turned out of the queue and headed back down the highway to Victoria. She drove into the city and spotted a grand-looking spa hotel. She decided to splurge and enjoy her evening.

After checking in, she changed and was soon pounding the wet pavement. She always packed her running things in an overnight bag just in case.

The sea was to the south and she followed the road to the coast. Cutting through Beacon Hill Park, where peacocks honked, she picked up the Waterfront Trail and headed east. Initially the route was flat and, with the wind behind her, she ate up the miles beside a grey pebble beach.

She often started her runs with a head full of thoughts, but after a few minutes all she could think of was her breathing and the pace. It was the perfect way to clear her head and de-stress.

She stopped thinking about the Jemila Dacks case and played with Scott's lateral thinking puzzle. How had Jack and Jill died?

When the trail ended, she took the ramp up to the road, dropping her head and pushing hard to the top. The beachfront was now screened by houses overlooking the straits. Soon the best route became less obvious and she followed a line of cyclists who she figured were also looking for the coast.

After almost a mile of what felt like the wrong direction she emerged on Beach Drive and was rewarded with by a pretty, sweeping bay.

Half a mile later she reached the most easterly point and took a breather. Walking across the edge of a golf course to the sea, she drank from a water bottle and looked out across the straits.

On a clear day, she guessed she could have seen the US. The Washington mountains maybe. However, today the view just faded and merged with a darkening sky. To her right were big houses with spectacular aspects. Plenty of money here, she thought.

The contrast with Grace LaBelle's estate couldn't have been more stark. Would the police have treated her any differently if she lived here? Would the police have made more of an effort to locate Jemila if she'd come from a wealthy, less troubled family?

Kate shook her head. It was the same the world over, it seemed. Live on the wrong side of the tracks and get the worst deal.

Time to turn around.

The choice was to loop back west to the centre or retrace her steps. The coast appealed more and so she took the descent and wended her way back to the trail and then the park and finally the main road north to the hotel.

Her mind went back to Jack and Jill. What big assumption was she making? Well, she only had limited information. They were dead but not by natural causes, so the assumption was that they'd been murdered. They were surrounded by water. Could it be more liquid than water? Could it be poison? No, that was linear thinking. But it could be ice. A block of ice could have landed on their heads... It was a possibility but not very satisfying. There must surely be another big assumption.

Exhausted from her run, she headed for the spa, showered and chilled out for an hour. A woman in the sauna struck up conversation and recommended Fisherman's Wharf for dinner. When Kate grinned, she asked why.

Kate had realized what the assumption was and why water was relevant. Fisherman's Wharf—fish. Jack and Jill weren't people. They were fish. The glass on the floor was their fishbowl.

With no other plan, Kate decided to take the woman's recommendation. Dressed and ready to head out, she noticed a message on her phone from Andrew, her software developer and gym club friend from the UK.

Are you up already? she texted.

Morning, kiddo came the response.

Couldn't sleep, so wondered what you were up to? What's the goss?

She messaged back that she was just going out for something to eat and would call once she had Wi-Fi. Immediately afterwards, she sent a quick message to Scott and asked how things were going with Ben.

Twenty minutes later she was in a sushi restaurant on a marina, watching the early evening activity in the bay. Lights on the boats provided a jewel-like display on the water.

There had been no reply from Scott, and she guessed he was too engrossed in guy-talk to check his phone.

She ordered food and then called Andrew.

"How's the software?" she asked.

"Brilliant. Still getting a regular income from the peer-to-peer stuff and now working on projects for a couple of start-ups. Actually, I've had more time to go to the gym and work out properly. Lost quite a bit of weight."

Kate tried to picture a slimline version of the man she had once likened to a silverback gorilla. "Really?"

"Nope. Just kidding. The more calories I burn, the more I need to consume. Vicious circle."

He asked after Scott and Tolkien before wanting to know about her latest case.

Andrew had always been easy to talk to, and she found it helpful to walk through the Jemila Dacks case with him.

"Are the police usually that annoying?" he asked.

"This detective is by far the worst I've dealt with, but it's always the same when we deal with a new unit. If we get a result with this one, next time they won't be so abrasive."

"*If* you get a result? Aren't you sure she ran away?"

"Not really. It just feels like a better solution—especially since Detective Stanley is so dismissive."

"It's a heck of a puzzle if she did get out without help. She can't walk through walls, can she?"

Kate laughed and waited for her food to be served before she said, "Funny you should say that. She identifies with a Marvel character called Rogue."

"Maybe she took someone else's powers—Silver Surfer. I think he could walk through a wall. Rogue absorbs other people's memories and abilities."

"I didn't know you were a superhero fan."

"Oh yes. Ever since I was a kid. Though I don't really keep up with all the developments and spin-offs. Just the original comic characters for me. Wait a minute..."

She could hear him tapping on a keyboard. When he came back, he said, "She ran away."

"That's my belief."

"No, I mean Rogue ran away from home."

"Where did she run to?"

Andrew tapped on his computer. "*The swamps* is what it says. Can't be more specific, I'm afraid. Any help?"

"Not really. There aren't any swamps around here."

Kate's lobster linguine arrived so she ended the call with a promise to talk more often. As she ate, she looked out of the window and watched the lights. She thought about Jemila Dacks and what Andrew had told her. Was it relevant that the girl thought she was a Marvel superhero? Maybe. But she didn't use super powers to get out of a locked room.

Kate pictured the bedroom. In her mind's eye she saw the comics. The girl was a comic fanatic.

And then it came to her.

It was so obvious when you realized, but then lateral thinking puzzles were all about assumptions obfuscating the obvious.

Kate dialled Detective Stanley.

"You still around?" he said.

"She got out of the room and ran away."

"Yeah, right. It's impossible—unless the mother was lying."

"No."

"How then? How did she do it when we both know there was no way out of that room?"

"Remember what you said to me down at the station?" She paused for effect. "You said, '*You're the intelligent one. You tell me.*'"

She ended the call with satisfaction. It was a cheap shot but it felt damned good.

ELEVEN

Kate set down her second empty glass of Chardonnay when her phone pinged with a message from Scott. He apologized for the delayed response, was just saying goodbye to Ben and would call her in a few minutes.

She was walking back to the hotel when he rang. She expected him to be full of his evening with Ben but it was all about his brother, Joe.

"He's alive!" Scott said.

Kate could hear the stress in Scott's voice. What should have been amazingly good news, wasn't.

"What's up?"

And then he told her the whole story, about ISIS, the attack on the aid convoy and the kill list. She stayed quiet and just let him talk it all through.

Eventually she said, "And you're sure? You're sure it's him."

"Unless someone has manipulated a satellite image… and why would they?"

He paused, and she guessed what was coming next.

He said, "I've got to go."

"To Syria? Oh, Scott." She stopped at the end of the wharf and just stared out into the darkness.

"I have to. If there's any chance… I'm booked on a flight in the morning."

61

Yes, of course he had to go. She snapped herself out of focusing on her own worries and said, "Right. I'll come straight home."

"I just checked the ferry times. It's too late tonight."

Her voice caught in her throat. She wanted to say that he couldn't go without her saying goodbye properly... not again! But nothing came out. She felt a tear on her cheek.

He said, "I'll be all right, honey. I've been trained for—"

It wasn't the same. Going to war, putting yourself in harm's way because it was your job was one thing. It's what you expected. This wasn't expected. He might be prepared, but she wasn't.

When her voice returned she managed, "What time... when's your flight?"

He told her.

"From Vancouver?"

"Yes."

"Then I'll meet you at the airport. If I'm late then you'll make the damn plane wait, OK? You aren't going without properly saying goodbye."

Aside from the lorry drivers who had spent the night in their cabs, waiting at the terminal, Kate was the first to arrive. She sweet-talked a BC Ferries manager who got on the phone and guaranteed she'd be first off the ferry at Tsawwassen. She almost kissed the guy, she was so relieved. However, the one hour and thirty-five minute journey felt like an eternity.

When she crossed the ramp, first off, a worker waved frantically for her to slow down but she ignored him. The Internet suggested it would take twenty-four minutes, but she knew better. This was rush hour.

62

She picked up Highway 17 and was soon on the 99. The tunnel under the Fraser River was clear and everything was going well until she approached the turnpike at Highway 91. Just weight of traffic or had there been an accident?

For five minutes, she barely moved. Then the traffic began to roll at walking pace.

Anxiety crawled up her neck. The flight would board in another twenty minutes. She wouldn't make it.

She called Scott, barely able to speak.

He said, "I've been on the phone to Ben. He's doing what he can to hold the flight."

"I could come off."

"The traffic will be just as bad, maybe worse. Only come off the 99 if there's an accident. Are you moving?"

"Yes."

"Then don't come off."

They kept talking, and hearing his voice helped her stay calm.

Then she said, "OK we're moving again. Yes. Yes. I'm up to thirty... forty... fifty now. It was just heavy traffic. How long do I have?"

"Maybe ten minutes, maybe longer if Ben can do anything."

"The satnav is saying twelve if I stay on the 99, and that's assuming there's no more congestion. Do I stay on or come off and take Bridgeport?"

Up ahead it looked like the traffic was slow going over the second river crossing. She made a snap decision and took the next ramp to the sound of a horn. *Whatever!*

Two minutes later, Kate turned left onto Bridgeport Road that cut the corner. Under the 99 and then... brake. Some damned lorry was in the road up ahead causing a tailback of traffic. People blared their horns.

What was this idiot doing, turning around on a main drag into the airport?

But he wasn't turning around. He'd somehow jackknifed, maybe reversing at a turn. Some kid at the wheel unable to sort the problem.

She still had Scott on hands-free and talking. She switched over to her phone and got out. Up ahead, just beyond the lorry, was a truck rental place. So, the kid had just picked up or was returning and couldn't handle the damned thing.

She talked Scott through what was happening. A guy came out of the rental place and started berating the kid.

"Come on!" Kate yelled, but her voice was lost in the cacophony of car horns.

The guy got the message and climbed into the cab.

"What?"

Scott said, "I've got to go, baby. They've held it as long as they can. I've got to run."

Her hands shook and she steadied herself against the car.

"Scott."

"Yes, baby."

"Dare Services—it's a stupid name."

"Yes, it is, but people recognize it. And that's important." He was breathing hard and she guessed he was running for the plane now.

"It won't be any good with just one of us." She choked up.

"Honey! I'm coming back. I'll be all right. I promise you."

She breathed long and hard, trying to stay in control. "I'm not going to dare you... you just bloody well better stay safe and come home."

"I promise. Four-one," he said, using their code. It had been the post office box where he'd left a message. It

64

kind of said: I'll be in touch and I love you and I'll be waiting for you all rolled together. She knew what it meant.

"Four-one," she said.

And then he was gone.

TWELVE

Barb Winter waved to Kate as she parked. For a second her neighbour stared before hurrying over. She pulled her red setter behind her.

"Oh my dear. Oh my dear. Whatever's the matter?"

Kate smudged tears from her eyes. Barb and her husband were a delightful couple. She was in her sixties and Bernie was probably ten years older, Kate figured. They had been next-door neighbours for over two years now—although "next-door" actually meant almost a hundred yards down the road. Barb came round and cleaned the house twice a week and, when they were away, she'd keep an eye on the place and feed Tolkien.

The elderly lady put her arms around Kate and let her blub. Toby, her red setter, sniffed around her legs. When he didn't get attention, he sat and watched.

Barb didn't say anything until the tears and quaking had stopped.

It was ridiculous, Kate knew. Logic told her that Scott took risks all the time. He'd taken a huge risk when he'd rescued the girl in Pakistan. There had been a firefight then and he'd been hit, but good old Kevlar had done its clever trick and he'd been fine. It was just the same, wasn't it?

No, it wasn't.

Syria was a war zone. IS fighters were religious lunatics and the US government were ready for a drone strike at any moment. Even if Scott managed to locate his brother without getting killed, there was no guarantee they wouldn't be vaporized a moment later.

Although Toby and Tolkien tolerated one another, Barb would never bring him into Kate's home. She tied up the dog outside and made a mug of tea the way Kate liked it. Then, like Toby, the elderly lady waited.

Kate blew on the steam and took a few sips.

"Scott's gone away for a few days." The way she said it, it must have sounded like Scott had left her.

"I'm sorry to hear that, dear."

Kate shook her head. "It's fine. It's just... It's a job." Which in a way it was.

"Oh," was all Barb said, and Kate guessed her neighbour didn't want to intrude. She knew they did sensitive work, although it had never made Kate cry before.

She felt an explanation for the tears was necessary, so said, "It's a dangerous job. I'm worried about him."

Barb smiled kindly. "Scott can take care of himself."

Of course he could. She knew he wouldn't take unnecessary risks, and, after all, he'd said four-one. That made her think about the twin brothers. The Mirrormen.

I lost one. I tracked him down and he was pretending to be the other one, who's dead. But he's not dead. Joe's alive and I lose Scott all over again.

She watched a black squirrel scamper onto the patio table, peel open a nut, nibble it and then dart away. Was all life so transient: one freeze-frame at a time? Pause, dash, pause, dash.

"Bernie is addicted," Barb said, disturbing Kate's melancholy.

"Addicted?"

"He's on his darned computer morning noon and night playing World of Warships. He's like some kid, and it's driving me crazy."

"I can't help I'm afraid. I have two seven-year-old nieces who drive their mother mad with their iPad games, and that's as much as I know."

Barb nodded, but, from the look in her eyes, Kate suspected she didn't know what an iPad was.

They chatted some more while Kate finished her tea. Never once did Barb ask anything else about what Scott was doing or where he'd gone, and Kate was grateful for the company.

Barb left to finish Toby's walk and reminded Kate she'd be back tomorrow to clean.

Kate went to their office and booted up the computer. She felt better and even chuckled at the thought of old Bernie being an online gamer. But that wasn't her intention now. She got out her notes and started tracing Grace LaBelle's two ex-husbands.

From the phone directory she got no hits on the name Bob or Robert Dacks, but there were four Dacks listed and she rang each one. The last one turned out to be a car workshop.

"Dacks?" a guy on the other end said when asked. He shouted into the phone and Kate figured he couldn't hear well above all the crashing and banging in the workshop. When Kate confirmed the name, he said, "I'll go get him."

Kate had to wait a good few minutes listening to what sounded like an ongoing train crash before someone else came on the line.

"Help you?"

"Bob Dacks?"

"Speak up."

Kate shouted.

"No, I'm Jed Dacks," the guy shouted back.

"I'm trying to trace Bob Dacks."

"You mean my brother Bobby."

Kate reeled off the ex-husband's date of birth.

"Yep, that's Bobby all right. But you can't speak to him."

"Oh, why?" she shouted. Suddenly the train crash sound stopped and Kate imagined Jed having to hold the phone away from his ear. "Sorry," she said at a reasonable volume.

"Bobby's been dead some eight years now. Got in a fight down town. Banged his head. Freak accident—well kind of. He was always asking for it, so it was just a matter of time."

"I'm sorry to hear that." The noise started up and she shouted again. "Have you seen or heard from Bobby's daughter Jemila?"

"Who?"

After a few attempts, Kate worked out that the brother had no idea he had a niece. She ended the call and, like all good investigators, followed up by checking the online record of deaths in British Columbia. She confirmed that Jed had died in 2009.

One down, one ex-husband to go.

Kate spent the next two hours trying to trace Steve McNamara. He was on the mainland, Grace LaBelle had said, which wasn't much to go on. However, Kate started in Vancouver, with the plan to move onto the national birth register next. She got twelve hits from the reverse directory search and one had the initial S. But it was a woman's voice on the answer service. She rang the other eleven and only reached three. Which wasn't surprising since it was during work hours. For the others, she left a message and hit pay dirt when one of them returned her call later.

"You're looking for Steve?" an elderly woman asked. "May I ask why?"

Kate said it was a personal matter, and the woman replied, "Well, I'm his mother. I haven't seen him for over a year, but he's around."

"His phone number doesn't appear to be listed."

"That's because he goes by the name Namara now," the mother said. "Dropped the..." And then she stopped, like she realized she'd said too much.

There was a moment of dead air and Kate decided to act like nothing had happened. She asked the same question she'd asked Jed Dacks about Jemila. Had Mrs McNamara seen or heard from her?

When she spoke again, it wasn't a nice old lady's voice anymore. Mrs McNamara said, "Let the past stay in the past." She paused like she was thinking about what to say and then said, "Goodbye." And the call ended. Just like that.

Kate immediately hit the online phone directories again, searching for Namara, but found none that didn't have a prefix of some kind. The mother's comment "He's around" suggested he was still fairly local, didn't it? And yet she'd had no luck searching. Which she guessed meant he either didn't use a phone or was ex-directory.

Scott's first flight was to Montreal and then on to Germany. She took a break from work by looking at flight paths and figured he'd be over England soon and then a few more hours after that they'd be able to speak.

She went for a run, heading down the road past Barb and Bernie's, took a left and was soon in the country. She followed the Pitt River and then trails through the

70

woods of Minnekhada Lookout before picking up the road again and turning for home.

Showered and in comfy clothes for the evening, she sat at her computer with a glass of wine and went through emails.

As usual there appeared to be a few messages from cranks, fans and trolls. There was a lengthy one requesting help regarding the problem of missing or murdered Canadian indigenous women. It was a regular theme because of the apparent scale of the problem. Kate and Scott had discussed it at length and agreed that they would consider each case on individual merit rather than group them as a wider issue. As Kate read through the latest request, she realized it was another generic request and not from a family member. She filed it with others on the topic.

The next email looked intriguing, being from the UK. Megan Stokes's brother, Danny, was missing. He was twenty-three and her full-time carer since Megan was wheelchair-bound. She went on to explain that the email was being dictated. Apart from the location, what piqued her interest was the next comment. It appeared that Danny was obsessed with the story of *I Dare You*. So much so, that his sister suspected he had deliberately disappeared so that Kate could find him.

Ordinarily, Kate would file this with the crank emails, but there was something else. Right before he disappeared he left a code. When Megan had asked what it meant, he said, "Kate Blakemore will work it out."

THIRTEEN

Overnight, Kate had a Skype call with Scott. She'd assumed he was flying into the Syrian capital, but he explained Damascus wasn't an option. Once there he wouldn't have been able to get to the north. "It's too far out of the demilitarized zone," he said. So, he was going to Turkey and from there by military plane to the US-controlled airfield.

She told him about the strange case in the UK and he'd asked if she was going.

"Not until the Jemila case is resolved. Or I can't do anything else."

"I'll text you once I'm about to board," he said.

In the morning, Kate had an idea and checked vehicle registrations for Mike LaBelle's car. It didn't take long to find what she was looking for. Then she switched her attention to husband number two. She worked the phone and search engines and eventually struck gold. She found the name Namara on an employer's noticeboard. Registering for something as innocuous as a charity event had been his undoing—assuming he didn't want to be found, that is. According to the site, he was an employee of Telus, the region's second-largest telecoms provider, which was ironic since he didn't appear to have a phone—but then maybe as an employee he knew how to disguise ownership.

Kate called the Telus headquarters in downtown Vancouver. Although she didn't get a contact number for Steve Namara, by the fifth attempt she managed to get a location. He was an engineer, and she discovered the district he was covering today.

Driving around Port Coquitlam, it didn't take Kate long to spot a Telus van outside an office block. When a man in overalls came out of the building and walked towards the van, she ran over.

"Steve Namara?"

"Who's asking?" he said with an intrigued tone rather than a defensive one.

Kate explained who she was and that it was about Jemila.

His eyes narrowed and his chest swelled like he was trying to look bigger. His fists clenched, and when he spoke again, his voice was laced with acid. "If you're here to threaten me…!"

Kate stepped back and raised her hands. "No! I'm definitely not here to threaten you. It's not like that at all."

His eyes stayed tight but the rest of him seemed to relax slightly.

Kate's mind was whirring. What was it? Why were Steve and his mother so defensive? Again, she played it straight and explained that Jemila was missing. "All I'm trying to do is find out where she's gone."

"Well she's not come looking for me." The way he said it sounded like it was the last thing on earth that she would do.

Kate started to speak but he cut her off.

"I'm re-married with two good children now. The past is the past. I've moved on and I don't appreciate anyone linking me with that girl."

"Why?" Kate asked, thinking that Steve had used a similar expression as his mother. "What happened in the past?"

He opened the door of his van, started to get in and stopped. His eyes narrowed, and if they could have shot arrows, they would have. He said, "If I ever see you again... If you ever come around causing trouble... If... well, you get it. If you do, then next time I won't be so civil. Next time..." And then he slammed the door and drove away.

Kate watched him go. She hadn't been intimidated by his words. A lifetime ago she'd have been a nervous wreck, but now she was just motivated. Motivated to find out what Steve Namara was so worried about.

It didn't take her very long. A search of BC criminal records brought it up.

Steve McNamara had been charged with sexual abuse of a minor. It didn't say who, but Kate was pretty sure it was Jemila. Her stepfather had moved away, changed his name, cleaned himself up and settled down as a regular husband and father. He didn't want anyone digging up the past and labelling him a paedophile.

It also told Kate something critical. If Jemila had run away, then Steve Namara was the last person she would seek sanctuary from. And more to the point, there would be no way that Steve, or his mother for that matter, would want her around. Like he said, he'd moved on. He had a family and a good job. He wouldn't want to jeopardize that for a girl who accused him of abuse.

★ ★ ★

74

Barb was in the house cleaning when Kate got home. She called out that she'd put the mail on the hall shelf and then something like: "There was someone here earlier."

Kate found the elderly lady tidying the cushions on the bed.

"You said someone was looking for me?"

"Did I?" She pulled an expression like she knew what she'd said and then regretted it.

"What's wrong?"

"Nothing, dear."

Kate waited but Barb carried on tidying.

"Barb?"

"Yes, dear?"

"You said something about someone being here earlier!"

Barb looked awkward and then said, "Sorry, it was nothing. Just that someone was looking for you earlier."

"What about him? Did he say his name?"

"No, dear."

"Did he ask for me or Scott?" Kate said, getting a little frustrated with the slow extraction of information.

Barb thought for a moment. "Both of you. One then the other. I can't recall which first though, if that matters."

"Did he say why he wanted to see us?"

"No, dear."

"Gas, electric...?"

"Oh no. He was in a suit." She paused, like she was deciding what to say. "Maybe he was a businessman."

Kate immediately imagined Ben Hurwitz and described him.

"No, this young man had short fair hair. He was also tanned, like he'd just come back off holiday and..." Barb hesitated, perhaps feeling she shouldn't have such thoughts. "He moved like he was in good shape, if you know what I mean. Like he exercised. Like Scott."

Kate's mind was whirring now. Like Scott? Just fit, or army-fit?

"Accent?"

"I couldn't place it. American, maybe from the south, but not strong enough to really notice."

"Anything else you can tell me?"

Barb placed an arm around Kate's shoulder. "Are you all right? Is there a problem?"

Kate didn't know, but there was something that seemed off. Maybe it was just because Scott was away. Maybe she was being jittery for no good reason.

At least that's what she convinced herself until Barb said, "One odd thing though. He came from the back, said he'd looked in the window in case you hadn't heard him ring. I did ask myself why you wouldn't have heard the doorbell, but he did seem like a nice young man."

When Kate spoke to Scott later she told him about the mystery visitor.

"You sound worried, honey," he said.

"No, I'm—" She cut herself short. Scott was dealing with real issues and here she was complaining about imaginary ones.

"Are there any signs of a break-in?"

"No."

"Is anything out of place?"

"I wouldn't know because Barb was in cleaning. Maybe there was. Maybe she tidied it away."

"I wish I was there," he said, and she wished so too, but he needed to do this. There was no point in her being weak.

"I'll be fine," she said, and saying it made her feel better. "I'll just take extra care…"

"Double lock everything. Set the downstairs security. Have your gun…"

"I will. I'll be fine," she said again. "Now, what about you?" He hadn't texted during the day so she'd assumed he'd been too busy. "Are you in Syria now?"

"Just touched down in Istanbul."

"You'll take care?"

Of course he would. He also promised text updates so she knew where he was.

When Kate's phone rang again, she'd put all thoughts of the stranger to the back of her mind.

"Grace?" Kate answered warily.

"I want to apologize."

"No, it's me who—"

"Shut up and let me talk. You didn't do anything wrong. I was tired and overly sensitive. The cops are convinced Mike killed our Jem but he didn't. I know him. He didn't. I was just being sensitive to your questions. I'm sorry."

"Well I'm glad you rang because I wanted to talk to you again. I have a theory and I want to tell you face-to-face."

"What sort of theory?" Grace LaBelle said sounding nervous.

"A good one, Grace. I promise it's a good one." Kate went on to tell her about the conversations with Jed Dacks and Steve McNamara. "Although Steve has shortened his surname to Namara. I know why too."

LaBelle said nothing.

"I'm sorry to ask but did your second husband abuse her, Grace?"

77

"He was a bum."

"You said you kicked him out. Is that really true?"

"Kind of."

Kate waited a moment before saying: "I think Jemila kicked him out—effectively. Would I be right?"

"Kind of."

"Grace, be honest with me, because I think this is important. Am I right that you knew he was no good—a bum as you described him—but it was Jemila's actions that got rid of him. She claimed he'd sexually assaulted her to make him leave."

"Yeah."

"So, he didn't really abuse her."

"Not sexually, no."

"And it wasn't your idea for her to make that claim?"

Grace made a swallowing noise. "Hell no! It was bad. She shouldn't have done it but she did and, well, it worked, didn't it?"

"I'm coming back tomorrow morning. I'll get the first ferry."

"You said it was important. I think you meant Jem's claim means something now."

Kate said, "The X in Jemila's blood by the door. I think it all makes sense, and I'll tell you in the morning."

FOURTEEN

Istanbul, Turkey

Scott blinked in the bright sunshine as he stepped off the plane in Istanbul. Heat shimmered over the tarmac. There was a man in a grey suit standing next to the shuttle bus looking hot and uncomfortable. Scott tagged him as a junior in the CIA.

"Bill Clinton?" the man enquired, using Scott's assumed name. "Follow me, sir."

There was a town car parked a few yards away and Scott climbed in beside the suit.

"Thanks for meeting me," Scott said. "Where now?"

The man turned out to be as talkative as a brick with a personality to match. He nodded like it explained everything, or just *in this direction*, and drove around the terminal to a hanger. There was a row of private planes parked outside. The guy stopped and nodded again.

Scott got the message and climbed out. Scanning the planes, he hoped the Jetstream would be his next ride, but when a pilot appeared beside a twin prop, he guessed the budget only stretched so far.

"OK, let's get you in the air," the pilot said with a flash of teeth. "Once we've got your bag in the hold."

This guy looked more like a local, but his English was excellent. He also turned out to be the exact opposite of the grey-suited CIA guy. As Scott buckled in next to him, the pilot gave a running commentary like on a scheduled flight. Flight conditions, flight time and the weather at the destination seemed to take on vital importance. Scott noted that the accents and idioms came from a range of states, and Tony—clearly an assumed name—admitted he'd learned his English through conversation.

"Never had a cotton-pickin' lesson in my life," he shouted above the engine drone.

The destination was Incirlik Air Base, which turned out to be in the southern tip of the country. Scott had assumed the next stop was Syria, but he didn't question Tony. Although the man talked a lot, there was never a hint that he wanted to know anything about Scott's business. Everything was light and friendly, covering football teams, movies, Tony's children—of which there appeared to be seven—Turkey's prospective membership of the European Union, and political figures in the United States.

Despite being in a diminutive plane, the flight, as promised by Tony, was velvet smooth. On the approach, just shy of two hours later, the pilot was directed to park up well away from the air force hangers. Once there, they remained in the cab until a jeep sped across the tarmac.

Tony reached out and pumped Scott's hand. "Hilary would have stood a chance if you'd been her husband," he said, and guffawed like it was the funniest thing anyone had ever said. "Good luck with whatever, Mr President."

The driver of the jeep could have been the CIA man's less talkative brother: bolt upright in his seat, no eye contact, no conversation. At all.

He stopped outside a block with the US Air Force crest above the door and pointed. There was a huge complex of buildings and a second secure area for the Turkish Air Force.

Scott slung his bag over a shoulder. "Thanks," he said, but the talkative brother just pumped the stick into first and drove away.

A blast of cool air hit Scott as the glass door *swooshed* open.

He walked across the tiled floor where a clerk waited expectantly at a desk.

"Welcome to the US," the guy said with a twinkle in his eye. He checked his paperwork as though a hundred civilians came through those doors each day, whereas Scott figured he was the only name on the list.

The guy looked up again. "Lieutenant Colonel Dao is expecting you, sir. Please take the stairs to the second floor. Right, and then fourth door on the right."

Based on the pattern so far, Dao should have been laconic and unfriendly. But he got up and shook Scott's hand before offering him a drink. Five minutes later they were sitting in comfortable chairs with excellent steaming coffee.

"I don't know all the details," Dao said, "but I do know the plan was to fly you into Rmeilan airfield in Syria."

"Was?"

"I've bad news I'm afraid. As of now, there are no flights in or out of Rmeilan. In fact, all Syrian ops are on hold. I'll be honest with you, I don't know when things are going to change. It's happened before for an odd day but... well, you know, this new government..."

Scott shook his head.

Dao continued after a *what-can-I-do* shrug: "All I'm saying is there's uncertainty right now. Mixed messages coming out of Washington. Once we get the go-ahead again we'll be in and out of there on a daily basis. After all, our guys in Syria need supplies…"

The air base at Rmeilan was under Kurdish and US control. The US were officially there as support and training. But Scott knew it was like the old *military advisor* euphemism. Officially, the US didn't have troops on the ground. Unofficially there would be Special Forces units operating out of the base. He figured that the light colonel was telling him all missions were on hold. Even if Scott got to Rmeilan, he wouldn't have military support.

Dao said, "I've got your kit." He pointed to a cellophane-wrapped package that mostly contained a navy blue Kevlar vest with the word "Press" emblazoned across it in white. "There's a pack with ID papers in there too. Though I don't mind saying, you're a braver man than me."

He scooted his chair around and showed Scott his computer screen. It was a map of the region. He pointed to a green area. "This big block in the north-east is under Kurdish control. Right up here in the corner is Rmeilan. ISIS are this grey swathe below the Kurds and it goes two-thirds of the way west. As they lose ground in Iraq, they're also pushing back into the Hasakah region—hence part of the reason for locking down Rmeilan. Too dangerous for us apparently. Anyway, to the west, ISIS have come up against this patchwork area." He circled the north-west with a finger. "The hashed area is under the Assad government control. They're pushing north. Then you've got pockets of Turkish control, Free Army, Kurds, al-Sham, and other rebel groups." He paused and seemed to study Scott for a moment, then said, "Can I ask where you're headed?"

"Around here, I think." Scott pointed to an area east of Aleppo.

Dao whistled under his breath.

Scott waited for a comment.

When Dao spoke, he was shaking his head. "Man, you do like trouble don't you. Even if you can get into Rmeilan…"

"What?"

"Look, we've got a billet here for you and you're welcome to stay as long as you want." He paused again as if trying to read Scott's thoughts.

Scott leaned forward. "What were you going to say before?"

"Even from Rmeilan, that's a heck of a distance. Mostly safe—relatively—but a heck of a distance."

"And?"

"I might have another option. Look, twiddle your thumbs for a while, and if you're desperate to get in… Well, I'll look into this other option."

"What is this other option?"

Dao raised his eyebrows. "I know someone who knows someone. You know how it works. If you're desperate, and for a price, they'll get you across the border."

"I'm desperate."

"All right then." Dao nodded. "It may take a couple of days, but leave it with me. In the meantime, kick back and enjoy the hospitality."

FIFTEEN

Kate caught the 7am ferry to the island. She'd been up for a few hours already worrying about Scott. They had spoken and texted and he'd finally admitted the problem. He was looking at other ways into Syria.

She'd spent time browsing awful news stories about the Syrian conflict. Car bombings, the chemical attack, helicopters that dropped barrel bombs on civilians, torture. And that was the Assad government. On the other side there were terrorist attacks, the kidnapping and beheading of foreigners, and the massacre of non-Sunnis. Jihadists, including ISIS, were on the rise. Since 2013, around four hundred thousand Syrians had died and there were over six million refugees.

If anyone would be fine it would be Scott, but she couldn't help thinking about it. Thank goodness he'd be under the protection of the US Army.

This morning, brilliant sunshine warmed the top deck and she stood in the wind, breathing deeply and watching the gulls swoop and dive before the ploughing bow.

It was a stark contrast to the weather two days ago. She'd also been incredibly stressed, fretting about seeing

Scott before he boarded his flight from Vancouver International. If the staff would have let her, she'd have stayed in her car waiting for the ramp to be lowered. But of course they wouldn't. Instead, she'd spent the stressful hour and a half staring through the lounge windows, willing the coastline to move faster.

She decided a cup of strong coffee would distract her and make up for the short night. As she turned, she could have sworn a man in a blue suit had been looking at her. The way he turned his head at precisely the moment she looked his way just felt wrong. Especially since he was now studying the paint on the bulkhead.

She shook away the thoughts. *I'm being paranoid now. Why the hell would anyone be watching me?* But her back brain processed his appearance. He had ginger hair and didn't have the build she'd pictured when Barb described the stranger from yesterday. No, this wasn't that guy. This was just a businessman who had looked her way and then, perhaps, got embarrassed.

Even so, she kept an eye out for him and was relieved she didn't spot him again.

As Kate approached the LaBelle residence, she saw a man she guessed was the neighbour Detective Stanley had mentioned.

"Mr Caan?" she called out, getting out of the SUV.

He yelled his Doberman away from the fence, then grunted, "Who are you?"

"I just want to ask a couple of questions."

"Said, who are you?"

Kate explained.

He spat. "That kid is a waste of skin."

Kate took a step closer and the Doberman pulled on his lead. She breathed slowly, grateful the big dog was on the other side of the fence.

"I'm sorry," she said, in her best placatory voice, "it does sound like she was pretty delinquent."

"Not the half of it," he said, and he proceeded to tell her about the things he'd reported.

"You say she wrecked your vegetable plot?"

"Garden, house, car, anything that little shit can do to piss me off."

Kate nodded. "And she's not been seen for over two weeks."

"That's right."

"What do you think has happened?"

"It wasn't me, if that's what you're thinking, missy."

"I wasn't." Again, Kate used the calming voice, and he seemed to believe her. "I was here a few days ago."

"Were you?"

"I noticed your garden then." This time she nodded towards the back of the house. There had been a green tarpaulin leaning like a shelter. This was now on the floor. So were a bunch of beanpoles. She continued: "Your garden didn't look like that last time. Correct me if I'm wrong, but it looks vandalized."

"You're not wrong. It's a damned mess and half my tarp is gone."

"Then…"

He shook his head. "Just because someone else has done this doesn't mean that little shit didn't do it before. If you ask me, someone has done us all a favour."

Kate realized he wasn't talking about the new damage to his garden.

He said, "No, I didn't do anything to her but if I ever caught her on my property I damn well would have. At least my dog would have." To emphasize the point, he

86

let go of the Doberman and it leapt to the fence, baring its fangs.

Kate didn't bother thanking Mr Caan for his help.

"Why are you smiling?" Grace LaBelle said when she opened the door.

"I just met the charming Mr Caan."

"And that made you smile?!" Mrs LaBelle moved aside to let Kate enter and then shut the door behind her.

Kate registered the *click* of the catch, probably loud enough to wake a light sleeper. But then Kate didn't think Jemila left the house while her mother was asleep.

She walked into the girl's bedroom and looked around. Nothing had changed. The comics were still on the floor, the computer chair at the same angle, the bed made, the wardrobe cupboards slightly ajar.

"I have a theory," she said.

Mrs LaBelle sighed. "Is it one I need to sit down for?"

Kate smiled again. "Not bad news, no. It's a theory that's supported by Mr Caan. Although he doesn't realize it yet because my theory is that Jemila is still around."

Mrs LaBelle sat on the bed and her weary eyes brimmed with tears. "So, you're sure she's alive?"

"I can't be one hundred per cent but, yes, I'm pretty sure she ran away—of sorts." Kate pointed to the X by the door. "If someone were being abducted, it would be pretty hard for them to put that very deliberate mark on the wall. Agreed?"

"I guess."

"It's more than a guess. That's blood, so something, presumably a finger, was cut. Let's assume for a minute that Jemila was gagged so you couldn't hear her scream in pain or frustration at being abducted. And yet she has time to stand by the door and draw an X? Surely the person abducting her is moving quickly and quietly. He's not going to give Jemila time to do anything. Even if she's gagged, she could kick the door, cause some sort of commotion to wake you. So that brings me to my first question: were you being totally honest with me, before?"

"What about?"

"Were you sober the night she disappeared?"

"Yes, absolutely."

"So, you're sure that any noise in addition to your husband leaving the house would have woken you?"

"I'm sure."

Kate nodded. It's what she expected, but she'd also noted Mrs LaBelle's question: *What about?* She needed clarification because there had been a lie.

"What wasn't true?" Kate asked.

"I don't know what you mean."

"I need you to be honest with me."

Mrs LaBelle said nothing.

Kate sat beside her and said, "Motive."

"Motive?"

"You painted a picture of a reasonably happy family life. Sure, she had problems and you needed to lock her down, but why run away? What was her motive?"

"I don't know."

"As I said, I spoke to husband number two. Originally, you'd said you kicked him out for being a bum but it wasn't you who got rid of him. It was Jemila. With her false accusation of sexual abuse."

Mrs LaBelle nodded.

Kate said, "And my theory is she wanted to get rid of husband number three. She put the X on the wall to implicate him. Because of his pendant. She wanted the police to think he'd done something bad—maybe not so bad that they could prove it. Maybe that was the plan for McNamara too. Just do enough to get rid of them."

Mrs LaBelle said nothing.

"She knew your husband had a secret, didn't she? She knew that he'd look suspicious and wouldn't have an alibi."

Kate saw she was on the right track. It was in Grace's eyes.

She continued: "Mike left early that day to do something he couldn't admit. And Jemila knew and that's why she disappeared that day. Mike did something illegal on that Wednesday morning, didn't he?"

"Maybe."

"When I was first here, you told me you were saving up to move from this house. Was Jemila happy about that?"

"Not really."

"And how could you afford to save?" Kate didn't wait for an answer because Grace's jaw had tensed as if refusing to open and allowing her to speak. "I also found out that your car is less than a year old. And it wasn't bought on credit. How could he afford that?"

Mrs LaBelle didn't answer. Kate hadn't known for sure. It had just been an educated guess since she'd found no evidence of credit. Mrs LaBelle's didn't deny it.

Kate continued: "You don't have to say anything. Just nod. Was Mike doing something illegal to raise money?"

Grace looked away, swallowed and then nodded.

"All right. I don't care about that side of it. I'm here because of your daughter. Like I said, I think she's still around—unless there's somewhere else she would go and you haven't told me."

"Not as far as I know."

Kate said, "Your neighbour's garden has been vandalized since Jemila went. Which is suspicious. Either someone else is responsible or Jemila did it since her disappearance. And then it struck me: he's growing vegetables. It's food. If she's around then she needs to eat, so why not take it from someone she hates?"

Grace brightened. "So, where is she?"

"First things first. I have an elderly neighbour called Bernie. Lovely man, but apparently addicted to online gaming."

"Like Jem."

"Exactly. How is she feeding her addiction?"

"She's staying somewhere with a computer?"

Kate smiled at that. "Oh yes."

"Where?"

"Like I said, first things first. What I want you to do is stack the comics and change their order. Make it illogical."

"Like?"

"Well, not in date order, and make sure the same titles aren't next to one another. Take a note of it and take a photograph of the pile."

"OK. Then what?"

Kate stood, placed a hand on Grace's shoulder and said, "Then you call me. You'll know when."

She left then and travelled back to the ferry terminal. It won't be long, she told herself. I give her a couple of days before something happens and Grace LaBelle calls me.

SIXTEEN

Kate checked her emails and, after removing the obvious crank messages, she read one in French from a woman in Montreal. Bruce was eight and had been missing for almost a week. The police weren't interested even though she called them every day. Kate spent ten minutes reading the lengthy email before the woman referred to Bruce as her best friend even though he was a pug. Kate binned the email without replying.

She read through some more and binned most of them. The final email had a large zipped attachment and the subject: "Please help us". Before downloading and opening the file, Kate ran advanced security checks on it. Everything came back clear.

It was a cold case from the US. Almost two years ago a John Doe had been discovered in a national park. He appeared to be in his seventies, had no means of identity on him and was dressed inappropriately for hiking. A taxi driver came forward explaining that he'd picked up the guy from the Cleveland Avenue station and dropped him at the foot of Mount Hood. Through CCTV, the police traced him back to Portland International Airport. From there they worked out who he was and that he'd flown in from Mexico. He'd also checked into an airport hotel with a suitcase, which the taxi driver denied seeing.

Eventually, because of his photograph in an article about the mystery, his sister contacted the police. They discovered his real name: Gerry Rosenberg. It wasn't the same one that was on his passport.

The police had ruled that it was death by misadventure. He was an elderly man out on a cold mountain in summer clothes. He died of a heart attack.

The email to Dare Services was from the sister's son, who was convinced that Gerry didn't die of natural causes.

Kate made herself a cup of tea and prepared to read through the detailed notes that the relative had sent. It was unusual to get such a good file on first contact and Kate devoured it.

Gerry was a loner and well travelled. The family had lost contact with him five years ago and believed he was living in California because his sister had received mail from there.

He enjoyed hiking but was the sort to be prepared. It was out of character for him to be in near-freezing weather wearing just a shirt and a thin windcheater. The second thing that the nephew highlighted was the cause of death. Gerry had a bruise on his chest by his heart. The medical examiner had judged that someone had attempted CPR, although no one came forward. In the nephew's view, the bruise was suspicious. Gerry was a fit man with no evidence of a previous heart attack.

The third odd thing was, as far as the family knew, that Gerry had never been to Oregon, let alone Portland, before. Why did he travel there?

And finally, he'd bought a return ticket and checked into the hotel for three nights. The police theory seemed to revolve around a lonely man who had decided to go somewhere picturesque to die. Really? A man planning that doesn't book a return flight.

Gerry's nephew was called Tony Wells. He asked if Dare Services would investigate the case. Although he lived in Chicago, he was willing to travel to Portland to meet them and go over Gerry's last few hours.

Kate's tea had gone cold. This was certainly a case that would interest them. The authorities appeared to have given up and accepted suicide rather than homicide.

Portland was just a short plane hop away. Maybe that should be their next case. Maybe she could get on with it while Scott was away. It would be a good distraction.

She fired off a reply to Mr Wells suggesting they talk. Minutes later he replied wondering whether they could meet in Portland. He was definitely eager but Kate needed a few days. She wanted to make sure about Jemila first. And secondly, she wanted to discuss the case with Scott.

She sent him an email and hoped he'd be able to read it. However, the good thing about this cold case was the lack of urgency—even if the nephew felt differently.

Thoughts of Scott and the dangers of Syria prompted Kate to get out and run. The last vestiges of sunlight streaked through dark clouds and she figured it would rain within the hour. Just enough time for ten miles.

At the bottom of the road, ten yards from her neighbours' house, was a black sedan. There was a man at the wheel looking at a map or something. If he was coming down here, he was undoubtedly lost, since Kate's was the last property on the road.

She cut left and headed for the river. Within a few minutes of focusing on the uneven surface and with fresh air in her lungs, she stopped worrying about Scott. By the time she got to the woods, she'd stopped thinking about cases.

She did a loop and came out close to the road. And stopped. Up ahead, a black sedan was crawling down the road.

Kate shrank back and watched it. There were two people inside. In the car at the bottom of her road there had just been a single man. She wished she'd paid attention and noted the make. It looked the same, but was it?

Am I just being paranoid? There are lots of black cars. And there are two people in this one.

The car continued down the road and disappeared around a corner. Tourists, probably, she decided. However, something told her not to run down the road just then and she started to jog around the loop through the woods once more. After a mile, her pace was back up and she'd forgotten the black car.

She passed a workout bench. There was a man leaning against it as though thinking about exercise, but he wasn't wearing training gear. Kate took another glance and confirmed what she'd subconsciously clocked: he was wearing a suit and baseball cap. But that wasn't all. The guy met her eyes and looked away. And then she knew she'd seen him before. It was the man from the ferry. The ginger-haired guy that had looked and then looked away.

Kate's heart gave a huge thump, like it was its last ever beat. She sucked in air, put her head down and ran hard. After almost a hundred yards she realized she was being stupid. Still out in the open, she was obvious and easy to follow. She veered off into the trees, changed tack and glanced back. No one was there. The guy wasn't following. And even if he was, she could outrun him. He was in a suit, for goodness sake, while she was in running gear.

Who the hell was he? What was he doing in the woods? Had the guys in the black car been looking for her?

She picked up a narrow trail that would lead her in the right direction for home. And then suddenly there was a man with a dog. She saw them in her peripheral vision. He was coming at her from behind and to the right. This guy was in running gear and moving fast, the dog almost pulling him along by the lead.

Kate ran harder but sensed he was gaining. Then he was behind her. She heard the dog's breathing.

This is it!

Kate dived to her left, rolled and grabbed a stick the size of a baseball bat. She squatted, ready, her heart pounding in her chest.

The guy looked at her like she was some kind of crazy thing. He didn't slow down and was soon out of sight running through the trees.

Jesus, he was really just out running with his dog!

When she stood, her whole body shook with adrenaline and fear. It took five minutes of walking before the shaking finally eased. Maybe the whole thing had been in her head? Maybe the guy by the exercise bars hadn't been the same man from the ferry.

For a couple of seconds, she held her head in her hands and breathed deeply. Then she shook the paranoid thoughts away and began to jog again. As she came out of the woods onto the road, there was a moment when she wondered if she'd see a black sedan crawling past. But she didn't.

The skies opened. It had come sooner than she'd predicted, and fine rain quickly turned heavy.

Kate turned into her road and seeing her house up ahead suddenly made her feel safe. Almost home. She sprinted the last two hundred yards and stood on her path breathing hard. Only this time it was through exertion rather than fear.

As she unlocked the front door she knew that she'd feel better as soon as it was bolted behind her. Imagined or not, there was nothing more reassuring than being safe in your own home.

She locked it and clunked the bolt into place and headed for the kitchen.

And then she froze. There was a man sitting in the lounge.

SEVENTEEN

Kate yelled.

The man started to stand and then she caught sight of someone coming for her from the kitchen. His hands reached out.

She'd trained for this kind of thing. Scott had been adamant that she should be prepared, but she was suddenly dizzy. She flashed back to the lodge on Bear Creek—the Arab waiting. The terror paralyzed her.

"Kate!"

Ben Hurwitz's voice.

She blinked and her vision started to clear. The man in the lounge was Ben, and he closed the gap between them quickly.

"Oh God!" she said, collapsing into his arms. She buried her face in his jacket and he held her until the quaking stopped.

"I thought—"

He said, "I'm so sorry, Kate. I didn't think. It was stupid of me to come into the house."

"I've been paranoid that someone has been following me all day." She sucked in air to finally calm herself. "I thought he—they—had broken in."

Ben guided her to the sofa. Now she looked at the other man, the one who had come out of the kitchen. He was in a suit just like Ben. CIA, she figured.

"What's going on?" she asked.

"Firstly," Ben said, holding up a hand. "It really was stupid for us to come in. Scott told me where the spare key was—"

"Why would he—?" There were a hundred questions cramming in Kate's mind right now. Ben had been here only days ago. Scott didn't say anything about him coming back.

"I promised Scott I'd look after you," Ben said.

Kate shook her head, not fully understanding. "Because he's gone to Syria?"

"No, it's a bit more complicated. When I was here a few days ago, it was a personal matter." He glanced at the other agent and shrugged. "I didn't tell you, Jonny, but I wanted to tell my friend that his brother was alive and might be on the kill list. That was where I disappeared to." Ben looked back at Kate. "But this is something else. This is something that affects you."

"Who were the guys in the black sedan? One of them had ginger hair."

"Our counterparts in Canada, doing us a favour. They were keeping an eye on you until I got here. You see, there's been a development. It relates to the Hamilton case."

"You're being cryptic."

"I don't mean to be. Let's see, I'll try and explain. You were in hiding three years ago. You'll remember I came to visit and that same day we heard that the congressman had died."

"Right."

"Well, he didn't. Basically, there was a hitman out to clean up the mess and that included you and Scott. With Hamilton dead, the hit was no longer required."

Ben was watching Kate's face closely. Too much eye contact, she thought.

"What aren't you telling me?"

"I don't know how much you know." Ben bit his lip. "I feel awkward asking. How much did Scott tell you?"

"Assume nothing."

Ben rubbed his hands together and blew on his fingers like he was preparing himself. Then he said, "The hitman was just up the road from your old lodge. He'd found you. If he'd not gotten the message in time, you and Scott would most likely be dead." He shrugged. "Hey, I'd most likely be dead too."

"Wow!"

"I know."

"No, I'm shocked that Scott didn't tell me. Be honest, Ben. He knew, didn't he?"

"Yes. Hey, but don't be mad. He had no reason to tell you about the guy. He was gone, and as far as we were concerned it was over."

Kate nodded. "But it's not, is it?"

"No, it's not. He knows Hamilton isn't dead and it looks like he's out to finish the job."

"And you're here to protect me?"

"Yes."

Kate stood and walked to the window. The rain pelted the patio doors and her reflection was distorted, like a melted waxwork.

After a long silence, she said, "You know the flaw in your logic, don't you?"

"What do you mean?"

"That you're here to protect me." She paused a beat, waiting for him to get it. "You just told me that this

99

hitman would have killed me and Scott. He'd have to be pretty good to kill Scott, but you said it as though you're a hundred per cent sure."

"I—"

"You also said he'd have killed you. Again with certainty. So how can you be sure you can protect me now?"

The agent called Jonny spoke next. "There's two of us, ma'am."

Ben said, "Last time we weren't definite and also didn't know exactly where he was. If I'd known he was out there, I certainly wouldn't have been alone. Agent Makaritis is here to watch my back as much as yours."

Kate spun and stared at him. "Wait, last time this guy was out there for a couple of years. Now you're saying he's *out there*. He's out there right now?"

Agent Makaritis said, "We don't know, ma'am."

"Would you stop calling me ma'am?" Kate snapped, and immediately realized how unreasonable she was being. "Sorry, I'm just a bit tense. Please call me Kate."

"All we know, is he's on the move," Makaritis said. "He's out there in the sense that he's off the radar."

Ben nodded. "We don't know where he is. There's one school of thought that he's either in hiding or waiting for orders."

"Does this hitman have a name?"

"A few." Ben looked away, like he didn't want to say more.

Kate spoke seriously. "Tell me what you call him."

"The Janitor."

She nodded and looked out of the window. The guy cleaned up other people's messes. They were Hamilton's mess.

She switched her focus back to Ben. "You said *one school of thought.* Do you have a different view about this Janitor?"

"He may well be hiding but he knows his orders. My thinking is that he's ready to finish the job, and that's the scenario we need to prepare ourselves for. And, like I said, I promised Scott."

Kate paced up and down as Ben described his plans. How they would stay overnight and move her in the early hours to a safe house in the US. Unlike last time, there would always be at least two agents watching the house and making sure she was safe.

"No," she said when he'd finished.

"What? You can't be serious?"

"I know you'll do your best, Ben, but I can't stay here. I need to go somewhere I'll feel secure."

"And where's that?"

She went over and kissed him on the cheek. "I'm going home. I'm going back to England."

EIGHTEEN

Two days ago, the man who called himself the Janitor fixed a camera to a tree opposite Kate's house and watched remotely until she went out.

He didn't expect to break in and knew there'd be a cat flap. He placed two drones, the size of insects, inside and retreated to the trees. Hidden from sight, he flew the first drone through the kitchen and hall before guiding it up the well of a spiral staircase. If the study door had been closed, he may have had difficulty, but it wasn't. He flew the insect to a position above the window, overlooking a computer keyboard. He imagined someone sitting at the desk and set off the second drone. This one he positioned on the opposite side, so if one view was obscured, the other should be fine.

Discovering the computer password would be straightforward. Getting into the house looked like a bigger issue. The last thing he wanted to do at this stage was warn the girl that he was active once more, that he needed to remove both her and her boyfriend from the equation.

And then, the following day, he got a lucky break. An elderly lady with a dog walked to the side of the property and picked up a stone, a fake stone. Inside was a key, and she used this to gain access.

She tied up the dog outside and was in and out again in a matter of minutes. Ordinarily the Janitor might have questioned what she was doing, but the opportunity was too good to miss. When she started her walk back down the lane, he fired up his U-Haul and headed for the locality. He stopped a mile from the house and cut through the woods like he had done the previous day. When he reached the tree camera, he repositioned it to view the road rather than the house.

Wearing gloves and overshoes, he was inside within seconds. He wore glasses with a lens that played the image from the exterior camera.

At the computer, he quickly entered the password he'd seen Kate use and accessed her emails and files. He uploaded software to monitor her activity just in case he didn't get what he needed now.

He copied the case files and skimmed through three new ones she appeared interested in. And then he stopped.

The old lady was coming towards the house again, although this time she didn't have her dog.

He closed everything down, positioned the chair as it had been and removed his two drones. At the door, he shoved his gloves and overshoes into his pocket and scooted around the back of the house.

"Hello?" the lady said. "Can I help you?"

He dropped the fake stone and hoped he looked like he was just walking around the grounds. There was no suspicion in the woman's face, just surprise.

"I'm looking for Scott and Kate," he said.

She said nothing, and for a second he could see she was processing this. Why was a man in a suit coming from the back of their house? Perhaps if he'd been in overalls he could have been checking out gas or electricity. But then he would have needed a truck at the front with an appropriate logo. He put his hand in a pocket and felt the cold metal of his gun.

He smiled and shrugged. "Scott's away..." he said, and she seemed to relax. He took his hand out of his pocket. "I know it's stupid but I wondered... you know... I looked through the patio doors in case Kate hadn't heard the doorbell." As he said it he realized his mistake. The front door had a knocker but no bell. Maybe he'd need the gun after all.

But then the lady said, "She's out. I don't know when she'll be back."

"She does keep odd hours!" The Janitor smiled again, and she seemed to relax.

"I tell her you called round?"

"Can you keep a secret?" He stepped closer and leaned forward like he was about to share a conspiracy.

"Of course!"

"I'm US security."

"CIA?"

He laughed. "A three-letter acronym. You probably know what it's like, they're changing all the time. A new administration and new acronyms." He flashed her an ID card with the crest of the United States and his photo. The words were too small for her to see. "But basically the same. One day soon it'll say OAP instead of NSA."

Now she laughed. "That'll be a long time yet."

They walked together to the road and he kept talking. "So I don't want you to say anything. Not yet. It would be better to come from us. I don't want to worry her."

"Is there something to worry about?"

"No, no! That's what I mean. I can't tell you and... Well I can tell you it's good news about Scott." He held a finger to his lips. "I need you to keep the secret. Can you do that?"

She nodded seriously.

"Good girl," he said and walked down the road. After twenty yards, he turned and waved. She was standing by the door watching him. Twenty yards later he glanced back, and she was gone.

NINETEEN

The red-eye into Heathrow landed thirty minutes late, as other passengers warned Kate it would. Her body clock said it was still Sunday night as she shuffled stiff-legged through the long queue at passport control. It always struck her as ironic that her fellow passengers from outside the country seemed to be processed faster.

Her brother-in-law, Tim, stood in arrivals with a warm smile and a hot Costa coffee.

"For you," he said, handing it over and taking her cases. "I know you're more of a tea drinker, but I guessed you'd need it."

"Darcy not here?" Kate looked around him, expecting her sister to jump out at any moment.

"Working."

They had started to walk towards the car park, and Kate stopped, taken aback by the shock news.

"Working?" Firstly, Darcy had always wanted to be a stay-at-home mum. Secondly, they'd had a baby boy only six months ago.

"Let's get in the car and I'll give you a proper update."

Kate was still shaking her head when Tim pulled out onto the airport perimeter road.

"I can't believe it," she said. "She…"

"She's her own woman. To be honest I'm surprised she lasted as long as she did. Especially once the twins started school. She began by taking some online courses and completed a marketing diploma last year."

"But she never said a word!"

Tim let out a small laugh. "She didn't want to be judged—by you especially. So I was sworn to secrecy."

"And now she's working, what, full-time?"

"Three and a half days a week. Small local firm with lots of flexibility."

"And what about Harry?" Kate had seen a hundred pictures of her gorgeous nephew on a photo-sharing site and Facebook. He always looked so happy. "Is he in nursery?"

"We have a nanny," Tim explained. "Darce wouldn't have it any other way, and she's brilliant with him. Also brilliant with the twins, does the school run and everything when we need her too."

As they headed west on the M4, Tim chatted about his family. Kate looked out of the window and realized how much she missed England, how much she missed her sister and the children.

When they could see the top of Windsor Castle, Tim said, "It seems like an age ago."

"Almost three and a half years. It is an age. I'm feeling terrible that I haven't seen the girls for so long."

"You FaceTime regularly."

"It's not the same."

"Well, if it's any consolation, I can tell you the twins are bursting to see you. You're a hero to them. So much so, in fact..." Tim suddenly sounded like he'd said too much.

"Go on."

"I didn't say this, OK? Promise me you didn't hear this and it won't affect how you treat Darce."

Kate promised.

Tim said, "The hero worship grates a bit with your sister. I think that was one of the reasons she got back into work. She wants the girls to respect her. She feels she has to compete with Wonder Woman."

"That's ridiculous!"

He shrugged. "Real or imagined, it's there. It doesn't help that the girls want to hear about your exploits the whole time—of course, we have to sanitize them, but they read between the lines. Plus, they get access to news. Oh, and they're gutted that the film is going to be rated 12A."

They came off the motorway at the Reading exit and Tim took the country lanes to their village.

Kate's phone rang with a US number she didn't recognize. Of course, it wouldn't be Scott. He was now in Turkey, kicking his heels, waiting to find a way into Syria. She decided to ignore the call.

An hour later, having met the nanny and spent time with Harry, the phone rang again. Same unknown number. She excused herself and answered.

"Hello?"

A man's voice said, "Kate Blakemore of Dare Services?" He had a lisp, and from his flat tone she placed the accent as maybe New York or Chicago.

"Yes?"

"Oh Hi, I'm Tony Wells."

The name rang a bell, but there had been so much going on that she couldn't quite place it.

He said, "Gerry's nephew. We exchanged messages about meeting in Portland. I just wondered whether you—"

Chicago accent, she thought. That twang is definitely Chicago.

She said, "I'm sorry—"

"What? You don't want to investigate the case now, is that it?"

"No. No, that's not it at all, Mr Wells. I was going to say I'm sorry I can't do it straight away. Something's... something's come up."

"Oh?"

He sounded so disappointed that she added, "Look I've just had to go to the UK for a few days..." She had to keep a low profile. She was effectively in hiding. She'd travelled under a different passport and even Ben had told her to restrict whom she told. But this was just a guy trying to solve a mystery about his uncle.

"Wait a minute," Kate said, breaking into her own train of thoughts. "How did you—?"

"Get your number?"

"Right."

He laughed awkwardly. "Did a bit of investigative work myself," he said. "When you didn't reply to my last email I found out your last case and spoke to a Mrs LaBelle. She gave me your number."

Wow! That was good detective work. The guy was smart. Kate promised to be in touch soon and ended the call. But afterwards, she had an uncomfortable feeling in the pit of her stomach.

TWENTY

Kate and Tim collected the girls from school and she saw first-hand how excitable they could be.

"Tell us about the man Uncle Scott shot!" Emma said.

"And tell us the story about the dead body," her sister India squealed.

"Enough!" their father barked, and the twins fell silent like expectant puppies, waiting for the signal to jump up again. "Auntie Kate will not be talking about any guns or shooting or bodies or anything like that."

"Oh!" the girls chimed in unison.

Kate hugged them long and hard. "I'll tell you about my latest case on two conditions. One, that you don't interrupt, and two, that you don't tell anyone else. Deal?"

"Deal!"

So on the way home, she told them a sanitized version of Jemila's case. It reminded her that she hadn't heard from Mrs LaBelle. She'd told her to set up the room and call her if anything changed. But it had been two days and there'd been no phone call.

* * *

"Why do you do it?" Darcy asked her later. No mention of the work-thing; the fact she'd kept it secret for almost two months. No, after a hug and a "hello" it was straight into questioning why Kate had qualified as a PI and why they were investigating odd cases.

"Because I can," she responded with a shrug. "To be honest, I haven't psychoanalysed myself lately. I do it because I enjoy it—and I feel I can make a difference. We can make a difference. I couldn't do it without Scott."

There was an unasked question, and she could see Tim and Darcy were uncomfortable about why she was here without Scott. Kate hadn't told them. She didn't want them to worry unnecessarily.

She'd already declined their offer of a bed.

"Now we've got Harry, he's taken the spare room," Darcy had said. "But you're welcome to the sofa."

"That's kind, but I have plans."

"Surely you're not staying at Mum's?" Since Kate had been gone, their mum's boyfriend, Terry, had moved in. It had been more than seven years since their dad had passed away, but Kate couldn't accept there was another man in Mumsie's life.

"No, I'm going to stay at a B&B. It's all booked." What she didn't say was that it was booked in another name again and for one night. She'd pay cash and move on. Each night in a different hotel.

Finally, over dinner, after the kids were in bed, Darcy raised the burning issue: "How are things between you and Scott?"

She threw it out there like it was a casual thing, like asking how she liked living in Canada or which cereal she'd eaten for breakfast.

"Everything's fine."

Darcy studied her with gimlet eyes. "I saw how you were with Harry."

"What do you mean?"

"You're broody."

"Am I?"

"Yes, you are."

Kate finished a mouthful of food and took a slow sip of wine. "You never told me whether Harry was planned."

"Don't change the subject."

"It's complicated." She looked at her sister and Tim and hoped they'd accept that as an answer. But they wouldn't, and so she told them that they couldn't have children.

"You or him?" Darcy prompted while Tim looked awkward at her frankness.

Kate's eyes welled up and her throat constricted.

"Sorry, sis." Darcy rushed around the table to give Kate a hug. Before Kate knew it, she was crying freely and the whole thing about Scott travelling to Syria came out. She didn't tell them everything, but she didn't like Scott hanging around waiting to begin his journey into Syria. If something didn't happen soon, he was liable to take matters into his own hands.

"I wasn't going to tell you," she said. "But I'm worried about him. I'm worried as hell."

TWENTY-ONE

Kate's B&B was on the outskirts of Windsor. It had looked better on the Internet and she decided it'd just be for one night.

Kate was in bed when she received a call from Grace LaBelle.

"You were right," Grace said straightaway and without apology, clearly oblivious to the time difference.

"About what?"

"The comics moved. They changed order and, like you said, I took a note of the editions and one has disappeared and one that I didn't take note of has taken its place. Does it mean…?"

"She's around," Kate said. "She's hiding and sneaking back when you aren't home."

"How did you guess?"

"She's addicted to the comics and her computer. Did the chair move at all?"

"No. I compared the bedroom with the photo each day and only the comics changed slightly."

Kate said, "And I think she was responsible for the recent damage to Mr Caan's vegetable garden. Either malicious or maybe for food. Maybe for something else as well. If you keep an eye on your fridge, you'll probably find she's taking a little from there—maybe just enough to keep her going but not too much to notice."

"So what do I do now?"

Kate had given this a lot of thought. "That's up to you," she said. "Really my job is over. She has run away rather than anything more concerning. However, there's a reason for it." She waited for a few beats in the hope that Mrs LaBelle would realize. She could hear her breathing, but there was no comment.

Kate said, "What are you going to do about your husband?"

Grace said nothing.

"You know where he was going on that morning she disappeared. You haven't told the police because it's illegal, isn't it?"

"Yes." Her voice was hoarse, like she was forcing herself to speak.

"Was it drugs?"

"No!"

"OK, but illegal is illegal, Grace. Why was he doing it?"

"To get money so we could move."

And then Kate had it. Jemila didn't want to move, maybe she didn't like sharing her mum with someone else. Maybe that was why she got rid of McNamara, husband number two. Maybe she didn't like her mum being with bums and criminals.

"Unfortunately, I think you need to choose between your husband and daughter. I think that's what this has all been about."

Mrs LaBelle was crying now. Either from the relief or distress. Relief that her daughter was fine or distress that she needed to choose. However, when she spoke, her voice was clearer. She said, "Jem. I choose Jem."

Treating herself, Kate booked her second night into a quaint coaching house in the equally picturesque village of Hurley, not far from Henley-on-Thames.

During the day, she'd focused on Jemila's problems and sent off some emails to contacts in Canada. She had some ideas how she might help Jemila Dacks and her mother.

She was satisfied that she'd done all she could for now when her phone rang again. It was her friend Andrew—the man who looked like a silverback gorilla but had the temperament of a teddy bear. They chatted briefly and he asked for an update on the girl obsessed with Rogue. Within the hour he was visiting Kate's hotel.

"I've never been here before," he said, as they strolled in the sunshine along the river.

"I don't think a lot of people know about this place. The only reason I discovered it was when Scott and I kayaked up the river on our semi-anniversary." She shook her head at the thought. So long ago, and it had been the time he'd told her his secret. At least part of it. It had been a time of innocence, before everything changed.

When they came to the lock, they sat down and she said, "And this is where he lugged the kayak along the towpath. We picnicked over there, on the grass by the weir."

After a reflective silence, Andrew said, "How are you, kiddo—really, I mean?"

"Really, I'm doing great. It's just…"

He said nothing as she collected herself. She was thinking about the past, about the people who had died. When she continued, she said, "I can't believe it about Lisa."

"Murdered. Went out to see an ex-boyfriend in the States, as I understand it, and got killed in some pointless random shooting. To be honest I don't know how you live like that."

"Canada isn't like America."

He shrugged and then leaned back to enjoy the sun. She thought he was going to fall asleep but he was just biding his time.

"You didn't really answer the question," he said, maintaining the repose. She guessed it was supposed to make her feel relaxed and open up. He continued: "A few days ago you were excited about that superhero case and now you're here. What are you running away from?"

Andrew was a good listener, and so she told him about Scott looking for his brother in Syria. "And then I got jittery," she said. "Turns out that the CIA think there was another hitman."

"What, in addition to the Arab?"

"They call him the Janitor. He had links with the congressman and might be looking to finish the job."

"After all this time?"

"That's what the CIA fear. They wanted to give me protection, which scared the bejesus out of me. Really, if he's as bad as they think then signposting me with security guys was the worst option I could think of. Anyway, I'm sure it's just in their heads. These spooks see danger around every corner. Quite frankly, I'm no threat to this guy or the congressman. Scott and his brother have the information and they're out of the equation for the time being."

"So what? This is just a holiday then?"

"Kind of, I suppose."

"And I don't need to go into hiding again like last time?" Andrew looked relieved, and she realized she'd worried him with talk of the Janitor.

"No, you're fine. Unless you have anything suspicious on your hard drive that you aren't telling me about?"

Andrew laughed, his whole body shaking, and at last she felt a weight lift from her shoulders.

A café by the lock-keeper's hut sold ice creams and Andrew bought them each a Whippy with a flake. It took Kate back to happy times, walking by the river in Windsor with her dad, being chased by fat swans desperate for the food.

They chatted about Andrew's work and how his software was now being used by a Belgian and two Italian companies. He was also in discussion with numerous other European lending businesses that needed to upgrade or launch similar products.

"It's going well. Better than I could have dreamed. Providing Brexit doesn't kill negotiations, that is."

Kate tossed the remnants of her cone to a patiently waiting pigeon. "Why should it?"

"No reason, except an attitude, particularly from EU politicians. There's a real possibility that there will be an irrational backlash against anything British, making it hard for us to trade with Europe. Making it cost prohibitive for European companies to buy my software and services. But don't worry about me. I'll be all right. I'll find a way even if it means slashing the price to compensate. So, what about you?"

"Brexit doesn't affect me."

"I mean what are you going to do while you're on this holiday? I know you, Katie. You're not someone to switch off and do nothing for what…?"

"A few weeks. Honestly, I haven't thought about how long I'm here for."

"There you go. What are you going to do?"

She'd already given it thought. She'd wondered about travelling around the country. Although born in the UK, there were many places Kate hadn't visited.

He said, "And after you've been a tourist?"

"I could do that for ages."

"On your own?"

"Well, OK, you make a valid point. There is this case..." And then she told him about the emails from a wheelchair-bound young woman concerned about her brother. She explained that they normally avoided anything like this since it could be fake or someone with a screw loose.

"Do it," he said.

"Do what?"

"Visit them. Maybe it'll be interesting. Worst case, you keep yourself occupied for a while. It'll help take your mind off Scott."

Kate dismissed the idea. Nothing could take her mind off Scott going into a war zone.

TWENTY-TWO

Three days later, Andrew turned up at her latest hotel.

Over a late breakfast he studied her like he was trying to read her thoughts. Eventually he said, "How's Scott getting along?"

"No progress. He's just waiting until the flights start again." Her voice quavered as she remembered what she'd been thinking yesterday when they ended their call. They'd spoken every day and Scott was getting more and more frustrated. He said he was waiting for the flights to resume but she knew him too well. He'd be looking at other options. He might even do something foolish.

Andrew put his arm round her. "I'm sure he'll be all right."

"Yes."

"When was the last time you took a break?"

"Well, this is supposed to be a holiday."

He laughed. "Then you should see a show in London, wander the capital, take in the sights and do a bit of shopping. Forget this case, and any other cases for that matter. Just switch off for the weekend—starting today—and enjoy the English Summer. After all, it only lasts a few weeks of the year."

"Wait a minute!" She felt her spirits rise slightly. "A few days ago, you were telling me to take this Stokes case."

He held up his hands: guilty as charged. "But all I'm saying now is take a few days to switch off."

So she let him take her into London for shopping and the theatre. With continued effort to avoid thinking of Scott, Kate called her mum and invited herself round for Sunday lunch. She hadn't visited for three years and that time had been a disaster because of her mum's boyfriend Terry—or rather because of her attitude towards him.

An email from Megan Stokes's arrived at the end of the day. This one had a different tone. She sounded desperate and begged Kate to come to England and help. Of course she didn't know Kate was already nearby.

Again, Kate's instinct was to ignore the request, but Megan's brother had sent a text to his sister saying Kate Blakemore could help, and then he'd finished it with the code four-one.

Four-one. The goodbye code. So what? He'd used their secret code. No biggie.

Except Kate and Scott had never told anyone their personal codes.

On Saturday morning, Kate knocked on the door of an ultra-modern house in Friars Cliff, on the south coast, east of Bournemouth. She'd called the woman straight after getting the email and agreed to meet.

An Asian woman of indeterminable age answered.

"Megan Stokes?" Kate asked, guessing this was not the woman who she'd spoken to yesterday.

"This way," the lady said in a voice that said it was all too much. She led Kate through a marble-tiled hall to the back of the house.

In a conservatory sat a young woman in a wheelchair. When she looked up, Kate realized she was blind.

"Megan?"

"Sorry, I can't get up," the woman said with humour. After holding Kate's hand, she spoke to the Asian woman. "Thank you, Aisha. You can leave us now."

Megan seemed to wait until the clack of shoes had diminished before smiling once more.

"It's been difficult," she said. "I mean, using a hired full-time carer after so long. Please. Please sit." She pointed to a sofa as though she could see it. Once she was sure Kate had sat, she swivelled the wheelchair so they were almost facing one another.

Megan said, "If you're wondering, I'm only ninety per cent blind. I can see tones. Which is good. And the story about needing help, well that's because Danny is missing. You see, he has looked after me since the accident." She started to talk about her brother but Kate interrupted.

"In your email you said he sent a text to you and used the code *four-one*."

"Yes, I replied asking what he meant, and he said to ask you. Only, I thought he was being funny. I didn't realize I wouldn't see him again after that. I think he was kind of telling me to get in touch with you. What does it mean?"

"Just something like *see you soon*."

"That makes sense."

"Do you know how he knew it—the code, I mean?"

Megan shrugged. "I have no idea, but he's obsessed with you. I wrote a couple of times but you didn't reply."

Kate had printed the last two emails. "Yes," she said thoughtfully. "I don't understand. Last Saturday you emailed that Danny was obsessed with *I Dare You* and you thought he'd deliberately disappeared leaving a complicated code for me to find him."

"Ah." Megan's neck flushed red.

"Yesterday you said he'd just disappeared and the four-one message. What aren't you telling me?"

"Danny wrote the first email—in fact, he's written a few over the last year. He thought you'd come if we said he'd disappeared."

"And then he really did?"

"Yes."

Kate stood. They were cranks after all. "I'm sorry, but—"

The woman in the wheelchair reached out for her, desperation in her unfocused eyes. "Let me explain. Please just listen to my story, because I think something bad has really happened."

Kate hesitated.

"Five years ago, to the month, we had a car crash," Megan said quickly. "We were all in it, Mum, Dad, me and Danny." She swallowed but continued and her voice betrayed little emotion. "Mum and Dad were killed outright. Danny was fine—on the surface, if you know what I mean. I... well this is what happened to me. I'm paralysed from the waist down. The blindness is something I've had all my life, so I can't blame anyone for that."

"But you blame someone for the car crash?"

"Someone rear-ended us on the motorway. We'd been in London for the day celebrating my twenty-first birthday. *Mamma Mia!* the musical—sad, I know, but I was such a fan. Anyway, it was late and maybe Dad wasn't driving fast enough, but a lorry hit us from behind and we went off the road. The investigators thought the driver might have fallen asleep at the wheel. There was another theory that our rear lights were out.

But that couldn't be proved because of the damage. Whatever the reason, we crashed, the other driver didn't stop and was never identified. Just one of those things, I guess. One second you're a perfectly happy family and the next your life is devastated. Sometimes I pray I knew who was driving so I could focus my anger on someone, but I don't and I never will." She briefly wrung her hands in her lap and then stopped herself. "Danny was just about to go to college and I had just graduated. He planned to study chemistry and I had a teacher training position lined up. But neither of those things ever happened."

"I'm sorry," Kate said, and placed her hand on Megan's. "But I still don't see..."

"I'm coming to it." The young woman forced a smile. "We were trapped in the crushed metal for over three hours. I don't remember it but Danny does. He was awake the whole time. He was hoarse with screaming by the time they cut us free."

"And your injuries were a result of the crash."

"All except the eyesight. That's congenital, although to compound things I now have two detached retinas— well mostly. So even if I hadn't been blind I would have been partially sighted as a result. Kind of ironic I guess."

"Megan, is Danny really missing?"

"Yes! Yes! The point is he sent the email last week. He sent the ones before too."

Kate didn't recall seeing any others and suspected Scott had just binned them.

Megan continued: "He would never have sent another one so soon. I sent the one yesterday because he really has gone."

"You still haven't explained."

"He was investigating the crash. He said he was making progress and then he was really secretive and on

123

the phone a lot. He was kind of excited and tense at the same time."

Kate thought for a moment and Megan reached out for her hand, seeming to know exactly where it was.

"Please help."

Still undecided, Kate said, "Tell me about the other code."

"Other code?"

"You said he'd left a code for me to solve."

"No. That was what he said in his email, thinking it would get you here. The only code he told me was four-one. And that was the other thing. His last text just didn't sound like him."

Kate said nothing for a couple of beats.

"Before you decide, at least let me show you around. You'll like the gym."

"Gym?"

"Please don't judge, but you probably guessed that we are rather well off. Dad made it selling his business, and then there was insurance. Basically we have more money than we know what to do with."

"If you don't mind me asking, what do you do with it?"

"A whole army of staff: Aisha is a carer—I know I said Danny was—well he is but he can't do everything for me and now he's gone. There's also a nurse who comes once a day, and a chef, a gardener, a cleaner. But most extravagant, I guess, are the chauffeur and personal trainers."

Again Kate said nothing.

"I knew you'd judge."

"Not at all! I was just thinking it would be amazing to have your own personal trainer, let alone your own gym. You were going to show me."

Kate stood and went to push the wheelchair.

"No!" Megan snapped, then immediately changed her tone. "Sorry, I need to do it for myself. I may not be able to do very much, but the least I can do is get around under my own steam."

As the young woman used her hands on the wheels, Kate realized it wasn't a motorized wheelchair. With her wealth, Megan could have afforded a state-of-the-art chair but she had chosen something manual.

The whole house had marble floor tiles and Megan explained that Danny had worked with an architect to make it suitable for his part-paralysed sister. Downstairs was open-plan and furniture sparse. A ramp took them into a basement where Kate saw the gym, one that wouldn't have disgraced any small sports centre. After that, they took a glass elevator to the first floor and here she found six bedrooms and three bathrooms. All the rooms had electric sliding doors, and Megan's bedroom had a side room like a nursery. Only this one was for overnight help.

"I need someone to stay every night since Danny disappeared," Megan explained.

"Another awkward question for you... how did Danny cope? With looking after you I mean."

"Not awkward—Danny was... Danny *is* great. We have a few arguments, like all siblings. Do you mean does he resent our situation? Absolutely not! He loves me and..."

"Maybe feels guilty that it was you and not him?"

"Yes."

"I want to understand him more. Understand his motivations."

"Of course."

Megan scooted around and went down the hall. The way she moved so smoothly, Kate would never have guessed she couldn't see.

"This is Danny's room," Megan said. It had a door and Megan bumped it open. "There you are. I'm sure you'll want to go through his things."

Kate stepped into the bedroom. The rest of the house was white and crisp, almost clinical. Danny's room was the complete opposite, reminding Kate of a dorm room. He had a Harley motorcycle in pieces at the foot of a king-size bed. One wall was taken up with a giant bookshelf with hundreds of books. There were model aeroplanes and *Star Wars* models hanging from the ceiling, a stack of vinyl LPs with a retro-style record player, a drum kit and six electric guitars. But none of those attracted her attention.

"What's the matter?" Megan asked, and Kate realized she'd been silent. An ice-cold fist had gripped her heart.

"Kate?"

There were posters all over the walls, mostly of rock bands, some movies and a handful of semi-clad girls. The one she now stared at was almost as tall as herself. On it were the words "I Dare You". Below was the photograph of a naked woman.

Kate was staring at a picture of herself.

TWENTY-THREE

The room spun in a blur and Kate leaned against the frame of the Harley to stop herself falling.

"I need to go," was all she could manage as she staggered to the door.

"Kate?"

Rather than get in the elevator, Kate went down the marble staircase. Even the thought of a claustrophobic cubical made her stomach lurch. She had to get outside. She had to get air.

Kate crossed the road and stood under a thin line of pines. She breathed in the salty air and stared out across beach huts and sand to the sea beyond. The Isle of Wight to the left looked closer than she expected. She could see the lighthouse and the row of chalk stacks known as the Needles. Straight ahead would be France, somewhere out there over the horizon. Or was it? In the recess of her mind she could hear her dad saying that the first landfall was South America. He also said you could see the illusion of a polar bear if you looked beyond the Needles. Kate couldn't work it out.

She knew she was avoiding, distracting herself from what she had just seen. How the hell had Megan's brother got a naked photo of her on his wall? Unless it was a Photoshop job, a created photograph using her face. After all, Danny was rich. Something like that, if you were obsessed enough, was probably easily purchased. Even if... no, it definitely wasn't her... but it still felt like a violation.

"Kate?" Megan's call brought her back. The young woman had wheeled herself to the edge of the road and, although she was looking straight at her, Kate suspected she couldn't see.

She walked over. "I'm still here."

"What happened in there? One minute we were talking and the next you were running out like... like I don't know what. Did something scare you? Was there something in Danny's room?"

Kate said, "Tell me about Danny's obsession."

"He idolizes you. In fact, it was his idea to contact you." She turned her chair around. "Could we go inside again? It must all sound strange, and I promise to explain." She started to roll forward and Kate saw she'd miss the path up to the house so she took the handles.

Megan said "Thanks", although Kate guessed the move had been deliberate.

At the door, Kate said, "I'm going now."

"No, don't I—" But before she could finish, Kate closed the door and walked away.

She found a hotel in Bournemouth and used the gym, training hard. But no matter how much she pushed herself, she kept thinking about Megan and the explanation.

Kate took a walk along the seafront and dialled Megan's number.

"How do you send emails?" Kate asked when the young woman answered.

"I dictate them. The software reads incoming ones to me too."

That made sense, so Kate pressed on. "And is Danny really missing?"

"Yes."

"What happened, Megan?"

"He really did disappear."

"Is he in hiding somewhere, hoping I'll find him?"

Megan didn't speak straight away and when she did her voice sounded like she was on the edge of tears. "I don't think so. I think something has really happened to him."

"Why?"

"Well, because he disappeared on Thursday. We didn't even know you were in the UK. And..."

Kate waited.

Megan cleared her throat. "I'm really worried because of the other thing. He said he was investigating our crash, who the driver was that night. He said he had information."

"And?"

"The night Danny disappeared was the fifth anniversary of the crash."

Kate watched a gaggle of surfers trying to make the most of the little waves. They paddled out and waited and waited. Every now and then one would race ahead of a wave and jump on for a ride that lasted seconds. It took patience and determination and for what? The reward was miniscule. Maybe that was what she had here.

"Kate? Are you still there?"

"Did you notify the police?"

"Of course. They pointed out that he's a consenting adult and to wait forty-eight hours. They've just been. A couple of cops came round and took a statement. They were in and out in half an hour. I don't think they're going to do anything."

Kate knew the feeling all too well. She could also hear the strain in Megan's voice and knew this was real.

She turned and headed back along the sand-swept promenade. The low sun was now in her eyes as she walked back towards her hotel.

"OK," she eventually said, "I'll see you in the morning. I want you to tell me everything you know, no matter how painful, no matter how awkward. Is that agreed?"

"Agreed."

TWENTY-FOUR

Kate took down the poster and rolled it up. Once the offending item had been removed, she began to go through Danny's personal things trying to understand him and, more importantly, find a clue to his whereabouts.

Megan came into the room, followed by another woman Kate hadn't seen before. This lady didn't speak but gave them both a mug of tea before silently retreating.

"More staff?"

Megan shrugged, *yes*.

"Tell me about Danny," Kate said, sitting on the bed.

Megan started by saying the family had lived in North London before their dad had made his fortune. "He first bought a ridiculously expensive place in Sandbanks, the other end of Bournemouth. There's a stretch people call Millionaire's Row. Apparently it has amazing views— Poole Harbour and the islands. Not that I could appreciate them. I was eleven and Danny eight. We were both in private school, so the move didn't matter. Mum used to do all the chauffeuring in those days." A flicker of a smile appeared, and Kate guessed she was thinking of her mum.

"What were Danny's hobbies back then?"

"Airfix planes and space." She pointed upwards and Kate realized she knew the remnants of Danny's childhood still dangled from the ceiling.

"Any sport?"

"Basketball, tennis, swimming... He was sporty but never too serious. He could play football but wasn't into any of the teams like his friends."

The way she said *friends* made Kate suspect there hadn't been many. "Was he a loner?" she asked.

"He still had friends." Megan sounded defensive.

"Genuine friends?"

Megan shrugged.

"Girlfriends."

"Some."

Kate almost asked if they were real again but thought better of it. Instead, she said, "Was there anyone special?"

"No. At least not that he told me about. He would go out and... nightclubs mostly, to pick up girls, but he never brought anyone back. I think he felt a bit uncomfortable. For me I mean."

"He liked to read." Kate nodded towards the bookcase as though Megan could see her. It was easy to forget she was blind.

Megan said, "Anything and everything."

Kate scanned the shelves: some text books but mostly fiction. *I Dare You* was there, as were a hundred other thrillers and adventure stories. The textbooks looked like a lifetime's collection, with moth-eaten *Star Wars* annuals and books on astronomy. There were also books on chemistry and maths that probably came from his last years at school, or maybe pre-college.

"He especially loved puzzles," Megan said, and Kate saw books on code-breaking and true-life stories like the breaking of the Enigma code. "I think that's why he loved your story. I enjoyed it too... the audio version of course."

"You left Sandbanks and came here. When was that?"

"After the accident. The house didn't feel the same without Mum and Dad, and it's a funny place: cut off and exposed to people gawping from the ferries. And because of my injuries..."

As Megan spoke, Kate opened the wardrobes. Unlike the rest of the room, they were neat and ordered. She figured a housekeeper did that. The clothes were designer and nothing looked more than a few months old, like he bought and cleared out on a regular basis. He had a set of shoe drawers, and again everything looked brand new.

Megan started again. "I had this place built for me... for us. It's quiet here without being so cut off."

Kate nodded even though Megan couldn't see it, but she wasn't thinking about the house. She was wondering about the brother. Could Danny be a figment of Megan's imagination? Maybe he'd died in the crash and this was all a weird coping mechanism.

Kate pulled out her phone. She knew the date so she searched for news about the crash. Nothing came up.

"Do you have any photographs of Danny?"

Megan shook her head, "There wouldn't be any point."

"Because you're blind."

"Yes." There was real confusion in her voice. "What other reason would there be?"

"But surely... before the crash."

"Oh, sorry, yes. There's some albums somewhere. Mum used to keep them... you know, when we printed photos out. Everyone just keeps them in the cloud these days, don't they?"

Kate agreed but was thinking, *Not every single photo, surely!*

"Could you find them, please?"

"I'll ask someone to look. They're probably in the loft. But if you think they will help…"

Kate was searching other cupboards, hoping for a box of nick-nacks, personal junk that might provide some clues. Didn't all men keep "man stuff"? She found nothing.

Kate sat on the bed. "Where's Danny's computer?"

"He didn't have one. He did everything on his phone."

"And where is his phone?"

"The police asked that. I don't know. I had people look for it but I guess it's with him. And it goes straight to voicemail every time I ring it."

Kate asked for the number and rang it. She hoped to hear Danny's voice but the message was just the standard carrier one.

Megan's cheeks were wet. "I'm worried… I'm really worried he's dead."

Kate tried to keep her voice reasonable, although her mind was telling her that he probably died five years ago. "Is it possible that he's just gone away for a few days? Is there anywhere he would go?"

"No. The police asked that. He never went anywhere except for trips out with me or to clubs… and he was always back the next day."

"Did he go to a club the night he disappeared?"

"No. He went to meet someone."

Kate thought back to what Megan had said before, about Danny investigating the crash. "So, you think it was to do with the accident? You think it was about finding the driver of the other vehicle?"

Now Megan brightened. "Yes, I do. That's exactly it. I told the police that but they just took notes. I don't think they believed me."

Kate said, "What else did you tell them? What else do you know about Danny's investigation?"

"Nothing except that he was excited about progress. I don't think he wanted to get my hopes up too much. That's why he didn't tell me anything else."

Kate was quiet for a long time. Danny's room faced the rear and an immaculate garden as pristine and soulless as the house itself.

"Kate?"

"Sorry, just thinking."

"You have an idea? Danny said you were really clever about these things. Like I said, he was a bit obsessed by you."

Kate placed a hand on Megan's shoulder and said, "I don't know. There's not much to go on. Not much at all. Is there anything else you can tell me?"

"Like what?"

"Anything that may help find him." When Megan didn't reply, she continued: "I'm going to ask a friend some things. In the meantime, I'd like you to find the photo albums. I'd also like anything personal of Danny's from after the crash. Just anything. OK?"

"What do you think?" Andrew said when Kate called him.

"That there are three possibilities. Either Danny is playing a game and he's hiding—"

"In the hope that you will come looking?"

"Right. Secondly, that something has happened, possibly related to this meeting he had, and then there's the final option."

135

"Which is?"

"That this is all some weird figment of Megan's imagination. That her brother is dead and died years ago, probably in the car crash."

TWENTY-FIVE

Kate returned to Berkshire and booked into a small hotel in South Ascot. Having lived in the area, she knew it wasn't horse racing season and so boutique hotels like this one offered reasonable prices.

She went to her mother's for a late Sunday lunch. Unlike three years ago, this time Kate made a big effort and found that Terry was all right. He might not be her father but she was pleased that her mum seemed settled and happy.

Kate spoke to Scott in the evening, and for the first time in a week he seemed more upbeat. He said there would be a meeting tomorrow and he was hopeful of positive news.

In the morning, Kate drove the short distance to Andrew's Victorian terrace house.

He gave her a big hug, like they hadn't seen each other in ages.

She followed him through to the lounge. "Remember the last time I was here?"

They sank into comfortable sofas and Andrew made a fuss with the chintzy cushions before saying, "Of course I do... when it all kicked off."

"I'm amazed you're still here," she said. To anyone else, Kate would have been more circumspect, but this was Andrew. She could say anything to him and he wouldn't take offence. "Partly because you're now rich and partly because of the break-in. I couldn't go back to my flat in Windsor even if I wanted to... just knowing he had been in there. It kind of feels like a violation."

"Did I never tell you this used to be my mum's old place? It would be very hard to leave. Plus, I love it and... for your information... I'm not that well off. OK I've done some good deals on the software, but it puts food on the table. It doesn't buy me a new table." Then he grinned. "Well, maybe I could stretch to a new table. I'm not a big spender, not like your Megan Stokes."

Before he would tell her any more, Andrew went to the kitchen and a few minutes later called her through to the back garden. The small yard had been professionally landscaped, with decking, a patio, shrubs and a water feature. He pointed to the outside sofa and started winding out an awning. On the table was a plate of sandwiches, fruit salad and still lemonade.

Kate said, "So not so much of a table, but a whole new backyard?"

"Something I'd always promised myself. A little luxury—at least when the sun is shining. Some people would rush out and buy a new car. Me? I just wanted a place to relax outside."

"I love it."

"You'll love this too," Andrew said, plopping a red foolscap wallet on the table.

"About the Stokes?"

He nodded. "The very same."

Kate pulled out a sheaf of papers that were still warm from the printer. Andrew had managed to find the article about the car crash in two places: the *Bournemouth*

Echo and another regional paper. They both had the same minimal details. They described the crash in the way Megan had. Nothing more. Nothing less. They mentioned the four passengers and that the two parents had been killed. They mentioned that both Megan (21) and Daniel (18) had been taken to hospital.

Kate looked through the pile of paper. "No follow-up?"

"Nothing about their conditions, but equally nothing about Danny subsequently dying. I also noted that it confirmed there were no witnesses and no evidence as to the hit-and-run driver."

Kate continued. She read an article about how Geoff Stokes and his partner had set up a satellite TV programme and that it had sold for thirty million.

"Ironic, isn't it?" Andrew muttered through a mouthful of ham sandwich.

"Which bit?"

"He made millions from a programme that no longer exists. A flash in the pan. Seemed to be a great success, he sold it and then *pop!* it's canned."

"Interesting. Do we know who the buyer was?"

"Three articles down."

Kate read through a business article about the purchase and how it turned out to be a financial mistake. The buyer was listed as a private equity firm.

"But that's not the most interesting piece." He pointed to the next article. "It seems Geoff Stokes pulled a dirty trick on his partner, Simon Germane. Seems Simon got his investment back but not a share of the profits."

"Photographs?"

Andrew turned a couple of pages and showed her a society photograph of the Stokes family. They were in evening dress and looked happy. It had been taken a year before the accident.

Kate went through page after page and saw why Andrew had referred to Megan as a *big spender*. The home improvements to their Friars Cliff house had cost two million. She'd also thrown some lavish parties, on more than one occasion booking an entire island in Poole Harbour and inviting hundreds of guests.

"And here's the odd thing," Andrew said as she flicked through the articles. "Not one of them, after the accident, shows a photograph of Daniel Stokes."

Kate put the papers down, took a drink of lemonade and reclined in her seat.

Andrew said, "You're thinking what I'm thinking."

"That he died?"

"Right."

"If I was in Canada I'd log on and look up the death records. Can I do that here?"

"Already done, though I suspect it's not as easy. You can't view a death certificate online but you can order one from the General Register Office. And…"

He was teasing her, so she let him and waited.

"And I searched but couldn't find anything. Doesn't mean one doesn't exist. The sure-fire way is to do it manually, go to the office in Merseyside with as much information as you have and get the experts to help."

"Liverpool?"

"Or there's an easier way."

She smiled. She'd known he was holding something back, but when he spoke again it wasn't what she expected.

He said, "I got a phone number of a personal trainer. Pure fluke that I came across this guy, but he has testimonials on his website and one of them is from Danny Stokes."

140

TWENTY-SIX

Near Incirlik Air Base, Turkey

The bar reeked of strong tobacco. The Turk sitting opposite Scott had a hard face but a disarming smile.

"You want to cross the border into Syria?"

"I need a driver to help me find my brother."

"In Syria?" The Turk shook his head, although the smile remained. "Are you mad?"

"Can you do it?"

"I can get you to the border."

"Colonel Dao said you'd do more."

The other man gulped his black sludge coffee.

"My name is Ali."

Dao had told him the man's name. This was pointless, the man was a waste of time. Scott couldn't help but let the frustration show. He'd been in Turkey a week. There was no sign of flights to Rmeilan and the clock was ticking. He'd spoken to Dao every day but all the man would say was "be patient" and "these things take time". But time was a luxury Scott didn't have.

He started to stand, and Ali caught his arm.

"It will cost money."

Of course it would. "How much?"

"I don't know. Maybe a thousand. Maybe two thousand."

"For you to act as my driver?" Scott pulled his arm away.

"Do you know how dangerous it is?" Ali lowered his voice as though he were telling a secret. "People enter the country to fight in the war, not to act like tourists." Then he shrugged. "And anyway, I wouldn't be your driver. I'm not so crazy. I will drive you to the border and there we will cross and meet my brother. He will be your driver in Syria."

Scott said nothing. He looked into Ali's eyes and tried to gauge the man. But all he saw were dark bloodshot eyes.

Ali said, "A thousand and I will get you into Syria with my brother." He shrugged again and also sat back. "Take it or leave it, my friend. You won't get a better deal unless you want to take your chances and do it yourself. In which case, I give you about ten minutes before you get killed. And that's if you are lucky. If some group decides you are worth more alive, then you will wish that they had killed you."

"I need more than a driver. I need a guide. I need someone to speak to people, to translate. I need someone to help me find my brother."

"Of course. Why do you think it has taken so long to organize?"

"All right."

"So you agree." Ali smiled for the first time, showing tobacco-stained teeth. "When would you like to go."

"As soon as I've gotten the money."

"Dollars."

Scott stood and signalled that the Turk should wait. "Half an hour," he said. He left the bar and walked around until he was certain no one was following. Then

142

he caught a taxi to the station where he'd left his bag in a locker. Within twenty minutes he was back at the bar.

Ali hadn't moved from the booth. He took a cigarette from his lips and let out a thin stream of blue smoke.

Scott said, "Let's go."

Ali held out his hand. "The money first."

"What do you take me for?"

The other man grinned. "An idiot who wants to go into a war zone."

"One hundred now and half when you hand me over to your brother."

Ali stopped smiling. "Do you want to go or not?"

"Two hundred now or I'll find someone else."

"A taxi to the border will cost you that much," Ali said, scowling, but then he shrugged. "All right, I need to make arrangements with my brother, and I will pick you up at 2pm tomorrow outside the air base gates."

Scott grabbed the man by the shirt, his temper flaring. "You said we could leave when I got back!"

"Just a misunderstanding," the Turk said, directing the comment to a group of men at the bar who'd been looking at them. Ali smiled sheepishly. "I have spoken to my brother and he can't meet us until tomorrow."

Scott released his grip and sat back.

"Tomorrow at 2pm Please, this is not a con."

Scott nodded reluctantly.

Ali surprised him by reaching out and shaking his hand. Then he flashed a smile, slipped out of the booth and left Scott to pay his bill.

Scott ordered a beer and sat for a while. He had mixed feelings: relief that he had a route into Syria but trepidation at what he might find there. Ben's plan had been to get him in supported by US Special Forces. They would have known the country, maybe the

143

language, and be armed to the teeth. Whereas Scott was armed with a press flak jacket.

By the time he'd finished his beer, he'd decided that Kate shouldn't know. He'd tell her the original plan was back on.

TWENTY-SEVEN

Lymington, England

Kate called the personal trainer but only got voicemail. She didn't say why she was calling and just left her name and number for a call back.

She had checked into another hotel, finding one in a small sailing town on the edge of the New Forest. She was flicking through the file Andrew had produced when he called to discuss the case.

"Andrew," she said, "we only talked a couple of hours ago and nothing has happened since, except I've left a message for the trainer to call me—got to go!"

She ended the call abruptly and accepted a call from Scott. He told her he'd be leaving for Syria tomorrow. He said he'd be accompanied the whole way so not to worry.

"Don't take any foolish risks, Scott."

He laughed. "Hon, I'll be fine. The guys will look after me. We'll be in and out."

"And if you don't find Joe?"

"Then I don't find him. At least I'll have tried."

"I love you," she said, and when they finally ended the call, she had the distinct impression that he hadn't

145

told the whole truth. He was taking a risk and didn't want her to know.

She went for a walk down a cobbled street to a pub on the river. It seemed familiar, and then she realized her family had been there years ago. When her dad was still alive.

Her phone rang. It was the personal trainer.

"Lee here. You left a message."

Kate said, "I'm hoping you can help me."

"I've a full client list at the moment but—"

"It's not about training. It's about one of your clients."

"I can't discuss my clients with you." He suddenly sounded defensive.

Kate softened her own tone. "I'm sorry. It's not like that. Nothing funny, I just have a question about Danny Stokes. You know he's missing, don't you?"

"Yes." He sounded less sure now, but he'd said yes, which meant he knew, which in turn implied Danny was alive. Didn't it?

She said, "His sister, Megan, has asked me to help find him. I just wanted to know when you last did a session with him. Can you tell me that, Lee?"

"Three days before he disappeared. In fact, he failed to show for our session on the day he went."

"I just have one other question, if you don't mind? You see I've been trying to find a recent photograph of him but can't find anything. Obviously, his sister doesn't have anything."

"Nor would she."

"No, because of the blindness."

"And his scar."

"His scar?"

"Yeah, didn't you know? He's got a bad scar on his face. From the accident, I think. Anyway he's really sensitive about the whole thing and won't have any photographs taken."

Kate ended the call and felt terrible. She'd convinced herself that Megan was delusional, that Danny hadn't survived the crash. But he had. He'd been injured and had become reclusive. No real friends. No photographs.

What had Megan said? *Danny was fine—on the surface.* Danny wasn't fine on the surface. His face had been cut and he'd never told his sister.

On the way back to her lodgings, she rang Megan, still feeling guilty.

"I was hoping to hear from you yesterday," Megan said.

"I'm sorry." Kate had thought about explaining, but what good would it do? Plus, she didn't want to say anything about Danny's looks if Megan didn't know. So instead she said, "I've been tied up with personal matters."

"I'd still like you to help."

"Great."

"The detective is fine with it too."

"Detective?"

"Yes, it looks like I was wrong. The police didn't ignore me. DS Keene is helping with the case and thinks he's got something. He's been trying to trace Danny's last-known movements using phone signals or something. I don't fully understand, but he's coming round again tomorrow. He'll be here at ten."

Kate flashed back to Vancouver Island and trying to work with Detective Stanley, about how rude and irritating he was.

"You're sure he's OK about it?" Kate asked.

"Yes, he's nice. Will you come, Kate? Say you will."

"I'll see you tomorrow."

TWENTY-EIGHT

Scott flung his bag on the back seat and climbed into the passenger seat of an old Mercedes. The inside of the car smelled like the bar where he'd met Ali: tobacco, coffee and booze. Maybe the additional aroma of a dog.

"I didn't think you'd come."

Ali grinned and gunned the engine. "But here I am." He pushed a music cassette into a player on the dashboard, filling the car with dreadful music—to Scott's Western ears, at least.

Scott turned it down.

"What's the plan?"

"I'll take you across the border and hand you over to my brother Uday. He'll take you from there... to find your brother."

Ali flicked the volume back up, signalling the end of further conversation.

Scott fished earbuds from the bag behind him, plugged into his phone and selected some more relaxing music. Before closing his eyes, he sent Kate a text to let her know that he was moving at last. On the phone last night he'd almost confessed that he wasn't under the protection of the US Army, but it would have served no purpose other than to worry her more. So he said they were heading for the US airfield in the north—back to the original plan—and he convinced himself that it was a possibility. So he hadn't lied. Not really.

He reclined the chair a couple of notches and did what all soldiers learn to do—switch off the brain and wait. He ignored the thick warm air and focused on the music to take him elsewhere. Occasionally he opened his eyes and saw fields rushing by. At one point the air became dry and he tasted dust. The Merc had slowed, and the condition of the road caused the car to jump and groan.

"I'm avoiding Antakya," Ali said when Scott pulled out the earphones. "This road is not good—quarry traffic—but it's better than the town. Since the war, the airport here has been very busy."

Scott hit the eject button on the awful cassette without complaint from his driver. He cracked the window hoping for fresher air but it was no improvement.

When they hit better roads again, Ali nodded towards a bus they passed. "Mercenaries," he said. "They fly into Antakya, gather there and the Syrian government lays on buses for them." They passed another. "You'll see that the border crossing is like a bus and taxi depot," he said. "In fact, if I wanted the work, I could shuttle people from the border all day... and all night." He laughed. "Though at night you run the risk of tangling with the smugglers."

"Smugglers?"

"Of people who don't have papers but can buy their way across. Where we're going isn't as bad as along the east. People climb mountains and cross miles of fields to get across—and face being shot by the gendarmes for their troubles. The smugglers pay off the gendarmes so they turn a blind eye—mostly." He laughed. "Of course, they make more money if they can get away without paying."

Scott checked his watch. They'd been travelling for two hours. Ali had promised a two-hour drive.

Scott asked, "How much longer?"

"Five minutes."

The five minutes stretched to forty. The sky had turned dark blue by the time they saw signs for the border. They were in a queue of traffic but moving at over thirty miles an hour. Fewer vehicles came the opposite way but clusters of people trudged along the fields edging the road. Behind them, Scott saw yellowed trees that looked as weary as the human tide.

Ahead, he could see the buses lined up like they would outside an airport. Young men stood in unruly ranks. Before reaching the area, Ali turned down a side road.

"Where are you going?"

"Look up," Ali said. It was a cloudless big sky like Scott was used to in the US Midwest. Ali nodded towards the sun. "We have another two hours until sunset. We are going to wait."

"Why?"

"You are white. You may have a beard but you stand out like a bacon."

"Beacon? A fire?"

"Yes. And you are planning to cross with your press jacket. That will get you through the border control, but there are many types of men here."

"What does that mean?"

"I told you about the mercenaries... the ones paid by Assad. Well there are many young men with many ideals." He lit a cigarette and took a long draw before speaking again. "Who knows, one of those young men might think a white man from the Western press will

150

make a good trophy. Some people think Allah has unusual desires." His guttural laugh brought up phlegm, which he then hawked out of his window. He cleared his throat and took another draw on the cigarette. "So, my friend, we wait a little longer."

Ali parked off the road under a tree that provided a little shade. They both got out and Scott squatted against the trunk.

Ali held out his hand. "Half of the money."

"No."

"You are within touching distance. Don't ruin it now. I need to protect myself. What if something should happen to you? What if you get turned away at the border? I will need to pay my brother. I also need to grease a gendarme's arm."

Under different circumstances Scott might have found Ali's mistake amusing, but this was serious. He deliberately hesitated before handing over another eight hundred dollars. He'd already separated the exact amount from his cash. The money wasn't an issue. He just didn't want Ali to know that.

Ali grinned and said he would be back in five minutes.

With the earphones back in, Scott watched the sun creep west until the sky behind him began to turn indigo and the hills glowed with the final embers.

He was just thinking about Kate and how long it would take for her to see the same sunset when Ali spoke.

"All arms greased," he said. "Time to go."

TWENTY-NINE

The Syrian border had a high fence topped with rolls of vicious-looking wire. Scott and Ali moved interminably slowly, half a pace then a shuffle towards the first of two buildings. The sun had gone down two hours ago and the light was fading faster than the residual heat.

On the Turkish side of the border there was a buzz of excitement that almost drowned out the sound of the cicadas. Everyone in Scott's queue was a young man. As they reached the fence and the first building, he could see the much longer queue on the far side. Thousands of people gathered in knots. Many appeared to be sitting or leaning against handcarts piled high with their meagre worldly goods. Based on the progress of Scott's queue and the ragged thin line that came out of the buildings from the Syrian side, most of the departing people would take days to cross.

Scott took a step into the building and warm stale air. It consisted of two rooms. The first had a queue to a typical passport control booth, but once people were past this, they waited in the second room.

Fans blew air towards the officials in their booths, but there was no such respite for the travellers.

Ali said, "You show them your papers and then wait to be cleared. Here..." He handed Scott a declaration form and pencil.

At the booth, the guard looked at Bill Clinton's passport, glanced over the official press authority and took the declaration form. He waved Scott through.

It wasn't until Scott sat down that he realized Ali hadn't followed him. He jumped up and strode back to the booth. Thirty yards away, he spotted the Turk sauntering away.

"Hey!" Scott shouted, but Ali didn't turn. Instead, a firm hand grabbed his arm and jerked him backwards. The barrel of an assault rifle jabbed into his side.

Scott held up his hands and the guard with the gun waved him back to the benches. Scott sat and waited, wondering whether Ali's brother would be on the far side. He doubted it.

Every few seconds a name would be called over a crackly speaker and someone got up. They went to the desk, had papers stamped and were shown the exit.

Scott heard someone close by explain in English that the papers got you through the next border post. The one in Syria. Anyone could go through the door, but without the stamp, you wouldn't get through the next building. They wouldn't stop you leaving here but you weren't really going anywhere without a visa.

After five people, Scott heard his pseudonym on the speaker. At the desk, he presented his papers. A surly officer looked through his passport and the form, held up Scott's press authority, seemed to scrutinize it and then handed the papers back without a stamp.

"Sit down please," he said, and reached to take papers off the next man.

Scott sat bemused as the man after him had his form stamped and left through the door. He watched another

153

two successful visits before Scott realized what was going on. He took out his wallet and put twenty dollars between the pages.

"Bill Clinton."

Scott walked to the desk and presented his papers. With the documents in his hands, the officer dropped them below the counter. When his hands came back the money had gone. There was no eye contact, no comment. The form was stamped, the papers returned and Scott was shown the door.

Outside, a high fence ran either side of the path. The second building was thirty yards away. On the other side of the fence was the road with heavy barriers. On the far side was a second pedestrian channel. Stark spotlights turned night into day for this short distance.

On the opposite side he saw what he guessed was a family: a man and his wife with five children. They scurried as though running a gauntlet, as though they needed to cross the space before someone called them back, before someone realized their mistake at letting them through. Scott hesitated, transfixed by the scene. One of the children was missing a hand, but there was worse, much worse. A child of maybe five looked like it was wearing a gruesome mask. Its hair was gone and the skin had melted. Only the clothes suggested it was a girl.

A nudge from behind brought Scott back to where he was, on the threshold of the second building. He turned and met the hard, dark eyes of a bearded man eager to get into Syria.

Scott stepped aside so that the other man could enter before him. There was no gratitude, just the hard stare.

Inside was the mirror image of the building they had left. He assumed this had once been manned by Syrian officials, but now the men with guns were in Turkish uniforms.

They stood by the door and checked each traveller had the stamped form. They glanced at it and waved them through. Beyond was an empty room. Once past these second guards, each traveller just went straight through onto Syrian soil.

Outside, they took two main routes. Most were shepherded into buses by men who could have been tour guides if not for their military uniforms and assault rifles. The others made their way alone or in pairs to waiting cars. The two groups were far apart. Two opposing sides, not yet ready to fight one another; one highly organized, the other more of a rabble.

Scott strolled in the direction of the cars but then hung back. He looked up and down the line as though trying to spot his ride.

Look confident, he told himself. Look as though you know what you're doing and you'll attract less attention.

It only took a few seconds to realize there were taxis. Not official, but cars available at a price.

He walked towards one at the head of what could be a taxi rank. He ducked down to speak to the driver and was about to when a man running towards him caught his attention.

"Mr Clinton?" the man said, breathless.

Scott nodded.

The man beckoned him away from the vehicle.

"Unless you have joined Ahrar al-Sham in the last hour," he said quietly, "I suggest we get away from these people."

"Uday?"

The other man didn't respond, and Scott jogged to keep up with him. They crossed a dusty patch of land the size of a football pitch before he stopped by a truck. He waved at Scott to get in the passenger side.

Once the doors were shut the man said, "Yes, I am Uday. You have money for me." It wasn't a question.

Scott considered arguing like he had with Ali, but his relief at finding the guy was real and so he handed it over.

Uday stuck it in his pocket without counting and immediately turned the key. After a splutter and belch, the engine fired and the truck bounced across the field to a road.

The Syrian said, "I am sorry I was late. I intended to meet you at what we laughingly call passport control. I am sorry. I was stopped and then I had problems with my engine. At least you didn't have any problems coming through."

"No, except for the delay while I figured I had to bribe the officer."

Uday glanced at him and then back to the road.

"Where are we going?" Scott asked after silence began to grow between them.

"Away from here."

"Where?"

"Somewhere safe... for now." The Syrian wouldn't be drawn further so Scott sat back and watched the headlights bounce and flicker. Every hundred yards or so they would light up refugees or wounded men as they headed for the border. One poor soul hopped along on one leg, using a branch as a crutch. He also lacked an arm. Scott couldn't help wondering what these young men felt, how foolish they had been to risk so much for glory or money or belief.

Uday pulled off down a rough track, and a short time later he parked by a barn.

"We rest here."

Scott said, "I don't need to rest," but the other man ignored him, stepped out of the cab and entered the barn. He lit a candle, and Scott saw fresh-looking straw on the floor and a table.

Uday pointed to a dark corner. "You can toilet there. You will also find a bowl and clean water to wash."

Scott freshened up before returning.

"Have you eaten?" Uday asked. Without waiting for a response, he opened a can of beans and handed it over with a spoon. They were cold but Scott ate them with a chunk of unleavened bread.

The Syrian watched as he ate. He said, "I saw you staring at the people we passed on the road."

"I saw a little girl..." The words caught in his throat.

Uday nodded when Scott didn't finish his sentence. Then he said, "You get used to it. No one is untouched by this war. Either you are horribly injured or killed or your heart turns to stone. It is the only way to cope."

"And the men we passed—the injured soldiers—will they get into Turkey?"

"If they still have their travel papers. Lose those and you won't be allowed back—without paying, that is. And the cost of my company is nothing compared to the cost of a Turkish visa... unless you want to risk the smugglers, that is."

"I was expecting Ali to come with me."

Uday shrugged. "I'm sorry it wasn't as smooth as intended. He will have paid for you to get through. There should have been no need to bribe anyone."

That's what Ali had meant when he said he'd greased arms. He'd paid the bribe in advance but Scott had still had to hand over twenty dollars.

"It wasn't a problem." Scott set down his tin. "So what do we do now?"

"We wait for dawn."

"Why?"

"We passed no road blocks on the road here. If we get stopped in the dark, I won't know who is stopping us. I won't know how to handle it." He studied Scott's face in the flickering light. "I won't know what to do about you. If we meet the wrong people, not only will you be dead but I will be dead also. So we wait and we prepare."

"Prepare?"

"Get some sleep and I will tell you in the morning."

Scott bunched up the straw and lay down, but he didn't sleep. The air was thick and warm. The candle burned out before midnight and Scott lay there in the pitch-dark, listening to Uday snore and the rats scratching in the rafters.

THIRTY

As fingers of light filtered through cracks in the barn walls, Scott heard a distant call to prayer.

Uday stood, rubbed his shoulders and cracked his neck. He lit a cigarette and took a couple of puffs, had to relight it and puffed again. The strong smell turned Scott's stomach.

After repeating the light-puff-light process a few times Uday said, "Are you awake, Mr Clinton?"

Scott sat. "Don't suppose you have any coffee?"

Uday threw him a bottle of water. "Use your imagination."

They sat and waited as it got lighter, until Scott could see straw dust spiralling in the cool air.

"You are expecting me to pray, perhaps?" Uday said, breaking the quiet. "I am Sunni, but not all Muslims are devout. You are American, right? You people think we are all the same, all Islamists."

Scott shook his head and then smiled. "And you are as guilty, no? Branding Americans as all the same."

Uday's features showed nothing. His face was rumpled like used bed sheets and his eyes were tired and yet piercing. Scott guessed the man was in his forties but looked sixty.

"I've been trying to decide," Uday said.

"What?"

"I've been trying to decide whether I am going to help you or steal your money."

Scott could have challenged the old man to have a go. As an ex-Green Beret, he had no worries he could deal with anything except a gun. But he didn't. He casually picked up the press jacket and slipped it over his head. Then he smiled. "Just a precaution in case you've made the wrong decision."

"I may have made the wrong decision," Uday said.

"Which is?"

"To help you, although I will not deliberately enter any Daesh-controlled territory."

"Did Ali tell you where I want to go?"

"He was vague but I know you are looking for your brother. You believe him to be in al Tabqab near Raqqa."

"That's right."

"I'm sure you know Raqqa is the main Daesh stronghold. I won't be going anywhere close, I'm afraid. However, if he is fighting—and I assume he must be— then it is likely he has moved to al Bab. Although I will not risk my life at the frontline."

"Get me as close as you can."

"You are willing to do whatever it takes to find your brother, I think?"

"I am."

"Then we will do this my way. Firstly, you will get rid of that stupid disguise. A reporter is no safer than anyone else. A white reporter will be a target of anyone looking for ransom money. As an American you are a propaganda target for any fundamentalist."

As a gesture of agreement, Scott flung the jacket aside.

Uday continued: "Good. But it is not enough. You have a beard but your skin is too white and your clothes are too clean. I will get you something to darken your skin. Outside there is plenty of dirt for you to mess up your clothes. Look at me. This is the image you should be aiming for. I will leave you for no more than an hour to get food and the skin colouring. Be ready when I return."

"I need a gun."

"That is not a good idea."

"I know that there are arms dealers at the border." Scott fished in his bag and pulled out a wad of notes he'd already prepared.

Uday considered the outstretched hand before taking the money and counting it. "What do you want?"

"A revolver and a couple of boxes of rounds."

"You could get a bazooka for this money." Then the Syrian laughed. "But it will be Russian and probably won't work. I will get your gun. Expect me to be longer. Maybe two hours."

Scott knew he was taking a big risk. Uday could now take the money and disappear, so he said, "When you get back, I will double the money and you can keep it all."

Uday smiled for the first time and Scott was surprised to see a perfect set of teeth, probably whitened.

The Syrian said, "You are very generous, but I would have returned anyway. In the box under the table there is a tin of peaches and some more bread. Have something to eat and don't go anywhere except to mess up your appearance."

Scott went outside and watched the truck disappear down the track. The old barn was in the middle of a field in a valley. To the west he could see hills in the distance. Beyond the ridge in the other directions was just sky.

161

The crop was green and probably young corn but it was tall enough to crawl through and not be seen.

Scott had no intention of staying put. Despite Uday's assurances, he would take no chances, so he started walking along the track. At arbitrary points, he entered the field to leave tracks in case anyone was searching. After two hundred yards, he doubled back and began a random route through the crop.

He got to the ridge and switched on his phone. He'd tried it in the barn but there had been no signal. There was still no signal. He switched it off to conserve the battery.

He dropped down, moving haphazardly again. In places, he crawled to dirty his clothes, and when he finally found a perfect spot to sit and wait, he got a stone and worked on thinning patches of his trousers.

He heard the truck splutter before he saw it moving slowly along the track. It stopped and the Syrian got out. Scott could see no one else in the cab but the cargo bed was piled with tyres. When Uday disappeared inside the barn, Scott looped around. He was thirty yards away but had a better view of the tyres. In theory, someone could have been inside, but it looked unlikely.

Uday reappeared and did a three sixty. Scott came out of the corn beyond the truck. He took a good look inside before joining the Syrian.

"You look a mess," Uday said as a compliment. He made no comment on Scott's caution and lack of trust.

"Thanks."

"Food for our journey," Uday said, holding up a shopping bag, "and a treat."

The treat turned out to be a jar of coffee. It was lukewarm but Scott drank it gratefully. He also examined the pistol Uday removed from beneath his shirt.

It was a used Browning Hi-Power. Belgian-made and stamped with what Scott guessed was the Syrian Army flag. It was a good weapon, if a little bulkier than he'd hoped. The thirteen-round capacity was a bonus and Uday had included a box of 9mm Parabellums.

"I could only get one box," the Syrian said with an apologetic shake of his head.

Scott stripped the gun and reassembled it and checked the firing mechanism. He loaded the bullets. Ordinarily, Scott would have test-fired the pistol, believing in the mantra that you should never fire a gun you haven't tested first. However, he had no idea who might hear a shot or how they would react, so he tucked the gun in his own belt and nodded.

He was ready.

THIRTY-ONE

Uday stuck Scott's bag in a hidden compartment under their seats and drove. They headed north and Scott soon saw what he thought was a village in the distance. It was only as they approached that he realized it was a refugee camp. Thousands of tents and ramshackle constructions littered the plain.

Uday stared ahead as though avoiding the sight. "These are the unfortunates who don't have money or papers. The latest count is a hundred thousand."

"Do they have food and water?" Scott said, shocked by the people's emaciated looks.

"Not enough. There's not enough aid."

The road continued to the border but Uday turned east. "It makes me sick to the stomach," he said eventually. "Does the rest of the world know this is happening?"

"Not necessarily the detail, but it's covered on the news."

"And still they do nothing. Human tragedy, and the world watches the TV."

Uday eased up on the pedal and his hands tensed on the steering wheel. "Checkpoint ahead," he said. "You are my dumb cousin. Say nothing and, if necessary, follow my lead."

There were six men standing by large oil drums on the verge. In theory Uday could have continued, but two of the men stepped forward and pointed their guns.

Uday stopped. He leaned out of the window and spoke. One gunman leaned into the cab. He said something that was directed at Scott and then laughed.

Uday smiled and Scott copied him.

Seconds later they were waved on and the checkpoint was soon dust in their side mirrors.

"They were friendlies," Uday explained.

"What did he say?"

"I told him you were an idiot, and he cracked a crude joke. If you hadn't been an idiot, perhaps you would have been offended."

There was a single wisp of cloud in the arc of blue, and Scott watched it rise as if chased by the sun. They travelled through wide plains and through cornfields. When they passed through villages, children lined the road selling all sorts of junk and red cans that Uday explained were mazut, a homemade mixture of oils that was used as a low-grade fuel. Then they were back into the endless plains.

"Do you mind me asking what your story is?" Scott said, breaking the monotony. "Your English is excellent."

"That's because I was an English teacher."

They passed through another checkpoint.

"Friendlies again?" Scott asked.

"It's always hard to tell... unless they are in black with the flag of the Daesh, then I suspect even my idiot cousin would recognize them. No, there are various brigades who hold small regions. Most of those are affiliated with what's become known as the Free Army, but their influence is dwindling. The Al-Nusra Front was also well established in the area but they have mostly

165

been taken over by the group called Ahrar al-Sham—also fundamentalists but more so. The struggle has changed. People now talk about the war being usurped."

"Usurped?"

"By Russia aiding Assad to gain influence in the region, by the foreign mercenaries, by Daesh supported by Iran and Saudi Arabia and then the Kurds fighting to establish their own—"

They crested a hill and Uday stopped speaking. Up ahead was another roadblock, only this one had a formal barrier and armoured vehicles.

"National Army," Uday said. "Same routine as before."

But it wasn't the same routine. The soldiers insisted that they exit the vehicle. One man jumped in the cargo bed and checked the tires. Another checked the cab while Uday was questioned. Scott hung his head and avoided eye contact. It was over quickly and they were back in the cab and driving.

"That was new," Uday said. "We're going to circle Aleppo, which is now controlled by the government."

They got onto a ring road and passed more soldiers but were waved through. Occasionally Scott saw burned-out vehicles, damaged concrete barriers and buildings. He'd seen pictures of devastation on the TV but now there was rapid reconstruction going on. Labourers filled holes in the road and there were cranes and construction vehicles everywhere.

"When will you ask about my brother."

"Not yet. Let's get around Aleppo and away from the government-controlled zone. If your brother is fighting then he is not here, I can assure you."

Scott saw road signs and thought they'd left the ring road for al Bab. He was surprised when Uday told him they would scoot around to the north and first head for Tal Rifaat.

"Why?"

"I'm not going into al Bab. It was held by Daesh until recently. They've been pressed to the south by a Turkish-backed group called the Euphrates Shield Unit. They're allegedly Free Syrian Army, but there's infighting with local battalions and the Kurdish Syrian Democratic Forces want it too. It's a powder keg."

Outside Tal Rifaat, Uday turned off the road and drove down a farm track for a mile. Then he asked Scott to get out.

Scott stuck the gun in his belt and climbed out.

"Sit in the shade," Uday said, tossing him a bottle of water. I'm going into the town to ask about your brother then—"

"—but I haven't even told you about him!"

Uday smiled. "You didn't need to."

Scott sat under the lemon tree that cast the best shadow and watched the truck's dust-trail disappear into the distance.

After two hours, he'd begun to wonder whether Uday was coming back when he heard something travelling fast.

Scott pulled out the gun and flattened himself on the ground. He hoped the thin trees and sparse grass could provide enough cover.

Three new-looking black SUVs roared towards him. The lead vehicle stopped. A man with an assault rifle climbed out and looked up the road and then right at where Scott was hiding.

THIRTY-TWO

The man with the gun swivelled it over his shoulder and urinated twenty feet from where Scott was lying.

Someone from the rear SUV shouted angrily and the man relieving himself gave a wave. He finished up and jumped back into the first vehicle. Within seconds the convoy was off again, driving fast over the uneven track.

Ten minutes later, Scott heard another engine. By this time he'd found a better spot to hide. But it was Uday.

"Sorry it took so long," the Syrian said when Scott climbed in. "There was a big queue at a checkpoint just outside the town. Looks like the Turks are threatening this area so the Kurds are being extra vigilant. There's also rumours of Daesh in the area."

When Scott recounted the story of the three SUVs, Uday nodded. "That sounds like Daesh. You were lucky, my friend."

"You were gone a long time. Did you find out anything about my brother?"

Uday shrugged. "Sorry. Nothing. I think we need to get near al Bab. Travelling these lanes across the north will be safer for us."

This was an agricultural area. They passed through small villages and met no checkpoints for many miles.

Scott said, "You call them Daesh but you mean ISIS, don't you?"

"Same thing." Uday gave a grunt. "It's Arabic for the same thing, but they don't like the name. It's similar to the Arabic words *Daes*, 'one who crushes something underfoot' and *Dahes*, which means 'one who sows discord'."

Scott got it. He wondered why the West persisted with ISIS. In Vietnam they had called the enemy the Viet Cong. It somehow seemed more dehumanizing and derogatory than National Liberation Front or Vietnamese Communists, from which it was derived.

They passed through two villages and Uday was more relaxed. There were no checkpoints and he said Scott could stay in the truck as he asked about the American.

As they left a war-damaged place Uday called Akhtarin, Scott asked, "So how did you know my brother was the one they call al Amriki?"

"He's American and he's involved in the fighting. I suspect he also looks like you. Am I right?"

"We're twins."

They drove south on a main road sign posted to al Bab. Wheat fields flashed past.

After the wheat fields came the endless plains. The car rattled and bumped along and Scott wondered how hot it was outside. He could see the air distorting the road ahead and figured it was at least as hot as Texas. Eventually the monotony sent him to sleep.

He awoke with a start, jerking awake as he remembered where he was.

"Good sleep?" Uday asked.

"How long?"

"An hour. You even slept through a checkpoint." Uday laughed. "It was a good job they were friendly. I said you were overtired and shouldn't be disturbed."

"Really?"

"No. It's remote out here. I noticed you keep checking your phone before you nodded off. There may be a signal here."

Scott switched his mobile on and saw a single bar of signal. There were three messages from Kate, updating him on her trip to the UK but mostly wanting to know he was all right.

He typed a reply saying he was now being driven through Syria and would call as soon as he could. He didn't mention the lack of military support and just said she shouldn't worry if she didn't hear from him because of signal problems. It took a few retries before it went and Scott then turned his phone off.

When he was done, Uday said, "The next town is Hazwan. There will be another checkpoint, probably Turkish-backed rebels. I'm hopeful we'll find news in the town—but I don't think this one will be safe for you."

Scott got out and found shade behind a tumbledown wall that may once have been a shed—but equally it might have been someone's home.

Uday was grinning when he came back. He also had bread and fruit.

"You know where he is?" Scott asked as he climbed in.

"More like where he's not. He's no longer in al Bab or its southern suburbs because of Russian bombing. If he's anywhere, he's likely to be east of here. Somewhere over by Manbij."

Scott didn't know it but he located it about thirty miles along the M4. He hoped Uday was going to take the motorway but soon guessed they wouldn't be because Uday turned off the al Bab road and took lanes heading east.

After a few miles of farmland, they saw a convoy of military vehicles coming the other way. There was no roadblock, but a man in the lead jeep flagged them down. The armour-piercing gun mounted on the top easily convinced them to comply.

Uday did his usual easy conversation while Scott pretended to be dumb.

Boots thudded into the cargo bed as someone checked their load, and then they were waved past.

Scott breathed out. He found that these moments didn't get any easier, despite the faction who confronted them.

"What now?" he asked as Uday put his foot down.

"We go to a place I know, north of Manbij. You'll get a better signal there. You'll be able to make a good phone call."

Uday was smiling, and for a second Scott wondered if he'd seen Kate's texts. Then he realized it was unlikely. It was easy to guess Scott was anxious to send a message home.

"Love is the most important thing," Uday said, nodding.

"This morning, you said you used to be a teacher. What happened?"

"I am from Homs. You know it?"

Scott remembered hearing the name on the news: a drawn-out battle between Assad's forces and the Free Army.

Uday continued: "I taught at a secondary school that no longer exists. Some teachers died. Children were killed. I survived."

Scott said nothing.

"You are wondering why I am not a fighter? I am a pacifist. It seems a strange word at a time of war and atrocity but I know that no good can come from fighting back. I was one of the early protestors against the regime. We were a band of academics and professionals who thought that peaceful protest could persuade Assad to change his ways. Maybe, looking back, we thought we could influence popular opinion and vote him out. But it did not happen, and once violence began, it was met with violence. We should have learned the lessons from the past. Of course, Gandhi eventually defeated inequality and prejudice by peaceful protest. We should have laid down, not fought back. But we are where we are and our beautiful country is lost."

After a silence punctuated only by the bump and groan of the truck, Scott said, "What did you mean by love being the most important thing?"

"My wife died two years ago—not because of the civil war—she died of cancer." Uday stared ahead for a quiet moment and Scott waited. "Life is fragile and we have such a limited time here on earth. I loved my wife more deeply than I can express. I miss her, and I don't know if I shall ever see her again."

"But your religion…"

"People who say they are certain of Heaven are either lying, deluded, or incapable of rational thought."

"That's cynical."

Uday gave a huge shrug. "It's my prerogative. Of course, I want to believe in an afterlife and I am told to have faith, but I do not truly know. It is the curse of the inquiring mind, of intelligence." He shrugged again. "Anyway, I digress. What I have learned in my short life is that, in the end, there is only one thing that truly matters. That thing is love. It is not money, or gain, or defeating the enemy. It is such a simple thing. Love."

172

They crossed a river and passed through another village and Scott noticed that, although it had clearly been in the war zone, the people went about their normal business. Old folk sat outside their houses and a group of boys kicked a football up and down the street.

"Do you have children?" Uday asked.

Scott shook his head.

"I have three. My daughter married and is living in Damascus. She's doing all right. I have two sons." The way he said it made Scott think the Syrian was immensely proud of them.

"Are they in Damascus too?"

"My eldest went to university. As soon as he finished he got a place in Vienna to study a master's degree. It was a way of getting out of military service. My younger son had to join the national army." He paused, and when he spoke again his voice cracked. "It is tough for a Sunni in Assad's army... especially one who doesn't really want to fight anyone... Razak, my eldest son, got him out. He knew a captain in the Austrian UN force... had his little brother smuggled across the border. He's now working in a restaurant in a town near Vienna. I brought up my sons on my own. I miss them but I'm glad they are safe and together."

"Brotherly bonds can be very strong."

"Like you and your brother?"

Scott nodded. "Is that why you are helping me?"

Uday laughed with real mirth. "No, that really *is* because of the money!"

THIRTY-THREE

There were dark mountains to the north, and Uday drove towards them down a farm track. At the end was a house that Uday said was safe. He had used it before. The roof was half gone, but inside it was more intact than Scott expected from the rubble outside. He realized an outbuilding must have taken a direct hit and disintegrated.

There were mattresses in every room and Uday explained that people used it when travelling through, sometimes soldiers, sometimes smugglers, but it was usually empty.

He left then, saying he would get more information, and Scott sat in the shade of the broken roof and watched the track.

Scott was used to waiting, and he now trusted that the Syrian would return. He checked his phone for a signal and called Kate. She told him about the case in the UK, that she'd just arrived in Paris and Andrew was with her. Scott was pleased she was busy and distracted from his ordeal. All he told her was that they were camping overnight in the north and hoped to make progress finding Joe tomorrow.

Afterwards, he judged it was mid-morning in New York and called Ben. After a couple of transfers, he was through.

"You've only got about three days," Ben said.

"I know."

"What's your plan?"

"I'm working on it."

Ben didn't need to say he was being crazy. He knew it. After dead air, his friend said, "If you do get him out—"

"—I have to."

"When you get him out, get back to Incirlik Air Base. I'll get the CIA there ready to interview him."

"And clear him."

There was dead air once more.

"Let's hope so," Ben eventually said. "Good luck, buddy."

The sun set, first shimmering gold and then a crimson streak. Uday's truck appeared almost three hours later.

He came into the house with a box of food and a map, which he spread on the floor. He showed Scott where they were. The Euphrates was to the east and they were about five miles from the Turkish border.

"Al Amriki isn't in Manbij. There is news of him fighting to the south of there. Although the news is confusing."

"How so?"

"I thought he was working for Daesh but now he seems to have left them for another fundamentalist group." He paused as he studied Scott's eyes.

"Does it bother you?"

"Not at all," Uday said with a melancholy smile. "But I expect it bothers you. Daesh being sworn enemies of your Western civilisation."

Scott shook his head. "And that's what doesn't make sense. Why would my brother do it?" He had told Uday about Joe's background, about being Special Forces and operating in Iraq.

When Scott didn't say any more, Uday pointed to Manbij. "I will take you outside of the town, where I have left a rented car—well, in a way. The rental market isn't exactly flourishing at present. It's a bit of a banger but I negotiated a good price for you. Then you are on your own."

Should there be no other option, they'd previously agreed what their story would be. Uday would say he was a hostage, that Scott had forced him.

Uday was sure it wouldn't happen. He could talk his way out of anything and, so far, there had been no trouble. Tomorrow they'd have a short journey and it was then all down to Scott.

They sat upstairs and Uday laid out a picnic of bread, olives, tomatoes, hummus and a yoghurt substance that he called *labeneh*.

As they ate, Scott said, "Why do you stay in Syria? You could go to Austria and be with your boys."

"This is where my heart is. No matter how broken, this is still my country. And one day I hope my boys will return to a better land, free of Assad, free of Daesh, free of sectarianism, free of foreigners."

"I could be offended."

"I don't mean you of course. I mean foreign fighters and other countries trying to land grab or gain influence." Uday smiled sadly and changed the subject. "Did you call your wife?"

Scott nodded. "The signal here is fine, and it was good to talk properly again."

"You love her very much?"

"I do."

Uday finished an olive, washed it down with water, and closed his eyes. "Love is not breathless. It is not excitement. It is not the promises of eternal passion. Love is what is left over when being in love has burned away. My wife and I had it. We had roots that grew towards each other underground, and when all the pretty blossom had fallen from our branches, we found we were one tree and not two."

"That sounds familiar."

"Louis de Bernières from *Captain Corelli's Mandolin*. Have you read it?"

"I've seen the movie."

"Ah."

"What does that mean?"

"Today people would rather watch than read another's words. In words, one can find much more depth." Uday sucked on another olive as though thinking. "On the road here, you told me you didn't have children."

Scott thought about his infertility and Kate. They had tried to have a child and failed. But it didn't matter, their love was as strong as ever.

Uday said, "The love of your partner can strengthen and define you. But the love you see in the eyes of your child. That, my friend, is the meaning of life."

"Is that another quote? Who said that?"

Uday smiled. "I just did."

They took it in turns. One slept while the other watched the road. In the cool hours of pre-dawn, Scott buried

177

most of his remaining money on the bombsite. He expected to need most of it to get home—if he made it this far. Before they had set off yesterday, Uday had asked what his plan was. But every soldier knows that when the fighting starts, all plans change. Scott just had an objective. He would find his brother and then find a way out of the country. It could be back here and the crossing to the north. It could be to a US base or it could be by another route. It didn't matter.

He stood with his back to a brick wall and watched the sky lighten and change colour.

When he went inside, Uday was hunched over a small stove with a pot on top. Using a shirt to hold the pot's handle, he poured coffee into a cracked mug.

"I thought you didn't have any coffee?" Scott said, accepting the offered drink.

Uday shrugged and grinned. "I was saving it. You should feel honoured. Normally we'd have sweet black tea for breakfast."

The coffee was thick and bitter and delicious.

"Thank you."

"This will be our last day," Uday said. He leaned against a windowless frame and moved his fingers through the first rays of sunlight as though he could touch them. He seemed lost in thought for a few minutes, before he turned, the light at his back.

"My plan was to leave you here."

Scott finished his drink. "What changed your mind?"

"Stupidity." Uday shook his head, bemused with himself. "I have a new plan."

"When the fighting starts, plans change."

Uday raised his hands. "Mr Clinton, I do not intend to get involved in any fighting, believe me. I will take you to the car and you can drive south towards Khirbat ar Rous. Although I don't think you will get very far."

"I just have to try." Scott held out his hand. "My real name is Scott."

Uday grinned. "I didn't think you were really the president. And, Allah be willing, you will find your brother."

"I thought you didn't believe."

Uday shrugged. "I said I didn't know. It never hurts to play the odds."

After they had shaken hands, Uday added: "And what then?"

"After I find my brother? I'll work something out."

"Once I have dropped you off, I will come back here. You have three days. Understand? If you can get back to this house within three days then I will take you across the border."

Scott nodded. "That's good of you."

Uday patted him on the arm and grinned. "Good of me? Remember, I'm doing this for the money. You get back here and we'll talk about how much you owe me."

In the truck, Scott sent Kate a text message. He said they were on their way and not to worry if she didn't hear from him for a few days. The signal was likely to be too poor. Afterwards, he took a long, deep breath and refocused on the task ahead.

As they bumped down the farm track, he took the map and memorized the roads in case he could get back. He tried to picture which armies were where and how to get as close to Joe's probable position as he could before he was confronted by IS fighters. Uday said that Daesh territory was about five miles south from where they would pick up the rental.

They passed through low hills with olive and pistachio groves and met their first checkpoint of the day. Uday said it hadn't been there the previous night, but it wasn't a problem. Uday wound down his window and spoke to them. Moments later, they were waved through.

When Uday drove off the road to find the car he'd bought yesterday evening, he stopped abruptly.

Ahead, by the car, a group of five armed men were pointing guns at them. They weren't IS fighters but they were just as unpredictable.

THIRTY-FOUR

The men waiting at the car had thick beards and dark scowls. There were at least twenty of them, all with weapons, and a bunch of vehicles, most with guns mounted to the roof.

"Trouble," Uday said unnecessarily.

Two of the armed men started to approach. They shouted and gesticulated with their weapons, at them and then away.

"They want us out of the cab," Scott said. He assessed the soldiers as poorly trained. They should have surrounded the truck first. He pulled out his gun and held it low, beside the seat. "Let's go straight to plan B. Tell them I forced you."

"No." Uday swallowed hard. "Some of these guys are so twitchy, if you say the wrong thing, they will just shoot you. Remember, I am Sunni. I can talk us out of this."

Then he opened the door and slowly stepped out with his hands up. Scott stared ahead with unfocused eyes and imagined he wasn't here. He saw images of himself and Joe, dressed in their made-up Mirrormen superhero costumes. Uday was talking calmly, and the two nearest soldiers seemed to listen.

Scott recalled the old lady who lived along the road. They'd seen her in town and helped her across the street, only to discover she hadn't wanted to cross after all. The memory made him smile. What was the old lady's name?

Another man approached and jumped in the cargo bed. Scott could feel the vibration as the man checked the cargo of tyres. When he jumped down, Scott glanced to the side mirror. The man had taken Uday's spare fuel canisters.

Uday pointed and complained but the soldier ignored him. He aimed his gun at Scott and gestured for him to get out.

Uday was talking rapidly, and Scott guessed he was arguing, trying to convince them like he'd convinced the others before that Scott was just his idiot cousin.

Scott kept his gaze forward and down like he was oblivious. But all the time he was watching. The second soldier broke away and rounded the truck.

Scott just had time to stick the gun behind him as the door was jerked open and rough hands pulled him from the cab.

Uday gave an angry yell.

Scott stumbled onto all fours, tried to stand but felt a boot on his back. He tasted dust and eased his face off the ground. But he remained prone, unthreatening and tried to stay relaxed. There was a small poppy growing in the dirt inches from his face and he focused on that.

The shouting continued and the boot lifted off, but Scott didn't move. He kept his eyes forward, his mind back in Palmyra, Virginia. Mrs Frolisch... that was the old woman's name. Six months after the crossing-the-road incident, they had found her by the river. She had slipped by the bank and broken her leg. Joe had gone for help while Scott performed first aid. He used strips of his clothes to bind her leg to a stick. A doctor said it would heal and his actions had prevented permanent mobility problems for the old lady. Their photos had been in the paper and the mayor gave them a medal.

Scott's attention was snapped back to the present as he was pulled off the ground. Uday was close, remonstrating with a couple of guards. He pointed to the truck and down the road. Maybe he was telling them he had an appointment and needed to sell his tyres.

Scott casually scanned where the soldiers were standing. If things turned bad, could he kill them before being killed? The nearest man was six feet away. He seemed less twitchy than the ones with Uday. The other men didn't seem to be paying much attention. Most were looking at and questioning other drivers. Go for the Browning or the nearest soldier's gun?

He glanced back at Uday and decided to go for the other man's weapon and use him as a shield. Then everything changed. In the corner of his eye, he saw someone marching purposefully towards him. At the same moment, the nearest man pointed his rifle and started jabbering.

Acting dumb, Scott glanced at the rifle. Jump up and grab it now? With the gun aimed at his head, the odds didn't look great. He started to move, very slowly, getting a better angle. At the same time, his body language said he was no threat.

The approaching man was five paces away, four, three…

The nearest soldier seemed to be getting more and more angry.

Scott shook his head. *I don't understand.* He raised his arms and half stepped towards the soldier with the gun.

Uday intervened. He stepped between Scott and the soldier and waved his arms. A rifle butt to the stomach abruptly shut him up.

Then the approaching man was right behind Scott, and in that instant, his left ear stung with a pistol whip that made a burst of stars fill his vision.

The soldier grabbed Scott's shoulders and swung him around. For a second they were face-to-screaming-face before Scott's knees were hit and he sank to the floor. Another blow to his head sent him spread-eagled in the dust. He felt the barrel of the rifle in his ear as hands patted his back.

And then they stopped as they found the Browning.

For a weird moment, everything seemed quiet. He couldn't hear Uday's complaints. He couldn't hear the shouting soldiers. Far off, he thought he could hear birdsong. Then the peace was shattered by a gunshot. And darkness rushed in.

THIRTY-FIVE

Two days earlier. Dorset, England

Kate couldn't help thinking about Scott, about when they first met, their amazing times together. How did you know when it was the right person? There were no rules, no formulas. But she had known. You want to spend every waking moment with someone. You want to share every experience with them. You're fascinated by everything they do. And being with them makes you feel a better person. Bigger, stronger, capable of anything. Like you can take on the world.

Although it hurts when you need to be apart, your love is still all-conquering. She knew that. She felt it. And yet, as she waited for Detective Keene to arrive, there was also the gnawing worry.

Scott said he'd let her know as soon as he was on his way. She'd checked the Internet overnight and read a few awful stories about people trying to cross the Syria–Turkey border. People getting shot, getting conned by guides, paying enormous bribes.

She knew the clock was ticking. Scott couldn't afford to wait if he didn't really have military protection.

Keene was late. She'd been waiting with Megan for almost half an hour when he rang the bell and was brought through to the conservatory by the carer.

Megan hadn't been able to expand on Keene's description so Kate had no idea what to expect. But she relaxed when she saw Keene's face. He was probably mid-forties, with a tan that set off his bright blue smiling eyes.

"It's a pleasure," he said, holding Kate's hand before sitting opposite.

She couldn't help but appraise him. British detectives were far less concerned about appearance than their North American counterparts. Or maybe it was salary related. He wore an unstylish grey flannel suit that looked a size too big. His shirt was buttoned down and adorned with a nylon tie. His unfashionable shoes looked old but polished so well that they had a reflective shine.

"You were nervous?" Keene said.

Kate smiled. "Can you tell? Dealing with the police... well, you never know what you're going to get. Sorry, I don't mean to be rude," she added quickly.

"No offence taken. I confess I hadn't read your story. Well, not until this weekend. But based on your past, I totally get your concerns." He handed over a business card. DS Kevin Keene, Dorset Constabulary, and then his phone number.

He said, "I also checked out your Dare Services website and understand that you normally assist people that have been let down by the authorities."

Kate looked at Megan, who was listening intently but gave no visual signals. Was there really any need for Kate to be involved?

Keene continued: "I know what you're thinking, Ms Blakemore—"

"Please, it's Kate."

186

"I know what you're thinking, Kate, that the authorities haven't let Megan down. So you're questioning why you're here. But perhaps I can give you an update..." He stopped and leaned towards Megan. "An exciting update, even from yesterday."

"Really?" Megan also leaned in.

"Sorry, I should slow down. Let me just tell Kate what we found out yesterday and then I'll get to this morning's news." He switched his attention back to Kate. "So, we've done a couple of things that you'd expect. We've put a trace on Danny's phone and also his credit cards and tried to work out his movements. He left home at two forty-five last Thursday."

Megan said, "We normally have our chauffeur take us everywhere but he didn't use Pat."

"No, he took a cab," Keene said. If he was annoyed at Megan's interruption, he didn't show it. Instead, he smiled disarmingly. "That didn't take much clever detective work. I just rang all the local firms and got lucky. He took the cab to Hinton Admiral railway station. The trace on the phone showed that he caught a train to London which was scheduled to arrive at Waterloo station at twenty-one minutes past five but was six minutes late. After that, his signal disappeared."

"Underground?" Kate asked.

"Twenty-five minutes later it pops up again at Kings Cross St Pancras. So yes, it looks like he took the Underground. From there it looks like he goes into St Pancras station, possibly a coffee shop, because he's there for fifty minutes and then the signal goes off again."

Kate said, "In the same spot or did he go back to the Tube?"

"Same spot. We figure the phone was switched off. Anyway, that was Thursday. Well, yesterday morning

187

the phone was switched on again. Briefly. On then off, but we got it. Still in St Pancras but two hundred yards away from where he was before." He nodded like he could read Kate's mind and continued: "Yes, I had the local guys take a look and yes we've got the phone."

Megan said, "You've got it?"

"Lost property. A guy working there was cataloguing items and just checked to see if it worked... at least, that's his story. We showed him Danny's photo—"

Kate couldn't believe what she'd just heard. "You found a photo of him?"

"Ah, not a photo but a computer-aged estimation. As I guess you know, there aren't any photos of Danny, not any recent ones at least. So we took an old one and computer-aged it a few years. Anyway, the lost property guy didn't recognize it but one of the staff at Pan something or other—"

"Le Pain Quotidien. It means *the daily bread*."

"Oh yeah, well, one of the staff thought they recognized the picture, but of course they get hundreds of people going through there a day and it was almost a week ago so we don't know if he was there alone or meeting someone."

Kate said, "You mentioned credit card activity..."

Keene shrugged. "Still too early. The warrant's been executed but we're waiting for the card companies to provide the data. From experience, it might take a few days—after all, we're just talking about a missing adult male, not a terrorist plot. Also, I just don't have the resources. It's just me and anyone I can call on to do me a favour."

He stood up and placed a gentle hand on Megan's. She gripped it hard for a long moment.

"I want you to know that I'm doing everything I can and that I am making progress."

188

She said, "Are you going already?"

"Things to do."

"What about Kate?" Megan reached out and Kate took her hand. "Kate's just come all this way."

Kate said, "It's not a problem, Megan. The main thing is that the police are investigating and things are happening. Like DS Keene said, we normally help out when that isn't the case."

What the detective did next surprised her. He winked and mouthed, "Talk outside."

He thanked Megan and said he'd show himself to the door. As he left the conservatory he held up two fingers and mouthed, "Two minutes?"

Kate nodded. She heard the detective's shoes tap their way down the hall and the door open and click shut. *What is he up to? What does he want to say that Megan couldn't hear?*

"I'm sorry if I've wasted your time," Megan said. "I really thought…"

"It's fine. You have my contact details. If you need me, just call or email." Kate held Megan's hand again as she saw tears spill over Megan's cheeks.

"He will be all right, won't he?"

"I'm sure he will be," Kate said, "and if there is any way I can help, I will."

Outside, Keene was standing where Kate had been the first time she'd visited, beneath the pines and looking out to sea.

She stood beside him and looked at the island. Breaking the silence, she said, "The polar bear…?"

"What?"

"I thought you could see a polar bear in the rocks of the Isle of Wight."

"Oh yes. Not from here though. It's an illusion formed by the cliffs on the far side of the Needles. You need to be on the Overcliff on the way into Bournemouth in order to see it."

"You wanted to tell me something."

"Walk with me," he said, and he started walking along the path.

She followed. "Is there bad news?"

"Nothing like that. Let's just sit down. I have something to show you."

He said nothing else until they had descended steps to the promenade and walked beside the beach. The air was warmer with no breeze. There was a long row of pastel-coloured beach houses. After two hundred yards they came to a café with benches outside. He said his car was parked just the other side and, while Kate queued to order coffee for him and tea for herself, he went to his car. When he returned, he was carrying a briefcase.

He placed it on the bench and sugared his coffee before opening it.

The first thing he took out was the computer-generated photograph of Danny Stokes. Kate smiled. There was something she'd discovered that the detective didn't know.

"He has a scar."

"Does he?"

"To be honest I don't know where or how prominent it is but the personal trainer said he'd been badly scarred in the car accident. Apparently, Megan doesn't know— or doesn't admit it to herself."

He nodded thoughtfully. "Which explains why he was so reclusive, why there were no recent photos."

"Right. But you didn't bring me here to show me his photo, did you?"

"No." He removed a phone from the case and placed it on the table.

"Danny's phone?"

"The very one."

He was teasing, being deliberately cryptic. She said, "And?"

"And we got into it and guess who the last call was to. Do you know anything about his father's history?"

"A little. I know he had a partner. I know they made their money selling a business that subsequently failed." Keene was nodding. "Was it the partner or someone from the company who bought the business?"

"Simon Germane, the partner. The disgruntled partner. Do you know about him?"

"That Megan's father somehow managed to get most of the money? Yes."

Keene cocked an eyebrow. "So it's interesting."

"Yes, but what does that mean?"

"The call log shows they spoke quite a bit the day before Danny disappeared and Thursday. And it all started with a text." He paused and raised his eyebrow again. "The text said, I know you did it."

"Wow!"

"Yeah. Here's my theory: Danny has spent the last few years trying to find out who the driver was, who caused the fatal crash. Something led him to Germane. The man had a motive after all. He got in touch and met him at St Pancras station last Thursday."

"And then disappeared."

"Not just that."

He was teasing again, so Kate waited for Keene to continue.

The detective said, "Germane hasn't been seen since last Thursday either."

Kate finished her tea and set the cup down like a statement. No more messing about. Straight talking from now. She said, "I get why you didn't want to say that in front of his sister. You didn't want to remind her of the

191

crash or suggest Germane's involvement. However, I don't understand what I'm doing here. Why are you sharing this with me?"

Keene picked up the smartphone and unlocked it. He seemed to open an app. He turned it around and showed her a text message.

He said, "It's another message from Danny Stokes to Germane."

Kate studied the letters and numbers.

"I'm showing you because I want you to help," Keene said. "I think you might be able to make sense of this code."

THIRTY-SIX

Kate sat in Andrew's lounge. It was early afternoon and she'd had the message from Scott that he was on his way and would message her once he was in Syria. Again he'd been vague about arrangements and timings, so all she could do was wait and distract herself. Danny Stokes's code was a good diversion from her concerns.

She'd written it out numerous times and stared at it.

S1E22-64 73 LXVI 1.4.10 0-691

Andrew had tried various standard approaches to cracking it but was none the wiser.

"How do you normally solve these?" he asked, flopping into a chair.

"This is the first actual code we've had. Normally it's just traditional detective work—only different. We try and do it from the individual's perspective, try and understand them first."

"And you found Scott because you realized what the first part of his code meant?"

"Because it was something personal between us."

"So, what's personal between Danny Stokes and Simon Germane?"

"The investment. Danny's father's business."

Andrew returned to the computer and dug out as much as he could find regarding the failed business. They spent another hour poring over the output.

Kate eventually said, "I'd really like to talk to Megan."

"Why don't you?"

"Because DS Keene asked me not to. He doesn't want her involved at this stage. Not until we have no other option. His logic is that we don't know if it's Danny or Germane who's in trouble. We know Danny sent the code, but since Germane is also missing…"

"Danny might have done something to him, you mean?"

"Yes. And anyway, what if Megan doesn't know either? I kind of get leaving her out of the loop for the time being."

Andrew rubbed at his eyes as though the thoughts were causing him eye strain. Then he shook his head. "Maybe it's something personal to Germane?"

"Right, both Danny and Germane would need to understand it. No point in just one of them getting the code and Danny sending it. I think we just keep on trying until something makes sense."

Andrew pushed his heavy frame out of the chair and stomped comically back to the office and his computer. "OK, boss," he called over his shoulder. "If an infinite number of monkeys can type the works of Shakespeare then one silverback gorilla can crack a simple code in less than an infinite amount of time."

How much time did they have? Kate had no idea, but a strange feeling said it wasn't long.

THIRTY-SEVEN

Kate spent the night in yet another hotel. She'd sent three messages to Scott asking for an update. Finally, after checking in, she'd received a text from him saying he was now being driven through Syria and was starting the search. The signal was patchy at best and he'd ring when he could.

Kate felt a growing sense of discomfort in her stomach. She knew it was probably worse for Scott. After all, he only had about four more days to find Joe.

She went for a long run through Windsor Great Park to clear her head. It was good to jog along the old route that she'd followed a lifetime ago.

Overnight she received an email from Grace LaBelle. The mother had written a letter to Jemila and left it in the bedroom. There had been no reply but the letter had disappeared. Jemila knew what they had guessed. She was sneaking back. She hadn't been abducted; she was just hiding.

Grace had wanted to know what to do next? Should she tell the police? Should they search for her daughter?

In Kate's view, it was better for Jemila to return of her own free will. Catching her would result in more lockdowns and running away. Next time, they may not find her. There was no mention in Grace's email of the husband and so Kate asked whether he was still in custody and what Grace's plans were.

Grace mentioned that her greatest wish was to return to their comfortable evenings, watching *The Young and the Reckless*, eating toast in front of the fire like they used to.

As Kate pounded the trails around the lake, she realized the obvious connection between Danny and his father's partner: the TV programme they'd created. S1E22 could mean: series one, episode twenty-two.

When she got back to the hotel, the first thing she did was search for the episode. Eventually she found it on an illegal download site. With just one "Seeder", the estimated download time was days! She showered and breakfasted before checking again. Now it showed only thirty minutes remaining. She waited impatiently as the pixelated progress bar turned green.

Then she hit *play*.

The programme was over two hours long. She started to watch and couldn't help wonder how this had ever been successful. Who the hell watched this rubbish? And then a thought struck her. S1E22-64. Could 64 mean sixty-four minutes?

She moved the timer to sixty-four and paused the programme. On the screen was the Eiffel Tower. Paris.

Kate called DS Keene.

"I was about to call you," he said, breathless with enthusiasm.

"Oh why?"

"You first," he said, and from his tone she could picture his bright eyes smiling.

"The first part of the code... I think I know what it means?" She paused and realized she was teasing him the way he liked to draw things out.

He was waiting, so she said, "S1E22-64. I think it's a reference to an episode of the TV programme Simon Germane worked on with Geoff Stokes." She paused again.

"Kate! Go on, you're killing me!"

She explained the episode and time frame. "It's Paris."

"Wow!"

"Wow?"

"The reason I was about to call you." He paused.

"Go on."

"We got the credit card transactions yesterday evening. The most recent one was four days ago at a hotel. And you'll never guess where... Paris!"

Kate was pleased when DS Keene asked her to go with him to France.

"You speak French, don't you?" he asked.

"Passable," she said, although working in Canada she'd found it easy to improve her school-standard language skills. "How did you know?"

He laughed down the line. "Just a hopeful punt from the way you said *Le Pain Quotidien*. Me? I struggle with hello and goodbye."

"There's a train from St Pancras at half three today. Could you make that? I'll get the tickets."

She agreed, packed her bags and drove over to Andrew's house.

"Very clever," he said when she explained the first part of Danny Stokes's code.

"Not really. It just took time to realize the commonality between them."

"So what's your theory?"

"I try not to have too many preconceived ideas. Jumping to conclusions is something we try to avoid. Like assuming what had happened to Jemila Dacks. The detective on Vancouver Island was so convinced of her stepdad's guilt that he wouldn't accept she'd just run away."

"To draw attention to the stepdad."

"Right."

"By the way, do you know what he was up to?"

"Not yet."

Andrew rubbed his eyes. "Well, back to Mr Stokes. Is it all right for me to have a theory?"

"Of course."

"Stokes believes that the partner—Germane—has something to do with the car crash. Maybe he paid someone to cause the accident. Maybe he just wanted to scare them."

"Is that it or do you have a theory about what happened?"

"Well, the Stokes boy sends a message to Germane and they meet at St Pancras, probably over coffee. It's all nice and calm, so nobody pays them any attention. But, afterwards, Stokes kills Germane and is now in hiding in Paris."

"Two things," Kate said. "Firstly, why was Danny's phone in lost property, and secondly, how did he dispose of the body, and why go to Paris afterwards? The Paris clue was to get the ex-partner to meet him."

"You said two things. That's three."

"I was thinking as I spoke. So...?"

"Maybe Paris means something more."

"I agree."

They had both watched the TV programme for additional clues but nothing seemed to jump out. Kate said, "While I'm away, perhaps you could go over the show again... look at things in the background perhaps, or incidentals?"

He grinned. "I'm already packed, Katie. I'm coming with you."

Before she could voice her surprise, Andrew continued: "I've a prospective software client in Paris. I've been putting off going because the chances of the deal happening are probably low, but with an excuse like this, how can I miss the opportunity? Plus, I want to make sure you're OK. I wouldn't forgive myself if anything happened on my watch."

"Andrew, you don't need to"—he held up his hand but she carried on anyway—"worry about me. After all, I'll be with a policeman and, despite your half-baked theories, there's no evidence of anything other than the case of a missing person. This isn't like last time."

"So you say," he said, "But I'm coming anyway. And even if you think you can refuse, you can't stop me buying a ticket and being on the same train. Oh, and just happening to find the same hotel. Anyway, Scott asked me to keep an eye on you—especially going to a romantic city like Paris with another man."

"Did he?" For a moment she was excited by the thought that Scott had been in touch.

"No, but he would have if... oops!" Andrew pushed up out of his chair and gave Kate a hug. "Sorry. I didn't think. I just..."

She wiped away the tears and smiled. "Shut up and get your bags."

THIRTY-EIGHT

DS Keene and Andrew shook hands and smiled pleasantly enough, but Kate sensed a little awkwardness between them. Was the detective disappointed that she had a chaperone? If he was, he quickly masked it and they were soon boarding the Eurostar; Kate and the detective in standard class, Andrew in business.

However, Kate and DS Keene sat at a table for four, and ten minutes into the journey, Andrew scooted up next to her.

"I was a bit lonely," he said. "Dinner isn't served for another forty minutes, so I thought I'd come and find you."

They relaxed in their seats and, after tea and coffee was served, Andrew asked, "So what's your theory, Inspector?"

"Detective Sergeant," Keene corrected him. "I assume you're asking me to speculate about Mr Stokes?"

"Where he is? What he's done? Why he's done it?"

Keene exchanged looks with Kate and pulled a tight smile. Before Andrew had joined them, he'd wanted to understand why her friend was coming.

He'd said, "I don't want him interfering with the case."

Kate had argued that Andrew was already involved. He was helping her. But Keene just shook his head.

He wasn't as blunt with Andrew because to him he simply replied, "Let's see what we find, shall we?"

Andrew nodded. "Nice holiday?"

Keene was surprised by the change in direction. "Holiday?"

"The tan. You have a tan, so I assumed you'd just been on holiday."

Keene raised his eyebrows. After an awkward moment, during which Kate thought he wouldn't reply, he said, "Spain."

"Oh nice. Where?"

"Where in Spain?"

"Of course."

"Madrid." The way Keene said it, fast and sharp, sounded like he was killing any further conversation, but then he said, "It was for work—an exchange. I did three months over there. They involved me in a few cases but it was mostly for relationship purposes."

Andrew knew Madrid, having worked there for the best part of a year. He talked about his favourite spots and restaurants.

Keene smiled and nodded politely, and Kate wondered if the ice between them had finally melted.

Keene asked, "Have you worked in Paris too, Andrew?"

"No, just a few long weekends." He paused and then said, "So did you pick up a bit of the accent while out there?"

"In Spain?"

"Yes."

Keene shrugged, like he was dealing with a child who wouldn't stop asking silly questions.

"Although I'm from the UK, my mother is Spanish. That's why I was chosen for the exchange, you see. I speak a little Spanish. I don't notice it, but maybe you can?"

Andrew nodded and looked out of the window as the Garden of England dashed past.

At the appointed hour, he slid out of his seat. "Dinner calls," he said. "Want to join me, Katie? There's a spare seat opposite. I asked and the hostess said I could have a guest join me to eat."

She excused herself and Keene got out his phone.

"You go ahead," he said, "There's some research I want to do anyway."

Three carriages later, Kate sat opposite Andrew and was served dinner.

"I'm amazed they let me," she said, sipping a glass of chilled white wine.

Andrew grinned and held up his hands. "Well, I did have to pay, but I thought your company was worth it."

She toasted him. "Keene isn't pleased you're here, but I'm glad you've joined me."

He raised his own glass.

She added: "You don't like him, do you?"

"You could tell?" Andrew took a sip of wine. "I don't know. There's just something about him. He's a bit smooth and creepy."

"No. He's just a nice man."

"Do you believe the story about Spain?"

Kate blinked her surprise. "Why shouldn't I?"

"It was awkward, like the only place in Spain he knows is the capital. And after being reluctant he then elaborated on why he was there."

"You're being ridiculous."

"Am I?"

"Yes, you are! He's a friendly copper."

"To you, maybe."

"But that's because I'm not making him feel uncomfortable with silly questions."

"He's just too smooth and charming to you."

And there she had it. Andrew was being jealous and protective. She reached out and gripped his paw of a hand. "All right, you're uncomfortable about him so I'll be wary. Does that make you happy?"

Andrew's eyes brightened. "It does. Now that's out of the way, let's enjoy this *croque à l'orange* before it goes cold."

Andrew fell asleep after the meal, so Kate slid out of the chair and returned to her original seat. Keene was finishing a sandwich as she joined him.

"Nice meal?" he asked, and his genuine smile relaxed her again.

"I'm sorry about my friend. He's just being protective of me."

Keene nodded.

She said, "How did the research go?"

"I was reading your story. The book, anyway." He flashed his smile again. "There's something I've been meaning to ask. I wondered why you're here on your own—without your partner, I mean?"

"Scott's on another case."

"Scott—Joe—it's confusing."

"And that was your research?"

"Oh no, no! It was about Andrew. He's John in the book, isn't he?"

The way he said it was like there was more to come. Like the fact meant something.

After she nodded, he said, "Is it all true? Well, the bits about Andrew, I mean?"

"Yes."

They came out of the tunnel and they both blinked as the sunlight burst through the window. Keene pulled the curtains closed.

He said, "He went through quite an ordeal."

She said nothing because she knew Keene had more to say on the subject.

"He was lucky he was never around when that bad guy—the Arab—was in Windsor and searching his house."

"Yes, he was," she said uncertainly.

"Too lucky maybe. Right place right time? A lot of other people..." He cut himself short, and she guessed he could see the distress in her face.

She said, "He's a good friend and has been for ages."

"Who found the calendar thing with the flashing light?"

"Andrew."

"Who found the memory card?"

That was Andrew too, but Keene already knew that.

He continued: "And who was it that suggested you go and find your boyfriend?"

"It wasn't really like that."

"But it was him, and you started to track Scott down before you were really supposed to."

Kate shook her head. "Enough! You're both as bad as each other. Andrew is a very close friend and there is no way—"

"Just be careful," Keene said. "That's all I'm asking. Andrew was involved before and now he's invited himself along on this case." The detective held her with his bright eyes. "I don't know what's going on with this odd case, Kate, but I know trouble when I see it. And I think your friend is trouble."

THIRTY-NINE

The first thing they did after arriving was to locate the hotel where Daniel Stokes's card had last been used. It was south of the river in the Latin Quarter, within sight of Notre Dame.

Keene must have rung ahead, because the receptionist was expecting him. He was given a key and the three of them were about to get in the lift when the detective faced Andrew.

"I'm sorry, but this might be a crime scene. I'd like you to stay here."

Andrew was about to complain but Kate flashed him a warning glare. They'd had another conversation in which she'd begged him to behave. Yes, she would take care but he had to stop irritating Keene.

So Andrew reluctantly stayed as they ascended to the third floor and located room 18. The boutique hotel had a theme of women ornately painted with ribbons and flowers. Keene explained that it was called Art Nouveau, and Kate remembered seeing a series based on seasons that were of similar style.

The bedroom, however, did not continue the theme. Here the wallpaper would have suited any major hotel chain, and serious church painting replaced the more flamboyant girls.

There were two queen-sized beds, and the furniture was clearly French in style, although they looked like low-cost reproductions. There were no clothes in the wardrobe or chest of drawers. The beds looked like they hadn't been slept in, but this was most likely down to housekeeping.

According to the receptionist, Mr Stokes had checked in five days ago and booked the room for ten nights. He used his real name and had paid in advance—which is why the credit card transaction showed as late on Friday.

The lady hadn't seen his passport and, when Kate asked, she couldn't recall checking the name on his credit card either. However, she did recognize the computer photograph that Keene presented.

"Doesn't look like he ever used the room," Kate said.

Single-paned, lead-framed windows looked out at a similar building opposite. Keene pulled back heavy curtains to reveal a door that opened onto a balcony. He stepped out.

"You can just about see Notre Dame between the buildings," Keene called over his shoulder.

Kate joined him.

The balcony was only wide enough for someone to sit on a narrow chair and enjoy the almost-view.

The floor was uneven lead, and a metal banister, green with age, ran the length of it. Kate placed her hand on the banister to steady herself and felt it move forward.

"Kate!"

As the rail moved, she saw Andrew on the ground below, looking up. For a split-second it felt like she would plunge towards him. But then she felt the detective's hand on her arm and he pulled her away from the banister.

She heard Andrew shout, "Kate, be careful!" but could no longer see him.

Then she was back in the room, with Keene guiding her. She sat on the edge of a bed.

"Are you all right? You've gone a bit pale, Kate."

She sucked in air and let his arm take a bit of her weight. "I'm fine," he said. "For a second I thought the railing was going to give way and I think I froze."

He knelt beside her. "Do you suffer from vertigo?"

"Not as far as I'm aware."

There was a bottle of water beside the bed. He filled a glass and she drank it down.

The door thumped open and Andrew barrelled into the room.

"Kate!"

"Get out!" Keene barked. "You aren't to come in here."

"Why? Because you said this is a crime scene? Well it almost was!" Andrew grabbed Kate's hand and eased her to her feet. "Come on, we're getting out of here and checking into a hotel. And not the same as yours!" he finished, with a glare at Keene.

Later, when Kate and Andrew had just checked into a modern hotel near Le Jardin du Luxembourg, her phone rang.

"How are you?" Keene asked.

"Seriously, I'm fine. And I'm sorry about earlier. Really, he's just being protective."

"And he doesn't like it that I was being protective too. Should I assume you no longer want to be involved?"

"No! I definitely want to help."

"Good, I'd like you to be, but it has to be on the condition that your friend butts out."

Kate hesitated before agreeing. Then she asked, "What's the plan for tomorrow?"

"I have to go to the police HQ and check in. The obvious thing to do next is check out the Eiffel Tower. I could join you there around ten thirty."

"We're looking for the next part of the clue."

"That's all we have to go on, so start without me. And Kate..."

"Yes?"

"I suggest you don't go up the tower... just in case you do have vertigo."

FORTY

Kate and Andrew walked around the Eiffel Tower and stood in the same spot where the actor in the episode had been.

Kate had told Andrew about her agreement with Keene, but he came with her anyway. And then the detective had messaged that he wouldn't be able to join her until later.

Andrew argued: "I can do the tourist thing. I just happen to be in the same place as you. And since Keene isn't here, what does it matter?"

Kate had accepted, but now, beneath the tower, no inspiration came to either of them.

"What would mean something to both Danny and Simon Germane?" Kate asked as they searched the pylons for something that might match the code. She read it out:

S1E22-64 73 LXVI 1.4.10 0-691

"The first part up to sixty-four was the TV episode, so we're now looking for the number seventy-three."

After two circuits, Andrew bought a guide and read it aloud as they queued for tickets.

Once in the lift to the first floor, Andrew said, "You used to be able to go up the stairs. Maybe we'll miss whatever the answer is."

"But Danny just left the code for Germane. If he could find it then so can we. We don't need to do something Germane couldn't have done."

On the first floor, they focused their attention on the telescopes. Beneath each one was a compass with places and numbers.

Andrew was still dipping into the guide. "It's a shame the number isn't seventy-two."

"Why seventy-two?"

"It's the number of names around the first stage. Gustav Eiffel had the names of the scientists, engineers and mathematicians involved engraved on each face."

Kate looked north. "What if seventy-three relates to the angle. Seventy-three degrees would be here." She pointed to the brass map beneath the telescope.

They descended to the first stage and purchased a map of Paris from the gift shop along with a pencil and ruler. Andrew spread the map on a table and aligned it to north.

"Are we sure the Eiffel Tower is the origin?" he said, placing the ruler on it.

"Until we have something better to go on."

"OK then." Andrew set the ruler at what he estimated to be seventy-three degrees from north and drew a line on the map. "Place de la Concorde?" he suggested.

"Or, if you keep going, there's Musée Grévin."

Andrew checked the guidebook. "It's a waxworks."

"Like Madam Tussauds in London?"

"It says 'depicting French history'. What do you think?"

"I think we've nothing better to go on, so let's check them both out."

Place de la Concorde was a little over a mile's walk, over the river and along the Champs-Élysées. A few clouds dusted the otherwise azure sky and the friends stopped off for a cool drink at the Pavillon café in the gardens.

I need to come here with Scott, Kate told herself as she relaxed with a coke and listened to the chatter of small birds all around. The call she'd had with him when she'd arrived in Paris had made her feel better again, but then a text in the early hours had brought back the worries. He just said they were on their way again and that she might not hear from him for a few days. Did he really have a military escort? How safe was he? Could he possibly find Joe?

She shook the negative thoughts from her head. Scott was a big boy. He could take care of himself and he would be coming back.

"Everything all right?" Andrew asked, with lines of concern on his face.

"I'm going to do the whole Paris tourist thing with Scott," she said, and forced herself to smile. "Stay at the Ritz Paris, do a boat trip along the Seine, climb Sacré-Coeur and have lunch in Montmartre…"

"You can climb Sacré-Coeur? Up the outside?"

"No, there are stairs that take you up and I think you're allowed across a roof."

"Sounds lovely. Can I come on that trip too?"

She laughed at his joke. "When is your business meeting?"

"Tomorrow morning."

"Then we need to get a move on and solve this puzzle."

* * *

Kate stood in the centre of Place de la Concorde. She looked across the road they'd just crossed and down the Champs-Élysées at the Arc de Triomphe, almost white in the sunlight. Beyond it, in stark contrast, she could just make out the giant modern square of the business sector, La Defense. The steady flow of tourists crossed towards her as the lights changed. Most of the people leaving the obelisk continued east to the gardens or the Metro. A large group of French schoolchildren pooled around the base of the obelisk.

"During the French Revolution, there was a guillotine erected here," Andrew said, reading the guidebook. "It's where Marie Antoinette was executed. Along with others of course."

"Any reference to seventy-three?"

"It would be the next set of numbers. Remember this is at seventy-three degrees."

"Right. I guess I'm struggling with the idea that Danny would expect anyone to take a measurement from the tower. It seems a bit obscure."

"Now you tell me!"

Kate shrugged. Maybe her mind just wasn't on this. Maybe she should give up and just wait for Scott to come home.

"Let's go with it for now," Andrew said in an understanding tone. "The next part is LXVI one dot four dot ten."

"So, anything in the guidebook that could match?"

"The obelisk is seventy-five feet tall. If you take off the golden cap—which incidentally isn't the original because it was stolen—you probably get seventy-three."

"I thought you just said—"

Andrew held up his hands. Guilty. "Well I hadn't read this bit about the height when I made my rash statement. I am only human after all."

"Apology accepted. So, what happened to the golden cap?"

"It was stolen in the sixth century BC and replaced with one made from gold leaf in nineteen ninety-eight." He looked up and shook his head. "It doesn't seem relevant, does it?"

"Then back to your original assertion. Let's look for something with the letters LXV and I."

The schoolchildren were herded away and the crowd around the obelisk thinned so that Kate and Andrew could get right up to the iron railings. The ancient stone section was covered in hieroglyphs that neither of them could interpret.

Andrew took a photograph on his phone for later examination. He also photographed the face of the more modern pedestal. Peering at the gold lettering, he said, "What does it mean?"

"It's Latin. I think it's a typical flowery recognition of how great King Louis Philipe the First was and that the obelisk was from a temple in Luxor, a gift from the Egyptian ruler. Although I doubt he had much say in the matter since Egypt was ruled by France at the time."

They moved to the next face, which had intricate diagrams, again picked out in gold, showing how the obelisk was removed and transported. Andrew took more photos and they continued their circuit.

The third face was in French, and Kate translated the recognition of an engineer called Lebas, who deserved the people's praise for his achievement. "Although not impressive enough to justify the inclusion of his first name," she added.

The fourth face was another series of pictures, as intricate as the others although less easy to interpret. While Kate tried to decide whether some of the drawings were of boats, Andrew went back to the French inscription and called her over.

He pointed to the date at the bottom. A Roman numeral: MDCCCXXXIV.

"What do you think? Could LXVI refer to a date?"

Kate shook her head. "The one dot four dot ten part is more likely to be a date. First of April nineteen ten or possibly two thousand and ten. LXVI in Roman numerals is sixty-six."

"Sixty-six!"

"What about it?"

"England beat Germany in the World Cup. Maybe Danny was referring to nineteen sixty-six and the name Germane."

Kate thought about it. "It's a possibility, although it doesn't point us in any direction unless it relates to Paris in some way?"

Andrew pulled a *don't-know* face. "Let's bear it in mind and take a look at the wax museum."

They crossed the busy gyratory and headed for the entrance to the Metro. The school group were in front of them and there was a cluster of young men rushing up the steps. Kate and Andrew tucked in behind the schoolkids, let the youths pass and then moved out to overtake the slowest children.

Andrew staggered. "Woah!"

Kate grabbed at his arm, but he spilled forward, took two giant steps and then fell. He skidded and rolled down half the flight before sprawling at the bottom.

Kate hurried down the steps. A teacher was already there, bending over him, checking if he was hurt. He sat up and rubbed at his elbows and knees. Suddenly all the children crowded round and Kate had to squeeze through.

"Il va bien," she said. *"Je peux le soigner, merci. Merci."*

The teacher nodded, realized that the children needed to be corralled, and moved away.

"You are all right, aren't you?" Kate said, helping Andrew to his feet.

He was trembling. "Someone pushed me."

She steadied him and was about to speak when he carried on.

"Someone actually pushed me, Kate. I know it was busy and people bump, but I felt an actual shove. Did you see the guy with the grey coat—the one in the hood?"

"No. And you really are unhurt?"

"Just my pride."

"OK. Let's get out of here and walk."

They went back up the steps with Andrew holding the rail the whole way.

Outside once more, Andrew took deep breaths and composed himself. "I'm fine," he said, after rolling his shoulders.

"This way then." Kate led the way down Rue de Rivoli, with the gardens on their right, to the fourth road on the opposite side. This led to Place Vendôme.

"I don't know if you know, but the Ritz Paris is here." She pointed to what looked like a row of town houses with awnings. The only clue to its grand status was the line of black limousines outside.

"Doesn't look like the Ritz in London," Andrew said, clearly unimpressed.

"I'd like to stay there all the same. And you get Napoleon's column right outside." There was sheeting around something tall in the centre of the square. "Although it's a shame we can't see it."

"It is sheet," Andrew said in a French accent.

"Are you trying to be funny?"

He laughed. "*Oui*, this is *sheeet*!"

"That's terrible."

They began to walk around and Andrew checked the guidebook. "The Vendôme Column," he read, "Forty-two metres tall. Finished in 1810 but commemorating a campaign in 1805. Which is ironic."

"Ironic? Is this leading to another bad joke?"

"No, I was just thinking. 1805. It's the year Nelson died. I wonder..." Andrew started to pat his pockets.

"What?"

He turned back the way they'd come. "My phone. I've lost my bloody phone!"

FORTY-ONE

Andrew checked around where he had fallen and Kate asked Metro staff. No one had seen the phone.

"I had it by the obelisk because I took photos," Andrew said, shaking his head. "I must have dropped it here."

"Then someone's picked it up and kept it. Doesn't surprise me. Do you have insurance?"

"Sure, but you know what it's like. It's backed up on the cloud too, but it's still a pain in the backside."

They went back up into the bright sunlight. There were fewer people around and Kate guessed they'd just been unlucky to meet a rush last time. It couldn't have been deliberate, could it? She shook the thought from her mind. No, that was just paranoia setting in again. Why would someone either want to hurt Andrew or take his phone?

She saw him studying her and kept her thoughts to herself. "I'm not sure the waxworks is worth it, you know?"

"I was thinking the same. Fancy an ice cream? There was a vendor in the gardens... at least there was half an hour ago."

They retraced their steps to the crossing by the obelisk and, once there, turned away and entered Jardin des Tuileries. They walked around the fountain to the ice cream seller.

"Small mercies, I didn't lose my wallet!" Andrew joked as he paid for two Cornettos.

"Back in the square, you were about to say something about Nelson, I think. Then you started to look for your phone. Something was ironic."

"I was being stupid," he said, sitting down by the water. "I wondered if Napoleon's column was a rival to Nelson's because of the date. But of course, Wellington was Napoleon's great rival, not Nelson." He ate some ice cream and started to whistle "Waterloo" by ABBA.

Kate couldn't help smiling. "I'm glad your spirits are up again."

"You can't keep a good man down," he said with a mouthful. "Although, apparently, you can push him down some steps."

They finished their Cornettos, enjoying the warm air and tranquillity. Kate tossed the remains of her cone to the sandy ground and it was immediately fought over by a brace of sparrows.

Andrew opened the guidebook at the Vendôme column again. "What's 1810 in Roman numerals? I was just thinking that it could be at seventy-three degrees."

"MDCCCX."

"That's a shame. Still nothing like LXVI." He looked from the obelisk and then turned one-eighty and nodded towards the Louvre. "How do you feel about taking a break?"

"Sounds good to me."

The friends spent the afternoon first walking around the outside and then in the museum. When they got back to the hotel, Detective Keene was sitting in the lounge with a cup of coffee.

He waved them over. "Any luck with the code?"

"Nothing," Kate said, noticing that he didn't comment on Andrew's presence. "Found nothing and lost something."

When Keene arched an eyebrow, Andrew chipped in. "My phone. I got pushed going into the Metro and either dropped it or... well whatever, someone took it."

"Sorry to hear that."

Andrew looked at Kate. "The more I think about it, the more I think it was the guy in the grey coat. And the hood was more like a cowl. I wouldn't be surprised if he actually snatched my phone when he pushed me."

Keene leaned forward, concerned. "But you're OK?"

"Mostly bothered by my phone. But at least I can get a new one. And thankfully I have all the details for tomorrow's meeting on paper."

"Tomorrow's meeting?" Keene seemed surprised and Kate realized she hadn't fully explained Andrew's presence.

"I build software and I've a meeting with a potential buyer in the morning."

Keene asked some questions, and as Kate listened to the to and fro, she wondered if the detective and her friend had finally accepted one another.

When they'd finished, she pitched in: "You haven't told us about your day. I hope it was more successful than ours?"

He frowned. "I'm sure you can guess what French bureaucracy is like. In fact, I think they invented it— bureaucracy, I mean. Anyway, I've been through the process and survived. The chief back home will be happy that all boxes are ticked. Anyway, sorry I didn't make it to the Eiffel Tower with you. I do have some news though, but let's save that for dinner. Are you OK for a couple of hours' time... say, meet here at seven?"

They agreed, but just as Kate was almost ready to leave her room, Andrew called on the room phone to say he'd stay in and prepare for tomorrow. "I'm sure Keene's news isn't too interesting or he'd have told us straight off. Plus, I think he'd rather I wasn't there."

The detective was waiting in the foyer and took her to an Italian restaurant a short walk from the hotel. It seemed like an insult to go to Paris and eat Italian, but his excuse was that he'd eaten a big French meal for lunch and wanted a simple bowl of pasta.

He'd brushed up nicely and turned on the charm, and she wondered whether he'd have been quite so charming if Andrew had been there. Probably not.

Keene's one nod to their location was to order a bottle of French white, although, being the cheapest on the menu, he'd have been better off with the Italian Pinot.

During the meal, Keene finally made reference to Andrew's involvement.

Kate said, "He was just accompanying me. If you'd been available he wouldn't have been there."

"So long as that's all."

She promised it was and reminded the detective that her friend was really here for the business meeting tomorrow.

When Keene accepted that, she said, "So what's your news?"

"I went to the city morgue. They had a bunch of unidentified bodies so I wanted to check in case either— or both—of our men were there. It would have saved a lot of time."

"I guess they weren't."

"No. I also went through their recent mugshots in case either man had been arrested. But that drew a blank too." He ate the chocolate beside the coffee cup.

She smiled. He was toying with her.

"That's not your news."

"It's not?"

She smiled patiently.

He finished his coffee, set down the cup and said, "I asked around about seventy-three. None of the officers had a clue. Except the weight of the tower is allegedly seventy-three hundred tons."

"And how does that relate to finding Danny?"

"It probably doesn't. Tell me again about seventy-three degrees."

Kate had told him about their day, about visiting Place de la Concorde and intending to go to the museum but ending up at the Louvre.

This time she described the inscriptions on the pedestal and showed him photos on her phone. She also mentioned Napoleon's column, although it had been hidden behind restoration panels.

He looked thoughtful. "How do you normally solve this stuff?"

"I imagine I'm the individual, try and get into their heads."

"So you think motive." He smiled, and she guessed it was because motive was a fundamental component of detective work.

"Danny's motive might be to get Simon to confess."

"And the investor's motive? Why would he meet up with Danny? Why would he come to Paris with him?"

"To get his money back."

Keene tapped Kate's phone. "Interesting that the obelisk has a golden pyramid cap and all the writing and diagrams are in gold."

"You think it's connected?"

"Do you know how much he invested?"

Kate shook her head.

"Five hundred thousand." He paused a beat, maybe waiting to see if it meant anything to her before continuing. "The golden cap on the obelisk is said to be worth half a million. So seventy-three means seventy-three degrees and takes him to the obelisk because of the gold."

Kate squinted, thinking hard, trying to make sense of it. Then she shook her head. "It all seems tenuous. Without Danny to explain, how would the other guy work it out?"

Keene nodded, and the look on his face suggested he was holding something back.

"Am I missing something obvious?" Kate asked.

"Not really. I told you that none of the police officers knew what the seventy-three referred to, but a girl from the typing pool overheard me asking and…"

"And?"

"She said there were seventy-two names around the Eiffel Tower."

"Along the edge of the first stage."

"All men's names."

"Right."

"According to our mademoiselle, Gustav Eiffel was a male chauvinist pig. He excluded a woman. A seventy-third person. A French mathematician"—Keene took out his phone and opened a note—"born in 1776. Died 1831. A pioneer of elasticity theory and came up with part of the solution to Fermat's Last Theorem—whatever that is. Her name…"

Kate held her breath.

"Her name was Marie-Sophie Germain."

FORTY-TWO

Germain. The missing seventy-third name from the Eiffel Tower was similar to Germane, the investor's surname. Surely that was too close to be a coincidence?

Kate thought for a second. "Even if we assume that Simon Germane understood the reference, where does that lead us?"

"I think we should visit her."

"But she's dead."

Keene checked his phone again. "She's buried at a cemetery in the twentieth arrondissement. It's called Père-Lachaise. I think we go there and find her tomb."

"In the morning?"

"Well certainly not now." He laughed. "The place looks spooky as hell, so you'll only get me there in the daylight."

Keene persuaded her to have a nightcap in the hotel bar. As she sipped a cocktail he asked about Andrew's software and she told him what she knew—although she had to confess her technical knowledge was limited.

"He sounds like a bright guy."

"He is. It's taken a long time, but he's finally succeeded in selling his program."

"Think this French company will buy it?"

She had no idea. "I don't even know who they are," she added.

"Oh?" He raised an eyebrow but said nothing else. He sipped his drink and seemed to be thinking. After a while he said, "You haven't mentioned Scott since the train. Have you heard from him?"

Kate said nothing.

"Oh," he said again. Only this time his tone said, *Sorry, I shouldn't intrude.*

What the hell? she thought. "Like I said, he's on another investigation. Only... only I'm worried about him."

"A dangerous mission then?"

"Syria."

Keene sat back. "What? He's gone to Syria? Don't tell me it's the war zone!"

"It is."

"Wow!"

Kate stared at her image in the mirror across the way. The lighting in the bar wasn't favourable. She looked tired and haggard. Worried.

"And you haven't heard from him since he went?" Keene sounded genuinely concerned.

"We've been in touch regularly, but there's been no contact since the early hours this morning."

"And you expected to hear from him?"

She shrugged. "Bad signal. He said he'd message me when he could and I shouldn't expect to hear from him for a few days. But I thought... I hoped..."

"There you go. He said not to expect anything. I'm sure he'll be in touch soon."

"Yes." She took a drink. "And he needs to be. He had two weeks and there's only a few days left."

The night seemed endless, but she must have fallen asleep because she dreamed her phone was ringing. And then she woke up. Her phone was really ringing.

She snatched it from the bedside table.

"Scott? Thank God!"

But it wasn't her boyfriend. Mrs LaBelle apologized. "If it's not a convenient time... but I couldn't wait. I have news I thought you'd want to hear."

"About Jemila?"

"She's home. I've got her home."

Kate was fully awake now and the news lifted her spirits. "How is she?"

"A bit skinny." Mrs LaBelle laughed. "But she's fine. You were right. She'd been staying in the electricity substation in the woods. And she'd taken Mr Caan's tarp when the rain got too bad."

"Have you talked about the reason yet?" Kate was certain it was all about the husband and trying to frame him. That's why she'd put blood by the door.

"Not yet. She's only been home a short time. And she's sleeping now."

Kate knew that the next few days were crucial. How the mother treated Jemila would determine whether she stayed or whether she slipped back into her old ways. Locking the girl in her room was not the answer.

Kate and Mrs LaBelle had discussed it before but they went over it again. The mother had other news, that her husband had been released on bail. Now Jemila was back, the case would be dropped. But Grace had chosen. She'd told Mike that he needed to leave. And if he didn't then she'd tell the police what he was really up to the night Jemila disappeared. Why he had left early and been caught on CCTV up near Beaver Lake.

They talked about it briefly but LaBelle wouldn't say what her husband was guilty of. Jemila was the priority and Mrs LaBelle confirmed that "he hasn't hurt anyone." That satisfied Kate for now.

It was almost three in the morning when Kate ended the call. She had an idea of how to help Jemila and fired off a couple of emails.

The distraction of Mrs LaBelle's call helped her switch off, and she was in for a surprise when she next woke up.

FORTY-THREE

The Janitor knew Paris. He'd been posted here for a couple of months, too many years ago. When he worked for the government. When his kills were sanctioned by the government.

The warehouse he'd used then would be perfect now. Providing the area hadn't changed. Providing it hadn't been regenerated.

As he walked the dark streets around the old port, he couldn't resist a smile. It was just as he'd known it. Just as run-down, with crumbling buildings, unused lots and plenty of options if things didn't go to plan.

He had a small black sack on one shoulder and its weight made him think. He'd debated whether the gun or the trap was the highest priority, but he figured he had time for both. Providing he didn't need a gun tonight of course.

He walked down to the water's edge and breathed in the sharp smell of the river. Or perhaps the smell came from a group of tramps, half sleeping, half out of their minds. No trouble from that quarter then.

He followed the bank and crossed a disused yard cluttered with crates and dumped machinery. At the far side, he climbed a fence and crossed a road. There were no cars here and the darkness seemed heavier, as though it pooled in low places.

His warehouse was here, silent and inviting.

The main doors were locked with a heavy chain. But he'd expected that. Almost blind in the darkness, he used his memory to round the building and find the drainpipe.

A quick test told him the pipe was sturdy and he climbed. Once on the roof, he crossed to the access door, took a metal rod from his sack and jimmied off the lock.

Inside was exactly as he remembered, although the dust hadn't been disturbed yet. It was a warren, a network of small rooms in which you could easily get disorientated. Near the middle was the room with the cage. He had no idea what it had been used for, although he figured it had been installed long after the business had failed. There were strange people in Paris, strange cults, and he suspected it had been theirs.

There were also TV sets with gantries and ramps for cameras and crews. He stayed for almost two hours before he was satisfied with the layout. He knew he didn't need to use the TV set, but it would suit his purpose well—if this was to be where it happened.

He used a spray can to make some marks. He realized they were probably unnecessary, but he was a perfectionist. These were final touches that made it as real for him as it would be for his targets.

When he left, he used a side door, breaking the lock and fixing it again. This way it wouldn't be too obvious.

"Hey, what are you doing?"

A dog growled as torchlight swept from the wall into the Janitor's face.

"Pardon! Pardon!" he responded, immediately changing his posture, making himself look startled and scared "*Je ne parle pas Français.*" He dropped one hand to his side, to show he wasn't a threat. With the other he shielded his eyes from the bright light. "*Español?*"

"*Non.*"

The dog continued to snarl and the Janitor figured it was on a tight leash. It was a good job he didn't have a gun yet. He didn't like killing dogs.

The other man quietened his dog and then said, "Speak English?"

"Yes," the Janitor replied in a meek Spanish accent.

"This is private. Private property. What are you doing here?"

"I used to work here. I was visiting."

"At night?"

"*Si.* It is the only time... I am sorry, I did not mean..."

The other man waved his torch towards the road.

"All right. Go and don't come back. Got it?"

"*Si.*"

The other man pulled his dog aside so that the Janitor could pass.

"I'll be here. Checking. Don't come back."

"I won't."

The Janitor walked the mile back to the Gare du Stade. He felt his blood surge. If a little encounter like that with a security guard could excite him, just how much thrill would he get from killing the two targets?

FORTY-FOUR

South of Manbij, Syria

Scott woke up and immediately assessed that he had no serious injuries. The gunshot must have been a warning aimed at Uday. The idea that Uday may have been killed saddened him. It was somehow worse than his own situation. His hands were tied behind him. He had the mother of all headaches from a blow to the back of the head. His face stung and he sensed bruises on his arms and legs. But he was alive.

He opened his eyes. Five men crowded in. Two held his arms and the others pushed and shoved and shouted.

"Who's in charge?" Scott said, standing straight and trying to sound confident.

His sudden outburst earned him a slap, and he guessed a previous slap had woken him up. The pushing and pulling increased. Then, from nowhere, a hood was put over his face and he breathed hot sacking.

Forced to the ground, his feet were tied and he was lifted. Two men carried him, and moments later he was dropped and a car trunk slammed down.

This is it, he thought. I'm being taken to Islamists. I'll be beheaded. I have no backup. And then the training kicked in and the mental strength took over. Military training had included such scenarios. *Stay alive. Look for options. Consider the what-ifs.*

He blanked out the cramped space, the bouncing and jolting and the lack of air, but he was still relieved when the trunk opened. Hands grabbed him and he let them lift him out. There was no point in struggling or fighting back yet. Let them think he was submissive.

After being dragged across stony ground, he felt concrete, and the change of air told him he was now inside another building.

Again he was held up by his arms, although this time there was no shouting and shoving. A blade was pressed to his throat for a second. But rather than cut him, his shirt was tugged and torn away. Then the knife roughly dug into his waistband and his trousers and underwear were shredded.

Naked, he was forced to kneel, and he convulsed as a bucket of cold water was dumped over him.

He heard the sound of feet retreating and there was silence. He listened hard but for half an hour he heard nothing except the occasional round of gunfire in the distance.

He killed time by counting the seconds, keeping his mind from fretting over his vulnerability. That's what they wanted. Leave him naked and vulnerable and he would talk. A classic interrogation technique.

The sound of boots approached and he reckoned it was three men.

The hood was removed and he was pulled to his feet. One man was standing either side of him.

A swarthy-skinned, thickly bearded man glowered at him. "Who are you?" he said in heavily accented English.

231

Scott said nothing. He thought about drop-kicking the man, using the men holding him to bring up both his legs, but the guy was just too far away.

The man on his left rabbit-punched his kidney.

"Who are you?" the man in charge repeated. "What are you doing here?"

Scott said nothing and was punched again.

As the man punched, he eased his grip on Scott's arm. It was a slight opportunity. Scott pictured himself trying to spin and jump, catch the man with his elbow. But then there was the man on the right.

"You are American," the man snapped at him. "Are you American Army?"

"No."

"American intelligence? CIA?"

"No." Immediately Scott grunted in surprise as the man on his right punched him. "I'm none of those things."

"Then what are you doing here?"

Scott had been avoiding eye contact. For the first time, he looked the other guy straight in the eyes. "Al Amriki," he said. "Al Amriki. *The* American."

The hood went back over his head, but before it did, he saw concern in the other man's face.

He was alone again, crouching blind on the floor for another hour before he heard the sound of a pair of boots coming towards him.

They stopped, and something cold and hard jabbed into the back of his skull.

AK47, he said to himself, and he prepared. There would be no pain, only sudden nothingness.

He heard a *click!* but the end didn't come.

Had the man forgotten to cock his weapon? Was it deliberate? Was it intimidation? Was he rehearsing?

Scott knew he shouldn't feel relieved. At any moment it could be over, and he wouldn't hear the click this time.

The seconds ticked by in his head. And then something slammed into his temple.

He had the sense of being picked up and moved. The heat and thirst made his mind swim in and out of consciousness. Or maybe it was the blow to the head.

He woke up suddenly. The ache in his bones told him he'd been here a while. Many hours, maybe a day. The hood was off and cold water made him convulse. He tried to suck the moisture off the floor but was pulled to his feet.

There were four armed men in the room. And another one. A younger man, maybe not even twenty. His face loomed large in front of Scott's half-focused eyes.

"*Haza hue!*" he said, his eyes wide with surprise. It's him!

Immediately, the hood was slammed back over Scott's head. He was pressed to the floor and then hands lifted him. After being carried a short distance he was dropped into a car's trunk again. This time the drive was longer and the heat and lack of air made his mind swim. He lost count, lost sense of time, and when he was lifted out, he could no longer support his weight. He was dragged backwards and, once inside a building, found himself lowered into a chair.

The hood was removed and he watched three men leave. The door clanged shut and he heard a key turn. There was nothing in the room except the chair. There were bars at a window and a peephole in the door.

A man in a black uniform came into the room after a few minutes. He had a bag on his shoulder and a gun in his hand, pointing at Scott. But then opened the bag, took out some clothes and offered him a bottle of water.

Scott gulped it down and then picked up a thin shirt and half-length trousers from the floor. When he'd finished dressing, he looked at the other man and thanked him. He guessed the guy was in his fifties, greying hair, neat beard, a tan that was more akin to Uday's than many of the foreign fighters Scott had seen since arriving in Syria. He had the air of a military man, an officer, maybe senior.

"What are you doing here?" the man asked in accented English.

"I'm looking for al Amriki."

"You are not al Amriki!"

"No, I said I am *looking* for him."

"Why?"

"That's between him and me."

The man looked at Scott hard and seemed to be considering his options. Scott felt more relaxed than he had for many hours and yet he knew things could change at any moment. Maybe this was good cop bad cop and a violent Islamist was just waiting for the signal.

Eventually the man spoke again. "You have caused us quite a lot of confusion." Perhaps he was about to expand on this, but he stopped abruptly. A knock on the door made him leave without another word.

When the door opened again there was a man with an AK47 and it was pointed straight at Scott's head.

FORTY-FIVE

Paris, France

Kate had overslept. There were three messages on her phone from Andrew: initially about meeting for breakfast, then a follow-up, then saying he was off to his meeting and would see her later.

She was too late for breakfast when she made her way down to the foyer. Keene was there reading a newspaper with a pot of coffee by his side.

"*Herald Tribune?*" Kate said as she clocked the paper.

"Morning," he said, folding it away. "Either it was a really good night or a terrible one. Looking at you, I'd say it was a good one."

She smiled at his charm. "I had a disturbed night, took a call and did some emails."

"News from Scott?"

She shook her head. "But it was good news about another case." She glanced again at the paper.

"Oh, the *Tribune*. The only English one available at the time. And anyway, it's always good to get a different perspective."

"Although in my view you won't get a good world perspective from an American paper. National news and an obsession with sport."

"I guess they have more national news than most. Bigger country and, of course, more sport... not just football and cricket." He got up. "So, ready to explore a graveyard?"

As they headed for the exit, she felt something nagging her back brain, something she couldn't put her finger on, but she put it down to slight grogginess and low sugar.

Outside, she persuaded the detective to wait while she bought a takeaway coffee and croissant. He was on the phone when she arrived back on the street but he ended the call and flagged down a taxi.

They climbed in and Kate spoke to the cabbie in French when he wanted to know their destination.

Once they were underway, Keene handed her a piece of paper: a map of Cimetière du Père-Lachaise. He pointed to a semicircular section.

"It's here, in division sixteen."

Kate studied the plan, which showed a huge area broken down into ninety-seven irregular areas. Division sixteen was one of the smallest.

"Should be easy to find," she said.

"Interesting fact: there are over a million graves in a cemetery the size of Vatican City. I'm not a great mathematician, but I reckon that means there must be ten thousand graves per section."

As they passed through the main gates, it felt like they were entering a fort. High stone walls were probably once needed to prevent grave robbers, Kate guessed. At least she hoped it was that, rather than keeping anything in. She wasn't a fan of zombie films but her imagination ran away with her as they passed between a jumble of tombs.

The irregular layout and frequent trees between the stones made it hard to gauge the enormity of the cemetery. Each path was signposted with street names and their division.

At division six, Kate decided it would be easy to get lost in there, even with a map.

"Jim Morrison," Keene said, breaking into her thoughts. There was a barrier propped up between tombs, presumably to stop people climbing over to reach the pop singer's grave. But it was clearly a token gesture ignored by the hardy fans, for the small stone had an array of beer and wine bottles on top with dead or dying flowers stuck in each. The stone itself was covered in graffiti, as were the larger tombstones behind.

"A shrine?" Kate said with disapproval. "It just looks an ugly mess to me."

They started walking again and Keene nodded. "Oscar Wilde's tomb is somewhere here too. At one point it was fashionable to kiss it, which soon became a need to cover it in lipstick kisses. It's all been cleaned up now, but I've seen photos and it was worse than Jim Morrison's."

"Some people have an odd idea of respect."

"Yes, they do." Keene looked up and down the path at the next junction. "We're close, but which way now?"

Kate checked the map. "We've missed it. This is thirty-one." The sign said XXXI.

As they turned around, Kate stopped. "I can't believe it took me so long to realize."

"Realize what?"

"The code LXVI. It doesn't mean sixty-six. It means L sixteen. Lachaise sixteen."

"My God, I think you're right!"

They retraced their steps as far as the last junction and then took the other fork. Here was division sixteen.

Kate took the base of the semicircle and Keene looped around the top, both checking the names on the stones as they went. A third of the way along, Kate spotted a tombstone between larger shrines and behind a tree. She squeezed past gravestones to get a better look and called out: "It's here."

The arched headstone had the simple inscription: *Here lies Mademoiselle Marie-Sophie Germain*. Beneath that were the dates 1st April 1776–27th June 1831. Kate stooped to read a plaque on the pedestal underneath: *To Sophie Germain. Students at the Sophie Germain High School in Paris.*

On the rear side, someone had sprayed graffiti. As she shook her head in disgust, a noise made her look up.

Thinking it was Keene, she started to say, "I don't see—" But it wasn't Keene.

It was a young man with a grey hood hiding his face. For a second she thought he was going to grab her, but he didn't. He spun and dodged behind the tree.

"Keene!" Kate shouted and rushed after the hooded man. When she burst out onto the path, she saw him twenty yards ahead.

"Keene!" she yelled again and started running.

The guy was fast, and as he dodged between gravestones and hurdled sepulchres, she decided he was young. He wore skinny black jeans and a black top under the grey hooded coat.

When she charged onto the next path he was now over thirty yards away. He ran up some steps and ducked through another division.

Kate's lungs burned but she pushed harder. After all, she was a runner, and no way was this guy getting away.

On the next path, she stopped. There was no sign of him to the left or right. Had he crossed over into the next plot? Had he doubled back? Had he hidden?

Instinct kicked in and she jogged left, sensing this was towards the middle of the cemetery. As she ran, she scanned left and right.

And then she saw him. He was walking, acting casual, like he didn't have a care in the world.

She closed the gap to thirty yards but hung back, keeping trees and tombs between them.

He stopped by a monument and glanced about. Kate shrunk behind a tree and peered round the side between the gravestones.

When he seemed sure that there was no one watching, he ran up some steps and went through a door into the monument.

Kate sprinted to the steps. She looked back, hoping to see Keene, but guessed he would have had trouble following her. There was no sign of the detective, nor anyone else for that matter.

She hesitated on the first step. It was too much of a coincidence. Andrew had seen a grey-coated guy who had probably pushed him down the steps. There must be a connection.

She pulled out her phone to ring Keene but there was no signal.

Damn! Wait and risk losing the lead or go through that door? Just in case, she decided she needed something to defend herself. Glancing down, she spotted a fallen branch. She took a deep breath, picked up the branch and walked up the steps.

The door was made of stone and had a large circular knocker. But the door was an inch ajar.

Kate listened but heard nothing. She tried to see through the gap but saw only stone wall and then darkness.

She pushed the door, and it moved easily on well-oiled hinges.

Raising her weapon, she slipped through the gap into the darkness.

Her eyes quickly adjusted and she saw a curving stone staircase immediately in front of her. She took it one step at a time, holding her breath.

At the bottom, she seemed to be in a large empty room. To her left was another staircase that she guessed was a mirror of the one she'd just descended. The eerie stillness made her hug her body, partly from the cold and partly for comfort. Ahead in the gloom she could see a wall and another door, only the wall looked odd, like it was covered in bubbles.

She took a step forward and then another. And then her blood turned to ice. The wall wasn't made of decorative bubbles. These were skulls. Hundreds of skulls built into a grotesque frieze.

Her gasp echoed in the strange room and then a noise made her turn.

An arm looped around her neck and she was dragged backwards.

FORTY-SIX

Kate heard Keene call her name and tried to shout, but her scream was lost in her assailant's arm around her throat.

The room lightened slightly and she heard feet on the stone steps. Then Keene shouted something.

He said it again: "Drop it! Let her go!"

She saw him at the bottom of the steps. Keeping his eyes on them, he bent down and picked up the stick she must have dropped.

Keene took a step forward. At that moment, Kate realized there was a knife in the other man's hand. In the corner of her eye she saw it move. The assailant switched it from her to pointing it at Keene.

In a blur of movement, Keene reacted. Brandishing the stick, he charged. At the same time, Kate was swung around and thrown towards him.

Keene caught her as she collided with him and sprawled on the floor. He looked at her and looked up towards the sound of running feet.

"I'm OK," she said. "I'm OK. Go! Get him."

Keene helped her to her feet and then ran to the far end, to the door in the wall. He was only gone for a minute.

He shook his head. "Can't find him."

"But…"

"He ran through that door, but it's a corridor with a bunch of small rooms off it. And he's just disappeared." He put his arm around her. "You're shaking."

"I'm fine."

He led her towards the stairs, his arm still providing support. "Let's just get out of this place."

Outside, he sat her on the low wall by the entrance and knelt in front of her.

"You sure you're all right? Did he hurt you?"

"No."

"Who the hell was he?"

Kate explained what had happened, how she thought it was the same guy who had pushed Andrew at the Metro, so she'd followed. "I called you," she said.

"I heard but couldn't find you. It was lucky I saw you come into this place." He looked back at the monument. "What the hell is it?"

Kate pulled out the map and tried to work out where they were. Of course! "The ossuary," she said. "Too many bodies for the cemetery so they put the overflow bones in here." She shivered. "What a gruesome place."

"Good."

She stared at him. "Good? What, good that it's gruesome?"

"No. Good that colour is returning to your face. You were as white as a… ghost… sorry, bad choice of words. Anyway, you were white when we came out."

She stood up. "All right. Let's go back in and find out where he went."

Keene steered her away. "No. He's gone. And we're going back to the hotel. You've had a shock and you're going to rest. We can come back tomorrow—and bring a torch next time."

She gave him an ironic smile. He didn't know how stubborn she could be.

"We are going back in," she said, determined. "Not least because I have a torch on my phone. But mostly because I saw something. Something that must be relevant."

FORTY-SEVEN

South of Manbij, Syria

Immediately behind the man with the AK47 was another man. Then another and another. Maybe ten men crowded into the room. All had guns. All pointed them at Scott.

No one spoke, and Scott realized they were waiting for something. Then to the group parted and a man moved between them. The others gave him a respectful space but the guns didn't drop.

This new man wore the clothes of a seasoned fighter and a bandana around his neck. The Stars and Stripes.

It was Joe. Darker skinned, harder eyes and longer hair, but there was no doubting who it was.

Before Scott could speak, Joe barked something in Arabic before switching to English. "Who the hell are you?" Naked aggression edged his voice, as though the wrong answer would mean certain execution.

"Joe! It's me, Scott." But as he said it, Scott doubted his brother recognized him. What had happened? Had Joe really become a terrorist?

"Stand up!" The threat of violence remained in the tone.

Scott pushed up from the seat, his brother's hard face inches from his own.

Joe barked, "Why are you impersonating me? Who is this Joe?" His eyes flicked left.

Before Scott could answer, and still wondering why Joe had looked away and back, his brother was speaking again.

"Who are you working for? Why impersonate al Amriki? What are you playing at?" As he said "playing", his eyes flicked left again and Scott got the message.

He prepared himself.

Joe shouted, "Answer me!" As he did so, he threw a right that connected with his brother's jaw sending Scott to the floor.

Joe shouted in Arabic and Scott was pulled to his feet.

"Answer me, scum. Who are you working for and why impersonate me?" Again the eyes flicked left.

The punch came and Scott rolled with it.

Joe barked in Arabic and Scott was dumped on the seat.

"All right. All right," he said, feigning defeat. "I'll tell you. I'll explain. But alone. Just you and me."

Again the Arabic, but this time the other men began to leave, hesitantly at first and then they were gone. Joe shut the door, locked it, and then rushed to his brother's side.

"What the hell are you doing here?" Joe said, hugging his brother.

Scott rubbed his jaw. "That hurt."

"Don't be soft. I warned you and you definitely rolled with it."

"Still hurt."

They hugged again.

Scott said, "Tell me you aren't this guy al Amriki."

"It's complicated."

"What, that you've become a terrorist?" Scott couldn't hide the despair. "You've turned against your country."

Joe shook his head. "Look, I said it was complicated. I'll explain later. First thing we need to do is get you out of here. We can't just walk away. We need a plan. At the moment they accept me because of my reputation, but there are people out there who would tear you apart. You've been lucky so far."

"I don't feel lucky."

Joe explained that the first group at the car had acted on a tip-off, but they hadn't known what to expect nor what to do with an American. So they had handed him off to an Ahrar al-Sham unit—for a fee. "They expected to get a ransom, maybe sell you on to ISIS, but then you confused them. One of them recognized you—at least, he thought you were me. But here they can see there are two of us, so the new theory is that you've been sent to impersonate me."

"What happened to the other man? I had a Syrian guide."

"I don't know. I'll see what I can find out."

Joe left and said he would work something out. Thirty minutes later he was back. There was a heavy-set older man with him. It was the first man Scot had seen there, the man who had said Scott had caused confusion.

"This is Sa'ad. We can trust him," Joe said, cutting Scott's bindings.

Scott nodded and rubbed his wrists and ankles. "Is there news about my guide? About Uday?"

"No one seems to have been killed," Sa'ad said, his accent thick but understandable. "Perhaps they let him go. And now we had better get moving too."

Joe helped Scott to his feet. "The plan is that Sa'ad will drive you out—"

"You have to come with me," Scott interrupted. "God, Joe, they've put you on the kill list!"

Joe said nothing for a moment, maybe processing this news.

"I need to get you to the CIA—"

"I can't trust the CIA. I can't trust anyone. Not after what happened. Why do you think I'm playing dead?"

Scott shook his head. "You trust me, don't you?"

"Of course."

"Then trust me that we need to do this or be vaporized. Which is worse? Taking the risk or waiting to be blown up by a drone?"

"How long do I have?"

"No time at all. It's imminent!"

Joe and the Syrian moved close together and spoke Arabic.

Scott interrupted: "Get me to a place about thirty miles north of Manbij. There's a safe house there. I have someone who'll meet us and get us over the border."

Five minutes later, with the hood back over his head, Scott was led back outside and to the trunk of a car. He heard shouts of protest, but as they sped away the voices were soon lost. After a few hot miles, the car stopped and he was helped into the back seat.

They went north on side roads and avoided Manbij. Scott no longer had any possessions so he borrowed Joe's phone and called Ben. He also tried Kate, but there seemed to be a problem. He sent a text instead, letting her know he'd call again.

Ben had said he'd sent the report as they were speaking. Any imminent drone strike would be suspended. Of course, they weren't safe yet, but Scott sank into the seat and relaxed. He wouldn't have felt so relieved if he'd known the Janitor was in Paris.

FORTY-EIGHT

Père-Lachaise Cemetery, Paris, France

On the wall of skulls in the ossuary was a symbol.

She pointed it out to Keene. "I dismissed it as graffiti on Marie-Sophie Germain's tombstone, but it's here too. I think it must be relevant."

The symbol was a cross with a circle at the top.

"Know what it is?" he asked.

Kate took a photograph, the camera flash briefly exposing the horror of the skull wall. She shook her head. "No, but I think it's a signpost. A marker. One on Sophie Germain's grave and one here. We need to find out what it means."

Using the phone's torch, she lit the way into the corridor and tried to ignore the idea that the hundreds of skulls represented as many dead people. The side rooms didn't have walls built from skulls but were covered with shelves and alcoves piled high with bones.

The air was cold and dry and eventually Kate felt her nostrils clogging with dust, although she thought she may have imagined it. They'd searched for ten minutes and found no grey-coated man, and no exit. He'd just disappeared.

Kate couldn't take any more and they retreated outside to the fresh air.

"I'll need to tell Inspector Fleurot," Keene said as they made their way to the cemetery exit.

"Who?"

"My French liaison."

"Ask him about the symbol too. I'll send it to you." She checked her phone. Still no signal, and there was none when she checked again in the taxi ride back to the hotel. There, she logged into the Wi-Fi and AirDropped it to him.

"Get some rest," he said. "I'll run my errands and let you know what the Paris police have to say."

After a long shower to remove the dust, Kate started to relax. She was surprised to see that she had two voicemails and a couple of texts. Her blood surged as she saw one was from Scott. It said he had found Joe and everything was fine. He would call as soon as they were safely back in Turkey.

Kate sat down, suddenly relieved. She wouldn't stop worrying until they were together again, but thank God he was safe.

The second text was from Andrew, checking she was OK since he hadn't heard back. Confused, Kate checked the voicemails and found that he'd left a message saying it was the third time he'd tried her and giving his new phone number.

She listened to a brief call from her mother before dialling Andrew.

"I've been worried," he said. "I couldn't get hold of you."

"Problem with the signal."

"In Paris?"

"I know… Maybe it's my phone that's playing up."

"So, you're all right."

"I'm more than all right. I've heard from Scott. Just a short message, but he's fine."

"That's great, Katie. And are you interested in my news?"

She could hear that he was teasing her. "Go on then. Tell me."

"They love it! They love it! Phillipe—my main contact at AuroTech—thinks it's a shoo-in. I need to go back tomorrow to meet the IT director who couldn't make it today, but that seems to be a formality. There's one condition though." He paused.

"What is it?"

"It relates to you."

"Really?"

"Phillipe wants to meet you. He's another fan, apparently. He's asked if we can have a celebratory dinner—albeit premature—tonight so that he can meet the star of *I Dare You.*"

Kate laughed. The guy probably expected the A-lister who was playing her in the movie. Nevertheless, it was for a good cause and she did feel like celebrating.

She spent the afternoon shopping for a little black dress and then chilling in the hotel spa. By the evening, in her dress and high heels, she felt like a new woman.

She was with Andrew and Phillipe from AuroTech in the foyer when Keene came through the doors.

After introductions, Keene gave Kate an appreciative smile. "Feeling much better then?"

Andrew looked at her with concern. "Did something happen today? I know about your message from Scott, but you haven't told me what you did today."

"I had a bit of a scare, that was all. Thankfully, Kevin was there to save the day." She could see that Andrew picked up on her calling the detective by his first name, but since he'd saved her it seemed rude not to.

The men listened with rapt attention as she recounted the chase through the graveyard and being attacked in the ossuary.

"The hooded guy had a knife but Kevin didn't hesitate."

Phillipe was impressed. "Wow! This is as exciting as the book. You were very brave to confront an attacker, Monsieur. He might have had a gun. Gun crime is more common here in Paris than you are used to, I think. Perhaps I should get your autograph as well as Kate's. Will you join us for dinner?"

Keene declined. "It's been a long day."

"Did you find out about the symbol we found?" She explained to the others about the cross with a circle above it.

"My friend in the police believes it could be an ankh, the ancient Egyptian symbol for life. Also used by a group calling itself *Société des Morts*."

"Society of the Dead," Phillipe translated. "I've heard of them. Who do you know in the Prefecture?"

"The who?"

"The Paris police. My brother is an officer."

"Oh. My contact is Inspector Fleurot."

"I don't know him, but of course it's a large force. And of course, he shouldn't use the title of inspector anymore. He's probably a captain, no?"

Keene laughed. "I guess. I don't care what he calls himself so long as he's of help."

"Of course," Phillipe said, shaking Keene's hand. "I'm sorry you won't be joining us this evening."

In the restaurant, Phillipe wanted to know all about the case and made Kate go over the details again and again.

Eventually he said, "My theory is that Danny set Germane up but, because of the phone being in lost property, maybe Germane forced young Danny to come here. The clues should have led the investor to the ossuary and he would have been killed there and his body disposed of. So perhaps it's happened the other way around and Germane has killed the boy. What do you think, Kate?"

"That you may be a detective in disguise."

He laughed. "I think I missed my true calling, that is for certain."

"Tell us about the ossuary." Andrew leaned forward, perhaps a glint of morbid fascination in his eyes.

But before Phillipe could respond, Kate chipped in. "It's like something out of a horror movie."

Phillipe said, "Not really. It is a very logical solution. There are only a finite number of graves, so old ones are moved to make way for new bodies."

Kate shook her head at the callous practicality.

"In the late seventeen-hundreds, the cemeteries were overflowing," Phillipe continued. "Bodies were being buried on top of other bodies. Some cemeteries started to collapse, and flooding in others brought bodies to the surface. Now that would have been something out of a horror movie! And so the ossuaries were founded, the largest of which is the catacombs."

Kate had heard of the Paris catacombs but hadn't visited them—nor did she want to.

"The catacombs are a network of tunnels two hundred miles long," Phillipe continued. "They are the ancient quarry mines under the city and contain an estimated six million bodies. You know you can get tickets?"

Andrew voiced the thoughts in Kate's head. "It's funny that the Khmer Rouge killed a million or so and horrified the world by pilling up the skulls. Here we have six million and they're treated like a tourist attraction."

Phillipe looked horrified. "No! No! No! Most people treat the dead with respect, and by accepting death do we not make ourselves more alive?"

Before they parted ways, the Frenchman wanted to talk about the case. He said, "In France we have a saying. Perhaps you have heard of it."

The others waited.

"*Quand le doigt montre le ciel, l'imbécile regarde le doigt.*"

Kate said, "When the finger points at the sky, only the fool looks at the finger, right?"

"*C'est bon.* We often use it at work, meaning don't focus on the problem, look at the solution. I only raise it because I wonder if there is a bigger picture that we are missing."

"Like what?" Andrew asked.

Phillipe gave a typical Gallic shrug. "I do not know, but I look forward to hearing what the solution is."

When they said goodnight, Kate was ready for bed and a truly good night's sleep with no worries about Scott.

"Nightcap?" Andrew asked. "Just a quick one."

Kate reluctantly accepted because Andrew needed to talk.

"What are your plans tomorrow?" he said at the bar.

"I don't know. I suppose I'm waiting to hear from Keene."

"You seem very pally together."

"Well, he really did save my life in that place."

Andrew stared into his drink. "I still don't trust him. He just seems odd. I couldn't put my finger on it before, but he's a bit overweight, right?"

"Yes."

"Like me?"

Kate felt uncomfortable but had to agree that Andrew had a few excess pounds.

"It's fine. I know I am. Always have been and no matter how much I go to the gym, I always will be. You can see I'm fat because I'm fat all over. Right?"

"OK." Kate looked at him uncertainly. What was his point?

"Next time you see our erstwhile detective, take a look at his neck. It's thinner than mine. In fact, I'd say there's no fat on it at all. Or his hands. There's probably no fat on his arms or legs either but we never see those."

"He's not that overweight!"

"Oh fine, and I am?" Then Andrew smiled ruefully. "All right, I accept I am, but he wears his clothes loose, like he's overweight."

"He just doesn't have any fashion sense, that's all. And why the hell would he pretend to be overweight?"

Andrew shrugged. "I don't know. Then there's the tan and his accent—"

"We've been over this before. He's been in Spain."

"Phillipe didn't know his contact and Keene used the wrong rank. They aren't called inspectors."

"I'm sure it was innocent. A mistake or a hangover from old times."

"And he uses Americanisms."

Kate hadn't spotted any but thought back to the morning and the *Herald Tribune*. It was the only available paper. She was so used to Americans that she guessed she wouldn't notice. But surely Andrew was just being plain silly. He didn't like Keene so he was seeing things that weren't there. And, she circled back, the man had saved her life.

"I think you're wrong," she said after a silence.

"I called the Dorset police."

"About what?"

"To check if he was genuine."

"And?"

"He wasn't available."

"Because he's in Paris."

"Sounded more like he was on sick leave."

Kate didn't know what to think. She was tired and a little tipsy.

Andrew gave her a deadly serious look. "Just promise me you'll wait until I get back. Don't go out alone with him tomorrow."

FORTY-NINE

Earlier, the Janitor had watched Kate shopping. It would have been so easy to snatch her then, but the time wasn't right. If it had just been about the girl, he could have got to her before she'd left Canada. In fact, he could have picked her up in the UK as well. But her partner was the problem. Scott wouldn't be so easily taken, and so he had drawn up his plans. And the one in Paris was coming together nicely. Providing Scott turned up.

Stalking Kate was fun for a while, but he had other things to do. First, he bought a new suit and then a black briefcase. Feeling like a businessman, he walked into his private bank and withdrew four thousand euros. Fifteen minutes later he was on the Metro travelling to Père-Lachaise.

The young man was waiting at the Aux Morts monument. He looked tired and irritated.

"You're late."

The Janitor ignored the insolence. The kid had been in the army and thought he was tough, but he didn't know the meaning of the word.

I could snap you in half in a heartbeat, the Janitor thought. But that's not how he operated. He wouldn't kill the kid unless he needed to. Unless the kid double-crossed him.

He smiled and nodded at the canvas holdall in the kid's hand. "You've got what I need?"

"Did I do a good job?"

The Janitor locked eyes with the kid. He knew what was coming.

The kid said, "The price has gone up."

The Janitor said nothing.

The kid said, "The sniper rifle was harder to come by than I thought. I got the spec you wanted but it cost me."

"We agreed a fixed price."

The kid broke the stare and shrugged. "And now the price has just gone up." Then he did something the Janitor didn't expect. He smiled and pointed behind him.

"What?"

"I'm not stupid enough to be here alone." He shouted over his shoulder and a voice answered. He smiled again at the Janitor. "You try anything and my friend will shoot you. No hesitation."

The Janitor raised his hands. This was getting out of control. A simple transaction could quickly become messy.

He said, "What's the new price?"

"Two thousand for the work I have done so far and the pistol."

The Janitor nodded.

"And two thousand for the rifle."

"That's everything I have," the Janitor said, indicating that he had the money in the briefcase. He was prepared for the increase but didn't want the kid to know that. "If I give you everything, it leaves nothing for—"

"—For whatever." The kid shrugged. "You're free to do whatever you like and I won't say a word."

"Three thousand five hundred."

"Four thousand. I need to pay my friend too."

The Janitor walked round the kid and up the flight of steps. At the top, he placed the briefcase on the ground and beckoned the kid to join him.

He said, "Before I hand over the money, show me the guns." He glanced at the trees, where he figured the other guy hid. "And no need to worry, because your friend has me in his sights."

"After I see the money."

"Fine." The Janitor picked up the briefcase and opened it.

The kid pointed to a bundle and, when it was in his hands, he flicked through it to make sure it was real. Then he stuck it in his pocket and placed the holdall on the wall behind him.

"This is how it's going to work," the kid said, reaching for the briefcase. "I'm going to leave. You'll stay here for five minutes before picking up the bag. Then you'll leave by the east entrance. To make sure there's no problem, my friend will keep his gun trained on you. Understood?"

Never buy a gun you haven't tested, was a pretty good rule, and one the Janitor subscribed to. He said, "You've checked the money. I want to make sure the guns are real."

The kid shook his head.

The Janitor sidestepped him and jumped the wall. "Look, I'm an even better target for your friend. I'm not going to risk anything foolish. I just want to check. Let me see the pistol."

The kid climbed the wall, unzipped the bag and let the Janitor look inside.

Pistol and rifle, both Steyrs with boxes of shells. At least five of each. The guns weren't new, weren't worth four thousand, but he didn't have a lot of choice. The

Janitor held out his hand and the kid placed the M-A1 in his palm.

The Janitor tested the action and then asked for the shells.

The kid's eyes widened. "No."

"They need to be real too. Don't forget, I'm a sitting duck here."

A box of 9mm Parabellums was passed over and the Janitor fed them in.

"Satisfied?"

"Not yet. You pissed me off."

The kid's first thought was that the buyer was going to run with the gun and money.

The black briefcase was suddenly in his face. And then he was dead.

There was a hole in the briefcase where the bullet had blasted through. An improvised silencer.

The instant he fired, the Janitor dropped the briefcase and rolled away. Then he sprang up and dived over the monument wall. He expected gunfire but none came. Instead, he heard the sound of someone running through the trees. So much for backup!

Jumping the wall, he snatched up the holdall and darted into the cluster of trees. He left the money. He didn't care about that. He didn't care what the authorities thought about the body, so long as he got away. All he needed now was news of Scott. And he'd get his wish even sooner than he'd hoped.

FIFTY

North of Manbij, Syria

That evening, they sat upstairs in the old brick house. Sa'ad had an assault rifle and kept watch on the single track in.

They drank water and ate fruit and talked. Joe wanted to know what was happening in the outside world. Scott wanted to know the whole story. What had happened to Joe, and what was the al Amriki thing all about?

Joe said he'd been a prisoner for a long time. There were two of them, both American, both ex-army and both potential pawns in an international game. The only difference between them was the other man was a Sunni fundamentalist with connections to the Muslim Brotherhood.

Joe said, "He was white like me but had been radicalized as a kid. That was all he'd tell me. He taught me to read and write Arabic. The only book we had was the Quran, and through this he tried to convert me to Islam. There was nothing else to do, so I listened and read and practised. I said I was interested, but I never really believed, not his version anyway."

Scott said, "How long were you held for?"

"We tried to keep track... three and a half years I think."

"Jeez!"

"I was drugged for part of the time. I vaguely remember being in a hospital."

"I saw you," Scott said. "I was told you were dead."

"The one I remember wasn't one of ours. I remember Arab doctors... and I was moved a few times. In the end it was basically a cell with a cot."

"Who was it? Who held you?"

"They never said. They just kept us fed and let us slop out... that's when I first talked to Muhammed— although I found out his real name was Jake. He said he'd changed it because of his religion. Occasionally we'd meet briefly outside but mostly we spoke through the walls. Muhammed kept saying his people would rescue him. I hoped the same, but it seems he was right. One day our jailors seemed panicky. We were shackled and bundled into a car. I thought we were being moved like we'd been moved many times before, only this time it was different. One minute we were being driven fast along a road and the next we were rolling. I remember noise and darkness."

Sa'ad said, "My daughter, Noura, found him. Something had hit the front and side of the SUV. The men in the front were dead but they'd also been shot. Noura didn't see Joe straight away. He'd been thrown clear but had serious wounds."

"I just remember waking up in Sa'ad's house. His wife tended to my wounds—"

Scott heard the Syrian mutter something like, "It is Allah's will. It is Allah's will," and Scott thought he saw tears in the older man's eyes.

"It took me a long time to recover, and there were times when Sa'ad's family hid me because of soldiers.

261

My memory was affected too and I didn't know who I was for a long time. Gradually it came back and I knew I needed to hide. I also knew that I owed Sa'ad a great favour for saving my life and giving me shelter. And so, when my strength returned, I joined the men of his family and worked in the fields."

Sa'ad said, "One by one our sons left to fight. Daily we would hear of the atrocities committed by Assad's evil regime, and it was natural for the young men to join the resistance."

"Until the family were left defenceless. There were times when soldiers came and raided the food."

"Which was not a problem, not really," Sa'ad added.

"Until the mercenaries came. Most of the women and the older men were harvesting when they came."

"Foreign *Takfiri*," Sa'ad said with venom.

"Probably mercenaries," Joe continued. "We don't know for sure because they killed everyone. They raped the younger women and then killed them all."

Sa'ad started muttering to Allah again.

"My friend's great aunt was the only one still alive, although she soon died from the blood loss. She told us what had happened. She also told us that Noura had been taken. She was only twelve."

Joe stopped and breathed out, composing himself.

"What happened to her?" Scott asked.

"We don't know. Sa'ad and I have been looking ever since. First we found the unit who were guilty and we killed them all. But not before they told us they had sold Noura to someone who traded in young brides. We then traced this man and he told us she had been bought for the soldiers in Raqqa, the ISIS stronghold."

Sa'ad said, "We joined the People's Protection Unit, a Kurdish group who were fighting ISIS. We hoped to get into Raqqa but we made little progress. And that's when we came across al Amriki."

Scott looked from one to the other. "But aren't you al Amriki, Joe?"

Joe grinned. "I am now. Let me explain... Most of the IS fighters work in independent units. We stumbled across Jake/Muhammed and his unit—"

"And beat them," Sa'ad interjected. "That's when we came up with a crazy plan,"

Joe nodded. "We took their clothes and I pretended to be al Amriki. It wasn't too hard. ISIS is a disparate organization and we looked similar enough that no one questioned who I claimed to be. We buried the bodies, took their clothes, and I wore the bandana."

"I saw the footage!" Scott said. "I was shown it as evidence that you were al Amriki wearing the bandana." He stopped and gripped Joe's arm. "How are we going to convince—?"

"You want me to prove I'm not him?" Joe pulled a piece of paper from a chest pocket. "I have a letter from a general of the YPG—the unit we affiliated with. It's my get out of jail card in case things didn't work out."

"Our plan was to walk into Raqqa and find my daughter," Sa'ad said, continuing the story. "The general approved and we got some intelligence out to him. But we didn't find Noura. When we got to Raqqa she had already gone." The big man's voice choked and he turned his full attention out of the window.

"Child bride," Joe whispered. "These jihadists call themselves men of God and yet think nothing of abusing underage girls, whether it's rape or official through the act of marriage. We found the husband two days ago but he'd finished with her. Can you believe it? Anyway, she's been sold on and Sa'ad won't rest until she's found."

"I understand, but you do need to clear your name with the CIA."

Joe nodded. He started to speak but Sa'ad beat him to it.

"Lights!" the big man said, sighting his gun. "There's at least one vehicle headed this way."

FIFTY-ONE

Sa'ad stayed by the roof and the brothers took up positions outside.

As the vehicle approached, it flashed its headlights and honked its horn.

Scott stepped away from his cover and into the lights. The vehicle stopped. For a moment nothing happened. Then the headlights went off and the interior light came on.

"Don't shoot, it's Uday!" Scott shouted.

His Syrian driver climbed out. In the pale moonlight, Scott could see the man's big grin.

As they embraced, Scott said, "I didn't expect you to come back."

"Neither did I, Mr Scott," Uday said, laughing. "Neither did I."

Uday pumped Joe's hand after being introduced, and he squinted at him.

"So this is the infamous al Amriki. Goodness, you really are similar. Tell me what happened."

"After I introduce Sa'ad," Scott said, and he led the group inside.

At first the two Syrians seemed wary of one another, but after bread and olive oil was shared round, the two men seemed to relax, although Sa'ad kept his gun on his lap and an eye on the track.

"What happened at the car?" Scott asked. "I was worried you'd been shot."

"I was lucky," Uday said. "One of the soldiers recognized me as his old teacher. I knew being a teacher was important. I just didn't realize it would save my life."

Scott recounted Joe's story so that Uday would know he'd been undercover.

Uday listened intently. "What about the attack on the aid convoy? I heard you were involved in that."

Scott studied his brother, perhaps hoping to hear that his eyes had betrayed him, that it hadn't been Joe in the jeep.

"We were there," Joe eventually said.

Sa'ad said, "We tried to warn them. ISIS heard a rumour that the US were unofficially escorting the convoy. They were waiting in ambush."

Scott recalled the video, the jeep approaching. The discussion. The man that left and the way al Amriki had executed the other two before speeding off.

"We had to make it look real," Joe explained. "I wanted to do more, but we couldn't blow our cover, so we warned them and sent one man to tell the others. I didn't actually shoot anyone. I fired into the ground and they pretended to be hit. But the IS fighters attacked before the US soldiers could prepare."

Sa'ad said, "We did our best, but you understand…"

Scott nodded. It was a shame their only witnesses had been killed. If any of the three men had survived, it would have been easier to convince the CIA.

Uday stood and stepped closer to Sa'ad. "And what is your plan now?"

"Make sure my friend is safe and then return."

"You can't go back undercover," Joe said. "At least with the two of us—"

"No, I will rejoin the YPG. General Yassim will have me back and I'll have to trace my daughter from the outside again."

"General Yassim," Uday said, impressed. "You know him personally?"

Joe pulled out his letter from the general. "Not only that, but I have a letter from him. It's the proof of my innocence."

Uday read it and then looked at Scott. "Have you still got your papers, your passport and visa?"

Scott had buried them in the rubble with the money. He'd recovered them as soon as they'd returned.

He nodded and Uday pulled out his phone. Scott didn't understand the call Uday made but the others seemed to follow it. When he ended the call Uday clapped his hands. "As easy as pie. We'll leave in two hours and be in Turkey by the morning. Since I don't need to smuggle you across, I'll drive you to the air base."

Thunder rumbled across the plains as they approached Jarabulus. The town was supposed to be in Syria but the border had moved south. Up ahead they could see a heavy military presence.

Sa'ad stopped and got out of his car. Joe followed and they embraced. "Farewell, my friend," Sa'ad said.

"I'll find you with the Kurds," Joe said.

"No, you have done enough. This is my fight not yours."

Joe gripped the other man's arm. "I'll clear my name and then come back."

Sa'ad nodded. Then he returned to his car, raised a hand in farewell and was gone.

Joe climbed into the truck next to Scott and their Syrian guide drove them slowly towards the new border, interior lights on and papers at the ready.

Uday grinned. "Next stop, Mr Scott, coffee in Karkamiş. Turkish coffee."

FIFTY-TWO

Paris, France

In the early hours of the morning, Kate finally received a call from Scott. He told her little detail but said they had crossed the border. They were now in Turkey and heading for the US air base at Incirlik.

Kate was too excited to go back to sleep and went for a run. She saw the sunrise spill liquid gold along the Seine. Back in her room, she was surprised when the hotel phone rang. Andrew maybe?

"Hello?"

"You need to get out of your room right now."

She didn't recognize the voice, and the urgency in the tone worried her. "Who is this?"

"No time. Get out now. Get down the emergency stairs. Move!" The call ended.

Kate grabbed her mobile and bolted for the door. She glanced up and down the empty corridor and then ran for the stairs. Just as she opened the door, she heard the lift arrive and the doors ping open. Two men stepped out and she shrank back.

After a pause, there was a loud knocking. She took a sneak peek and saw the men outside her door. They were dressed alike, both in black jeans and dark leather

269

jackets. The quick look told her they were scruffy and unshaven.

They knocked again, this time more urgently. Who the hell were they? She peeked again. One man was kneeling by the door handle and then she heard a *snick* as her bedroom door was unlocked.

She didn't wait to find out any more. Those guys had broken in to her room. There was no good outcome here. Turning sharply, she ran down the stairs. The bottom could take her outside through a fire exit, but it was alarmed. Go through there and the men would discover she was on the run rather than simply out.

She glanced into the lobby. There were two house phones in booths to the right before the bar. To the left was open space, then the lift, and finally the reception. The young male receptionist seemed distracted with something below the front desk. Kate decided to take cover behind the phone booths and duck into the bar. From there she could take a few paces and be out of the front door, hopefully before the receptionist looked up.

As she stepped forward, the first house phone rang. Out of instinct, Kate picked up the handset and turned her back so that the receptionist couldn't see her face.

She said nothing.

The same voice that had given her the warning said, "Café on Rue du Bac in ten minutes. Right out of the hotel. Second left and then second left again. Ten minutes." The call ended.

Kate put the phone down.

The receptionist was looking at her but there was no real interest in his eyes. Maybe he was just thinking that it was odd someone had taken an incoming call. Maybe he recognized her from earlier and wondered why she was going for another run. Or maybe he was just bored.

270

She forced a smile and walked confidently to the door.

"Mademoiselle," the young man called out, but she ignored him.

Outside, she sprinted along the road and took the second on the left. Two minutes later she was outside the café. It had traditional red awnings and tables on the street. A smattering of people sat outside drinking coffee, reading papers and smoking. She glanced through the open double doors. There was a barista behind the bar and a customer leaning against it.

Stepping inside, she scanned the interior for any other customers. There were none.

The customer at the bar turned and looked at her. He smiled.

Kate stepped towards him, but just as she approached, the man was served coffee and a croissant. He took them and moved away.

The barista asked her what she'd like. She shrugged and watched the customer take a seat outside. He didn't glance her way. No one did.

The barista was talking again and then she heard her name.

"Sorry?"

"Are you Mademoiselle Blakemore?" the barman repeated in French.

"Yes."

"I have a message." He gave her the name of another place.

"Where's that?"

The barman smiled and gave her directions to a street close by.

Kate thanked him and immediately headed for the street. She was halfway there when she became aware of someone walking close behind her.

"Keep walking," the voice said. The same voice.

"Who are—?"

"Soon. Let's just get somewhere safe."

He gave her instructions and a few minutes later they were in a small restaurant—not the café the barista had named. The room was empty except for a lady behind a counter.

"Sit," the man said, gently. He pointed to a table in the farthest corner. When Kate hesitated, he added, "I'll explain everything. Please take a seat."

As she took a chair with her back to the wall, he called to the waitress in accentless English to bring them two coffees. Kate changed the order to one coffee and a cup of tea.

The stranger sat down opposite Kate.

Her first impression was of a fit middle-aged man. He had a confident air and bright eyes.

"Are you OK?"

Kate nodded. "Who are you? What's going on?"

"You're in danger." Maybe he was going to say something else but he stopped as the waitress placed two cups the shape and size of small bowls in front of them. The coffee looked strong and good.

He watched the waitress retreat.

Kate said, "You were saying I'm in danger."

He shrugged. "Yesterday a young man was murdered. Shot in the head."

"How's that relevant?"

"It was at Père-Lachaise."

That piqued her interest. "I was there..."

"Yes, you were. In fact, you broke into the Aux Morts monument."

"How...?"

"CCTV. That's how they knew. You were attacked by a man after you followed him inside."

Ice started to form around her heart. "The man who attacked me..."

"A young man."

Kate waited.

"The same young man found dead last night. Kate, the police think you're the main suspect."

FIFTY-THREE

Kate took a gulp of weak tea. The man opposite sat impassively, his eyes searching as though trying to read her thoughts.

"Who are you?" she said.

"Your question should really be: 'Who is Detective Sergeant Keene?'."

"Who is he?"

"Not who he claims to be." The stranger paused, still watching her closely. "Where was he last night? Where has he been when he's not with you?"

Kate shook her head as she tried to process the fragments of information.

"Who is he?" she asked again.

"Honestly? I don't know. I don't know what he's up to, but he's up to something and he's dangerous."

"Tell me what you know."

"DS Keene told you he was a policeman. Did he also tell you he had been to the French police?"

"To visit his contact."

"But you didn't see that man. And you didn't see Keene go into the police HQ—it's the big building close to Notre Dame, you know. Thirty-six Quai des Orfèvres."

Kate knew it, although the man opposite pronounced the street name as *Orfefers*. She'd visited Sainte Chapelle, famous for its stunningly beautiful stained-glass window. The chapel was surrounded on three sides by the Paris police and law courts.

She squinted at the stranger. "How do you know all this?"

"Because I've been watching." He raised his hands in defence. "Whoa, before you judge, hear me out. The men who came to the hotel this morning were homicide detectives. As I said, you are their main suspect in a murder. They would have whisked you away and taken you somewhere, although I suspect it wouldn't have been to the HQ."

"Can you stop talking in riddles? Who are you and what's going on?" Kate started to stand. "If you don't tell me right now—"

The stranger reached for her arm but Kate twisted away. She now regretted the choice of seat and braced herself in case he jammed the table against her.

"Mademoiselle," she called to the waitress.

The stranger held up his hands again and suddenly seemed less threatening. "Just hear me out," he said. "If you—"

The waitress came up behind him. "Is everything all right?" she asked.

Kate exchanged looks with the stranger and then back at the waitress. She forced a smile. "Just a pastry, please. Anything you have that is warm and fresh."

When the waitress retreated, the stranger asked what she'd said.

"I told her to call the police if I screamed," Kate said with an eyebrow raised, and she fixed him with a glare. "Now tell me or I walk."

"First of all, let me tell you what I know about you. Then my story will make sense."

Kate shrugged, and the stranger told her that she had gone to Danny Stokes's home near Bournemouth because he was missing. He knew about her meeting Keene there and that they had first gone to St Pancras and then travelled on the Eurostar to Paris. He also knew that her friend had come with her, although he didn't know Andrew's name.

"Just one thing," she interrupted. "Is my friend in danger too?"

"Not that I know of. Can I continue?"

She nodded, but the waitress chose that moment to deliver a pain au raisin.

The stranger smiled, probably realizing Kate's earlier bluff.

When he continued, he said that she had gone with her friend to the Eiffel Tower and then Place de la Concorde. After that they had walked around and ended up in the Louvre. He frowned then and said, "Though I'm not sure why you did that."

"Tourists," Kate said flatly.

"The next day Keene took you to the Père-Lachaise cemetery and you looked at gravestones. You split up and you then chased the murdered young man to the monument. Keene saved you, didn't he?"

"Yes."

"Rather convenient, wasn't it?"

"What, being attacked?"

"No. I think Keene wanted to build your trust." He smiled without humour this time. "It was a set-up, Kate. Not only that, but it was Keene who shot the man yesterday. He bought a gun off him and then killed him with it."

Kate was going to speak again but the stranger stopped her. "I think you were at the cemetery because you were following signs, following clues." He took a napkin and drew a cross with a circle and turned it towards her. "It's called an ankh," he said. "And it's a clue that Danny left."

"How the hell do you know all this?"

"About Danny? About the man calling himself Keene?" He stopped and looked around. There were now three other people in the restaurant but no one close enough to overhear.

"Well?" she prompted.

"I know this..." He held her gaze. "I know this because my name is Simon Germane, and those clues were meant for me."

FIFTY-FOUR

Simon Germane—Danny's father's old partner. The man who allegedly felt cheated out of a fortune. The man who Danny suspected had arranged for the car crash that killed his parents and crippled his sister.

Kate's head spun with a thousand questions. Germane spoke before she knew where to begin.

"Let me take you back," he said, "to a point before you were involved. You see, I did get a message from Danny Stokes. He texted me and suggested we talk."

"He sent you a code."

"Not at that point, no. Is that what Keene told you?"

"Keene showed me."

Germane shook his head in wonder. "Then he edited the records or something because Danny came straight out with a request to meet."

"And you met him at St Pancras station?"

"No. That's the worst thing about all of this. I didn't meet Danny. I wish I had because I wanted to talk. Yes, I wanted some money but I also wanted to end all of the bad feeling."

Kate waited. She took a bite of the pastry and a sip of the now cold tea.

Germane said, "It wasn't Danny who I met, it was Keene. He said he was a detective investigating Danny's disappearance and asked for my help. That's when he showed me the code. And like you, he brought me to Paris."

"To solve the code?"

"I guess so. That's the whole frustrating thing about this. I don't know what he's up to or where the code really leads. Did Danny leave it? Is he at the end or—as I suspect—is there money involved here?" He shrugged. "I just don't know. But what I do know, is that Keene is a fraud."

He paused, and again Kate waited for him to continue.

"Keene made the mistake of introducing me to a man he called an inspector helping to find Danny, only I knew something was up because he was using a fake name. I saw his ID. A real policeman, but only a sergeant, and the office where we met wasn't the headquarters. I think Keene only introduced him to add to his own credibility, but it backfired. That night I called the police station and asked for Inspector Fleurot. I then asked for Sergeant Berne and got put through to the man. When he answered I used the other name and he panicked. So did I, I can tell you! I got out of that hotel as fast as I could."

That tallied with Andrew's concerns, and last night, Phillipe had said the job title was wrong and he didn't recognize Fleurot's name.

Germane continued: "I didn't know who to trust—if anyone at all. I certainly couldn't trust the police."

Kate nodded. "And that's why you said I was in danger?"

"Because I bet those policemen who came to get you were bent too. I suspect you would have been taken somewhere and... well, I don't know what they planned."

Kate's mobile started to ring and she fished it out of her leggings. It was Andrew. He must be wondering where she was.

But, just as she answered it, the man snatched it out of her hands and switched it off.

She stared at him. "What the hell?"

"What the hell do you think you're doing?"

"Answering—"

"Your phone needs to be off. We don't know what they can do... you've probably had trouble with your phone. It never seems to work when Keene is with you, right?"

Kate said nothing.

"My guess is he's blocking the signal somehow. Probably afraid of who will call or message. I don't know, but I'm sure the bad guys can trace your phone." He waved his arms around. "This whole cloak-and-dagger thing hasn't just been for fun you know!"

"The *bad guys...*" she said, slowly. She extended her hand towards the phone. He handed it back but glared at her as though half expecting her to switch it back on. She didn't.

"Who was it?" he said, his voice still edged with tension.

"My friend Andrew."

"The guy you came with?"

She nodded. "I need to speak to him. He'll be worried."

The other man shook his head. "I don't trust anyone. *You* can't trust anyone."

"I trust Andrew."

"I don't care." Then he thought for a moment. "You follow my rules or I walk out right now and you never see me again."

"And I care because?"

"Because, like me, you want to know what's going on. Together we have a chance of solving this thing, maybe finding Danny Stokes. On your own, I give you an hour or so before you find yourself locked up and probably charged with the murder of the guy in the cemetery."

Kate tapped her fingers, glanced at the phone and then back at Germane. What he was saying made sense. She was in danger and had no idea what the next move should be. And she wasn't someone who walked away from a challenge like this.

"I need to speak to my friend," she said.

Simon Germane sighed but then gave a slight nod. "What are you going to say?"

"Two things. I'm going to tell him what's going on..." She raised a hand to stop his anticipated challenge. "Don't worry, I won't tell him where you are."

"I'm not worried about that. I won't be here. Meet him someplace. Don't name it directly. Arrange somewhere that only he could work out and tell him to make sure he's not followed. What was the other thing you were going to say?"

"I need my clothes." She pointed at her running top. "I can't stay in this stuff, and I guess I can't go back to the hotel."

"Good guess."

"Right, then I need Andrew to bring me my things."

"Fine, but use a public phone. Go to the meet—"

"—And make sure I'm not followed."

"Right. And remember to tell your friend to make sure he's not followed. If I think you're leading them to me then you won't see me again." He gave her an address near the Moulin Rouge. "Be there in two hours or—"

"—I won't see you again. Yeah, I get the message."

281

"When you get the chance, get a burner phone. And," Simon Germane said, leaning forward and looking even more serious, "you might think you can trust Andrew, but don't. It's not worth the risk. It would be best if he were to go home. Less risk for you, less danger for him. Got it?"

She got it.

FIFTY-FIVE

Kate stood against a wall in the Place Vendôme. "The ironic column," was what she told Andrew, and he was there within thirty minutes. He approached from the north carrying her bag and stood by Napoleon's column that was hidden by the restoration sheets.

After making him wait a few minutes as she checked for anything suspicious, she pinged him a message from her new pay-as-you-go phone.

It's me. I'm against the wall directly opposite the hotel.

Andrew looked up from his phone and turned in her direction. Spotting her, he walked across the square.

"Oh my God!" he said, almost in tears. Dropping her bag, he engulfed her in a bear hug. "I've been so worried, Katie. What the hell's going on, and why the new phone number?"

She told him everything, about the phone call at the hotel warning her that the police were about to arrive and then meeting Simon Germane in a restaurant and what he'd told her.

"He's worried," she added.

"I'm worried—about you I mean."

"I'll be fine. Now that we know the truth about Keene—whoever he really is... Anyway, I should have listened to you."

Andrew held her at arm's length and looked into her eyes. "There was a lot I was suspicious about. But the police... I don't like the sound of running from the police."

"But they may be dodgy. If they're working with Keene then I can't take any chances. You and I both know I didn't kill anyone and yet the police think I'm somehow guilty. If they lock me up for God knows how long, then I won't be able to get to the bottom of what's going on."

Andrew nodded slowly, seemingly accepting her argument. "So what do we do now?"

"*We* don't do anything. *You* go and have your meeting with AuroTech and then go back to England." He looked like he was about to complain but she stopped him. "I'll be better off not worrying about you."

He shook his head. "What about Keene?"

"I've sent him a text so he thinks I've given up. You going home will help convince him that I have too."

Andrew shook his head again.

"It's not negotiable, Andrew. Germane is nervous as hell and barely trusts me. He certainly doesn't trust you. If I'm to solve this thing then it's without you." She hugged him. "I'm sorry."

"I'm not happy."

"I'll stay in touch."

Germane wasn't waiting for her in the café near Moulin Rouge. She sat alone and felt uncomfortable. The lights were so dim she couldn't read the menu on the table in front of her. She was also the oldest person there and still in her jogging gear. Avoiding eye contact, she found herself reading old posters that advertised bands she'd never heard of. Probably too trendy for their time and too French for international fame.

A young man dressed all in black, something halfway between a goth and a punk—he had a silver chain connecting his nose to his right ear—leaned over the table. When he moved away she realized he'd dropped an advertising flyer. She could see handwriting across the top. Unable to read what it said, she used the excuse to exit to the street outside.

It was an address. A flat two doors along.

Simon Germane didn't answer when she pressed the buzzer. She tried it again and was just starting to wonder if the flyer hadn't been meant for her when she sensed someone at her shoulder.

The proximity made her turn sharply and step aside.

It was Germane.

"Cripes! You made me jump."

He ignored her and quickly opened the door. Seconds later they were inside and climbing a flight of stairs. The stairwell was dingy with the smell of mildew, but once they were through another locked door, into the flat, it was clean and airy. Only then did he turn to her and speak.

"Sorry about that. I've been staying here and I'm twitchy about being spotted. If Keene or his police buddies find out about this place... well, it would be over."

Germane sat in a chair that looked like an antique. In fact, as Kate scanned the room, she wondered if everything had been made in a Louis-the-something's age.

"What?" he said, watching her.

"I don't suppose you have a shower here? I could do with getting changed out of these jogging things."

He told her there was a bathroom on the third floor. The dining room and kitchen were on this floor, there was a lounge on floor two and the top floor had a bedroom and bathroom.

The rest of the apartment was furnished like the dining room, with sumptuous chairs, a sofa and a chaise longue in the lounge. Heavy green and gold curtains blocked the light, and when she flicked the switch she saw a stunning central chandelier. The bedroom had the same curtains and a smaller version of the light. The queen-sized bed was high off the floor in an ornate frame and was adorned with a green silk quilt. There were chairs, a dressing table and cushions everywhere. Kate decided the room smelled like lavender and lilies.

There was no shower in the bathroom, just an iron roll-top bath with huge taps.

Kate locked the door and the room soon filled with steam as water gushed into the bath. It might not be a shower, but at least the water was piping hot.

As she waited, Kate couldn't help but be nosey. The shelves were filled with bottles and jars. She found a bath soak that was the source of the lavender-lily scent. She decided against using it. Soap would have to suffice.

"Feel better?" Germane asked as she reappeared twenty minutes later in jeans and a T-shirt.

She nodded and took a seat at the table opposite him.

He was smiling.

"What?"

"I've obviously only rented this place. The décor isn't my taste."

"I should hope not!"

"Belongs to some old dear—probably as ancient as this furniture. If I'd checked into a hotel, they'd have my passport number. Keene and his buddies could have tracked me down, no problem, if I'd done that. You don't want to know how much this relic has cost me, but it serves a purpose."

It seemed a smart move, and despite the curtains—presumably kept closed as a precaution—the apartment wasn't offensive. The layout reminded her a bit of her old place in Windsor. That thought triggered thoughts of Scott. He'd moved into her flat for a few months before he'd mysteriously disappeared.

She needed to check on Scott, find out whether he'd reached the air base yet.

Germane snatched her phone from her hands.

"You're starting to annoy me," Kate said, reaching for her phone. "That's the second time you've done that."

"Did you get the burner, like I said?"

"Yes, but I need—"

"Yes, but nothing." He opened the back and snapped out the battery. Then he popped out the sim card and handed them to her.

She shook her head and started to replace the battery.

His features creased with a scowl. "You don't get it, do you? These guys are dangerous."

"I need to stay in touch with Scott."

Germane's features relaxed. "Your partner. I read about the two of you. Is he not still in Canada?"

"He's been on a mission and is now in Turkey."

"Message him on your burner. I'm sorry to be strict but you can't call him—just in case. I don't know what these guys are capable of technically. Just text and let him know your new number."

Germane stared at the patterned wallpaper. He said nothing for a while and when he spoke he surprised her.

"Napoleon died because of his wallpaper. Did you know that?"

Kate shook her head.

"It was green and it had gotten damp. The French used to use arsenic in green paint. The water released the fumes and he died. Killed by a wallpaper paint. Quite funny really." He smiled, but it soon faded when he saw she wasn't amused. His tone switched to serious once more. "Look, Kate, I need your help. To be honest we may even need Scott's help."

"Scott?"

"No disrespect, but you don't strike me as a fighter."

"I can handle a gun."

"That's not what I mean. Your partner is trained. I've read about your exploits. It's what he does. Look, I don't know what we are going to come up against but I do know they aren't afraid to use guns... and if it comes to a fight then we'd be better off with someone who can handle himself."

Kate had to agree. She texted Scott using the disposable phone: **Change here. High risk. 4 1 day at least. At airport yet? May need yr help. SMS only. x**

When she put the phone down, Germane said, "So where do we start?"

"We start by you telling me everything you know about the message Danny Stokes left."

288

FIFTY-SIX

Germane wrote the code on a piece of paper.

S1E22-64 73 LXVI 1.4.10 0-691

"Keene brought me to Paris to solve this," he said, tapping the paper. "Just like he did with you. I realized straight away that it was about the episode with the Eiffel Tower. It didn't take me long to figure out that seventy-three referred to Sophie Germain. It took me a bit longer to decide to go to her grave site."

"So, Keene knew all along?"

Germane nodded. "If he didn't tell you upfront then he wanted you to work it out—or make it look like *he* had."

"What next?"

"Well, like you, we saw the cross with a circle at the top symbol that we later discovered was called an ankh and Keene found out about the dead society—or whatever they call themselves."

"Société des Morts."

"Yeah, that's it. We then went to the catacombs where they allegedly hang out. Although there are miles of tunnels, we just did the tourist thing and saw the skull-lined walls and the caverns with thousands of bones on the shelves."

Kate nodded. It sounded just like the ossuary she'd seen at the cemetery.

"Anyway," Germane continued, "that afternoon Keene introduced me to the man he said was a police inspector. As I said before, that's when I got suspicious and, after checking him out, I did a runner. So I didn't get any further than you in solving this."

"But I didn't go to the catacombs."

Germane shook his head. "For all I know, that was a dead end."

"What did you do next?"

"Well, firstly, I ran back to England, but then I couldn't bear it. I wanted to know what was going on so I called Dorset Police and confirmed that Detective Keene wasn't in Paris. Then I gambled. I figured the fake Keene would either need me or Danny—or maybe his sister, Megan. So I surveilled their house. Lo and behold you turned up and the fake detective wasn't far behind."

Kate nodded. "And you followed us."

"I followed you."

"And now what?"

Germane pointed to the pile of books on the table and then slid a pad of paper across to her. "Let's work on this code. Two heads are better than one."

Kate wrote the code on the top sheet of paper for herself. It immediately brought back memories of the time she was in Washington trying to crack Scott's code. A cryptologist had tried multiple techniques to no avail. This was not some clever mathematical puzzle. It was a simple code that Germane should have been able to solve but he couldn't. Like she had, he was probably overthinking it.

She said, "Someone I met yesterday told me a French axiom: When the finger points at the sky, only the fool looks at the finger."

"What does it mean?"

"Just that maybe we're going about this all wrong? Maybe there's a bigger picture."

"I can't think of one," he said, and picked up a book on the catacombs.

"Let's just bear it in mind."

Most of the books were all tour guides of Paris. Kate selected one and started to search for anything that might have part of LXVI 1.4.10 0-691 in it.

At some point, Germane offered her coffee and she asked for tea. He made it too weak and added sugar without checking.

Kate took a sip and left it. She opened a book on the architecture of Parisian hotels. It prompted a thought about the Art Nouveau hotel in the Latin Quarter.

"What about the hotel where Danny Stokes used his credit card? Did Keene take you there too?" As she said it, she realized there was a discrepancy. Keene had said Danny used his card a week ago. That must have been about the time Kate got involved, which must have been after Germane had escaped.

"Same hotel," Germane said.

Kate shook her head trying to make sense of it.

"What?"

"I don't get it," she said. "He'd been there before and then used his card again..."

Germane stood. "Let's go."

"Where?"

"To the hotel. You speak French, so let's ask at the hotel. Let's find out if they know anything about Danny."

Kate was surprised that Germane didn't take her to the Metro. Instead, he took her through the back streets of Montmartre, to the far side, away from the tourists in narrow streets where the sun never touched the dusty and littered ground.

She'd asked him where they were going but he didn't respond. When he finally stopped by a flight of stone stairs that descended below ground, she pulled at his sleeve.

"What's this?"

He forced a smile. "An underground car park."

"You have a car?"

"I rented one in the suburbs. Thought it was safer than public transport."

She accepted that but waited above ground until a small Citroen, grey and inconspicuous, appeared beside her. He wound down the window and nodded for her to get in.

As they drove, Germane had her check for suspicious vehicles, any potential tail. Rather than go across the city, Germane took a circuitous route, going west out onto the *Périphérique*, exiting near Roland-Garros and then crossed the river by the huge Georges-Pompidou Hospital, that she initially thought was a series of low-level, ugly glass offices. His style was often described as brutal but this was simply massive and dull. At least the Pompidou centre showed creativity.

After that, Germane drove through the 15th arrondissement to reach the boutique hotel in the Latin Quarter.

Germane marched into the hotel ahead of Kate and asked the elderly male receptionist if Danny Stokes was still staying there. The man looked flustered and Kate suspected he hadn't understood, so she asked in French.

"You are not the police. I am afraid I cannot share that information with you," the receptionist said, and Kate translated.

"There was a middle-aged lady here when I came with Keene," Germane said.

"Same for me." Kate smiled at the old man. "Please could we see the lady receptionist, Monsieur?"

The man scurried off surprisingly fast for one who looked infirm. Germane took the opportunity to lean over the desk and take a look at the ledger. He stepped back guiltily as the woman receptionist came through a door.

"Can I help you?" she said testily.

Kate said, "We are really worried that we haven't found our friend. Remember, we came before…"

The woman looked long and hard at Germane. Maybe there was something in his face, but she seemed to soften.

"Yes, I remember."

"To days ago, you said you'd seen our friend Mr Stokes…"

Germane added: "And before that, when I came with the policeman, remember that too?"

"Yes."

Kate said, "Madam, this is really important. So, our friend came here and left and then came back again."

"That is correct."

"Has he returned since?"

The woman hesitated. It was almost as if she were considering her options, but then she shook her head. "No, definitely not."

"Could the other receptionist—?"

The woman's face suddenly hardened again. "I've answered your questions. Please now leave or I will call the police."

Kate exchanged looks with Germane and he shrugged and turned towards the door. She followed him out.

"Weird," she said in the street.

"Danny's movements or the lady back there?"

"Both, I guess."

He shrugged again. "French people. They don't think like the rest of us. Anyway, we've confirmed that Danny was here and he came back. So Keene wasn't lying about that."

"I'd convinced myself that he was," she said, looking up at the balconies and recalling how she'd almost fallen. If it hadn't been for Keene, maybe she would have, but then maybe that was his plan.

As they walked towards the car, Germane said, "The catacombs are close."

"I thought you said it was a dead end."

Germane didn't speak again until they were in the Citroen and the little engine shook into life. "It was a dead end for me. That doesn't mean you won't see a connection."

Two minutes later they were in a square with a giant statue of a black lion in the middle. Germane pointed to a building. Incongruously attached to its side was a large shed-like structure. Kate watched a few people come out of the shed door. Nothing said catacombs or place of millions of dead people, but this was the entrance.

Germane said, "Let's just take a quick look."

"No."

"I thought you wanted—"

"Of course. I want to find out what's going on but I'm not going in there."

Germane parked and swivelled in his seat so he could get a good look at Kate. "Why?"

"Why don't I won't to go into a grotesque place of death?"

Germane said nothing.

"Think about it," she said. "I was attacked at the ossuary in Père-Lachaise. It'll bring back bad memories." A narrowing of one of Germane's eyes suggested he understood that, so she continued: "Plus I think it really was a dead end. No pun intended. Danny Stokes has left you a trail. The connection to the catacombs is tenuous. I don't believe he would do that."

"But the ankh is linked with the society of the dead. Their member attacked you and now he's been murdered. There is a connection."

Kate didn't respond. She resolutely sat back in her seat and waited for Germane to drive away. It only took him a minute to realize there was no point in arguing and he pulled out of the parking space. They drove back in silence. She looked out of the window and noticed that he took a different route back, this time going east.

He dropped her on the street outside the garage, and after he had parked, they walked back to the apartment near the Moulin Rouge.

They still hadn't spoken when he put the key in the lock. She'd used the time in the car thinking about the code but had begun to suspect he was sulking. But then he surprised her.

"Hungry?" he said.

She stepped into the damp-smelling stairwell as he kept hold of the door. She was hungry. It was early evening and she'd only had half a Danish all day.

"Famished."

"The brain needs energy." He smiled. "If we are to solve this then I need to make sure I feed you. The best brain food? Studies suggest it's Chinese. You like Chinese I hope?"

"Yes."

"There's a great takeout close by. Make yourself at home and I'll be back in thirty."

And with that he closed the door behind her.

FIFTY-SEVEN

While Germane was out, Kate received a message from Andrew saying he was home. She received another from Scott. He'd reached the airport where the CIA were waiting to interrogate Joe. He was worried about her news but she replied using the code four-one again so that he'd know everything was fine.

Germane returned with enough takeaway Chinese to feed an army.

"Didn't know what you'd prefer," he said. "I may have overdone it a bit."

He pulled out a bottle of red and poured himself a glass. Kate declined. She wanted all her wits about her.

She'd been reading a book about the Eiffel Tower in case they'd been mistaken about the meaning of seventy-three. If that had been wrong then they needed to go back to the start.

She put the book aside and tucked into the food.

"Good?" he asked after she leaned back unable to eat another thing.

"Very. Is Chinese really the best food for the brain?"

"I might have made that up." He laughed and she felt herself relax for the first time that day.

"Well I like the theory. Let's hope it helps."

They cleared up and Germane threw away his untouched wine. He must have seen her surprise.

"Following your lead," he explained. "Food, yes. Alcohol, no. I may not know about the benefits of Chinese food, but I'm sure alcohol won't help."

Kate nodded and picked up where she'd left off, reading about the Eiffel Tower. Germane selected a book and also began reading.

Over the next two hours they rarely spoke. Occasionally one of them would read a passage out loud to the other but nothing seemed to fit.

Germane got up and paced the room. He opened the rear curtain and Kate saw that the sun had gone down behind the building beyond. Nightfall was probably an hour or so away.

"Germain and Germane," he said with his back to her. "It's too much of a coincidence. I think we accept that seventy-three refers to her."

"OK."

"Which takes us back to Père-Lachaise and Sophie's grave. What if it wasn't the ankh? What if there was something else? What if we missed it?"

"You want to go back to the cemetery?"

He turned then and looked either serious or concerned or maybe both. "I know it'll be hard for you but it's our only real lead."

Kate sighed. She could see the logic. "Fine, as long as I don't have to go into the ossuary again."

"Great!" He grinned and suddenly became animated. "Come on, let's go. We've at least an hour until the cemetery shuts." He stopped when he must have seen her face. "What?"

"Tomorrow morning. The gravestone will still be there in the morning, and there's no way I'm going there tonight."

And that was the end of the discussion. She wasn't budging and she could see he knew it.

The Janitor strolled through the streets of Paris. He couldn't sleep, and he walked for miles, soaking up an atmosphere unlike any other city he knew. The warm night was complemented by the orange sodium lights, like a log fire's glow.

There was no point in trying to sleep. He could feel his mission coming to its conclusion and there was electricity in his blood. He'd forgotten that feeling. It had been too long since he'd done this and he had a sense of the early days when he'd been a soldier. The things he'd gotten away with. But he needed to control those urges. He had controlled those urges. He was a professional, an assassin, and that left no room for indulging in the pleasure of death.

There were people on the streets: tourists, lovers, street cleaners, other workers. It was like daytime with a fraction of the population. He particularly liked that there were no drunks or thugs on the street—none that he saw, at least. He walked through the gardens at the end of the Champs-Élysées, took a seat on a bench near the obelisk and breathed in the warm air. From there he walked around the square and stood outside the American Embassy for a while, recalling days gone by.

He bummed a cigarette off the guard outside and made small serviceman talk as he smoked it. He shared no specifics but it felt good to chew the fat for five.

Afterwards, he followed the river to the Île de la Cité and crossed the Pont Neuf. He'd always assumed it meant "bridge nine" until someone had explained it was "new bridge".

Outside the police headquarters at 36 Quai des Orfèvres, he leaned on the embankment wall and watched the activity, the constant flow of police—mainly men—in and out of the entrance. At one point three unmarked cars shot out of the underground garage, their lights and sirens already on. In the US they would have been big Fords, like the old Crown Victorias or new Dodge Charger Pursuit vehicles. But here the police drove small Peugeots. On the surface there was something comical about these guys. However, the Janitor had been inside the headquarters with its harsh black-and-white lino and staircases with metal nets to prevent prisoners jumping to their deaths. They had group meeting rooms where suspects would be interrogated without a lawyer. It was a hard, ruthless place, and the Janitor liked how these men weren't tangled up in stupid public protection laws. The rest of the world could learn a thing or two from their speed and precision—if not their choice of transport.

He continued his stroll and walked around Notre Dame. There were prostitutes here, which he found ironic due to the proximity of the cops. They seemed typically French, stylish and cool, even though he suspected most were Eastern European. He ignored them but still felt a frisson of excitement as he walked away. Maybe he would indulge. Maybe it would ease the electrical charge running through his blood.

It was a long walk north but he had all night. Eventually he reached the foot of Montmartre. The gardens were closed but he saw kids in there, listening to music, smoking pot and having fun.

The Janitor could have climbed the fence, like the kids must have, but instead he walked around and up the steps to Sacré-Coeur. Even after two in the morning there were still people up there enjoying the spectacular Paris skyline with the Eiffel Tower lit up in the distance.

The *place* beside the white basilica didn't have any artists or market vendors at this time, but a couple of bars were open and the Janitor could hear jazz coming from further down the hill.

A girl was leaning in a doorway. She held out a cigarette as he passed and asked for a light. At least he figured that's what she'd said.

He studied her and she stepped out from the shadows. She was pretty in a large-boned way. Her blonde hair was undoubtedly dyed but she had a nice mouth and inquiring eyes.

"I don't have a light," he said, "but I have some cash."

"For what?"

He gave her his best little-boy smile. "Just straight. Nothing kinky."

"Do you have three hundred for thirty minutes?"

He decided he'd been wrong. She sounded like a Parisian. Maybe second generation, probably a student or ex-student.

He smiled again. "You have somewhere?"

"But of course."

She led the way down the hill and turned left at the bottom. After a short distance, she stopped by a narrow entrance and pushed open the door.

The Janitor had kept an eye out for signs of trouble; he knew unsuspecting punters could be an easy target for muggers, but he had his pistol. More concerned about attracting attention to himself than shooting a foolish attacker, he stood in the doorway and waited a second to be sure no one was following. He put the latch on the door and followed the girl upstairs. On the fourth floor, she used a key to enter a studio flat. The lights were dim but it didn't smell offensive and he figured she either lived there or shared it. He was sure he'd been right in picking this girl. She wasn't the chattel of some gang. This girl was small-time and private. Her price had told him as much.

She nodded towards the bedside table and, after counting out the money, he wedged it under a lamp.

After he checked the door was locked, he removed his jacket. The gun was in a pocket, and he folded the jacket for easy access beside the bed just in case. He'd barely straightened when she moved in close and began her act, teasing him, undoing his buttons. When she'd undone everything, she fell back on the bed, inviting him to remove her clothes.

"Straight," she said.

He knelt on the bed over her. "Let's do this, but please don't talk."

Her eyes seemed to smile at his politeness, but it was soon gone, replaced by a faraway look. He didn't care as he climbed on top of her. The truth was, he found himself thinking of his target—how he could have her like this at any time. How surprised she would be when he caught her! At first she would be confused, trying to make sense of what was going on. Then she would understand and anxiety would rapidly become fear. Her next reaction would be to fight, but by then it would be too late. She would struggle until the fight left her. That's when resignation would set in.

He found his rhythm and felt the girl respond. He focused on her briefly, her bleach-blonde hair spread out behind her head longer than Kate's, though he now noticed that their jaws and necks were similar.

He placed his hand on her throat and his mind went back to being in control. The way captive girls would give up. It had been a long time ago, but the memories were still strong now he closed his eyes.

They would convince themselves that there was hope but there wasn't. When the final moments came they would see again the hopelessness of their situation and then real fear would set in. And they would know that it was then a matter of how they died. They would pray for a quick end.

Suddenly he felt the girl beneath him again and was snapped back to the bedsit. Her eyes bulged with alarm. He was squeezing her throat, throttling the life out of her.

She couldn't scream because she couldn't get any air. He placed his other hand over her mouth and released the grip. Her gulps for air sucked noisily through his fingers.

He let her get just enough before flipping her over and pressing down on the back of her head. Forcing her face into the bedspread, preventing any noise.

She still fought, and he half regretted choosing such a big girl. But then he wouldn't have got off on a small one.

With practised ease, he put pressure on her carotid artery and she was unconscious in less than a minute.

He climbed off her and shook his head. *Dammit!* He'd almost lost control. Almost returned to the man he'd been in the army, before he became more professional.

She'd be fine. She'd wake up before dawn with a headache, but be she'd be alive.

He dressed, pulled out his wallet once more, and tossed another two hundred on the bedside table. After all, he was a reasonable man.

FIFTY-EIGHT

The cemetery gates were opened at eight in the morning. After a week of glorious sunshine, today the sky was leaden. A fine drizzle coated Kate's thin denim jacket within seconds even though she had an umbrella she'd taken from the apartment.

Last night, Germane had been the perfect gentleman. He'd insisted that Kate have the bedroom. After all, he claimed, he'd only slept on the sofa since he'd been there. He didn't like the lavender scent and the bed was too soft.

The bed was ridiculously soft, almost engulfing her as she lay on top of the covers. She didn't get undressed. However nice Simon Germane seemed, she didn't know him and it didn't feel right to wear night things with a virtual stranger in the same house. Perhaps it was a combination of the lack of sleep the night before and the super-soft mattress, but she fell asleep within minutes. She didn't wake up until Germane had knocked at six with a cup of tea for her.

The cemetery was even more dismal in the rain. Water clung to everything and big droplets fell from the trees.

Now that Kate knew the location of division sixteen and Sophie Germain's grave, she walked a direct route. But all the time she glanced left and right.

"Everything all right?" Germane asked at her shoulder.

"Just twitchy."

"You believe in ghosts, Kate?"

"It's not that," she said, laughing unconvincingly, "I can't help but worry that another hooded guy will jump out."

"He's dead. Keene killed him."

"Another one. If he was from that *société* then there are more of them and we don't know what their motivation is, whether they're involved in this."

He touched her arm. "You're right, I'm sorry. I'm just as edgy about Keene and the police, so I get it."

"Thanks."

She cut through the edge of division six and pointed out Sophie Germain's grave. But then she remembered he already knew. Keene had brought him here as well.

Of course, the inscription hadn't changed. There were just the dates and a plaque underneath. What were they missing?

Germane started to search the stones that lay beneath the headstone. Kate went around and took another look at the rear of the stone. It was slick with water and mottled with age but there was nothing else except for the golden ankh symbol.

When she heard Germane grunt, she looked over the top of the gravestone. "What's up?"

"There's something here."

She scooted back round just in time to see him pull up a triangular stone. He stood up with a grin on his face. "I think this is it."

"A triangular stone?"

305

"A pyramid. Use your imagination. It's a 2D representation of a pyramid."

"I don't see it."

He was chuckling. "Something I read last night. One of the original plans for the cemetery included a huge pyramid." He rubbed his face, thinking. "Now I'm wondering whether your seventy-three degrees idea was right. It took you to the obelisk, right?"

"Yes, but..."

His enthusiasm seemed to fade. "Oh. I get it. Why send us here to realize we should have been there?"

That was her thinking. It didn't make sense. Sending them back to the obelisk wasn't a linear progression, wasn't logical if Danny was leaving a trail.

"The Louvre!" Kate realized. The modern glass pyramid at the museum. Ironically, she'd been there with Andrew—although they'd been playing the tourist, and they'd stopped looking for LXVI and the rest of the code.

Germane nodded. "So, we go to the Louvre, right?"

Kate was about to agree when someone spoke in French close by.

She jumped, half expecting to see a guy in a cowl. It was a gardener in an Australian-style trench coat and holding a rake.

"*Pardonez?*" she said.

He said, "*Pyramide.* You want to know about the pyramid?" He shrugged in the Gallic way, shoulders up, lips pouted. Rainwater ran from the epaulettes on his trench coat. "I heard you speaking. The plans for this cemetery included a very big pyramid."

Germane stepped towards him. "Where would that be?"

"The chapelle," the gardener said. "In the plans, it was originally going to be a pyramid. In fact, there is a pyramid inside." He shrugged again. "Sophie Germain and pyramid numbers…"

The man clearly enjoyed an audience and started to tell them about how she had solved an important part of Fermat's theorem and how it related to pyramid numbers.

Germane interrupted him. "You were saying there's a pyramid in the chapel."

"But yes."

"Would you show us?"

"You must find a tour guide. I am just a gardener." To illustrate his status, he waggled the rake in his hand. "I have work to do."

Germane pulled a wad of notes from his pocket and handed them over.

The gardener stuck them in his pocket and winked. "You are very persuasive, Monsieur. This way please." He leaned the rake against a tree and led them up the path towards the centre of the cemetery.

"One dot four dot ten," Kate asked as she hurried to keep up. "Does any of that mean anything to you?"

"But of course. They are the numbers that support Fermat's claim." He said something about geometry and n triangular numbers and counting dots.

Germane said, "So the dots in *one dot four dot ten* literally means dots?"

"I don't know. Maybe, Monsieur. But they are the triangular pyramid numbers: one, four, ten. The next number is twenty. Mathematicians count dots whereas you might count balls."

They had reached a drive that went up to an ugly stone block of a building with two pillars that almost reached to the top, contrasting horizontal lines and a dome that may have once been gold but was now tarnished. On either side they could see what looked like cloisters. It was an architectural mess but the gardener seemed proud. Under the entrance pillars, he shook the water from his coat, stamped his feet and took them inside.

It was a plain, high vaulted room. A large featureless box with a wooden floor and row upon row of chairs. Unlike a church, Kate saw there were no icons and guessed it could satisfy any faith—or none. Perhaps that was why the exterior was such a mishmash of styles.

The gardener marched to the centre of the room and pointed to the floor. Here, inlaid in wood, was a design that could have been nautical—concentric circles and lines like a compass. In the centre was a square with a cross through it.

"This is where the centre of the great pyramid would have been," he said with enthusiasm. "And this"—he pointed to the square—"is your pyramid. Seen from above of course."

Kate and Germane stood over it, looked down and looked around. It didn't seem to be telling them anything unless there was something about the compass. But her companion beat her to it.

"These lines," Germane said, pointing to what could be directions, "is there anything unusual about them?"

The gardener's face contorted. "What do you mean?"

Kate said, "Anything not what you'd expect or has another meaning?"

"Not that I know."

They stood in silence for a moment. Just as she sensed the gardener was about to leave, Kate smiled encouragingly at him. "You've been very helpful, but before you go… I can't help but notice you know a lot about maths. Perhaps you know the meaning of the next numbers."

"I know a lot for a simple gardener, you mean. I may not have gone to university, but yes, mathematics is a hobby." He gave another Gallic shrug. "Tell me your numbers and I'll see what I can do."

"Zero dash six nine one."

"You are looking for someone."

Germane was suddenly more interested. "Yes! Yes, we are."

"Then I can tell you were they are. It is not a zero, it is an O. It stands for *Ouest.* You want west six hundred and ninety-one. You'll find it down there. They are all numbered." He pointed to a door on their left. Then he smiled. "This is the columbarium."

Germane shook his head. "The what?"

"Where we keep the ashes. You are looking for someone's ashes, correct?"

Kate's immediate thought was that Danny Stokes was dead, that this was some sick joke leading to his ashes. They thanked the gardener, went through the door and found themselves in what Kate had assumed was the west cloister. It was a covered walkway but it was never designed for priests or monks. This was the resting place of thousands of people, all in a wall of four by four boxes, like pigeonholes. Each box had a number engraved in the stone above and each was different. They were various colours, although most were marble, with writing and designs; the cremation equivalent of a headstone.

Germane was moving quickly along the bank of boxes, searching for six hundred and ninety-one. Kate was two steps behind and saw his surprise as he found it.

"Well I... Another Germain!"

The box had a brown marble front with a thin golden cross with the name Germain AGNUS beneath it.

"Must be it. But what does it mean?" Kate said, looking at how other boxes had more detail, not least dates. Many had small flowers, and she saw one had a medal. Agnus Germain had nothing.

Before she realized what he was doing, Germane pulled out a penknife and worked it around the marble. In seconds, he had levered the cover off.

"Simon!"

He reached inside, pulled something out and pushed the stone back in place.

"It's all right," he said, almost to himself. In his hand was a small piece of paper that he started to unfold.

Kate held her breath and watched intently.

Germane glanced at the paper and then his hand dropped to his side.

"What does it say?"

He turned towards her and his face looked as though he'd forgotten she was there. "It's an address." He opened and closed his mouth like it had suddenly become dry, blinked and met her gaze. Then he nodded. "Kate, I know where we have to go. I know where this all ends."

FIFTY-NINE

Andrew spent the morning at home fine-tuning the software for AuroTech, but his mind wasn't on the job. He was worried about Kate. He was especially worried that Keene was still around.

He picked up the phone and dialled Dorset Police and, like he'd done in Paris, asked for Detective Sergeant Keene. He got the same message that Keene wasn't in the office.

"I think he's being impersonated," Andrew explained. "I need to talk to someone who can help." When he got a lukewarm reaction, he added: "It could be a matter of life or death."

That got him put through to a DI called Dishwater, and the man agreed to meet him.

Two hours later, after a stop-go journey south on the M3, Andrew was sitting in the canteen at the Dorset Police HQ.

It turned out that the inspector was called Deshorter, but he didn't seem to notice when Andrew got his name wrong as they shook hands. The man had a friendly smile and was probably intrigued at Andrew's life-or-death statement.

"Tell me from the beginning," Deshorter said, although he made no move to record Andrew's statement.

So Andrew began by explaining that his friend Kate was investigating the disappearance of Danny Stokes.

"I know of him."

"Well, Kate met a man calling himself DS Keene, and all three of us followed his trail to Paris."

Deshorter nodded. "And what makes you think that DS Keene is fake?"

"First of all, he behaved mysteriously, only sharing some information. He also said he was dealing with a police inspector in Paris, but according to their ranks, the man would be a captain not an inspector. And it turned out he might not be genuine either."

"Did you meet him?"

"No."

"Then how do you know?"

"I have a new client... I sell software and my client is also in Paris. Anyway, long story short, my contact there has a brother in the police and he thought it was suspicious too."

"Anything else? Tell me why you think your friend is in danger?"

"Because Danny Stokes is missing and, for all we know, might have been murdered."

"That's a stretch. You don't seem to have any evidence of that, or am I misunderstanding? Why do you think this man wants to hurt your friend?"

"I don't know. I don't know what his motivation is. It might be money. As I'm sure you know, Danny Stokes is worth a pretty penny."

"And you left her in Paris with someone you thought was dangerous?"

Deshorter's tone had been shifting. Now the man blatantly disbelieved what Andrew was saying. Andrew felt his blood pressure rising and stood. "I'm wasting my time."

The inspector also stood. "Let's get a cup of tea. I get grumpy when I'm thirsty. At least that's how other people see it."

Andrew followed the policeman to the canteen bar and they ordered tea. Deshorter had a slice of fruit cake. For a sugar deficiency, he claimed with a smile.

Back at their table, Deshorter said, "You are worried about your friend."

"Yes."

"And what can we do to help."

"Get involved." Andrew took a gulp of tea. It was better than he anticipated. "Contact the Paris police and get her protection."

Deshorter cocked an eyebrow. "You do see how tenuous this is? I could humour you by asking for contact details and promising to pass them on and then not doing it."

Andrew said nothing. He took another sip and tried to stay relaxed.

Deshorter bit into his cake and sat back. "OK," he said, "I'll contact the French police, but it's obviously out of our jurisdiction…"

"When I rang for Keene last time, I was given the impression he was on sick leave. Perhaps I could also speak to him. Maybe he knows something."

The DI shook his head. "Like you've just said, he is on sick leave. I can't go and provide you with his personal contact details. But I will tell you that he was interested in the Stokes case—before he took leave."

And then the blindingly obvious thought struck Andrew. He knew what the man calling himself Keene looked like. Impersonation of a police officer was a serious crime. Why wasn't Deshorter picking up on that?

He said, "Can I see a photograph of DS Keene?"

The inspector hesitated and then nodded. "I'll be back in a minute."

Five minutes later he returned with a sheet of photographic paper. He turned it around so Andrew could see. On it were the mugshots of ten police officers. Each one had their name underneath.

Andrew took it from Deshorter and stared at it. "Oh my God," he said, his voice catching in his throat. "I need to call Kate."

SIXTY

When Keene received Kate's text telling him she was going home, he hadn't believed her for a minute. He'd called her mobile, which had gone straight to voicemail. He'd tried again later and decided she had switched it off, which confirmed she was avoiding him.

He'd spent that afternoon watching the hotel in case either she or her friend returned. Neither did, and he suspected she'd deliberately delayed sending the message until they had both checked out.

He'd called Fleurot to ask for help tracing her. But the man was too busy.

"Can you at least lend me a car?" Keene had asked.

"That would be difficult…"

After a bit of backwards and forwards, the other man had finally agreed to provide a motor scooter. Keene could see it on the pavement outside the café he was now sitting in—an eVivacity. Cream with a blue seat. And he had to confess it was better than a car for getting around Paris.

The café was opposite the cemetery. He had a theory that Kate would start from scratch in trying to find Stokes, but he thought the Eiffel Tower was unlikely since she'd exhausted her search there before.

He'd spent the previous evening in the café and seen no one who looked like Kate or her friend. But he had an instinct for these things and had returned before the streets were barely awake. He was wet from the drizzle, which was the major disadvantage of the nippy scooter, but he'd only care if this was a wasted stake-out.

He ordered a large, strong coffee, waited and watched. From his vantage point, he could see two Metro stations, but he expected her to arrive by taxi. She'd also come to the main gate, because she knew the way from there. And she didn't know he'd be watching for her.

However, he was surprised when he saw her. He'd just glanced at the main entrance to the cemetery and she was there. At least he thought it was her. She hadn't walked up from either Metro and there was no sign of a taxi.

She had an umbrella and a denim jacket with the collar turned up. It was hard to tell from this distance, and there was a man with her.

Who was he? He wore a coat with a hood pulled up. It wasn't her oversized friend, but that's all Keene could tell before they disappeared under the arch and into Père-Lachaise.

Tossing more than enough euros onto the table, Keene calmly walked outside to his scooter. With his helmet jammed over his head, he bumped off the pavement and cut across the road. At the entrance, he hesitated. There was a drive through the grounds but if he went in he might miss them—and he couldn't exactly drive around on the cemetery footpaths looking for them. So, he changed his plan. He put the scooter on its stand but stayed on it, ready to move as soon as he saw them again.

It was half an hour later when they appeared. Keene turned away and watched them in his mirror. The way they jogged past him made him think they'd found something. They had purpose.

And the way they were together made him think of Kate's partner. Could it be Scott back from Syria? He felt a frisson of excitement. Had the two of them cracked this already?

They didn't head for the Metro, nor did they flag down a taxi. Instead, they climbed into a small grey car and seconds later were weaving through the Paris rush hour traffic. Keene kept a good distance that he varied so he wouldn't be an obvious tail. The spray and drizzle blurred his vision and he got in to a rhythm of using his hand to wipe the visor every thirty seconds or so.

The grey Citroen headed north and, as Keene saw signs for the N1, he wondered if they were going to continue north. The Stade de France was up there. Perhaps that was the destination? Maybe they were leaving Paris altogether and heading for another town in the north. However, as his mind tried to picture a map of northern France, at Porte de Chapelle, they picked up the *Périphérique* and went west.

After a couple of miles, the Citroen took the off ramp and turned right. They were going north again, only this time Keene didn't know the area and he needed to be careful. The traffic was light, so he hung further back. However, the Citroen didn't follow major routes. He saw signs for the Olympic Stadium and then a port.

At a roundabout, he lost them momentarily as he wiped the water from his visor. Then he spotted the car on what was called the main port road. But as soon as he started along the road, they left it.

He took the same turn and found himself in a run-down industrial sector. Perhaps there had once been

317

investment there but it looked like it had fled thirty years ago, maybe more. Some factories looked deserted and what looked like once-thriving convenience stores were now semi-boarded or with bars at the windows. There were residential houses too that reminded him of some of the worst terraces in England. He guessed anyone who still lived here was either out of work or paid so little they couldn't afford to move.

No cars were parked on the street and the only occasional vehicle was a lorry. The Citroen was nowhere to be seen. At least the drizzle had stopped.

Keene cut left and right, zigzagging through the tired streets, vainly searching. He reached a large section still active with containers and cranes. Turning back, he took the next spur and reached a dead end at the river. Again he turned, followed the dock, and looped around the next one. There were warehouses and factories. There was a brewery and some warehouse and storage areas, which were in use, but the majority had sunk into disrepair, with high fences and empty car parks.

And then he saw the little grey car. It was tucked between two buildings, deliberately hidden from plain sight.

Keene parked a hundred yards away and slunk alongside a corrugated iron fence until he was close. It was empty and he couldn't see anyone around. So where had they gone?

He didn't expect them to be in either of the two nearby buildings but he checked anyway. As far as he could tell, both were empty, and he found no way inside. He returned to the car and walked round it. The concrete ground was covered in a creamy substance, probably fine dust from a concrete factory he'd passed. The rain had turned it to liquid.

Beside the car, Keene could make out footprints, and there was a clear direction they'd taken.

The route took him to a gap in the fence and then another road. On the opposite side of the road was a giant warehouse with smaller ones on either side. But it wasn't the buildings that attracted him, it was the fence opposite. The chains had been cut and peeled back. Of course, that could have happened at any time, but there were also security signs around. Surely if there was security then they would repair a hole like this?

Keene pulled back the fencing, ducked through and jogged to the larger of the three warehouses. It had metal sides and darkened windows. The main double doors were securely closed with a heavy chain and padlock.

His gut said this was where they were headed. But just in case they had continued through to the far side, he went to the rear of the warehouses and looked through another security fence, across the road. He could see rail tracks, more rough land and a storage area beyond that.

Yes, his quarry was here, most likely in the larger of the three warehouses. He went back and checked it for open windows and doors. In the alley between the two buildings he was rewarded. An emergency exit was open a crack. Without hesitation, he slipped inside.

SIXTY-ONE

In the car, Kate had received a text from Scott saying he would be leaving Turkey soon and asking where they would meet. She replied with the address that Germane gave her—the one from Agnus Germain's cremation box. In the message, she included the code four-one to let him know she was all right.

As he drove, she chatted. "Do you mind me asking if you were ever in the military?"

"Why?"

"Something about you reminds me of Scott."

"I'm gym-fit rather than army-fit." He laughed. "Maybe that's it. I pump iron rather than shoot lead."

She guessed that was it.

Although she didn't know about the docks to the west of Paris, she saw signs once they left the *Périphérique.* The run-down region looked much like any other that had long passed its glory days.

She saw a row of boarded-up houses. Shops that looked open had bars at the windows. "How do you know this place?" she asked.

"It's special. You'll see why when we get there."

She looked at him, curious, but he didn't elaborate.

They parked in a shadowy space between buildings and he explained that this wasn't the address. He said he was still being cautious in case anyone had followed them.

Once out of the car, he led the way to a gate onto a road and the next block. Here the chain link fence was eight feet high with barbed wire on top, but he spotted a place where the chains were broken. After a few tugs, he had widened the gap enough so they could climb through.

In front of them were three metal-sided buildings, one of which was as big as a football stadium.

Only now did Germane explain. "We were here before," he said, indicating the largest warehouse. "Me and Danny. We came here for the shooting of episode sixteen."

"I didn't see that one. What is this place?"

Germane didn't respond. Maybe he hadn't heard, too focused on getting inside. He tried the main double doors, but there was no way in without a serious bolt cutter or maybe a bulldozer.

"Let's go around," he said, and he headed left.

They had almost finished circling the building before he stopped and pointed.

Kate stared. There was a golden ankh spray-painted onto an emergency exit. Germane pulled out his phone and seemed to take a few snaps of the image.

He glanced towards the road and fence before reaching for the door handle.

He said, "This can't be coincidence."

"Careful—" she started to say, but swallowed the rest because he'd already tried the door and found it unlocked. As he started to open it, Kate put her hand out to stop him. "Simon!" Her voice was a hoarse whisper.

"What?"

"Slow down. We don't know what's going on. We don't know if there's someone in there waiting for us."

Germane shrugged and continued to pull the door open. "I don't care," he said. "I need to know what's going on."

And then he was inside.

Kate followed into the darkness and held her breath, listening.

Germane stood motionless, listening hard too. Then he signalled for her to follow and took cautious steps. There was a staircase to their right. He glanced up and hesitated as if considering whether to ascend, but instead he continued towards another door.

Germane eased the door open. They listened again and then stepped into a monochrome space. Faint light came from somewhere above but Kate found it hard to see. Dust swirled in the bone-dry air.

"What is this place?" Kate whispered.

Germane didn't answer, and she followed his slow, careful steps past wooden crates and cardboard boxes. At the foot of a metal staircase he stopped and looked up again. Then behind. Then at Kate.

She was holding her breath again and listening.

Far off, she thought she could hear the faint sound of metal on metal. She raised her eyebrows.

Is someone here?

He shrugged and then nodded to the stairs.

They took them carefully, like they were walking on fragile paper. Even so, Kate's shoes squeaked twice and Germane's made a scuffing sound before they reached the top.

Now they were on a suspended metal footbridge and she could see bars that came down from the ceiling. Dust motes spiralled around them, lit by vents way up high. From this vantage point, even in the half-light, she could see the enormity of the space.

They moved forward and she realized part of the area was divided into sectors. She stopped over one and looked down on a set.

"A studio," Germane whispered. "I think this one was for a soap."

Even his whisper seemed loud up here. He must have read the concern in her eyes because his next words were: "I don't think anyone's here. It's too quiet." He still spoke quietly though.

They walked forward again and he pointed to the space on the other side. "Another studio."

"How do you...?"

"This warehouse is, or at least was, owned by a French TV channel." He was almost speaking normally now and the tension lifted. There really was no one around. It was a giant cavernous space in which time seemed suspended.

He continued: "I know this studio because we were partnering with them here. We visited and used some of the stuff to film over here. That first room was one of many storage areas—props and stuff." He walked more confidently now and she hurried to keep up.

The gantry swayed with their footfall.

"This next set is my favourite." He pulled up and pointed down to the right. "There."

All she could see was a dark shape. It almost filled the whole studio area but she couldn't quite focus.

"What is it?"

"Remember the movie *The Cube*?"

Kate shook her head. Something he'd said jarred with her. But she dismissed the feeling as insignificant as Germane continued.

"You should, the original was Canadian. It's one of the cult successes of the nineteen nineties."

"Afraid not."

"Well," Germane said, clearly enjoying the role of guide, "the French created a game show based on it. Contestants were locked in a cube and needed to escape, but you never knew which cube they would find themselves in next. Much of it is Perspex and some walls are mirrored. And the French being the French, of course, they called it *Le Cube*."

Kate leaned over the metal banister to get a better look.

He said, "It wasn't a great success."

She wasn't surprised, but then game shows weren't her thing.

"It's dry in here. Are you thirsty?" He handed her a bottle of water after unscrewing the top. Kate took a drink and handed it back.

She was about to ask what he thought they should do next when Germane held up his hand, his eyes wide.

Listening hard again, her heart pounded in her ears, but she heard nothing else. Germane, however, seemed to have picked something up. He held a finger to his lips and pointed along the walkway.

Then he started to move, stepping lightly but going faster than before. Kate followed.

After twenty paces, they passed the end of *Le Cube* studio. There was pitch darkness to their left and right and Germane continued.

After another ten paces, he stopped and listened. Ahead was another ladder. This went down to a corridor.

Suddenly he bolted.

Something had moved in the shadows below them. A person, maybe?

Germane raced down the short flight to the corridor. Kate hurried a few steps behind.

There were doors to the left and right along the dark corridor. And she couldn't see its end.

A creak and a click. The sound of a door closing.

Germane hesitated for a fraction and then started to run along the corridor. "This way," he hissed.

Kate fumbled for her phone and switched on the torch as she ran. When she looked up, Germane had a door open. She followed and found they were in a small room. Then through another door and another. Each time, Kate's light flashed around, illuminating boxes and desks and Germane's back. She heard their feet and other noises. Other doors. Other scuffling and running.

And then the light briefly caught someone ahead.

Germane grabbed the door handle but it wouldn't open.

"Stokes!" Germane shouted. "I know it's you."

There was no response.

Germane fought with the handle. "He's holding it," he said to Kate, and then to the person on the other side of the door: "Let's talk. Danny, you've got me this far. Let's just talk."

"Step away from the door," a man's voice responded.

Germane let go and took a step back.

Kate's phone pinged but she ignored it. Her light shone on the door as the handle turned.

SIXTY-TWO

The door opened a crack and then stopped.

She heard footsteps, like the person stepping back.

"Now come in."

Germane looked at her, looked back and stepped forward.

Kate's phone pinged for a second time and she glanced at it. A message from Andrew.

She could read it on the locked screen. It said, I was wrong. DS Keene is genuine.

What did that mean?

Ahead, she saw Germane push the door with one hand. Only now did she realize he had a gun with a silencer in his other. He must have had that under his coat the whole time.

Germane stepped into the next room. Kate stayed by the door, stuck her phone away and glanced into the gloom.

The other man was about ten yards away. She could see his shape but not his face.

"There's a light switch by the door," the man said.

Germane turned and flicked.

Danny Stokes stood before them in a room probably four times the size of the others. Behind him, in the centre, was a cage—a human-sized metal cage with bars.

"Danny," Germane said in an almost friendly tone.

Stokes looked at the gun in Germane's hand and then at the door.

"You're not alone. Kate Blakemore is here."

Stokes grinned. "No bullshit!" He took a step forward.

"Kate?" Germane called over his shoulder. "It's OK, show yourself."

Kate stepped into the room, half behind Germane.

"Wow! It really is you!" Stokes was still grinning. The scar ran down his face and looked like a grotesque mask. Plastic surgery gone wrong, Kate wondered. Then she blinked, because her eyes seemed to fog for no reason.

She said, "What's going on, Danny?"

"Did you like my code, Kate? It was clever, wasn't it?"

"Yes." She kept he voice flat. "Yes, Danny, it was very clever. You got us here."

"Thank you," he said, looking at Germane. "I never thought I'd get to meet the real Kate Blakemore. And yet here she is." Back at Kate: "Here *you* are!"

Kate blinked again to clear her sight. Her head felt funny. There was so much going on, it was confusing. Why hadn't Germane moved? He was in control. He had the gun pointed at Danny Stokes but he was just standing there.

Keene is genuine. What did it mean?

Germane said, "Did you deal with the other thing?"

"Easy," Stokes said without taking his eyes off Kate.

And then she had it. She stepped away from Germane and saw his gun switch to her.

She took a breath. "What's going on?"

Now, Germane smiled. "Quid pro quo," he said. "I needed Danny's help to get you here, and he was desperate to meet you."

"Detective Keene is genuine," she said.

Danny stepped towards her. "And dealt with. Good job you spotted him."

"Stop!" Germane barked at Danny.

Kate's legs felt weak. She wobbled.

Germane's hand was on her arm. The grip hurt but seemed somehow far away. Like her arm was stretching.

Danny backed away and she saw the cage loom up. The next moment, she was inside and the door closed.

Danny was right there. "Why?"

Why what? she was thinking, but Germane answered.

"I don't know how long I'll have to wait."

"But we've got her."

"No, Danny-boy, I've got her. You're surplus to requirements."

"No!" There was panic in Stokes's voice. And then Germane fired.

The last thing Kate remembered before slumping to the floor was the burst of red from Danny Stokes's head.

SIXTY-THREE

Kate's temple thumped and her shoulders ached. The water. Germane had drugged her with the water. That's why he hadn't drunk any. She moved slightly, and although her wrists burned, they weren't tied. Neither were her feet. She figured they must have been. How long had she been unconscious?

Through closed eyelids she could see light. Far off, she heard something scrabbling, maybe cogs grinding. She remembered the cage in the room with Danny Stokes. She wasn't in the cage. Then she remembered Germane shooting the young man.

She listened hard and kept her breathing slow. If there was someone out there, she didn't want them to know she was awake.

Then an electronically distorted voice boomed loud. "Stop the act, Kate. I know the difference between unconsciousness and faking it."

She opened her eyes and was dazzled by colourful spotlights. She was in a Perspex box about eight feet by eight feet with twelve squares drawn out on the floor. Each square was a different colour. The lights shone through the front and top of the box, which were translucent. The sides were made up of four by four multicoloured squares just like the floor. Except one, which was dark.

She remembered seeing the structure from above, through the half-light. There were many such cubes, stacked, and she guessed, because of the spotlights, that she was at the front and top.

Noises close by reminded her that she'd heard scrabbling before. Her box was empty. Was there something in the next box, the one to her right?

Kate stood.

"Don't move," the voice said.

Now she looked into the light, shielding her eyes. Maybe there was a man standing about thirty feet away with the lights behind him. Although he was just an outline, she knew who it was.

"Germane."

He said, "Welcome to Le Cube, Kate. Like I said, don't move until I say. Each of those squares is different. Most will give you a nasty shock. But it's not your turn to play yet." With that, the spots went out and burst into life to her right. The dark square was in fact a Perspex window. It wasn't perfectly clear, but inside the next cube she could see a man testing the walls, maybe trying to find a weakness.

Kate heard Germane through speakers in the other cube. "Welcome contestant number one. Your cube is now active," he said in a game show voice.

The man took a step away from the wall, screamed, immediately jumped forward and crouched.

Germane laughed. "I warned you, contestant number one. That blue square was a mild shock."

The man in the other cube said something but it was lost beneath Germane's voice over the speaker. "Other squares have different outcomes, some worse than others. One is a trap door that will drop you into another

cube. And one is a chute. The *chute* is your way out."
He emphasized chute strangely.

The man in the other cube stood up and did what
Kate had done, shielding his eyes against the light.
"What the hell? Who are you?"

Kate recognized the voice. "Keene?"

The man heard her and turned towards her cube.
"Kate? Kate, is that you?"

She took a step on to the next square. Nothing
happened. No shock. Nothing. As she suspected, there
was only one active cube at a time and it wasn't hers.

She stepped again and reached the right-hand wall.

"Keene," she shouted through the Perspex window,
"it's Germane. He's up there doing this."

"Germane? Why? What's he doing here?"

The man at the spotlights laughed again. "So many
questions, Kevin. You tried to tail us on a moped. You
aren't very good it, you know. Then when I got here I
sent a message to Danny to deal with you."

"Danny? Danny Stokes? Is he here?"

"I'm sorry," Kate said, ignoring Germane. "I thought
you weren't who you said you were."

The voice from the speakers said, "Oh, this is
interesting. Why don't you two just have a chat?"

Keene said, "Is that why you pretended you'd gone
home?"

"Andrew was especially suspicious because he
couldn't get hold of you at work."

"Because I was here!"

"But they said you were on sick leave."

Keene nodded. "The gaffer said I couldn't come.
Said there was no justification, no evidence of a crime, so
I claimed I was sick and came anyway."

"And Inspector Fleurot? We found out he's really
Sergeant Berne." As she said it, Kate realized her

331

blunder. It had been Germane who claimed Berne was Fleurot's real identity. She said, "Is Fleurot also real?"

"Of course."

"But..."

"Retired. I was off the grid so I used someone I knew from the past."

That must have been why he used the old title of inspector rather than captain. With all that doubt about the man, no wonder she bought Germane's lie that Fleurot was really someone else. If only Keene had told her what he was doing, maybe then she wouldn't have suspected him. Maybe she wouldn't have been fooled by Germane.

"Have you two quite finished?" Germane asked.

Keene said something else but Germane spoke over him, turning up the volume. "Number one, you can't just stand there. The objective is to escape. You need to find the chute. As such, the squares will change in three, two, one..."

There was a whir and suddenly Kate's cube was rotating; Keene's was too. When it landed on its side, the floor took on a new multicoloured square pattern.

Keene screamed.

"Oh," Germane said, "I've turned up the voltage to make it a bit more interesting. In fact, if you don't move within a minute, your square will become hot—and by that, I mean it will give you another nasty jolt."

Keene didn't move. A minute passed and then he screamed and jumped onto another square.

Keene stayed there and a minute later screamed again and jumped.

"Germane!" Kate banged on the front of her cube. "Stop it! What the hell do you want?"

"I want to show you how the game works, Kate. Please be patient, your turn will come. Now, contestant number one... good."

Keene had stepped onto another square. This time nothing happened.

"You've tried four, so eight to go, contestant number one. Eight to find the *chute* or drop into the next cube."

Keene stepped onto another square.

There was a *snap!* and Keene crumpled to the floor.

"Did I say chute?" Germane laughed. "I meant *shoot!* An easy misunderstanding. Thank you for playing, contestant number one."

Kate looked through a semi-transparent square at Keene. He wasn't moving and she guessed a rapidly growing dark patch was blood spilling from his head. There was a bullet hole in the front wall. Germane had shot the British detective.

"You're sick!" she shouted.

Keene's lights went out. Kate's lights went on.

"Contestant number two, are you ready?"

"Tell me why you just shot him!"

Germane said nothing for a moment. When he spoke, his voice was no longer that of a game show host. It was cold and calculating.

"To show you I'm deadly serious."

"I know you're serious. Why did you kill Danny?"

"Because this isn't really about Danny Stokes!"

"You used him to get me." Her mind was working now and pieces started to fall into place. The way the lady at the Art Nouveau hotel had seemed uncertain. She'd been checking with Germane to make sure her answers were right. Of course, she had said she recognized the computer-aged photo but didn't mention the scar. She'd have remembered the scar.

Kate shook her head at missing the clue. "Danny never stayed at that hotel, did he?"

"I couldn't risk you finding him too soon."

"But why did you need him? After you got the code…"

"I work with contingencies. And he turned out to be useful. When I pretended to photograph the ankh outside, I messaged Danny that we were being followed. It turned out that your intrepid detective just stuck his head into the darkness and let Danny whack him. Pretty stupid and unprofessional, don't you think?"

Kate felt bad about Keene. If she'd trusted him maybe this whole thing would have been different.

"The detective was an idiot," Germane said as though reading her thoughts. "Danny too. Blinded because he was so desperate to meet you."

Kate was thinking again. If Danny was working with Germane, then who else? "The kid from the cemetery," she said. "You set that up. And Andrew's phone. The kid was working for you."

"Why would I do that? Why have the kid attack you?"

"To make me trust you."

"Well done."

And then Kate had it. She said, "You aren't Simon Germane, are you? Are you even British?"

"Originally American."

"Why the elaborate trail? Why have us running around Paris? Why not just bring me straight here?"

"Because it was fun, because it got you here on your own free will and because we had time to kill."

"Why do we have time to kill?"

"Because this is as much about your boyfriend as it is about you. You see, I need to finish a job I started a few years ago."

"You're the assassin."

334

"I never really liked the term. You know the Hashshashin were the original Islamic fundamentalists. Ironic, don't you think? Anyway, I prefer to think of myself as someone who cleans up other people's mess."

"We aren't anyone's mess. We don't know anything."

"I let you go before because I thought the job was over. But it wasn't. My employer is still alive and I have a contract to fulfil."

Kate leaned hard with both hands pressed against the Perspex, trying desperately to see him. "You know that my partner is Scott? Joe was the one linked to Hamilton and he died in Iraq."

"Doesn't matter."

"So, you're just going to play a game and then shoot me, like you did with poor Detective Keene?"

"We've still got time to kill. We need to wait for Scott to arrive. He'll be here in about an hour, I figure. We exchanged texts." He paused and she wondered why. Maybe he wanted her to think about that, because he chuckled. "You think I don't know about your silly code! Of course I do. *Four-one, Scott. Everything is fine, just meet me here.*"

Kate felt for her phone. Of course, it was no longer in her pocket. She said nothing but felt her heart drop an inch.

"It would have been so much easier if you'd met me in the States, in Portland."

Kate's mind flashed back to emails about the mysterious case of the man found dead on Mount Hood in Oregon. The phone call with his nephew who wanted her to meet him urgently.

He repeated himself, only this time in a voice she'd heard before—a Chicago accent. "Recognize me, Kate?"

It was the man who called himself Tony Wells.

SIXTY-FOUR

Kate straightened and wiped her hands on her jeans. There were marks on the Perspex where they'd been, and for a second she imagined a hole appearing as a bullet came through.

She shook the negative thought away. *Keep him talking*, she told herself. "That was you on the phone? You pretended to be Tony Wells?"

"I had it all set up, nice and simple, in the States. Instead, you had to go to the UK and I had to improvise."

"So, Danny Stokes... Was that whole thing fake?"

"This is where it gets clever," he said, and she heard the pride in his voice. Perhaps she could use that to her advantage? He continued: "You see, I was in your emails. It was easy enough to pick up on Danny's obsession and play on it. I just got there before you did." She sensed a smile on his mouth as he said, "I set it all up beautifully."

"You told him to use the code four-one."

"I knew it would get your attention."

"But why France?"

"You think delaying is going to help you?"

Kate carried on regardless: "You created this whole elaborate thing. The clues were brilliant."

"They were mostly Danny's, though I helped. At first I pretended we were going to trap his father's ex-partner. But then I didn't need to. He just wanted to impress you."

Kate nodded. She didn't know how well the hitman could see her but she wanted him to think she was impressed. She guessed he could see her pretty well, maybe from multiple angles. Maybe he was even filming it.

"You knew this place from before, didn't you?"

"Sure. I was here a while back. I saw the original show. It was good, maybe too good for an unappreciative French audience. Why France? Because I had contacts. I knew this place and I knew how to get a gun."

"One thing I don't get. How did the kid in the grey cowl disappear in the ossuary? He ran into the dark. We looked afterwards but didn't find him."

"There was a hidden door. A tunnel went up to the chapel."

"Did you kill him—the kid in the grey coat? Was that you?"

She heard him say yes, but he was a distance from the microphone. She squinted into the light, wondering what had distracted him.

Get his attention back, she told herself. "You aren't Simon Germane," she shouted. "You don't like being called an assassin. So what *do* I call you?"

When he spoke, his voice was loud again. "You're still trying to delay, Kate. But fine. Until recently I was known as Señor Max, but you can call me the Janitor. Like I said, I clean up other people's messes."

Suddenly the lights went out. A theme tune played off in the distance and then the Janitor spoke. "Intermission,

Kate. I suggest you get some rest until the real action starts."

The light was fading fast as Scott stood beside the little Citroen. He'd circled the docks and this was definitely the address Kate had texted him. It had been two hours ago and she'd used the four-one code. Maybe she had moved.

He sent her a message: **Arrived. Where are you?**

Kate immediately responded with directions close by. She told him to go through the side door and then straight ahead past the stairs. She ended: **Look out 4 1 nightwatchman. Can't wait to see you.**

Double checking. What's the address? he replied.

Kate responded with an address and directions. She mentioned an open side door and again used four-one.

Scott didn't take a direct route, and a hundred yards later he found a brand new looking scooter hidden in the shadows. He felt its engine. It had some slight residual warmth. Maybe two or three hours old?

He left the scooter, wondering how that fitted in. Kate hadn't mentioned getting a car. So he'd figured she was with the guy helping her. So the scooter meant a third person. Someone following them?

He kept low and reached the road. Ahead he could see the entrance gates were locked. He figured Kate and her friend had found another way in but he didn't search for it. Instead, he found a place, away from the gates, where he could climb the fence. As soon as he was over he jogged across the lot to the main building. Rather than go straight for the side door, he circled all three structures and drew the conclusion that everything was locked up tight. If necessary, he could climb the walls, since there were plenty of handholds.

The large warehouse roof and the one on its right were flat. That would mean an access door and stairs, so a quick exit could be possible. As a defensive point, the largest building had windows all around and high up. There would be a reasonable panoramic view if you could move quickly and easily on what he figured was the top floor.

Scott completed his reconnoitre and located the open door. He noted the graffiti and remembered Kate telling him about the ankh symbol when they'd spoken two nights ago. He wondered what had happened to her since then. The snippets exchanged by text said so little except that she was all right but may need his help to resolve things.

She hadn't mentioned why they were in this giant warehouse, whether they were hiding or preparing, or something else entirely.

He regretted not getting more information, but the last few weeks had been intense, not least the time at Incirlik being interrogated by the CIA. Joe must have had it a thousand times worse, but they'd accepted his story, the assumed identity and fighting ISIS from the inside. A letter from the general in the YPG vouching for him had undoubtedly helped his claim.

Scott checked up and down the alley between the buildings and lightly stepped inside. And listened.

He heard nothing, waited a few beats and walked to the bottom of the stairs. They were metal, the type used as external fire-escapes, with lots of spaces and holes for the rain.

He glanced at the door ahead of him. But then instead of going through it, he took hold of the stair rail and began to ascend.

* * *

Kate had no idea how much time had passed. She was curled in a ball on the central squares. Her eyes blinked open and she coughed. A metallic taste in her mouth told her there was something in the air. A bottle of mineral water was within reach and she took a long drink to quench her thirst and remove the taste.

"Thank you for the water," the Janitor's voice said almost softly through the speakers.

Kate sat up. "What?"

"You should thank me for the water."

"What's in the air?"

"Just something to help you sleep. I didn't know how long we'd have to wait. So, you should thank me for that too."

Kate said nothing. She knew the Janitor was enjoying this. Fear didn't begin to describe how she felt, but there was no way she was going to show him, let him have that satisfaction. In fact, she now felt a weird calmness. Maybe it was the gas that made her relaxed, but there was no point in panicking. There was no point in scrabbling about like Keene had.

There was no way out of here unless the Janitor opened her cube.

But then of course she had hope. Hope that Scott would come. Hope that Scott would rescue her.

The far-off music began again and the Janitor put on his game show voice. "Welcome back to Le Cube, ladies and gentlemen."

Kate stood and shielded her eyes, waiting for the spotlights. But when the lights burst on they weren't aimed at her cube, they were on the one to her left.

The Janitor continued: "Welcome, contestant number three. Welcome, Scott Ranieri!"

340

SIXTY-FIVE

Kate's legs buckled. She could now see more clearly through the square in the wall. Was this a different cube? Stepping nearer, she peered through. There was someone on the floor.

He stood up awkwardly, hands tied behind his back.

"Scott!"

He turned towards her, confusion on his face as well as a trickle of blood.

He looked back at the lights. Had he not seen her? Was this square like a two-way mirror?

"Scott, I'm in here!"

She banged on the wall but her fists made no sound.

The Janitor said, "Contestant number three, your cube is now active."

Scott said nothing.

"I'm sure you know the game. You have sixteen squares to choose from—until Le Cube rotates, that is. Some squares are good and some are... shall we say... not so good. One square will give you a *chute*. That is your escape."

Kate yelled to warn Scott of the Janitor's meaning but her voice was lost.

"Some squares are safe, but you only have a minute to move again, because after a minute they... shall we say… aren't so safe anymore. In fact, you may find it a bit shocking. Contestant number three, your minute starts… Now!"

Scott didn't move. Kate found herself counting the seconds in her head, desperate for him to move to a safe square.

The buzzer sounded and Scott yelled as electricity made him jump. He landed on a new square.

Nothing happened.

"Well done, contestant three, you have found a safe square. But remember you only have a minute."

"Enough!" Scott shouted. "Who the hell are you?"

The Janitor switched to a different voice. "I'm the man who's here to clean up. Oh, and you have twenty-five seconds left."

"Clean up what?"

"The mess with the Saudi prince. Ten seconds."

The buzzer sounded but Scott moved a fraction before it. But he yelled anyway. His new square had turned into a bed of needles and she now spotted his bare feet. He remained on the square.

"Very good," the Janitor said. "You have two minutes on a bad square."

When Scott spoke again, he sounded calmer. "You realize it's all over?"

"That's what they wanted me to think, but my client is still alive."

"So, you're cleaning up the witnesses?"

"Just you two to go. Your buddy Hurwitz is already dead. Ninety seconds."

"But I'm not who you think I am."

The Janitor laughed lightly. "Really? You are Scott and were impersonating your brother Joe to entrap the Saudi prince."

"As a diversion from your client. But he was playing a similar game. A longer game."

"One minute."

"We are both soldiers. We have both been pawns."

The Janitor said nothing.

"You don't really know what's going on. For all you know—"

"We may be soldiers, but I'm getting paid." The Janitor laughed. "You have thirty seconds."

"For all you know, you could be playing into the hands of the enemy."

The Janitor laughed again but this time it sounded forced. Perhaps Scott was getting to him. When he spoke, he said, "How quaint. A sense of right and wrong. Goodies and baddies. Ten seconds."

The buzzer sounded in less and Scott yelped and stepped from his square. He then screamed out and began to dance on a square glowing with heat.

"Better move before your skin burns off," the Janitor said calmly.

Kate saw Scott tense up and make a step.

"Oops!" the Janitor said. There was the same sickening *snap!* she'd heard when Keene had been shot.

Kate screamed, "Noooo!" and Scott dropped to the floor.

SIXTY-SIX

She slumped against the wall. Tears flowed freely and she felt all the strength she'd been holding inside flood out.

It seemed like an eternity but, in reality, only seconds passed before the lights in her cube came on. She didn't move. She expected the Janitor to play the game show host again, to announce contestant number two, but he didn't.

Was he just going to shoot her now? Was the game over?

And then a voice came through the speakers.

"Kate?"

She sat up. "Scott? Is that you? Are you all right?"

She jumped to the window into the next cube. Scott was still on the floor but he was sitting up. He was gingerly touching his feet.

And there was no bullet hole in his cube's wall.

Even though she knew it was ineffectual, she banged her fists on the wall. "Scott!"

He looked at her then and smiled. But he didn't move from his square.

A popping sound pulled her attention away. She looked up and saw a door in her cube's ceiling begin to open. And then a ladder descended and a man's shoes were at the top.

For a horrible moment, she thought it was the hitman, but then she saw that the legs were wearing combat pants. The Janitor had worn chinos. Scott was wearing combat pants! She glanced back into the other cube, but Scott was still there nursing his feet. So it wasn't him. *Who the hell...?*

"Kate!"

She looked up and did a double take. "Scott?"

He rushed to her then and took her in his arms. Eventually he eased her away, kissed her and said, "Come on, we need to check on Joe."

Joe was in the other cube, and grumpy as hell when they climbed down to him.

"Took your time!" he said.

"You shouldn't have been captured so quickly."

"He blindsided me. And *you* had the gun!"

"Well, then it was a good job I did!"

Joe showed the soles of his feet. "I reckon I've got first-degree burns."

Scott hugged him. "Sorry, I got lost. There are a hundred rooms back there. And then I found myself on the wrong side of the set. When I got back up top, I couldn't find the bastard. The only lights were on your cell."

"It's a cube," Joe corrected. "And I never ever want to see one again. In fact, if either of you even mentions a Rubik's Cube in the future—*ever*—I'm going to have to kill you."

Scott brought the car around to the gap in the fence and carried Joe down to it. He explained that they had flown into the US air base in southern Belgium and then borrowed a car to drive to Paris. The drive took three hours but they'd been delayed almost an hour getting the car and a gun.

"We wanted assault rifles but the M9 was all I could mooch."

Mooch, Kate knew, was Scott's expression for the British word *blag*.

"And just the one," Joe added. He lay on the back seat with his bare feet raised.

"How did you know I was in trouble?" Kate wanted to know.

"You said there were bad guys," Scott said. "When you texted from the burner, you said you needed help." He glanced at her. "Did you just *humph*?"

"I just realized Germane told me to get a *burner*. I should have known it's an American expression. A Brit would normally say pay-as-you-go or disposable. But you still haven't explained. I didn't use the code for ambush."

"That's a stupid code," Joe grunted.

"Ignore Grumpy back there," Scott said. "I texted that I wanted to *double-check*. Germane somehow knew four-one but should have used eight-two."

They rode in silence for a while and Kate couldn't help thinking about how afraid she'd been. How she'd felt real despair. How she thought she would die.

Finally, Scott broke into her thoughts. "Time to make that call?"

Before they left, Scott had checked on Keene. Although rigor hadn't yet set in, he'd been dead for a few hours. In his pocket, Scott found a card with Fleurot's phone number.

Kate dialled it and spoke in French to the man who answered. Fleurot confirmed Keene's story. He was ex-Prefecture, retired, and had given the British detective some help. Kate gave him a quick summary about being trapped at the warehouse and he was shocked that they had been danger.

"I had no idea," he said. "I thought Detective Keene was just following you to find someone else. I had no idea."

She said nothing, let the old inspector connect the dots and realize that something bad had happened.

"Mademoiselle, please tell me Simon is all right. That he is with you now."

And then she told him Keene had been shot and killed by the other man.

Fleurot switched to a formal tone and insisted on details and that she contact the Paris police.

She told him about Le Cube and said that Keene should be recognized as a hero. She said, "I can't tell you who rescued me, but our attacker is dead and I'd like it if Detective Keene could be confirmed as the shooter."

They discussed it more and she made it clear that neither she nor the rescuer wanted to be involved any further. Finally, Fleurot said he'd do what he could.

"Sounded awkward," Scott said as he sped north towards the Belgian border.

"He wasn't happy that we didn't stay around to leave statements."

"But he believed you."

"Yes."

Joe grumbled something from the back seat.

Kate turned, "Do you want to stop? Can I get you anything?"

"An explanation," Joe said. "I want to know how you could possibly think I was Scott!"

"You're twins... and anyway, I wasn't expecting you."

"We may be twins, but I'm the better looking one."

347

She laughed. "Then my only excuse is that the Perspex window into your cube was obscured."

"Apology accepted," he said with a grin.

Then she asked about Syria, and for the next hour he told her his story.

By the time they had arrived at Chièvres Air Base in Belgium, she had noticed a wistful tone to his voice.

"Do you miss Syria?" she asked.

"It's been a big part of my life for a long time now. I've seen a lot that I thought I could walk away from. It's a mess and may never return to its former glory... And..."

"Yes?"

"I made a promise. I said we'd either rescue Sa'ad's daughter or find justice for her."

"You're going back, aren't you," Scott said, a catch in his voice.

"I've been thinking about it these past few hours. It's something I need to do. There are things in life that define us."

"You're a Mirrorman, Joe. I get it."

"We used to think we were superheroes to save the world." Joe smiled, although his eyes looked sad in the faint moonlight. "We can't save the world but sometimes we can make a difference."

When they parted, Scott hugged his brother hard. Joe would catch a flight back to Turkey and the others would go home to Canada, although there would be a short hop via Germany.

Joe had had his feet treated, bound and been given crutches. They stood on the tarmac, a US Air Force plane being loaded in front of them. A member of the ground crew said Joe should board.

"Come find us when you're done," Scott said with tears in his eyes.

"You bet." Joe gave him a punch on the arm and then tucked his crutches under his armpits, ready to go.

"Joe!" When his brother turned, Scott added, "You got one thing wrong."

Joe looked confused. "What's that?"

"I'm the good-looking one."

"In your dreams." Joe laughed. He declined the offered support of the groundcrew and hobbled across the tarmac.

SIXTY-SEVEN

On the flight home, they agreed there would be no more cases for a while. "An indefinite sabbatical," Scott called it, although Kate hoped it would become more of a holiday. Maybe one day they'd vacation in Paris, but not for a while. For the time being she contented herself with discovering more of Canada.

Ben Hurwitz met their flight. Scott had called from the Belgian air base and discovered he was alive and well. Why had the Janitor claimed Ben was already dead? Some sort of weird psychology was how they explained it, but they would never know.

What they did discover was how the Janitor had gained access to their information. A security expert swept the house and checked computers. He found the insect-cameras and spyware that the Janitor had installed remotely.

Kate put two and two together and guessed the Janitor had been the man Barb Winter had seen snooping around the house.

The Janitor had gained access to the emails and picked up the strange case of the man found near Mount Hood. That's how he'd known to pretend to be the nephew Tony Wells. If Kate had met him in Portland, she had no doubt the Janitor would have held her there until Scott returned home.

Kate had told Wells she was in the UK, and he'd read Megan's and Danny's emails. He'd flown to London and conned Danny into thinking he'd help. Whether it was to trap Kate or the real Simon Germane, she'd never know. But the Janitor had told Danny the four-one code that would get her attention. Then he and Danny had created the trail.

The French media reported on three bodies found at the Paris warehouse which had been a TV studio. There was also the discovery of another body in an apartment near the Moulin Rouge. An elderly lady had been smothered and left in an understairs cupboard. It wasn't connected to the deaths at the port, but Kate realized the Janitor hadn't really rented the lavender and lily scented apartment where she'd spent the night with him.

Detective Keene was hailed as a hero in the British press and there was a quote from DI Deshorter about how Keene had taken personal leave to help the Stokes family. Danny's role in entrapping Kate wasn't mentioned because no one knew. Megan told the media that the other man had probably conned her brother. Maybe Danny thought he was tracking down their father's killer. There was some speculation that the real Simon Germane was involved. But he could never respond to allegations because he was never traced. Kate's theory was that the Janitor had killed him as part of the deal with Danny.

Joe rang one morning with the news that he'd joined up with Sa'ad searching for Noura. He was also providing the CIA with intelligence on the ground. He had a rant about the US policy of funding the fight against ISIS because it had shifted to Ahrar al-Sham. The group also wanted an Islamic caliphate and were almost as extreme as ISIS.

"We wouldn't fund the Taliban to get al-Qaeda, so why does the president think this makes sense?"

Scott didn't have an answer. The only thing he knew was that sometimes the government just took military actions for political reasons. It was the way of the world. What else would you expect politicians to do, especially when it came to playing soldiers? It's why military intelligence was an oxymoron—because the politicians were always behind it.

In Joe's view, the answer was to support the government. He hated to say it but he felt the Russians had a better strategy, the only difference being the conditions that should be imposed. Assad should be forced to embrace democracy and a fairer, more secular society.

"And yet you're working for the CIA!" Scott challenged him.

"First and foremost, I'm an American," Joe said, and then he laughed. "When I said I pass on intelligence, well, I tell them what I want our government to hear."

There was no news of Noura, but they remained hopeful that she was still alive.

They ended the call with Joe promising to call again.

In the weeks that followed, Hamilton was indicted and charged with treason. The press referred to Joe as soldier R, but he wasn't required to give evidence, although his statement to the CIA in Turkey was pivotal to the case.

Kate stayed in touch with Grace LaBelle, and when it was Jemila's sixteenth birthday, Kate received an invite to the celebration. She travelled with Scott, taking the ferry to Tsawwassen and driving down Highway 17. When they passed Beaver Lake she reminded Scott about Detective Stanley and his annoying assertion that Jemila was buried there.

"Did you ever tell him how you knew how she'd escaped from the bolted bedroom?"

"I thought it was better to keep him in the dark." Kate laughed.

She knew Grace's husband had left the island and that she no longer had plans to leave their home. Jemila was happy. Grace still wouldn't tell Kate what her husband had been doing that night, but the police had found no drugs or anything else incriminating.

Kate had called in favours and social services were giving Jemila and her mother a chance.

Grace rushed out and hugged her when they arrived. Jemila followed and shook her hand awkwardly.

"Wow!" Scott said. "You do look like Rogue."

"See, Mom." Jemila grinned. Then she invited them in to see her latest paintings.

As they walked up the path, Grace said, "Thank you. The trip to Marvel's offices worked miracles."

Kate's calls from Paris had been to contacts who could pull strings. Jemila had been invited to see where the comics were created and to visit an exhibition of some of the most famous Marvel superhero artwork.

Grace continued: "They thought her artwork showed real promise. They said she was almost guaranteed a job, providing she went to art school first. And guess what..."

Kate waited, a smile forming on her lips.

"...She's determined to go to college. Already started applying, would you believe?"

"I'm so pleased for you both," Kate said, and she gave Grace another hug. She sensed the woman had also cleaned up her own act. The house smelled fresh, and the little things, like fruit in a bowl on the lounge table, spoke volumes.

After admiring Jemila's paintings, Scott glanced around the girl's bedroom and asked, "So how did you get out? You were locked in with no means of escape."

Kate said, "She didn't."

"How did you know?" Jemila asked.

"When there's no obvious solution, you have to think outside the box."

The girl laughed. "Only this time it was inside the box, right?"

Kate nodded. "You were here the whole time. When your mum unlocked the door in the morning all you needed to do was wait for her to leave." Kate stood by the cupboard and opened the door. "You were up there on the top shelf."

"It was a squash. I broke open a cardboard box and used it to hide behind."

"I saw the broken box."

Jemila nodded.

"And you had to move your comics."

"That was the hardest part—and leaving them, of course."

Kate said, "I'm so glad you hope to go to college."

"I'd like to but..."

"But what?"

"It's going to be tough."

"Nothing worth doing is easy. And a smart man once told me to focus on the sky rather than the finger pointing at it."

"What does that mean?"

"You tell me."

"Aim high?"

"That'll do," Kate said with a smile. "Aim high and be a hero—or a superhero, in your case."

When they left, Jemila thanked Kate for not judging her. For believing in her. As she gave Kate a peck on the cheek, Jemila whispered, "Stolen goods. He was making his money by acting as a middleman."

They pulled apart and the girl acted like she'd said nothing. She shook Scott's hand and waved goodbye.

On the journey home, Kate told Scott.

"Jemila found out her stepdad was crooked. Mike LaBelle was getting money so they could move but she wanted to stay there with her mother. She thanked me for not judging her."

"You've made a real difference to that girl's life."

"That's why we do this. It feels good."

Scott was silent for a while as they headed for the ferry and she knew he was thinking. Finally he said, "It felt good to find Joe and clear his name."

Even though he'd been successful and Joe had been in touch, Kate sensed the experience had affected Scott. He'd been more pensive, and she'd caught him following *Free Syria Media* on Twitter.

"I can't help being affected," he'd explained. "It's very sad, and I totally get why Joe had to go back."

One afternoon, as they strolled along the river, Scott finally confessed to what had happened to him in Syria, how he'd crossed the country without an armed escort. The suffering he'd seen, the desperation. He also told her about Uday: the man's hopes, dreams and beliefs. How the Syrian had risked his own life and then met them again at the bombed-out safe house. Uday had not only driven them across the border, but all the way back to Incirlik Air Base.

Uday had only asked for enough money to cover expenses, but Scott had given him considerably more. Uday said he'd continue to Austria and visit his two sons.

Kate had already suspected that Scott had crossed into Syria without US Army support but she still gave him a hard time for being so reckless. "You'd better promise you'll never, ever pull a risky stunt like that again!"

He held up a hand. Scout's honour.

On the top deck of the ferry, with the wind in their hair, Scott put his arm around her and held her for a long time. After she kissed him and they were face-to-face, he said, "I think we should also try again."

"Try again?" She had no idea where he was going with this.

"Uday told me that the love of your child is the most rewarding thing, the meaning of life," he said. "I'd like to try IVF."

"That's one smart guy," she said, and kissed him. "One very smart guy."

"Does that mean yes?"

"Of course it means yes!"

After a hug, he placed his hands on the railing and leaned into the wind. She copied him and tasted the salty air.

"We're good at what we do... and we enjoy it."

It had been nine weeks since they'd been back and she'd been thinking the same thing. "Yes."

"Then I also think we should get back to work. Let's find the next case to solve."

Kate looked at the beautiful hills of Vancouver Island. Seagulls danced through the air behind the ferry. The sabbatical was over. Dare Services was back.

Acknowledgements

Firstly I want to recognize my wonderful wife, Kerry, for her support and encouragement. You will always be my North Star.

I'm grateful to my advisors for helping bring locations to life: my friend Rami Sabeh for Syria, and my uncle Bill Murray (not the actor) for Canada. Thanks also to Matyas Csiky for exchanges on his experience of the UN's role in Syria.

My unofficial editor and friend Pete Tonkin deserves a mention for his considered comments on an early draft. Also, thanks to Richard Sheehan for his official editorial review. As always though, any mistakes are my own.

A special mention goes to Sophie Liang for her enthusiasm. And a thank you to the other readers of *I Dare You*, who have encouraged me to write this second instalment. Hopefully there will be a third.

Singapore 52

Chinese New Year 1952 Ash Carter had to leave the Middle East in a hurry. But when he arrives in Singapore he finds himself in the middle of a much bigger problem. No one knows where, or when, or who but someone is planning an attack. Carter is told to make sure it doesn't happen. With pressure from politicians and the army and with Chinese Secret Societies watching his every move, he has other plans. He is more interested in finding out who killed his friend.

Read the first few chapters of Ash Carter's initial adventure here…

What they've said about Singapore 52:

"Think Jack Reacher with a dash of James Bond, set in Singapore. Thrilling!"

"Simply gripping! Perfect for an on-screen thriller"

Singapore 52

ONE

Friday the first of February 1952, the sixth day of the Chinese New Year and my first in Singapore. I was here for two reasons: partly, because a friend had asked for help but also because I needed to get away from Palestine. Quickly.

On the flight from India a young army lieutenant told me everything he knew about Singapore. Which wasn't much. He said it was run by the British and strategically important both militarily and for trade. He said it was the best place to get posted and get laid. Nestled in the tropical jungle, the place was as exotic as the women were beautiful. He told me it was the size and shape of the Isle of Wight but upside down and with ten times the number of people. I'd never been to the small island on the south coast of England but I guessed it wouldn't have been as packed as the streets where I was now. I was in the Chinese quarter of the city and heading for the docks where my friend worked.

I sidestepped a street vendor who tried to block my passage with his tray of steaming noodles. He touched my arm. "English. I have something you like."

Even before he'd spoken I knew it was more than noodles he wanted to sell me. He had a large bag over his shoulder. A protective hand hovered over the opening. He'd have stolen goods in there. Watches maybe. I stood out, a white man in shorts and a short-sleeved shirt. Not an army uniform but not a labourer. If I didn't buy his watch maybe the plan was someone else would pick my pocket. I moved on.

Observation and deduction. We do it every day, often without realizing it. It's instinctive and vital for my line of work. My previous line of work. The crooked street vendor selected me because he spotted me and deduced I was a prime target. It works the other way too. Recognizing something that's out of the ordinary, out of place.

The first rule of covert surveillance is to blend in and act natural. Tailing someone is easier when there's two or more of you, but a good operator on their own should be fine when in a crowd. And this was a crowd. The man I'd spotted could have been a dock worker, dressed in brown overalls and a cap. After all, the docks were about a mile away and there were other labourers dotted around. Most of them were in clusters and walking with purpose. This guy acted more like a tourist. He slowed down and sped up and never overtook me. The real give-away was his shoes. Not dockers' boots, not army boots. Smart brown shoes. Probably Brogues.

I had two choices: evade or confront. It was an easy choice. We were in public and the guy didn't look a threat. I continued to walk along the street as though acting like a tourist without a concern. Rain drops, the size of small marbles, smacked the exposed skin of my arms and I glanced up. People around me started to scurry. A tropical downpour was coming. The timing was perfect. I saw an opening to what looked like an undercover market and stepped inside. It smelled of roasted chicken, incense and dust.

Doubling back, I stood by the entrance, hidden from the approaching tail. He'd come inside and I'd grab him.

Ten seconds passed. Twenty seconds. The guy didn't enter and he didn't walk by. A whole minute must have passed before I was tempted to step back into what was now a torrential downpour. The sound of trade was masked by the rain as it crackled like an intense wood fire on the canvas roof above. And then I heard another noise above the racket. Shouting.

I looked around. Smoke wafted, green in the thick air. The undercover market extended for at least a hundred yards and probably had offshoots I couldn't see. Stalls and customers were everywhere with hardly any space to move. At six-two I could see over the heads of most of the crowd. And then I saw a definite movement like a wave of heads. In an area about a third of the way down people were moving away, hustling, pushing one another. There was no panic, just an urgency to get away. Some of the people at least. It seemed to be the source of the commotion too.

I headed in that direction and as I drew closer I could see the problem. A stall had been overturned, the wares scattered on the cobbled floor. Three British soldiers were remonstrating, shouting and throwing things around.

I moved closer still. There were just two rows of people in front of me now.

I heard one of the soldiers say something about dirty Japs and I moved through the last remnants of the crowd. I could see him now: a fourth person, on his hands and knees. With a white band tied around his forehead and a red dot in the centre, he was clearly supposed to look like a Japanese suicide pilot.

One soldier kicked the prone man in the rear while another forced his boot into his face and indicated that it should be kissed or licked.

"Enough!" I shouted. Either they didn't hear me or they were distracted by a young white woman who threw herself at the nearest soldier. She flailed her arms and screamed and was batted away like an annoying fly.

I helped her to her feet. She was just a teenager.

"You all right?"

There was dust all over her pretty white dress and tears streaked down her cheeks but I could see she wasn't hurt. She sobbed something about protecting the vendor and I nodded.

In the voice I'd used many times in similar situations, I bellowed, "Military Police!"

For a moment even the crowd fell silent. All three soldiers stopped, frozen to the spot. Then the guy who was clearly the leader stared at me, eyes cold and hard. I could read doubt on his face.

"Military Police," I shouted again. "Get out! Get out now!"

Two moved. The leader didn't. Then he laughed.

"Bugger off. You ain't an MP. Where's your red cap?" The other two closed ranks, pushed out their chests.

No point in getting into a discussion. I skipped forward. One step. Two steps. Punch. It was a straight right to the guy's nose. Just a tap, but it spun him around. Before the blood appeared I was already sidestepping to hit the next guy with a left hook.

The third man was a problem. He was the one behind the Japanese vendor who was starting to rise. Still only half upright, the vendor was pushed and fell towards me. I instinctively caught him which was a mistake. It slowed me down. The bloody-nosed leader was up and also lunging. I tripped on something on the floor and we fell together, knocking over a trestle table.

I felt a blow to my head, scrabbled to my feet and blindly tangled with another of the soldiers. I hit him hard but again found myself tumbling to the ground.

And then suddenly there was an eruption of noise: whistles and shouts. Strong hands pressed down on me, pinning me to the ground. I expected more blows but there were none. I breathed in the hot dust. *What the hell?*

"Stand up!" a voice barked in my ear. He spoke with the same authority I'd tried just a few minutes earlier.

With my arms locked behind my back I was pulled to my feet and held by two men in uniform. They had red caps. Royal Military Police.

A major glared at me. Behind him I could see the three soldiers I'd been fighting, each of them also held in an arm-lock.

I saw the girl in the white dress. She was kneeling by the vendor, offering him a drink. She looked over and seemed to smile, perhaps apologetically. The items that covered the floor looked like Japanese war memorabilia which made sense for a Japanese vendor. I spotted a sheathed Samurai sword under one of the over turned trestles. Thank goodness the soldiers hadn't noticed that. I looked at the trouble makers. Not one of them could have been twenty. Just kids probably high on booze and adrenaline. They hung their heads now, no fight left in them. Which was a good thing because you don't mess with the military police.

The three men were dragged away and the crowd immediately parted to let them through.

My captors didn't move and the major continued to glare at me, unblinking.

I nodded. One officer to another. "Thank you."

The major said nothing.

He seemed to wait until the last of the three was almost out of the covered market. Again I nodded. "Right. You can let me go now."

Only now did he change his expression. The glare became a kind of smirk.

"Let you go?"

"Yes. I was just—"

The major barked, "You are going nowhere, matey boy." He spun on his heels and I was nudged forward, my arms locked behind my back. "You are under arrest."

TWO

I blinked in the bright sunlight. Water sloshed from pipes and ran over the cobbles down the street. A truck with military police markings was pulling away and I figured the other three guys were in it.

A second vehicle waited, its rear doors open.

"I'm a civilian," I said to the major but he ignored me. He walked to the front of the vehicle where a beetle-browed sergeant opened the door for him.

A second later I was bundled into the back of the truck. At the last moment, I caught a glimpse of the guy who'd been following me earlier. He was leaning against a wall, cigarette in mouth, watching. He inclined his head, perhaps as a courteous nod. It was the first indication that maybe something was going on.

The MPs snapped cuffs on me behind my back then attached the cuffs to a metal bar in the rear of the truck. Once secured, they sat either side and slammed the door shut.

"Where to, lads?" I asked trying to lighten the atmosphere. They didn't respond but then again I didn't expect them to.

I couldn't see outside but the bumpy ride took no more than ten minutes. We were still in the city. When we stopped, I heard the front passenger leave. Then the two in the back got out and shut the door again. It was hot inside, maybe eighty degrees Fahrenheit, maybe more. I tried to stay relaxed with shallow breaths. *Don't think about the heat.* I knew what was going on. I'd done or instructed the same thing many times. This was about weakening a prisoner's spirit. Exhaust him, break him and gain control.

Thirty minutes later, the doors opened.

The sergeant with the eyebrows looked at me. I'm sure I was dishevelled, my short hair plastered on my head, my clothes soaked with sweat. Not an impressive sight. But that was the point.

"Welcome to Hotel Bras Basah," the sergeant said in a Welsh accent.

He climbed in and detached the cuffs from the bar. My arms ached from the uncomfortable position.

"Could you uncuff me, Sergeant?"

"When we've got you inside, sir."

I could see from his eyes that he'd made a mistake, shouldn't have called me sir. But there was no point in confronting the situation, not yet anyway. I may have been hot and bothered and thirsty and quite pissed off, but I was also intrigued.

We were parked on a street behind a Land Rover. The other truck was there too, the one from outside the market I guessed. Since I hadn't heard anyone get out of it, the squaddies were either still inside or hadn't been kept waiting.

We were outside a single storey brownstone, just wider than the parking space for the Land Rovers. It had large windows and glass doors which were wide open to the street. Five stone steps took us into a foyer. There was a long desk in front of me and three MPs behind it, one an admissions clerk. They all looked hot and I figured that was why the doors were open, trying to get some air into this hothouse.

The corporal behind the desk watched us approach. He would log the prisoners in and ask for the usual details: name, number, rank and regiment. He'd also note the reason for arrest. I knew that the majority of soldiers that I'd seen were on shore leave. The three I'd fought were from the Staffordshire regiment and had come ashore a couple of hours earlier.

"Causing affray," Eyebrows said. The admissions clerk wrote it down and then reeled off the usual questions aimed at me.

"Ash Carter," I said. "No number. No regiment. Civilian."

Even though I put emphasis on the last word, the clerk didn't bat an eyelid. He just grunted, "Cell one."

Eyebrows led me around the desk to a corridor. On the left was a door that I suspected led to a couple of offices. On the right was the main cell. It could probably take over twenty men comfortably. Double that uncomfortably. But there were just three today. The squaddies. They sat on the bench, looking sorry for themselves—especially the one I'd jabbed on the nose. It was stuffed with cotton wool and his face was swollen.

To a man they looked up and tracked me through the metal bars as I was led past the pen and through a door at the back. There were four individual cells here. Each about eight by six feet, each with a stubby wooden bench.

Eyebrows opened the gate and I stepped inside. He removed the handcuffs, stepped outside and locked me in. He left me for a minute before returning with a metal mug of water.

I drank it and sat on the bench to wait. Through the door I could see the corridor that led to the foyer. I couldn't see the large pen or the squaddies but sometime during the next two hours, I heard the three Staffordshires close-quarters marched out. I heard one of the guards say the name of a troopship and surmised they were being taken to brig aboard the ship. Soldiers would never be retained on land if their ship was about to leave. But they wouldn't be free. All troopships had their own equivalent of these cells.

Later, I heard two drunken soldiers dragged in and dumped in the pen. Unlike the Staffordshires, the two new prisoners argued and, when the clerk shouted at them to shut up, their abuse turned to him briefly before they resumed their argument.

I had been dozing when I heard my door unlock.

Two guards stood in the corridor.

"You're to see Major Vernon," one said.

The other one said, "It's a long walk."

I stepped outside the cell and they stood one in front and one behind as though we were about to march close-quarters. The one in the front stepped forwards smartly and I waited for the inevitable prod in the back. It didn't happen.

The guy in front opened the door to the corridor and I took a casual step forward. The guards walked awkwardly for five paces and then stopped. I stopped.

The man in front opened a door on the right and we filed through. As suspected there were two offices here, one on either side. He knocked on a door and we waited.

After a count of twenty, a voice called, "Come."

The guard opened the door and we stepped in. I was wrong. It was more like an interview room than an office.

The major stood with his back to us, looking out of an open window. There was a large oak desk between us and one large chair on his side, one small chair on my side.

The guards left.

"Sit, Mr Carter," Vernon said.

I remained standing.

He turned and glared at me. He had small, cold eyes and a half-bald head. As a civilian he may have been tempted to shave it all off or have a comb-over to hide the lack of hair. Instead, he had shaved his scalp halfway like two heads had been stuck together, one bald and one not. It was some kind of signature look. Whatever, he was clearly proud of the unusual hairstyle because he smiled after I looked at it.

On the desk was an open book. He glanced down. "Causing affray, it says here."

I said, "The three Staffordshires were bothering a local market trader. A girl was knocked off her feet. I stepped in to help."

"They were on shore leave. A little merry from drink and having a bit of fun."

"I judged the situation—"

"Judged?" Vernon shouted. He slammed both hands on the desk and leaned forwards. "Who the hell are you to judge?"

I didn't respond.

Vernon made an exaggerated show of turning a page.

"Witness statements," he said, spitting the words.

"Good."

"Not good." He stood ramrod straight, maybe trying to look big though he was a couple of inches shorter than me. "Have you wondered why you are here rather than in a police cell?"

I didn't respond.

"I have witness reports that say you shouted, 'Military bloody Police'."

"Without the bloody."

Vernon said, "Military Police. Impersonation of a military police officer."

"Who were the witnesses? Did you get a statement from the Japanese market trader?"

"Impersonating a member of His Majesty's armed forces—a military policeman not least—is a criminal offence." He trotted off some regulations and then waited for me to say something.

I met his glare and said nothing.

"The witnesses all claimed you started the fight."

They hadn't interviewed anyone from the market. It wasn't standard procedure, not unless there had been criminal damage or grievous bodily harm. All Vernon had were three statements from the Staffordshires.

I shook my head and waited.

Eventually he flicked over another page and pointed to a line of type that I couldn't read upside down.

"Palestine," he said in a tone that was almost reasonable.

"That's right."

"Just off the boat yourself?"

"No, I caught a flight into Changi."

He waited. When I didn't elaborate he said, "Captain Ash Carter. Assigned to Royal Military Police seventy-fifth Provost. Special Investigations Branch. Palestine."

It seemed to be the only information he had about me. I nodded and said, "Retired as of two weeks ago."

The cold, hard stare returned and I wondered if he ever blinked.

I added, "Honourable discharge."

Vernon puffed himself up again. His teeth were clenched as if he wanted to say something but was unsure what it was.

Finally he bellowed, "Guard!"

The door opened and the two MPs stepped smartly inside.

"Take Mr Carter back to his cell."

THREE

Night approached and slinked slowly across the corridor leaving just a dim light from the room beyond. I leaned on the wall and dozed. Something you learn in the army is to sleep when you can. You also eat when you can but all I was given was a chunk of bread and another mug of water. It was lukewarm and tasted of tin.

During the night there was a lot of noise and activity. Many drunken soldiers came and went from the pen next door. At one point the sergeant with the eyebrows came through and asked if I wanted a blanket. The heat was unrelenting so I used it as a pillow and curled up on the floor.

It was still dark when I woke up just before six in the morning. I rubbed the stiffness from my joints and returned to the bench. A guard brought me a mug of tea and a billycan with watery porridge.

"What's next?" I asked him.

"No idea," he said. "Except..." He looked uncertain.

"Go on."

"Well, sir, you've caused a bit of a kerfuffle." That was all he would say before he left me.

Thirty minutes later, Eyebrows came back. "Sleep all right?"

"I've had better nights. But I've also had worse."

He nodded. "You're staying at The Queens?"

They'd obviously checked up on me whilst I'd been in the clink. "In theory," I said. "I checked in but haven't actually stayed there yet. Yesterday was my first day."

Eyebrows cracked a smile. "Well then, welcome to Singapore." He led me into the corridor. I counted eight men in the pen, looking tired with hangovers and bruises from fighting no doubt.

Eyebrows checked me out at the desk and showed me a map.

"This is the Military Police Head Quarters on Bras Basah road. Your hotel is here—" He pointed to a crossroads not far away. "A maximum of ten minutes' walk. Get yourself cleaned up and I'll pick you up outside the hotel at oh-eight-twenty."

"Pick me up?"

"Yes," he said and became more serious. "I'm to take you to Government House."

I expected a vehicle, but I was wrong. *Pick you up*, just meant that Eyebrows would meet me at The Queens Hotel and we would walk. Showered, shaved and with clean clothes I felt like a new man. On the steps of the hotel I formally introduced myself.

Eyebrows replied with a nod. "Sergeant Dave Hegarty."

We set off at a brisk pace.

"What's at Government House, Dave?"

"Sorry, sir, that's all I've been told." After that, he said nothing.

We walked in a straight line with the rising sun at our backs. There were occasional blocks of shop-houses—two storey buildings each with a retail shop downstairs and living quarters upstairs—but within minutes we were in the area I learned to call the Government sector. White Georgian properties gleamed in the sunlight.

Hegarty stopped at a shiny black door with a silver knocker and door pull. He knocked and the door was opened by a Malay butler who bowed curtly.

Hegarty indicated that I should enter and said he'd wait outside.

The butler led me down a corridor and parquet flooring clicked under my shoes. I glanced at large oil paintings and expensive looking ornaments. He stopped at an open door and waved me inside.

The room looked like a cosy private library. There was a plush rug and leather armchairs. It smelled of cigars and polish and was cool compared to the street with a giant fan turning lazily in the centre of the room.

A man wearing a black suit and white wing-collared shirt sat in one of the chairs. His legs were crossed and he had an unlit cigar in one hand.

"Captain Carter," he said rising. "Very pleased to meet you." The way he stood made me think he either had a false leg or a knee problem.

I shook his hand. It was soft.

"And you are?"

"Secretary Coates."

He was a small, relaxed man but with a natural air of authority. Public school and army, I figured, but a long time ago. He was over fifty and gone to seed though his pale eyes were still bright.

We both sat and I decided his movement suggested the leg was indeed false. Between us was a round mahogany table. I placed a hand on it and said, "Secretary?"

16

He smiled. "I work for the Governor. As I'm sure you know Singapore is a Crown Colony. We have a Legislature, a government if you will, and I'm the Secretary responsible for internal security."

I nodded and took in the room. The books crammed on shelves were leather bound and looked more like journals or record books than for entertainment. There was a globe to Coates's right—the sort that was really a drinks cabinet. I could see Asia, but Singapore was too small to make out.

He saw me looking. "Strategically important," he said. "Raffles realized it as soon as he spotted the island and pictured it as the gateway to the Orient. Pretty much everything going east or west by sea goes through Singapore." Then he pierced me with his bright eyes and asked abruptly, "What are you doing here?"

"I believe you wanted to see me."

"I mean in Singapore."

"I'm visiting a friend." Which was true. I'd received a telegram from an old school chum, Tom Silverman.

SINGAPORE GREAT BUT SOMETHING AMISS -(STOP)-
INVESTIGATING -(STOP)- NEED YOUR HELP -(STOP)- PLEASE CALL

I could do better than call. I needed to get away from Palestine and had nowhere better to go, so a few days later I jumped on a ship to Egypt. Then I caught a ride on a DC 9 to India and then another flight to Singapore.

Coates was appraising me with his bright eyes. Maybe he doubted my story, but I saw no reason to elaborate or prove its veracity.

I smiled. "Perhaps now, you could tell me what I am doing here. In your office I mean."

Singapore 52

The politician lit his cigar with a motion that was both languid and considered. After it was lit he took a long draw and the space between us filled with blue smoke.

I said, "You had me followed. Before I was arrested I spotted someone tailing me."

"We knew you were coming." He took another long draw and set the cigar down. "Captain Ashley Carter."

Only my father called me Ashley.

I said, "I prefer to be called Ash."

"You resigned your commission from the Royal Military Police two weeks ago after seven years of distinguished service. Why would you do that?"

I looked over his shoulder at an oil painting of elephants in the jungle. The detail was almost good enough to be a photograph.

Coates said, "You were awarded the Distinguished Service Medal. Which is ironic really. I understand you were instrumental in stopping a bomb plot against the United Nations building."

"It was more the occupants—the international delegates—than the building but apart from that you are correct."

"And then you resigned."

"Yes. It was time to move on."

"Really?" He picked up his cigar and blew another cloud between us. I wondered if he was using it as symbolism—a smoke screen. I wasn't going to tell him anything he didn't know. And then I discovered he knew more than I expected.

He said, "You resigned because you were unhappy. You were unhappy because your snitch—if that's the right term—was murdered and you could do nothing about it."

It was much more than that. I tried to stay relaxed and not let my face betray my feelings.

Coates said, "The suspected perpetrators—four of them—were found dead three days ago. The same day you left the country."

I said nothing. It had been the day I'd left. Coates knew a great deal but not everything. I suspected he was filling in the gaps in his intelligence with educated guesses.

He continued: "As an MP you were powerless to take any action against the murderers. So I think you resigned and took independent action. You found the perpetrators and you killed them. You revenged your snitch's death."

"That's pure speculation," I said.

"For now."

I stood. "Thank you, Mr Coates. It has been an interesting meeting."

"Sit down, Ashley."

I remained standing and looked at the fine detail of the oil painting.

He said, "I have a proposition for you," and pointed to the chair. "Please sit."

After I had taken the seat, he rang a silver hand bell and the butler appeared. "*Stengahs*," he requested. When the butler returned with two tumblers, Coates explained that they contained weak whisky and soda. He took a sip in the same languid fashion that he smoked.

I waited.

"I want you to work for me," he said with a beatific smile.

"I'm in Singapore to visit a friend. I'm not staying."

"Let's be frank. You aren't leaving without my approval. Since I suspect you of murder, I could incarcerate you here on the island."

"Under what charge?"

Coates waved a hand. "I don't think you understand the situation here, my boy. I am responsible for the security of the island. I am responsible for the police and the law as it concerns the wellbeing of the population. My God, man, do you not know we are at war?"

"I'm aware of The Emergency," I said. Since 1948 we had been fighting the communists in the north. It wasn't the scale of the war in Korea, but it could develop. I was well aware of the tensions.

"Bandits are everywhere."

I nodded. Bandits were what they called insurgents back then.

Coates continued: "And it's just a matter of time before the Reds attack us at home. In Singapore."

"And this affects me, how?"

"I want you to make sure it doesn't happen."

"You have the police and the army for that. You said yourself that you're in charge."

"I want you between them."

"That's Liaison's job."

Coates took another slow sip of his watered-down whisky. "I don't want a liaison officer. I want action. I want someone who can work with the army and the police. I want someone who can also be independent."

"And I'm your ideal candidate?"

"Although you're a civilian, you'll be accepted by the army." He gave me the smile again. "I also know who your father is. And because of your father I know the new Commander-in-Chief for the Far East won't have a problem either. General Gaskill is based here on the island."

This was crazy. Coates was well informed about my recent past and, despite the angelic smile, could make it seriously difficult for me.

"All right," I said, "I get why you've chosen me but why now?"

"Because of two things. There's a rumour that someone is buying arms on the island. Someone—most likely a group—is arming themselves."

"And the second thing?"

I was intrigued when he pulled a piece of paper from his pocket. He leaned forward and handed it to me.

It was about six inches by four with red symbols on one side. It looked like an advertising flyer. There was a circle with a paw print in the middle. Underneath were four characters that I assumed were Chinese.

"What is it?"

"Precisely? I don't know."

"How did you get it?"

"From a reliable source."

"And what do they think it is?"

"Best guess is it's a secret code."

I handed it back but he wanted me to keep it. "A code for what?" I said.

He finished his drink and for the first time I thought I detected a chink in his façade. He was worried.

"What do they think it is?" I asked again.

"An attack," he said quietly. "There's suspicion of a plan to attack us—an imminent security threat."

FOUR

Dubious of the Secretary's motives, I walked back to The Queens Hotel, thinking. At the reception desk, I asked if I could use the telephone. There was only one for the whole building. At first the receptionist dismissed me so I told him I was working for the government. I couldn't get in any more trouble, could I? I flashed my old warrant card, like the police show and moments later I was alone in the manager's office and speaking to the operator. She put me through to the colonel of my old regiment, Dexter. He was pleased to hear from me and gave no indication that he knew why I'd left so abruptly although he must have guessed.

I cut to the chase. "Colonel, I need to know—what's the situation there?"

Dexter didn't immediately answer. I knew him well enough to know he was choosing words carefully. When he spoke he said, "Everything is tickettyboo. There is no problem."

So I wasn't wanted in Palestine for murder. "Thank you," I said. "It's just that someone here seems to think there is."

"Army?"

"No."

"Government?"

"Yes."

"My advice would be to play the tourist somewhere else. Or go home to Blighty."

I didn't say anything.

"Ash?"

"I'm thinking of staying. For a while at least."

"Take care and if there's ever…"

I thanked him and ended the call. While I was speaking I twirled the warrant card between my fingers and imagined it was the government ID card Secretary Coates had promised me.

When I'd said I'd think about his offer, he'd responded, "You have twenty-four hours," and I reckoned that would be plenty of time to check out how serious the threat was and see my friend. If I then needed to get away, I was certain Tom could help. He was an engineer at the docks and could get me on a boat and off the island.

Outside the hotel, a porter hailed a trishaw for me. These, I was told, were everywhere in the city and better than a taxi for short distances.

As skinny as a whippet and speaking no English, I guessed the driver was Bangladeshi. However, he understood when I asked for the docks and we set off at a brisk pace.

After the Esplanade, which everyone called the *Padang*, we passed an obelisk and crossed the Anderson Bridge. Its white, arched girders resembled a rail bridge. On the far side we went through a square crammed with cars. As we approached the docks, the road became dense with traffic and the air filled with choking fumes.

We made slow progress through a gaggle of people and animals before stopping by a pier. I located the harbour masters office and was told that the maritime engineers were based at the end of the main docks. The office was a stone's throw away but we needed to circle around to Keppel Harbour.

Using sign-language, I directed my driver back to the long congested road that took us to the docks supervised by the navy. The navy's shipyard was to the north of the island but they had an HQ here and oversaw both the troop and commercial shipping.

At the entrance, a manned barrier ran between high fences and we were stopped by a Masters-at-Arms, the naval equivalent of an MP. He let me enter and I signalled the trishaw driver to wait for me.

There were no troopships in and, apart from a commercial ship being unloaded, the docks were quiet. The ship was to my right and I could see half a mile of storage areas and warehouses. Just inside on my left was an MT yard, a compound inside which included a motor pool. There were various size trucks and three identical pale blue cars. I'm not a car expert but I could see they were all Ford saloons.

I continued on past the yard and the dock swept around. Here was a long warehouse, workshops and offices. The Master-at-Arms had pointed to the far end of the wharf and I could see a couple of guys working on something that looked like a giant pulley system.

As I approached, I called out, "I'm looking for Tom Silverman. Is he about?"

When they looked up, I read something in their faces: uncertainty or concern maybe. They exchanged glances and one pointed to a door.

Ducking inside, I saw men working at benches and others sitting around a table drinking tea. The air was filled with a hum of machinery and screech of metal.

There was no sign of Tom. I asked the group drinking tea and again received the look.

A voice behind me said, "Who wants to know?"

I turned and introduced myself to the guy who explained he was the gaffer.

"He's my friend," I said. "Something's wrong isn't it?"

"I have bad news, I'm afraid."

I waited and could tell he was unsure how to explain.

"Just say it," I said.

He shrugged, released from the need to be sensitive and just said, "He's dead."

FIVE

Instantly, my guts constricted. "Dead? What the hell...?"

One of the men at the table spoke up. "A car crash at night out on the road to Nee Soon."

"When? How'd it happen?"

"Ten days ago."

"We don't know the detail," the gaffer said. "Really bad downpour. An accident. Just lost control they think."

"Who thinks?"

"The police."

I nodded. That made sense. But an accident? He'd sent me a telegram asking for help ten days ago, so he'd died that night.

"Did he tell anyone of any concerns?" I swept my gaze across the group. To a man they all looked baffled. I switched back to the gaffer. "And the police definitely think it was an accident?"

"That's right." Now he looked uncertain. "Are you suggesting otherwise?"

"I don't know but you can be sure of one thing. I'm going to find out." Again I turned to the group. "If you find out anything, hear anything that might be remotely significant, please let me know."

"How will we…"

At that moment I decided I was staying. I also knew I was moving out of The Queens Hotel. "Get a message to me. My name's Carter. Ash Carter. I'll be at Gillman Barracks."

Gillman Barracks was the home to Singapore's Military Police 200 Provost Company. I figured I needed to be either close to the police or MPs and my background made the army the obvious choice. Of course there was also the consideration that they had quarters whereas I didn't know the situation with the police.

Back at the hotel I spoke to the operator again and was put through to Secretary Coates.

"I have two conditions," I said. "Firstly, we draw up a proper contract. I will work for you until the incident you are concerned about occurs or three months. No more. After that, I am free to leave the country."

"What's the second condition?"

"You get me into Gillman."

Coates actually laughed. "Of course, dear boy. I'll agree to both of those. I'll have our agreement drawn up by the end of the day. In fact I'm one step ahead of you. Major Vernon is already expecting you at the barracks. I'll also send you the government warrant card in case you need it."

I checked a map and decided to get a proper taxi. However, before that, I walked to the police HQ. It was an imposing building on the corner of Hill Street and River Valley Road. There was an open door on the corner and I went through. I expected it to be a staff entrance, however it led to a piazza and what looked like a parade ground. There was no one around. I continued round the side and found a door marked *Public*

Entrance. Oversized, aged teak doors were closed but opened as I pushed one. Warm stale air and the smell of a day's worth of body odour immediately assaulted me. Giant fans slowly turned in the vaulted ceiling causing air to circulate, but do little else. It was warmer inside than on the street.

The room was crowded, people standing in the centre or sitting on benches around the side. For the large number of people, I was taken by how quiet and calm they were. Or weary. I eased my way to the desk where a sergeant was dealing with a small Chinese lady surrounded by a gaggle of children.

The sergeant, himself Chinese, glanced at me as I approached and called something over his shoulder that I didn't understand. A moment later another sergeant appeared. This one was maybe Malay but spoke excellent English.

"Can I help you, sir?"

I looked around at the many faces watching me. I had jumped the queue but saw no malice.

"I'd like details of an accident—I have discovered my friend was killed in a car crash ten days ago." I showed the sergeant my new warrant card and he almost leapt out of his skin and then stood to attention. He took a couple of beats to compose himself and then ushered me around the desk. Moments later I was sitting in an office. The window was open and I moved the chair to get as much air as available.

"My name is Inspector Anand Rahman." The man in the doorway had a generous smile on his Indian face. He held out a bony hand and pumped mine warmly.

I introduced myself.

"Yes," he said, "I've been expecting you. Secretary Coates himself spoke to me this morning. Welcome Captain."

"Please, just Ash. But that's not why I'm here." I went on to explain about my friend's unfortunate death and asked if I could view the file.

He nodded and then shook his head. "I am afraid I do not know about this accident. As I am sure you appreciate, there are many, many incidents that occur each day. Most of those involve the soldiers off the boats and my role is to work with the military—the military police in particular. But if you would excuse me for a minute, I will request the report... Mr Silverman you say." He checked a calendar. "On the twenty-third."

He spoke to someone in the corridor and I glanced around the office. It had certificates on the wall and a photograph of a large family gathering. There was a clock the size of a dinner plate that ticked slow and loud. His desk was small and functional: just an in-tray and out-tray with papers and nothing personal.

When he returned he gave me the generous smile again. "It won't be long, Captain... Ash."

While we waited he asked about my background and experience in Palestine. Half an hour went by and he talked about the need to work more closely with the MPs. An operation had recently gone wrong because of failed communication. The MPs had ruined an investigation into drug smugglers by chasing a soldier who had tried to deal in the stuff. Rahman grinned. "I think with your help, we will find we work so much better together."

"How do you find the Special Investigation Branch officers here?"

He cocked an eyebrow and waggled his head. "I have never met them."

I was surprised, being SIB myself—at least I had been until two weeks ago.

"I believe they are mostly in Malaya because that is where the trouble is."

And yet the inspector had just described a classic SIB issue: a soldier involved with drug smugglers. I took a mental note to ask about it at Gillman. For now I moved on and handed him the flyer of the circle with a paw print and said, "Secretary Coates gave this to me."

Rahman studied it, turned it over, studied it some more and handed it back. "What is it?"

"Coates's evidence of a security issue. Have you seen it before?"

"No. But then..."

"What are you thinking?"

"Well, I wondered whether the source was us, the police. And we have a large force—almost a thousand men. So it could have come from us. I'll try and find out. I was also thinking about the numbers."

"Numbers?"

"The writing appears to be a series of numbers: four, ten, two, ten. I'll ask around about those. I'll also ask whether anyone has come across a lion's paw in a circle before."

"Lion's paw?"

"That's what it looks like to me. Of course lions feature a lot in Chinese imagery."

He passed the flyer back to me as a young policeman came into the room. He gave the inspector a file and I noticed how deferential the junior man was towards his superior. The chap practically bowed as he backed out of the room.

Rahman opened the file in front of me. It was typed and in English but consisted of two pages of foolscap paper and five photographs about eight inches by six. I read it. The report was by an officer called Sergeant Kee and was reasonable for someone whose first language wasn't English.

Tom had been driving south on the road from Nee Soon to Singapore City. The road was made of small stones called laterite and was rutted in places. There was thick jungle on either side of the road. It was judged to be about one in the morning. The sky was overcast and it had rained heavily in the hours before. It was totally dark except for the headlights of his small car. It was referred to as a Toyota SA Compact. I didn't know it.

There were no other vehicles on that stretch of the road. The report said the car was old, the tyres were bald and the windscreen wipers broken.

During a sudden torrential downpour, the car hit a rut and the driver lost control. He couldn't see where he was going and drove at speed into a tree. He travelled through the windscreen and died immediately from the impact.

I put the report down and studied the black and white photographs. There were two from the front, one focused on the impact and the other on my friend's body trapped between the car and tree. The windscreen was in two main parts but looked like it had come out whole and broken when it hit the ground.

The third photograph showed a tyre with no tread. The next was a shot from the rear showing the ground and what looked like a skid mark. The back of the car was clearly visible on this photograph. However the next picture showed a dip in the road. It was filled with water and the stones again appeared to show something heavy had skidded over it.

I sat back.

"Satisfied?" Rahman asked with a smile.

"No," I said with concern. "There are many things wrong with this report."

"Really?"

I handed the inspector the photograph of the skid. "I'm not convinced this was an accident."

Singapore Girl

As a thunderstorm approaches, Ash Carter stands on the strip of no man's land between Singapore and Malaya. A headless body has been placed on the causeway and it seems to be a message. The number 221 is painted on its back.

Carter is told to investigate because it seems drugs related. And drugs surely mean the involvement of Chinese Secret Societies. Following the clues, Carter soon comes up against an old adversary and a humanitarian aid unit that aren't all they seem.

Travelling through Malayan jungle and Penang, Carter unravels a well-disguised but simple scheme. One for which the Singapore girl holds the key.

The second instalment of the Ash Carter thriller series is out in spring 2018